ABOUT THE AUTHOR

Richard Cobourne writes with a production background in the broadcast, corporate, music, global events, and communications industries. He has worked in the business-of-show all over the world for many years – and as a result has a deep understanding of the shenanigans of the industry. He began his career working for the BBC, initially in the sound department of radio, TV, and outside broadcasts. After fifteen years he left to co-found On Screen Productions Ltd, which he sold in 2015 to pursue a career as a freelance consultant creative producer, occasional voice artist, and to enable him to write full-time. He is a member of The Ivy Club, BAFTA and the National Liberal Club.

This is the second novel in the showbiz thriller trilogy. The third, maybe final (who knows?), is in progress.

Richard Cobourne lives with his wife on the Welsh side of the Wye Valley and in Fuerteventura.

The author can be contacted via www.Cobourne.com

ABOUT THE BOOK

Real people, real events, real organisations, and real places are frequently mentioned in this trilogy – there is no suggestion of any wrongdoing, they are there solely to add authenticity and context, nothing more. You may like to think that this is entirely a work of fiction – but that's up to you...

RED LIGHT AND BELL

AND BELL

RICHARD COBOURNE

Matador
Unit E2 Airfield Business Park,
Harrison Road, Market Harborough,
Leicestershire. LE16 7UL
Tel: 0116 2792299
Email: books@troubador.co.uk
Web: www.troubador.co.uk/matador
Twitter: @matadorbooks

ISBN 978 1803135 878

British Library Cataloguing in Publication Data.
A catalogue record for this book is available from the British Library.

Printed and bound in the UK by TJ Books Limited, Padstow, Cornwall
Typeset in 11pt Minion Pro by Troubador Publishing Ltd, Leicester, UK
Cover designed by Vikki Byrne at www.HelloOSP.com

Matador is an imprint of Troubador Publishing Ltd

'All the world's a stage,
And all the men and women merely players;
They have their exits and their entrances,
And one man in his time plays many parts.'
William Shakespeare, *As You Like It,* Act 2, Scene VII

'Be sure your sins will find you out'
Numbers 32:23

AUTHOR'S NOTE

COVID-19 Pandemic

This trilogy was conceived and born well before words such as 'lockdown', 'tiers', 'social distancing', 'unprecedented', 'Zooming', and 'you're on mute' had entered the everyday lexicon. In *Bandwagon*, the opening novel in this series, there is no mention of the plague – whilst it was being written the significance of COVID-19 simply wasn't known.

The publication of *Bandwagon* coincided exquisitely with the first of the many restrictions with which we have learned to live – as a result all promotional launch and media activities were put on hold; the TV production deal was cancelled; many bookshops closed, opened, re-closed, re-opened (repeat *ad nauseum*).

This book, *Red Light and Bell*, the second of the trilogy, continues a few seconds after the conclusion of *Bandwagon* – leaving me as I was writing it with somewhat of a dilemma. I had little choice – COVID-19 and the new way we live our lives simply had to be ignored. Perhaps this is for the good, as many of us have already lived, breathed, and survived through it and will continue to do so. For those who have suffered and are suffering, who have lost friends and family, we do not need reminding.

BREXIT

The combined effect on the entertainment industry of both COVID-19 and Brexit is almost a perfect storm. The devastating stage of the pandemic has (hopefully) died down and the UK's artists have resumed touring – but with massively higher fuel, transport, and energy costs.

The end of decades of unrestricted movement across the (current) twenty-seven countries in the EU means red tape and shrinking margins could cause lasting damage to artists' careers and the concert business on both sides of the English Channel – not to mention the hideous border delays and customs' impedimenta. You might wish to lobby your MP: https://allpartymusicgroup.org.uk/

Recent national events have demonstrated the immense talent of the UK's AV, media, theatre, events, and touring production teams, cast and crew. The industry is rising Phoenix-like to the challenge but needs your support please – so get out there and enjoy yourself.

Whatever happens, for everyone, please enjoy this escapist yarn.

Richard Cobourne, October 2022

"CAPTIVITY"

MARTHA'S GLOBAL NUMBER ONE!

Shut up on my own, no friends, no work, no phone
Thought I'd lost my freedom
Got it oh so wrong
Because I am not free
I'm what they want me to be
A picture painted years ago
Not allowed to breath or grow

Under your thumb
So scared my race was run
Let you decide upon my truth
Turned away from those who loved me,
lost my sister and my youth

Alone here with my demons
Getting older, no shoulder to lean on… to dream on
My crazy life so far away
The locks and bars holding the world at bay
Finally no place to hide
I have to face just what's inside

But with time to reflect, I begin to suspect,
that the truth I was sold was a lie
If I change my life, I won't die
It might just help me to survive.

Chorus
I found peace in captivity
Whom I'm supposed to be in captivity
A brand new me in captivity
And finally I'm free

Lyrics by Alison King

PROLOGUE

THURSDAY – THREE WEEKS LATER

INEVITABLY IT WAS RAINING. NOT A HEAVY downpour, more a drizzle – a *ceobhrán* or *brádán* as Enniskillen's locals might say. Innocuous at the time, yet somehow manages to soak through every layer of the mourners' clothing. Not that there were many mourners considering this was meant to be a commemoration and interment for the death-in-service of a locally born UK Metropolitan Police Officer.

Within Enniskillen's Saint Macartan's Cathedral, there was no media scrum unlike at the cremation in London nine days earlier. There was just one stringer with a camera from the local newspaper, *The Impartial Reporter*; a very few local family, mainly cousins; not many friends from school and growing up; two officers from the Royal Dragoon Guards in dark suits and regimental ties; and a couple of the deceased's former close colleagues from around the United Kingdom of Great Britain and Northern Ireland made up the paltry numbers in the mostly empty pews. A funeral is a public event – accordingly, anyone can attend, but no others chose to exercise their option except for the watchers. And the watchers, watching the watchers.

The deceased's ashes in a simple council urn, sat in lonely isolation on a small table covered with a plain violet pall between the empty choir stalls at the foot of the wooden altar table – an allegory for his life.

Journalist, Danny Owen and PR, Daisy deVilliers sat surreptitiously hand-in-hand. The pew, several rows in front of them, was taken with Detective Chief Superintendent Bill Kelly, Detective Sergeant Rob Andrews, and Detective Sergeant Anastasia Spencer-Hatt – not hand-in-hand.

In the tower, high above them all, the solitary tenor bell weighing over one ton added to the occasion – its ominous tolling seemed somehow lazy, almost lackadaisical. Fewer than a dozen parish churches in Northern Ireland have towers with peals of eight or more bells where campanologists can exercise their skills. Saint Macartan's Cathedral watching over Enniskillen is one of those – for this sombre day the single bell left the seventy-year-old ringer unchallenged. He would be rewarded with a few drinks later – and then a few more.

The forty-minute service did not include the full Catholic mass – which was probably just as well considering the damp

2

cold had managed to penetrate every mourner seated in the almost three-hundred-year-old cathedral.

Detective Chief Superintendent Bill Kelly was invited to say some, 'Words in Remembrance.' He spoke for just over four minutes. He had decided to keep the more salacious stories, suitable for the black humour of his police colleagues, for the wake later.

The deceased could not be described as a good Catholic – DCS Bill Kelly was one of the very few who knew some of the extent of the sinning.

Townsfolk had heard in the distance the strains of the service's hymns. Traditionally, *Abide with Me* and controversially for some in Northern Ireland, *I Vow to Thee my Country*. A few locals crossed themselves in anonymous respect for someone they didn't know – it was just something they did when funerals were heard in the distance at the top of the hill.

None, except those in the know, spotted the surveillance teams sitting in the gallery high above the nave; or concealed outside around the perimeter; or the heavily armed teams in body armour hidden in nondescript vans parked on the roads leading to and from the cathedral.

For a celebration of a deceased life there were surprisingly few tears and even fewer opportunities to laugh. The service for the late Detective Sergeant Michael Maguire's ashes concluded – huddled under umbrellas outside, the mourners watched as the urn was lowered into a small grave in line with the Catholic Church's recommendation of burying the ashes of the deceased.

None felt they could leave in seemingly undue haste until they had shaken the hand of the Reverend Patrick

Quigley, the Dean of Clogher, thanking him for *a wonderful commemoration* and other traditional funereal platitudes. Once duty done, most felt they could, at last, leave to escape from the all-encompassing omnidirectional damp.

'How long do we have to stay here? I'm soaked to the bloody skin,' demanded Danny Owen watching the others depart. Journalists can be known to be a crabby lot.

'I'm working, so have to stay until everyone has gone.' Bill Kelly surreptitiously put his finger to his ear, listening to a message from one of the watchers via his concealed walkie-talkie. He clicked the switch in his pocket twice to silently transmit he had received and understood. 'And if I'm here you can bloody well stay too.'

PR, Daisy deVilliers gave the pair of them a filthy look that said so much. Somehow, she always managed to look elegant whatever the occasion or time of day or night. The black knee-high Celtic & Co Popper Boots perfectly matched the black North Face Women's Apex Bionic Trench Coat – both bought especially for the occasion. *They would come in useful for when Martha's tour resumes,* she thought. A chill ran up her spine at the thought of the events that caused the enforced postponement. She pulled up her collar as she looked around – most mourners had departed for the *after-show party* as Daisy insisted on calling the wake.

The Level Seven Bar within Blakes of 'The Hollow,' just down the road from Saint Macartan's Cathedral was already doing brisk business. Its literary, theatrical and music score ambience seemed appropriate – it is allegedly one of the most famous and oldest pubs in Ireland. Its warmth was beckoning the last of the remaining mourners.

4

'Okay, let's call it a day. Stand down.' Bill Kelly spoke into his concealed microphone – those in immediate earshot ostentatiously heaved a sigh of relief. He turned to Danny and Daisy – she had been hopping from foot-to-foot trying to keep her feet warm despite the boots, 'Looks like there is nothing to see here. I'll see you at the wake in twenty minutes or so. I'll just clear up here.'

Without further asking the pair walked away from the cathedral, still hand-in-hand, and down the lichen-covered stone slabbed path. They turned left onto the road. Daisy cwtched her arm around Danny's.

Their thoughts were interrupted by a boy's voice shouting at Danny, 'Here, mister. A bloke told me to give you this.'

The boy, without dismounting from his flamboyantly decorated mountain bike, held out a white DL envelope with the name Stanislaw Nowak written in thick black felt pen on the front. 'He said you'd give me five pounds.'

'What man?' asked Daisy, snatching the envelope from Danny.

'Up the road,' replied the boy turning around to vaguely point somewhere in the distance. The road was stubbornly empty. Not even an abandoned car in sight.

Daisy fumbled in her handbag for the allegedly-promised five-pound note – she'd claim it back when she did her expenses. The crisp plastic note was exchanged for the envelope, which she stuffed in her already packed handbag. The boy cycled away – his legs pushing hard. The video surveillance would be analysed later.

'Don't you want to open it,' asked Danny.

'Not addressed to me,' replied Daisy. 'And anyway, a large gin and tonic is beckoning.'

Daisy was famed for her encyclopaedic knowledge of the world's gins – and disdain for house tonic *dispensed from some hideous CO_2 contraption.*

Meanwhile Detective Chief Superintendent Bill Kelly was frustrated – he needed to fully understand the reasons why his former colleague, Detective Sergeant Michael Maguire was so publicly murdered, and by whom.

'This is very irritating.' Kelly said to no one in particular.

The frustration was getting on top of him – unusual for the normally calm senior detective. He thought back to what was meant to be a joyous celebration – the return of Martha and her fabulous first night.

Its awful finale.

DAY ONE
THURSDAY NIGHT

THE O2

THE O2 HAD NEVER HEARD ANYTHING LIKE IT – twenty thousand people cheering, whistling, applauding, stamping their feet, hugging, some in tears of happy emotion.

Stage centre, there she was – the reinvigorated and relaunched pop-megastar Martha, wearing the long, gold evening dress that she had worn at the top of the show just two fabulous hours ago. The gold discs sewn into the fabric sparkled like personal mirror balls from the six follow spots illuminating her from back, front and sides. The dozens of massive video screens which made up most of the staging brought her face in super high detail, almost intimately, to her devoted fans.

I'm back she thought through waves of elation, as she took long, deep bows. The once-familiar, long-ago forgotten buzz of audience adoration almost overwhelmed her. A buzz that no chemical could replace – legal or otherwise.

'Thank you... Thank you... Thank you, every single one of you for coming tonight to celebrate with me.' Her voice was crystal clear helped by the massive hundred-kilowatt time-aligned PA system.

She held both her arms out wide in a visual embrace to her fans – the almost invisible, head worn Shure microphone, specially adapted for Martha's show, allowed complete freedom. Her front-of-house sound balancer working with Michael Jackson many years ago had *acquired* the unused Shure Special after Jackson's sad and premature passing – his loss was Martha's gain. Martha, in her reinvigorated career, had taken a while to embrace not having to hold a normal radio microphone – the old ways were sometimes more comforting to a performer but, like the custom made in-ear monitors, she realised how much they helped to improve her performance and the audiences' experience, so could never go back.

The crowd noise reached new levels. Martha looked out from the elaborate stage towards the u-shaped auditorium of the O2 Arena with its four layers – to her it looked like a gaudily decorated birthday cake with too many candles. The corporate boxes, with their champagne sipping clientele, were ringed around the central layer like the jam and cream in the middle.

The ten banks of 5x5 Par30 LED light matrixes high above her head mounted on the specially designed proscenium arch illuminated the audience so she could clearly see her fans – and the fans could see each other sharing in their elation.

Martha gesticulated with her hands to calm them down. On cue as a visual signal, the audience lights dimmed, and the crowd quietened. 'Thank you... Thank you... As this is the first night of the *Martha Movin' Out* tour, I'd like *you* to help *me* thank some especially important people who have made my journey here today possible.'

More applause and cheers – up went the lights. Martha waited smiling and laughing for the noise to subside. Once again, her face showed every emotion on the many screens behind and around her. The audience lights dimmed again to settle the crowd.

'First of all, I'd like to introduce you to my wonderful sister. My twin. My unexpected muse. Someone who helped me to write my new songs whilst we were in *captivity* together. Please give it up for my gorgeous sister, Vikki.'

The band reprised an over-orchestrated version of the song, '*Captivity*.'

The huge scenic doors at the back of the stage, bedecked with the immense video screens, opened in a backlit cloud of smoke and dry ice to reveal Martha's twin sister, Vikki, wearing exactly the same costume as Martha. It was remarkable – two peas in a pod. Identical. Martha and Vikki burst out in joyous laughter – no-one had told Martha that tonight, Vikki would be her perfect doppelgänger. For a moment, the audience cheering subsided – as one, they gasped. The audience lights were now up at full brightness; the noise ramped up to yet another seemingly impossible level. Vikki walked forward to centre stage – where the two girls hugged for ages. The massive auditorium sparkled with the combined effect of the two mirrored dresses as the cheers and applause continued. Eventually the clamour subsided – a little. The audience lights dimmed; the noisy crowd took this as their cue to reduce their heat from frantic boil to a gentle simmer.

'As you know Vikki and I were kidnapped and held in *captivity…*' cue more cheering at the mention of Martha's new album, Captivity '…held in *captivity* together. Every cloud has a silver lining. We got to know each other again. Proper sisters. And sisterly love. Vikki helped me to write the new album. She helped me break the creative block of the past seven years. My muse, my gorgeous sister, Vikki – thank you.'

Captivity had rocketed to number one on the back of the very publicly televised release from their kidnap ordeal in the Wye Valley a few weeks before. It had broken all records as the fastest selling CD and download reaching number one, bar Elton John's *Candle in the Wind 1997* – which sold 1.55 million copies in its first week and over half a million on the first day. Martha's new future seemed to be assured.

The cheers and stamping of feet continued unabated. After a final public hug, Vikki took an extravagant bow, waved, and exited stage left. The band reprised the final bars of '*Captivity*' – finishing with an extraordinary octave halved downward contra-bass glissando and orchestral major chord. The music and the lights did their thing to control the crowd – if only they realised how they were being manipulated.

'Thank you to my promoter and producer, Stanislaw Nowak who had the vision and courage to bring me back *to you* after too many years away. To have faith in me. Thank you.'

Cheers – no-one really cared about Stanislaw Nowak, they were consumed by their love for Martha, and now also Vikki.

Nowak sitting up-stage left in the second tier of the O2's reserved VIP and celebrity seating struggled to his feet. Two follow spots perfectly illuminated him as he reluctantly waved. He didn't look like a man who was happy to be thanked – ever the showman outwardly, he tried to show a mixture of some joy and pleasure. Fear, verging on terror remained inscrutably hidden as he acknowledged the applause – he blew a kiss towards Martha and promptly sat down. Few knew the reality of the stress and pressure he was under – and had been under for the past months. How he nearly lost, might lose everything – including his life. *This should have been my crowning moment, a respected member of society,* Nowak thought. He tried to fold his massive, flabby body out of sight. Daisy deVilliers – Martha's tour publicity manager – was shocked at his behaviour. She thought her boss, Nowak, would have been loving the praise, the attention, and the adulation. Instead, he was shying away from it all. *He seems to be afraid of something*, she thought, *really terrified.*

Several celebrities nearby caught in spill from the intense beams of the follow-spots, preened and postured – *never miss an opportunity to be photographed and seen* was their collective introspection.

'There are many, many people who I have thanked in private – but there are three groups of people to whom I owe my life and I would like your help thanking. Firstly, to the Special Forces who rescued Vikki and me from *captivity*,' Martha attempted to continue, but had to take an enforced break for the inevitable light-induced cheering. 'You saw them in action on TV and in the newspapers. Their bravery and selfless dedication to their jobs is an inspiration to us all. They are here tonight as my guests, they know who they are, but for obvious reasons I cannot tell you who or where they are. The words thank you are simply not enough. But thank you.'

Everyone looked around to see if they could identify *their* covert heroes. No-one could. More applause. Thirty Vari-lights circled across and around the auditorium and across the domed ceiling, dazzling, tantalising, and mocking – *where and who are our heroes?*

'To Detective Chief Superintendent Bill Kelly and his team from the Metropolitan Police, for your persistent dedication – without you, my sister and I wouldn't be here today. Thank you.' Some of the Met Police team, sitting in the VIP and celebrity seats in the row in front of Stanislaw Nowak, sat up straight, and in embarrassment half-heartedly waved and then had no choice but to applaud each other less-than-enthusiastically – they were all well and truly out of their comfort zone, sitting far too near to Stanislaw Nowak, a person-of-interest for far too long. One day their turn would come to put him behind bars. As if Nowak could hear the Met Police's combined thoughts, he turned around to face Bill Kelly sitting two rows behind and gave him one of his sickliest bravado grins. *If only they know what I know*, Nowak thought. Kelly remained outwardly impassive.

'And finally, last but not least, Danny Owen and Daisy deVilliers – thank you for your love, support, and unselfish dedication in helping me and Vikki in so many ways. Most of you will know Danny from his radio shows on Starshine. He and Daisy, my publicist, were instrumental in so much, helping me over the last few weeks. They put themselves unselfishly at risk to ensure we can all be here today. I love you both.'

Without the benefit of stage make-up, the follow-spots' intense bright white light made them look ghostly-pale. Danny squeezed Daisy's hand as they stood to acknowledge the cheers – they waved with their free hands. Both had become minor celebrities in their own right, having spent hours on the radio and TV, and in the papers telling and retelling their story in the rescue of Martha and Vikki. *Or that part of the story that could be told.*

Yuliet Spooner, sitting beside Danny and Daisy leant away from the blinding light; she had asked that her name be kept out of the public approbation. Her anonymity wasn't one hundred percent guaranteed but working at the Centre for Covert Media Studies meant she needed to remain as low profile as possible – it wouldn't do for a covert investigative journalist to be outed to this massive crowd. She, more than anyone, knew the full extent of Stanislaw Nowak's criminal past and present. The file in her Chubb Trident Euro Grade Six safe at her office near Kings Cross Station, with copies secreted in her house and in another location, contained sensational information that would be revealed in a series of yet to be published exposés to the discomfort of not just Nowak, but several other high-profile individuals. The police, sitting around her, would give their eye-teeth to see it – if only they knew of its full contents, or the identity of the person from whom she had obtained it.

Martha blew Daisy and Danny a kiss – the audience cheered, half-heartedly. They'd done enough thanking and wanted to get on with it. The audience lights went out.

The main stage lighting cross-faded to a deep, deep blue – almost ultra-violet. A single follow spot and two rich gold back lights were trained on Martha. The band took their cue from the show-caller for what was meant to be the final song of the night, Martha's massive number one Christmas hit from ten years ago, 'Missing You, Loving You' – it stayed at the top for seventeen weeks. Once again, the cheering and whistling and applauding ramped up as the massive crowd realised that they were going to hear *their song* from younger days. Memories flooded back. Those in relationships, and some who weren't, held each other's hands. Many hugged. Several kissed passionately ignoring those around them.

Martha spoke over the opening bars of the music. 'Please join in with me. Sing with all your hearts as we all remember those friends and family we love. And especially those we still love but who are no longer with us…'

Mobile phone torches and the centrally controlled multi-coloured illuminated wrist bands were waved high above everybody's heads – memorial candles. The emotional effect on everyone was breath-taking.

Martha sang the words in a moving, intimate tribute to her siblings and parents who were killed in the terrible crash many years ago in thick fog on the M1 north of Watford. She often thought *what her life would have been if they were still alive. Would she even have had the success without their death spring-boarding her career? Would they have been proud of her? Or would she still be touring the booze-soaked social clubs of the Midlands of the UK scraping a meagre living?*

Pull yourself together, she told herself as she sang. *That was before. This is now. Come on. Perform. Give it everything you have.*

Her performance soared even higher. *Oh yes. I'm back.*

Every single person in the O2 Arena was mesmerised. Except one – whose mind was elsewhere, preparing.

Theatrically revealed on tiered decking at the rear of the stage were members of *The London Community Gospel Choir* in white trousers and jackets, some in surplices. For most of the concert they had been in the vocal booth or in amongst the band providing BVs – backing vocals. The sight and sound of their close harmony choral vocals added poignancy. The choir, driven by the altruistic vision of peace, love and unity created an infectious passion and charisma. It was a major coup for Jimmy to persuade them to join the *Martha Movin' Out* tour – the choir has a global reputation having collaborated, performed, and recorded with Elton John, Madonna, Paul McCartney, Annie Lenox, Sam Smith, Ellie Goulding, Jessie J, Adele and many more. Martha was as excited to have them on stage with her, as they were to be on stage with Martha.

'*I'm Missing You, I'm Loving You, forever... and ever... and ever...*' Martha's coloratura soprano voice was superlative. The final notes drifted away accompanied by a suspended soft stick roll on the cymbals – for a few seconds there was almost silence as the sentiment washed over everyone. Then the roar grew and grew. And grew.

The crowd chanted Martha's name.

'*Martha, Martha, Martha, MARTHA, MARTHA...*' which continued for over five minutes.

Martha couldn't leave the stage. She was genuinely gobsmacked. Not one of the sometimes-cynical technical team or musicians had ever heard an ovation like it. Tour manager James 'Jimmy' Patrick conferred with Martha's musical director on their comms packs. The show caller, sound, lights, and the rest of the tech team confirmed they were ready to go. The band cued up the unscripted reprise of '*Captivity,*' Martha's most recent stellar hit.

Martha needed no asking – she gave a performance that some say was the best of her life. The crowd's collective singing of the chorus was breath-taking...

I found peace in captivity
Whom I'm supposed to be in captivity
A brand new me in captivity
And finally I'm free

Once again, as the song finished, the crowd reached new levels of elation – a staggering collective ovation for Martha. She took her fifth bow after the unexpected second encore. The audience wanted, demanded, more.

Martha looked out across the sea of affection – everywhere brightly illuminated.

'*Martha, Martha, Martha, MARTHA, MARTHA…*'

Martha looked off stage to Jimmy, the tour manager. She raised her eyebrows in a silent request. *Another encore?*

Jimmy ignored her. He was deep in conversation on his radio talkback system. 'Mute Martha's mic,' he instructed the sound team. Suddenly, and unexpectedly, he rapidly walked onto the stage with a strained smile, took Martha theatrically by the hand and, waving to the crowd, started to escort her off the massive space.

'What the fuck are you doing?' demanded Martha, through a forced public smile unheard by her adoring fans. 'They wanted more.'

Jimmy's grip on Martha's hand tightened.

'Smile and wave.' Jimmy was insistent.

Martha reluctantly flourished her free hand high above her head in an enforced fond farewell. She might not have liked it, but she trusted Jimmy's judgement. She tried to give her best stage-smile as she reluctantly waved. Confused thoughts bounced around her elated mind. *What the fuck is going on?*

The crowd cheered and booed – they wanted more of Martha. She was *their* Martha. The star of *their* lives. *Who was this man who had the audacity to drag an obviously unwilling Martha off stage?*

As soon as they were out of view of the audience, at the side of the stage behind the leg lines, Martha turned on Jimmy. 'I repeat. What the fuck are you doing?'

Jimmy said nothing, except nod at Martha's close protection team, who surrounded her and hassled her to her dressing room collecting Vikki on the way – the two men stood guard outside and the two women entered the room with her. All looked worried as they listened to the multiple reports on their earpieces.

Outside in the auditorium amongst the foot stamping, cheers, whistles, and joyous shouts could be heard the beginnings of terrified screams.

Daisy deVilliers had, for the first time in her thirty-odd years, seen the inner contents of someone's head distributed over a wide area – her first reaction was amazement that something the size of a small football could contain so much. Perversely she then worried about how she was going to get the nauseating mess off her floral jacket, blue striped blouse, black trousers and black J'Adior pumps given to her by Christian Dior's PR manager.

Sitting beside her, Stanislaw Nowak tried to push the heavy, lifeless body off him – it was knocked back onto him by the heavy round's kinetic energy from the sniper's rifle. He was drenched in warm pumping blood and the remains of Detective Sergeant Michael Maguire's brains.

Then reality kicked in. Unlike many fans in the tiers of public seating above, besides, and immediately in front of her, Daisy did not scream – everyone reacts differently to traumatic shock. She instinctively leapt to her feet, looked down to her left at the shuddering body in its death throes on top of the squirming Nowak – her mouth unable to form any words.

Danny, on Daisy's right, leapt to his feet. He automatically, lovingly, tried to take Daisy in his arms – snapping her back to reality. Danny was equally spattered with blood, mucus, and human brain even further daubing Daisy's already blood-sodden party-wear.

Daisy ignored him, pushed Danny and Yuliet away as she scrambled across the other guests in her row, distributing even further the dead body's detritus. In panic, she stamped on their feet and tripped over their legs in her escape to the aisle on the far side. Few noticed, as they tried to absorb and reconcile what was going on.

Danny Owen, once investigative journalist, now reluctant celebrity reporter on Starshine, the London-based independent radio station was on high alert – his adrenaline pumping. He had met the victim only on a couple of occasions in the meeting rooms of New Scotland Yard, yet this was still personal. He and Yuliet were the only journalists in the immediate vicinity of the terrible event. All the other media were in the Golden Circle immediately in front of the stage – and too far away, or their sight lines obscured, to be able to make sense of the scene going on above them to their right.

Danny tried to chase after Daisy. His way was blocked by VIPs and celebrities struggling too to make their escape. His journalist instincts kicked in – he pulled out his iPhone 14 Pro Max with one hand and started taking pictures.

Detective Chief Superintendent Bill Kelly, who had been sitting two rows behind Nowak, and away from his Metropolitan Police colleagues and families, attempted to take control – he had seen the effects of a bullet too often. He shouted, 'Sergeant Andrews, Rob, get everyone away from here as quickly as possible. VIPs, celebrities, and AAAs to the green room. Don't let anyone else from nearby leave the

O2. Detective Sergeant Spencer-Hatt… Anastasia call it in – request full back up. We'll need the lot.'

'For fuck's sake, get those lights off us,' Kelly pointed at the audience lights just recently used as a catalyst for joy – he had escaped the bloody drenching, but didn't want every self-appointed citizen journalist photographing the carnage just in front of him.

He looked down at the body, Nowak and then to Danny 'What the hell are you doing?'

'What it looks like? Taking pictures,' humphed Danny, continuing to snap away. 'You'll want some for scene-of crime – best to get them now whilst everything is fresh and untouched.'

'As long as I don't see them online, the TV or in the papers.' Kelly was terse.

Danny didn't reply. His iPhone was attempting to synchronise his images to his Cloud account – but even with the allegedly lightning-fast 5G it seemed painfully slow.

Alongside and around them members of the audience could see some of what was going on – an almost head-less body on top of a struggling man with deep red blood distributed around the seating area, onto the concrete floor, and amidst the VIP and celebrity guests. As is often the case at a time of modern tragedy the camera phones were out – the screens distancing the photographer from reality. Several war-reporting news cameramen in conflicts around the world had been killed simply because they thought they were isolated by the viewfinder.

The chaos began to build and build, as nearby onlookers eventually accepted the reality of what they were seeing illuminated by the dazzling audience lights – some were sick, some were transfixed, whilst others tried to make sense of it. What was unanimous was their total horror as phones-in-hand they began to race for the exits – little encouragement needed.

Then came the hysterical scream, no one knew whence it came. 'Oh my God, it's a bomb.'

And that was it.

The cry of *'bomb'* was repeated like an aural Mexican Wave. The terror and panic grew. Word and rumour spread like an uncontrolled viral infection – the screams were long and piercing. Once happy, Martha's adoring fans now scrambled for the exits, pushing, shoving, falling over each other.

The capacity crowd of over twenty thousand people, some with the end of Ariana Grande's Manchester concert flooding back, rushed up and down the stair ways, stair wells and foyers to escape. The ordinary and emergency exits of the O2 were jammed as people fought to pass each other in obscene selfish panic.

Frantic parents, friends and families lost contact – later to begin what would be the hours-long search for their children, and those from whom they had been separated when the rush to apparent safety began.

Once outside some took to social media posting photos with increasingly desperate guessed, misinformed and downright fake news – which was picked up by TV, radio, and the press across the world. The less professional media abandoned any semblance of verification from independent sources preferring *citizen journalism* to grab the headlines first before their rivals. It wasn't long before truth and fiction completely parted company, forever consigned to the inexplicable customs of social media and sensationalised rolling news.

Daisy deVilliers' began to process what she was seeing a few metres away from her. The uncontrollable shaking began to subside as she gripped the handrail on the side of the stairs. People passed her, knocked her, and banged into her as they made their irrational panicked escape.

Daisy held fast. She knew she would have, did have, a job to do. Her phone started to go nuts – at first one or two WhatsApp and text messages, then it ramped up dinging every second. She couldn't reject phone calls fast enough. As the *Martha Movin' Out* tour's PR, every journalist she had personally invited seated in the Golden Circle directly in front of the stage wanted to know from her what was going on – and wanted a quote from Martha.

Oh my God, Martha, she thought. 'I must see Martha,' Daisy demanded over the increasingly strident uproar.

'She will have gone,' Danny shouted in reply. 'You saw Jimmy take her off stage. He knows what to do, she will be in her car well away by now.'

'I'll call her,' panicked Daisy. But her phone was not allowing her to make outgoing calls, overwhelmed by the incoming demands of the baying media. Then the whole internet and mobile phone networks ground to a halt. The system was swamped as more than five hundred emergency calls were made by the public from inside and outside the entertainment complex.

Ambulances, police officers, first responders, radio reporters, TV news trucks with satellite up-links, and the thoughtless who are never happier unless they are watching other people's anguish unfold, rushed to the plaza outside the massive dome.

Ten-year-old Camden Town native Amelia Cohen, Mia to her friends and family, was the second person to die that night – the life crushed out of her by the selfish stampeding crowds. Her death passed unnoticed by almost everyone – such was the bedlam.

Yuliet Spooner had surreptitiously moved – she now sat at the top of the seating block quietly observing from on high, taking the occasional picture and making notes – no one noticed her in the pandemonium. To her experienced eye something wasn't right – her career had taken her all over the world to what are euphemistically called *hot spots*. She had witnessed random shootings and calculated assassinations – even speaking with the gunmen, all too eager to show off. She just escaped with her life on the last 'plane out of Kigali the day after Rwandan genocide began – she was there to interview Agathe Uwilingiyimana, the late Prime Minister of Rwanda, who had been slain earlier that day.

Stanislaw Nowak, the producer of what, up until then, had been the culmination of months of work was in shock. He was exhausted from unsuccessfully attempting to remove the leaden almost headless corpse from on top of him. Sergeant Rob Andrews levered away Detective Sergeant Michael Maguire, his former colleague, to release Nowak. He shouted, 'Get out Nowak. Go to the Green Room and stay there.'

His shouted command was ignored – so he grabbed Nowak by his blood-soaked shirt pulling him to his feet, 'Get out of here. Green Room. Now!'

Nowak, who had been sitting immediately behind

Maguire, gazed at Rob Andrews uncomprehendingly – these bodily fluids were not what Nowak normally enjoyed in his sordid private life.

Andrews tried again. 'Now. Get backstage and stay in the Green Room. Do not, I repeat not, move from there.'

Nowak snapped, suddenly switched to attention – he lumbered up the stairs brandishing his AAA pass, Access All Areas. He was none too gentle with anyone who got in his way – pushing them aside. Some stumbled. Some fell. Some swore. Some recoiled in horror at Nowak's disgusting bloodied state. But he didn't care. He crashed through the security gates and into the relative serenity of the backstage lift.

The Green Room, booked for the private after-show party, was filling with an increasingly noisy throng of cast, crew, musicians, a few journalists, and 'friends and family,' the hangers on who know someone – or know someone who knows someone. Everyone demanding to know what was happening and why they were locked in there. *Don't you know who I am?*

Many made the most of the lock-down, unaware of the gory details of what going on outside – the free bar was doing brisk business. Waiting staff, wearing gold Martha Movin' Out aprons, distributed small plates of food – which were disappearing as fast as they could be served.

Nowak burst into the Green Room to be greeted by hysterical shrieks. He was an appalling sight, covered by the scattered contents of Maguire's skull – in hindsight it was agreed that Nowak together with the other bespattered VIPs and celebrities should have been kept isolated.

Nowak collapsed into a chair in a corner – he was uncontrollably shaking and on the verge of tears.

The glitterati in the Green Room lost their appetite for the gourmet grub – but found an increased need to load up with free alcohol. Some returned from the lavatories with an intense feeling of happiness, inappropriate sexual arousal, loss of contact with reality, and a remarkable effect on the reward pathway in the brain. A few had left careless evidence of white powder around their nostrils, further corroborated by remarkably dilated eyes.

Up in the catwalk high above the rapidly emptying auditorium Aleksandr Makarov looked down at the results of his day's work – his *moment in time*, as he liked to call it. He alone was impervious to what he considered to be the collective stomach-turning emotion generated by Martha's fans below him.

Aleksandr Makarov wasn't the name he was given at birth, but instead one the philologist engaged by the FSB had given him – the Russian Federalnaya Sluzhba Bezopasnosti, more commonly known as the Federal Security Service. Makarov had long ago determined his name was suitably anonymous and could see no point in changing it back to his family and given name when he left the FSB twenty years ago to pursue a lucrative freelance career as a hired assassin. He had decided this would be his last job. The police and security services had never caught up with him – luck and careful planning on his side. *They only have to be lucky once, I must be lucky all the time* he told his fellow assassins announcing his retirement via an encrypted message on the dark web. His hope was he could settle down to enjoy his accumulated wealth with his recently acquired girlfriend, who knew him only by his given name and who had no idea that he was an international gun for hire. She thought he was a highly successful, freelance global pharmaceuticals sales consultant.

Just before pulling the trigger, he checked his mobile phone. The signal was strong and the battery good – he had not been stood down by the UK mobile phone number. He calmed his breathing and steadied his heart rate for what, for him, was an easy shot. As soon as the subsonic round had left the rifle Makarov was on his way – saving a precious one and a half seconds. He did not need to see the certainty of his marksmanship – like a rugby player knowing when the ball was kicked safely between the posts. He just had time to see a head catastrophically distribute its blood and jelly-like contents onto those seated near his target before he was temporarily blinded by the dazzling effects lighting.

He made his escape quickly and unseen – his instructions had been, under all circumstances, not to be discovered. He regretted that he would have to leave behind the Vintorez rifle, originally issued to him by the Russian special operations units controlled by one of the main military intelligence services of the Spetsnaz. One of several he had *forgotten* to return when he changed careers – his fee for today's work easily covered its cost. Not that he needed to replace the weapon.

He quickly looked around for anything that might give him away. With his gloved hand he had already picked up and pocketed the single spent SP5 cartridge that had recently done its duty propelling the Teflon-coated subsonic 9mm x 39mm hollow-point round across the diagonal of the O2 arena at 263 metres per second.

As Aleksandr Makarov carefully retraced his steps along the elevated catwalks he had taken much, much earlier that day, he arrived at his chosen hiding place for his weapon. The maze of cables and air-conditioning conduits had offered several choices. He carefully opened the access hatch with his multi-purpose pocket-knife – a Russian imitation of the ubiquitous Swiss Army Knife. The rifle wrapped in black cloth would not be seen by anyone casually inspecting the area in a first pass. The rifle, inevitably, would be found – but its location would hopefully confuse for a short while the forensic teams trying to establish from where the shot had been fired and at whom he was aiming. Of course, the detailed inspection by scene-of-crime and forensic officers would inevitably discover the weapon, but this would buy time – not that there was anything to personally identify him with the Russian weapon. All identifying marks had been filed off and then acid-etched away. He relocked the hatch.

He wouldn't be seen as it was forbidden for anyone to enter the walkways above the auditorium when people were present below – and it was almost impossible to be seen by most casual observers at arena level. There was little he could do about the disturbed dust – as a distraction earlier in the day he had deliberately scuffed and buffed various other areas by taking various paths along and around the elevated catwalks close to the taut PTFE-coated glass fibre fabric roof of The O2 entertainment complex on the Greenwich Peninsula in southeast London.

He brushed the remaining obvious dirt from his clothes and made his way back down into the public levels to join the panic-stricken throng hurrying from the O2.

In the chaos he planned that no-one would see him make his escape; the spent cartridge to be thrown later into the nearby River Thames to join centuries' worth of trash, treasure, firearms, and inevitable supermarket trolleys that one day might be discovered by the mud larks.

The clothes he was wearing would be given the following day to a homeless man he had identified during his recce – he had checked there was no nearby CCTV to capture his altruism.

With a spring in his step, he briskly strolled along the newly created *The Tide*, London's first elevated park, towards North Greenwich Pier to take, as planned, the next Thames Clipper River Bus.

My slow boat to safety, Makarov mused.

DAY ONE
THURSDAY NIGHT

THE UNEXPECTED ALWAYS
HAPPENS UNEXPECTEDLY

THE BEST LAID PLANS SOMETIMES FAIL FOR extraordinary reasons as in Aleksandr Makarov's case or, more often, simply bad luck. On this occasion both.

Makarov hadn't considered the effect of seventeen Special Forces soldiers in the *Martha Movin' Out* audience having a well-earned treat – some with their partners and children.

Several, those without family or children with them, were covertly armed with the Swiss-made Sig Sauer P228 pistols chambered with thirteen 9mm rounds. The Government, led by recommendations from the various security agencies –

including the SIS, the Secret Intelligence Service, AKA MI6; the Security Service, AKA MI5; and SO13, the Anti-Terrorist Specialist Operations branch of London's Metropolitan Police Service – had collectively decided that, due to recent random terrorist attacks, covert weapons would be carried by some 'off-duty' fully-trained authorised personnel, especially in situations that might attract unwelcome activity, such as concerts and large sports events.

Sergeant Ritchie Macpherson – known as *Gherkin* to all – thought he saw a muzzle flash just before the screaming started. He wasn't certain in amongst the phone torches, wrist bands and the show's pyrotechnics but he was suddenly on high alert, like a Meercat sensing a predator. Meercat sentries give different alarm calls depending on whether the predator is a mammal, a bird of prey or a snake. Gherkin's colleagues saw him stiffen and immediately joined him in high alert in an attempt to assess the threat – almost certainly a mammal or a snake.

'What is it?' demanded *Doughboy* – a fellow regimental sergeant.

'Thought I saw a muzzle flash,' Gherkin hesitated, 'Delete that. Certain I saw a muzzle flash.'

Doughboy started to reply, 'You need to calm down mate, this is— '

The build-up of screams and panic that was spreading around and along the audience confirmed that something had happened. The off-duty troop, without hesitation, transformed from husbands, fathers, wives, mothers, and partners back to their day job.

Gherkin was a trained sniper, so instinctively knew what the subtle tell-tale sign of a muzzle flash from a rifle looked like – in the noise of the auditorium and in amongst the pyrotechnics there was no chance that the semi-suppressed report could be heard.

They all carefully scanned the most likely sniper vantage points. They kept their inspection low key so that anyone high up in technical chaos of the roof space should not notice – unlikely in the densely packed crowd.

The nickname *Gherkin* had been with Sergeant Ritchie Macpherson since he joined the Paras, many years ago – and the name had been adopted by the Special Projects Team, the official name for the Special Air Service's anti-hijacking counter-terrorism team trained in close quarters battle, sniper techniques and who specialise in hostage rescue in buildings or on public transport. In the armed forces, nicknames stick with people for the rest of their life – Ritchie Macpherson gained the epithet simply because he hated gherkins in his Maccy-D. *'If I had wanted fuckin' vegetables with my meat, I'd have gone to a fuckin' poncy place.'*

Doughboy – Sergeant Greg Bounds – was lumbered for life with his moniker from an earlier age as a simple squaddie because he refused to eat a meal without some sort of bread. He, like many of his regimental sergeant colleagues, had enjoyed 'baptising' new recruits – payback time passing on the same ridicule to those that they now led: *'Do unto others as you have had done unto you.'*

But it was *Cilla* who spotted Aleksandr Makarov. 'Far end, high, two o'clock from stage, above block four-zero-niner' she raised her voice so her colleagues could hear, 'access door at roof level.'

It was the opening and closing of the small hatch that drew her eye to it – a sudden flash of light and then gone. Sergeant Olivia Black – *Cilla* – had only been in the Special Projects team for four months, but she had already earned the respect of her colleagues in an operation at Stansted airport, the designated hijack airport where police and the SAS regularly train for such an eventuality.

Captain Stephen Jasper, troop commander, pecked his wife on the cheek, 'Keep the families here. Away from the panic. You should be safe. Back soon – keep your phone on.' Mrs Jasper did as she was told corralling the partners and children – as the wife of any officer would do. Captain Jasper then took command of his team.

'Cilla take Gherkin and Doughboy to where you saw the light. Are you armed?' asked Jasper.

Without a further word, the unarmed Gherkin was surreptitiously handed a pistol by one of his armed colleagues. No-one saw – *no point in causing more panic,* he thought. And with that they were off at a steady trot – looking like any other panicking member of the audience.

'You lot get outside – look for anyone acting suspiciously or too nonchalantly. Hopefully, you'll know what you are looking for when you see it, but it will be difficult – but we do difficult. We don't have our normal comms – we'll use the WhatsApp group we set up. Remember our families and children are on it too – so keep it clean. I'll talk to HQ. Terry and Spud with me. Looks like a commotion up there.' Stephen Jasper pointed to the mid-tier seats to the right of the stage, at where Detective Chief Superintendent Bill Kelly was trying to take control.

'Right then, let's see what's occurring.' For a *Rupert*, Jasper was well-respected by his troop having fought with them on a couple of very tricky missions – *tricky* being a troop euphemism for *'fucking outrageously dangerous.'*

Jasper, Terry, and Spud carefully wrestled their way through the exiting crowds – the panic seemed to have subsided a little. On the way Jasper called his HQ Officer Commanding at Stirling Lines, Credenhill via his secure mobile phone.

'I don't fully know what we are dealing with here,' Jasper was crisp and precise, he gave a succinct sit rep. 'Recommended putting Blue Thunder on standby. I'll get back to you ASAP. Standby.' He ended the call and put the phone in his inside zipped jacket pocket.

Jasper's CO took the recommendation. Blue Thunder, the 70-strong unit trained in tackling domestic terror scenarios, moved to five-minute standby. Two Chinook helicopters were wheeled out of their hangers 170 miles to the east-northeast of the O2 Arena.

A couple of security guards tried to prevent the three-man team from entering the VIP and celebrity seating area – none of them had seen the distinctive MoD passes before, but they quickly got the drift following some assertive interaction. Neither were going to argue.

Bill Kelly was, at first, not pleased by the arrival of three strangers. He was about to order them to leave.

'We saw the muzzle flash.' Was all that was needed to be said. Jasper showed his pass and thrust out his hand. 'Captain Jasper, MoD. I led the team who rescued Martha and Vikki.'

Kelly shook his hand more in an instinctive reaction than in greeting. He introduced himself. 'Detective Chief Superintendent Billy Kelly, I think we spoke on the phone.'

Jasper nodded and continued. 'One of my team saw someone high up in the grid. I have three of the team going up there now. More of the team are outside on the plaza, seeing what they can see. I don't hold out much hope in the crowds, but we thought we should try?'

'I was off-duty,' Kelly was equally straight to the point, 'Not now. One of my officers is dead. Not a lot left of his skull.'

Captain Jasper looked down at the bloody remains of Maguire, now lolled in the aisle where he had been unceremoniously dumped by Nowak and Rob Andrews. Like Kelly, he had seen it all before in more places than he cared to remember – Mogadishu, Sierra Leone, Helmand, Iraq, Ukraine… Death is death. It is never pretty – he knew what he was seeing.

'Probably a hollow-point bullet. Expands when it enters, so makes a bigger hole, causing more damage. Hollow points usually stop inside their target, so they impart more kinetic energy, which means they are more lethal. But from the mess, this round looks frangible, intended to disintegrate upon impact – meaning less likely to harm those around the target.'

Bill Kelly assessed Captain Jasper's dispassionate summary. 'So, my man was the target?'

'Looks that way. But you are the policeman.' Jasper replied. 'We are trying to catch the shooter for you. That's all we can do. Excuse me.'

And with that Captain Jasper, Terry and Spud left.

Meanwhile Cilla, Gherkin and Doughboy were lucky. Just as they reached the upper level, having forced their way upstairs through the oncoming crowds desperate to leave – and wrecking a couple of security doors on their way – they spotted the figure of Aleksandr Makarov coming out of a door marked *'Authorised Access Only.'* Health and safety regulations demanded that no-one is allowed on the catwalks high above the audience unless they are in pocketless overalls. Show crew normally wear working blacks with the O2 Arena logo embroidered on the front. Makarov was on his own, in normal casual clothing, looking supremely confident, almost cocky – his back was to the three special forces soldiers.

'That must be him.' Cilla was on full alert. No-one else had ventured from that direction. The issue was getting close enough to be able to restrain him without endangering civilians or creating more panic. Firearms were out of the question – for now.

The three followed Makarov from about thirty-five metres away – they wouldn't be spotted walking briskly with the escaping crowds, down the escalators and along the O2's *The Avenue*, towards the south of the round dome and onto the main entrance.

As part of the emergency evacuation plan all entertainment venues, shops, cafés, and restaurants within the dome had been closed adding to the chaos. Sirens and alarms were sounding everywhere – a dispassionate female voice on a digital loop asked visitors not to panic and to leave quietly by their nearest exit. Bills were left unpaid in venue-sanctioned *runners* – to the inappropriate glee of many and the chagrin of waiting staff who would receive no gratuities.

Cilla WhatsApp'd the rest of the team. 'Eyes on. One point eight five metres. Slim. Blonde hair. Tan leather jacket. Blue Jeans. Just passing *Bar Indigo* on his left. Heading for main entrance.'

Jasper replied. 'Cilla, Gherkin and Doughboy stay with him.'

He ordered the other nine to take up strategic positions – three loitering outside the main entrance and the rest watching the routes to the bus station, taxi rank, underground station, and the paths to the car parks. 'Remain inconspicuous, we can't draw down weapons in this crowd. Follow the target and update. Restrain if you can without endangering civilian life. Terry, Spud with me towards North Greenwich Pier head. Hopefully one of us will catch him.'

Makarov had reconnoitred his escape options a couple of days earlier posing as a tourist with map and camera in hand. His KGB training officer, a former British member of the UK´s secret service now residing in Moscow, reinforced the importance of his eleven Ps: *Proper Prior Planning and Practice Prevents Piss Poor Performance*; adding *and always take a Pre-action Precautionary Pee.*

Makarov had carefully considered all possibilities – bus, the Jubilee Line on London´s underground maybe changing onto the DLR or Queen Elizabeth Line, taxi, hire car, chauffeur, the Emirates Air Line – the cable car across the river Thames. He decided that the Uber-sponsored Thames Clipper river buses were the least obvious route and therefore his preferred getaway.

Two weeks earlier Makarov had taken a one-month rental on an anonymous Airbnb studio flat one stop on the Docklands Light Railway from London City Airport. His choice of river taxi should work well – the studio flat just two hundred metres from the Royal Wharf pierhead. From the boat to the flat he had planned a circuitous route that found several CCTV black-spots where he could reverse his jacket, don a flat-cap, and put on heavy framed glasses – he also would change his walking style from brisk to slow with curved back and short paces. In the studio flat he had secreted an expensive leather briefcase, with passport, Euros, credit cards, and boarding pass all in a tested alias that would not alert the authorities. Necessary precautions but it was unlikely that the Police would ever find out who he was.

He planned to depart very early the following morning in a dark pinstriped suit, white shirt, black brogues, and old school tie; crisply stride to Pontoon Dock station and take the driverless DLR train to London City Airport to join the throng of city-types travelling on the first flight of the day to Zurich. He was a master of disguise.

Makarov continued to execute his exit plan – he briskly strolled towards North Greenwich Pier to take the next Thames Clipper river bus down river. At first he was not aware of his followers or that he was walking straight towards Jasper, Terry, and Spud. However, as he approached the jetty, his KGB and FSB training kicked in – he instinctively thought he noticed his followers in the distance. *Was he being paranoid? How had they possibly picked him up so quickly?* He surreptitiously increased his pace – the Thames Clipper *Monsoon* was readying to depart.

Jasper, Terry, and Spud increased their pace confirming Makarov's fear. He had no idea by whom he was being followed and how they had spotted him in the developing chaos.

Even if they were in contact with the Police, with all the bedlam and distractions it was unlikely that they would be able to get their act together in the few minutes it would take the boat to sail downstream to the newly opened Royal Wharf Pier on the other side of the river.

They do not look like police, so who are they? he worried. *Maybe a wet team paid to eliminate me to tie up loose ends.*

He ignored the direction signs and the patiently queuing passengers as he trotted down the inclined walkway trying to look like a selfish idiot not wishing to miss his boat. Several waiting passengers responded with typical British sangfroid managing sotto voce tutting and the occasional, 'Well honestly' combined with hopefully *meaningful stares.*

He didn't like it but was now committed to this escape route. He had no weapons on him apart from the small knife. All other routes were now not an option – keep moving forward was his dictum.

The crew of the *Monsoon* began casting off its lines tethering the river taxi to the floating pontoon. The gap very gently widened. Makarov sprinted the last ten metres, leapt over the barrier and lunged for the stern of the departing boat.

The plan would have worked had it not been for the green slime from constant wetting of the River Thames making the decking on the wrong side of the barriers slippery. What should have been an easy jump was doomed as soon as

Makarov's feet had left the pontoon – like skating on ice. He nearly made it to the good ship *Monsoon* to the astonishment of the crew carefully coiling up the thick mooring lines. His chest hit the edge of the afterdeck with some force, winding him. His hands attempted to get a grip on the stern rails of the departing clipper, but his momentum was not enough. He slid down towards the water.

Had the *Monsoon* been one of the more modern vessels driven by waterjets he would probably have survived. But the *Monsoon* was propeller driven by two powerful engines. His animal-like scream as his legs were entangled in the rapidly spinning brass propellers was the second traumatic experience for many of the departing fans that evening.

Captain Stephen Jasper turned to his troopers, some now assembled on the pontoon watching the traumatised crew shutting down the engines, 'Right stand down – not a lot we can do here. Doughboy, tell the others and the families. See you back at the HAC Mess – my round. We don't want to be involved with this. As usual speak to no-one, we weren't here. I'll talk to the Police and HQ to straighten things out.'

No-one could endure Makarov's level of pain for long – for him, it seemed like time without end.

In the floodlights illuminating the river and gently bobbing floating pontoon, the Thames around the stern of the clipper turned from murky brown to vibrant red as Makarov's body was dragged down. Within his blood and oxygen starved brain he enjoyed a moment of pride – he would be remembered and celebrated by his industry for yet another professional job well done. Reputation was all – even as he bled out

In exquisite pain there are no villains or heroes – death was a glorious release.

His final regret was his future life would not be fulfilled. He would never be aware that he had failed in his mission.

DAY ONE
THURSDAY NIGHT

SCENE OF CRIME

'BILL, HOW ARE YOU? THIS IS A BIT OF A HORLICKS?'
Detective Chief Inspector Harry Bodkin surveyed the scene.

'You got here quickly Harry,' responded Bill Kelly to
his old friend. Harry Bodkin and Bill Kelly had been at the
Hendon Police College together many years before. They
had remained good colleagues and inevitably distant, yet
firm friends. They shook hands as Bodkin looked around.

'Your sergeant called it in. I just happened to be near
the control room,' explained Bodkin. 'Realised it was serious
and blue-lit it here. Had hundreds of calls – some said there
had been a bomb. Armed support. Anti-terrorist squad.
Uniform. Mobile control rooms. The whole team is setting

up outside. All being inundated with the press and bloody politicians wanting to be seen to be seen demanding to know what is going on.'

Harry Bodkin was not as ambitious as Bill Kelly, preferring to stay with good old-fashioned assault, burglary, and murder – unlike Kelly whose rise in the National Crime Agency had been steady rather than spectacular. Both were good investigators with loyal teams.

Detective Chief Superintendent Bill Kelly headed up a serious organised crime investigation team at the National Crime Agency – qualified in covert surveillance, source handling, hostage negotiation, and responsible for numerous national and international investigations into serious and organised crime, from international financial fraud through to human trafficking, arms dealing and drug trafficking. Tonight in 'civvies,' not his normal work-day M&S off-the-peg suit and restrained tie – he now felt uncomfortable in his camel-beige chinos, blue canvas deck shoes and Harlequins' rugby shirt with the famous jester logo.

Detective Chief Inspector Harry Bodkin headed a Major Investigation Team – the specialised homicide squads of the Metropolitan Police in London, tasked to investigate cases of murder, manslaughter, attempted murder where the evidence of intended threat and other investigations identified for specialist needs.

'This looks like another fine mess you've got me in. Have you IDd the victim yet?' asked DCI Bodkin. Police black humour helped to keep a distance from the human tragedy of death.

'He was one of mine. DS Michael Maguire.' Kelly forgave Bodkin's facetious question.

'Oh. Christ. Sorry. I didn't know.' Bodkin felt uncomfortable and looked at Kelly for a sign of forgiveness.

Kelly patted his old mate on the arm. 'Nothing more to be said.'

Curt exchanged nods acknowledged the end to any misunderstandings.

Bodkin was dressed in his work-day dark grey suit, white shirt with Metropolitan Police cufflinks, and a plain blue tie. His black shoes were perfectly polished. He was an imposing figure at one metre ninety tall with his body in proportion for his height. His parted greying hair matched the colour of a simple moustache.

'My sergeants and the rest of the team will be up here presently. You know that you and your team cannot continue to investigate this – you are witnesses and too personally involved.' Bodkin tried to put on his most friendly voice. He knew that Kelly would be hurting for his colleague.

'I suppose so, but this *is* personal.' Kelly stopped. He wanted to consider his thoughts before he could no longer retract anything.

'So, what happened?' Bodkin needed to know as soon as possible what led up to the shooting. Before Kelly could answer Bodkin's phone rang. 'Sorry, must take this. My sergeant.'

He listened without saying anything. His response was a simple 'Okay, I'll be there as soon as I can.'

He looked at Kelly with an ashen face, 'A young girl has

been killed in the panic. And now there is a mutilated body in the water by North Greenwich Pier.'

Then Captain Stephen Jasper arrived. The uniformed Police Constable who had been trying to restrain him was red with exertion.

And then another arrived, 'Hello I'm Virginia Stephani. Met Police PR and Comms Team. I was in the audience.'

Kelly, Bodkin and Jasper looked at each other in wonderment. Kelly was first with the acerbic comment, 'Who next I wonder? Colonel Harry Llewelyn with the British Show Jumpers to come thundering down the stairs? Or the Jamaican bobsleigh team?'

Stephani, Jasper and Bodkin gazed at Kelly – events were clearly getting to him.

'I know about the body in the water,' Jasper was crisp. 'I am pretty certain it was your shooter.'

'Who are you?' demanded Bodkin of Jasper.

Kelly responded by first asking Virginia Stephani to leave. 'We'll be back to you as soon as. This is confidential for now.' Bodkin was confused but nodded his assent.

Bodkin and Kelly both took Stephani's business card. Kelly pointed at Daisy deVilliers, clearly in shock, sitting at the far end of a row in one of the seats that wasn't blood splattered. 'That's the concert's PR, go and speak with her. We'll need to issue a statement and schedule a media conference.'

Kelly introduced Bodkin to Captain Stephen Jasper and explained his role leading the team that rescued Martha and Vikki a few weeks earlier from their enforced captivity in the Wye Valley.

'That was your lot was it, was it? A right media frenzy you stirred up. But why are you here?' demanded Bodkin.

'Martha invited us as a thank you. We were delighted to accept on condition that we remained anonymous. One of my team saw what they thought was a muzzle flash – which turned out to be correct. We saw someone in the catwalks over there,' Jasper pointed. 'He was seen escaping through an access hatch. We followed him in the crowds – and I sent a team to intercept.'

Bodkin interrupted, 'Are you armed?'

Jasper ignored the question. He continued, 'His escape route was to be on one of the Thames Clipper boats – he must have seen us. He attempted to jump onto it as it was departing, but he slipped and fell into the propellers. Not nice.'

'Is he definitely dead?' asked Kelly.

'I would have thought so. Not a lot left of his legs – the remains of them in the water.' Jasper was passionless.

'And you are sure he was the shooter?' Bodkin's turn.

'As sure as we can be. He was in the right place at the right time. And increased his pace when he saw us.' Jasper wasn't offended. 'Clearly a professional as we were pretty inconspicuous. Only a trained eye would have spotted us.'

'Right. This is all getting out of hand. Bill, you stay here and protect the area until my team arrive.' Bodkin looked around to see Danny taking pictures on his iPhone. 'Who is he? And where is everyone else?'

'I'll vouch for him. He and Daisy, the PR, helped in our previous investigations. The rest of my team are escorting the VIPs and celebrities to the back-stage Green Room where

45

everyone is waiting to be interviewed.' Bill Kelly was trying to balance being seen to help and a personal determination to find out who had murdered one of his team – *and was this a connection to the past?*

'Right Captain Jasper, explain what your people saw?' Bodkin realised he was speaking to no-one. Jasper had gone.

Out of Bodkin's and Kelly's earshot, Danny stopped taking pictures and was speaking on his iPhone contributing a live report via Radio.co's Pocket Streamer app into Starshine News, his radio station. He stuck to the facts, not mentioning how close he was sitting to the, for now anonymous, dead policeman – Danny following the age-old journalists' adage that they are not to be the story. Basic journalism training ensured he did not reveal names or details of the deceased until the police had the opportunity to contact relatives. Danny was one of the remaining professional journalists in a world where accuracy was often trumped by speed.

Later, in the Green Room, Danny used his iPhone with a professional microphone to record vox pops with enthusiastically helpful celebs all wanting to grab the headlines – all gushed how awful it was and how they had been deeply affected. Not one expressed any feelings for the dead policeman or his family and friends.

Me. Me. Me. I. I. I. Bloody puffed-up half-wits was Danny's private assessment.

Danny photographed everyone he interviewed for inclusion on Starshine's web pages and social media. He could honestly say that he had an exclusive – unlike several of the journalists, some still corralled in the golden circle in front of the stage. Danny uploaded the unedited vox pops to the newsroom's media server along with additional in- and out-cues. He spoke with the overnight duty news editor and arranged to come in an hour earlier than normal to package everything up for his breakfast show contributions. He wasn't going to get a lot of sleep that night.

Only Daisy, in her interview with Danny, had expressed any sympathy for the not-named-Maguire's colleagues, friends and family, carefully spinning the story to ensure it was reported that these were Martha's words. Not surprisingly, Danny gave the lion's share of airtime to Daisy and Martha by proxy.

Gordon, Starshine's breakfast DJ, with his girlfriend-of-the-night left the VIP seating area quicker than almost anyone, arriving first at the Green Room's free bar – the premium offerings supplied as part of several sponsorship deals arranged by Daisy.

Gordon downed a large *Sun-Rum Honey Mojito* on the rocks and was on his second as the other VIPs and celebs arrived. His girlfriend went for a large *Psychopomp's Old Tom Gin* mixed with *Double Dutch Cucumber and Watermelon tonic* over lots of ice and slices of fresh mango. She was already fed up with DJ Gordon's egocentric histrionics and was on her third – she had decided to ditch Gordon and make a beeline for a famous actor whose name she couldn't remember but looked fit enough to take her home for some horizontal de-stressing. If they got as far as home.

It was not unknown for Gordon to be worse-for-wear or even still drunk when he hosted the breakfast show the morning after the night before. The production team exchanged foul-mood reports as a matter of course – all knowing, hoping, that Gordon's days were numbered in a management-planned reshuffle. Audience numbers had been steadily in decline.

Away from everyone Daisy planned a hastily convened press conference with the Police's PR Virginia Stephani – they had got on well enough after a poor start, but it was clear that professional rivalry, albeit well hidden, meant they were never going to be best of friends despite gushing rhetoric otherwise.

Virginia addressed Daisy 'This is what you need to say—'

'I speak on behalf of Martha only. No more. No less.' Daisy had interrupted her. She wasn't in the mood to be told what to do. 'I am not speaking for the police. I will say Martha is devastated at the news that an off-duty policeman was killed at the opening night of the Martha Movin' Out Tour. Her thoughts are with his colleagues, family, and friends at this exceedingly difficult time. Martha asks for privacy for the dead policeman's family and for Martha. We will provide more information about tickets for the remaining tour dates as soon as we can, keep visiting www.MarthaMovinOutTour.com. Remember no G. No questions for now, a further statement will be issued tomorrow when we have more information. That's it.'

Daisy snapped her notepad shut. It was more or less what Virginia wanted – but then she added, 'No mention of the little girl who was killed.'

Daisy was horrified, this was the first she had heard of either. 'What little girl?'

Virginia explained.

'Oh my God, but that's awful. Why do people behave like that?' Daisy was clearly upset by Mia's death. She hesitated, considering her thoughts, 'For now, Martha mustn't know. It will push her over the top. We'll liaise tomorrow to decide when we are ready to announce the news about the death of the little girl. I'll then let Martha and our team know in advance so no one is taken by surprise.'

'We agree. But I'll have to liaise with and get approval from the senior investigating officer,' Virginia responded.

Daisy saw red before telling herself to calm down. 'No statement is issued about this event, the tour, or Martha without my prior approval. I don't care what your boss says.'

Virginia was about to object, but she looked at Daisy and decided that now wasn't the time to take this further as emotions were running high. She smiled non-committedly.

'Right then, before we meet the press, I'm going to get some clean clothes, Maguire's red isn't my shade.' Virginia laughed out loud at Daisy's gallows humour.

Half an hour later Danny, in clean clothes supplied by Daphne, was one of the seventy or so invited journalists rammed into the O2's media room alongside twenty TV cameras and press snappers – word was spreading as the shooting of a policeman at Martha's concert became an international story that would lead the news cycle for several days to come.

The press conference hadn't gone that well. Bodkin had fronted it on behalf of the Police, introduced by the force's PR, Virginia Stephani. Now also in clean clothes and Nike trainers supplied by Daphne, Martha's tour wardrobe mistress, Daisy deVilliers spoke as agreed on behalf of Martha and the tour only.

All they could or would say was that a policeman had been shot and the time of his death. His name was being withheld until family had been informed; and investigations were continuing. There followed the inevitable barrage of questions. Many of the press seemed more interested in whether Martha's next concerts at the O2 would be cancelled and would the paying public get their money back, rather than the dead policeman.

Kelvin Edwards' question was the final of the night, 'Is the policeman's death connected with the kidnapping of Martha and her sister Vikki?' Before anyone could answer Virginia Stephani abruptly stood announcing that was the end for now and further details would be released in due course – she led Bodkin and Daisy out of sight. Before Daisy left, Kelvin Edwards gave her a hard stare – there had been *previous* between them.

Ultimately there was little new to learn for Danny – he had covered most of the bases earlier with his Green Room vox pops, but he stood quietly at the back of the room supporting Daisy hoping no-one from the massed fourth estate would recognise his involvement.

Kelvin Edwards, the showbiz, and gossip columnist from *The Daily Tribune* – allegedly the UK's leading celebrity daily newspaper and on-line blog spot – decided it was time to call in some favours. He had spotted Danny at the back of the room and, as the others left, collared him. Danny inwardly shuddered. Kelvin was the last person he wanted to talk to. Outwardly he put on a show of friendship.

'Kelvin, how are you?' Danny's outstretched hand was ignored.

'What the hell happened? Who was killed and by whom?' Kelvin tried and failed to be friendly. No verbal foreplay – straight to the point.

'Sorry mate, can't help you.' Danny tried to be assertively regretful with a half-hearted smile.

'You were right there beside it all.' Kelvin didn't believe Danny.

Before Danny could reply a uniformed policeman escorted him out the door that the other three had just used – Kelvin tried to follow but was forcibly stopped by the long arm of the law. 'Sorry sir, invited guests only.'

Kelvin knew when he couldn't win.

It had been a long day for both Daisy and Danny – and would be an all-nighter for most of the Police. It was well after one in the morning before Daisy and Danny were able to leave. The London Underground Night Tube, although open to Balham near Danny's flat, didn't appeal – they took the electric black cab ride. Daisy snuggled under Danny's outstretched arm, the carrier bag with their bloodied clothes on the floor. There was little more to be said or could be said with the possibility of being overheard by the driver. They soon both dozed to be awoken, what seemed like only a few minutes later, by the taxi driver asking for forty-five pounds. Danny gave him a fifty-pound note and asked for the receipt.

DAY ONE
THURSDAY NIGHT

MARTHA

Inside her Camden Town, North London flat, Martha was right on the edge – Sky News, playing on her waterproof TV recessed into the wall above her bath, was not helping. Its repetitive rolling news becoming addictive as rolling news often does. BREAKING NEWS scrolled across the screen in the lower thirds: 'Policeman assassinated at Martha concert.' She wondered how long it took for *breaking news* to become *ordinary news*. She rather hoped that there would be yet another no confidence vote, maybe an MP caught in a bizarre sexual ritual, or perhaps taking money for questions – knocking tonight's unwanted news off the top spot.

Martha was aware something was not right when Jimmy had escorted her off stage quickly and forced her to her backstage dressing room. She didn't have a chance to wipe off her stage makeup or remove her stage garb before the close protection team ushered her and her twin sister Vikki away. Neither had heard or seen the panic, such was the efficiency of the security team. Without consulting the Police, they had both been whisked home in Martha's chauffeur driven all-electric Mercedes-Benz EQC.

Martha's driver had been told not to answer any questions other than to say there had been a security incident – not unheard of with fans at high profile events who thought they personally owned a piece of the star. However, Martha had insisted her driver switch on the radio – it wasn't long before Danny's live report on Starshine's eleven o'clock news revealed the extent of what had happened.

The media had arrived surprisingly quickly and were already camping outside Martha's home. They were being held at bay by two of Martha's close protection team who had been urgently despatched as a now-needed precautionary measure. Technicians seated in the back of gaudily sign-written TV vans were extending their masts and raising the satellite uplinks. Enthusiastic in-vision reporters, microphones in hand, breathlessly delivered pieces-to-camera. And, as self-important TV-types are wont to do, they all ignored the double red lines – newsroom managers would sort these tiresome administrative issues out with the police and council the following day.

The blue-white TV lights cast dancing shadows on Martha's fourth-floor bathroom ceiling – reminding her that for some time she had been meaning to have Californian shutters installed. As she reclined in her luxurious roll-top bath, it was strange seeing the outside of her five-storey apartment block live on the news.

What the red tops would give for a picture of me naked under the suds, Martha thought in a perverse moment. *That would distract the headlines.*

She reached for her iPhone to take a selfie in the bath. 'Stupid bitch. Am I mad?' she whispered to herself out loud, putting the iPhone back on the bath-side table.

Her twin sister, Vikki, was in her bath at the rear of the apartment with a large glass of Rioja. No TV. 'All I Need' by Air featuring Beth Hirsch playing quietly on the guest room's music system – randomly selected from the chill-out playlist. Vikki was still on a high from her brief on-stage appearance with her sister. She was already planning how she would spend the royalties from co-writing Martha's latest stellar release.

Meanwhile as Martha laid in her rapidly cooling bath, she realised that, unlike Vikki, she had become accustomed, maybe immune, to paparazzi and the sometimes-unwelcome media attention – but this was different. Death and illness at her concerts whilst not regular, certainly wasn´t unusual – heart attacks, heat-related, alcohol-driven or fans simply overcome with emotion. Stewards and first aiders quietly attended with as little fuss as possible. Few in the audience, and rarely those on the stage, ever knew something was happening.

But Murder? Martha mused. *Bloody hell! Murder?*

A chill quivered up her spine. Her skin tingled. She told herself to calm down.

The news channels and other media thrive on league tables, they claim *for context* rather than morbid titillation – on this occasion they *shrieked*, in carefully orchestrated outrage, the rankings of deathrates at various other global events. Outside of the UK this single death would have barely rated a mention had it not been for Martha's celebrity currency combined with the *murderous assassination* by sniper of a policeman, albeit off-duty, which trumps the deaths of ordinary civilians and so cynically bumps it up the atrocity indices and challenges the tautological creativity of the headline writers.

Assassination by gun fire at large events is normally a random act reserved for the USA driven by its absurd constitutional right to bear massively powerful assault weapons. Outraged right wing US politicians champion that guns don't kill people, it's people that kill people – the work of deranged zealots, supremacists, and those with mental health issues.

For the UK press outlets though, the shooting would catapult the event to the top of the atrocity charts for a few days. All used this shooting as an excuse to remind readers of the bombing at the Manchester Arena just after the conclusion of Ariana Grande's concert – there twenty-two people were callously murdered.

Death, depravity, deprivation, devastation, destruction, disease, desolation, despair, and disaster sells newspapers said one alliterative editor in an expansive mood late one night after a well-refreshed dinner in the private room of a press club. His fellow diners, also editors, nodded sagely – then passed the third decanter of Port to the left.

Now wrapped in towels and dressing gowns, fresh from their scented bubble baths, Vikki and Martha sat on the long cream leather sofa watching rolling TV news – nothing new, just more rehashes of the bones of the story updated every fifteen minutes accompanied by the inevitable urgent music. Self-appointed terrorist experts and celebrity commentators were queuing up at every TV and radio station ready to voice their opinion unencumbered by the benefit of knowledge.

'Those who know anything say nothing, those that know nothing say anything.' Martha, nodding at the TV, was fed up with the so-called experts commenting on her own life – she rarely knew who half these people were. 'They are ultracrepidarians.'

'What?! Ultra what?' demanded Vikki with a laugh.

'Don't you know the old nineteenth century word? Shame on you,' teased her sister. 'Presumptuous critic – one who loves to give opinions on matters they know very little about.'

Vikki looked askance.

'Susie Dent. Countdown. Dictionary corner.' The result of Martha's guilty pleasure watching day-time television on catch up – or often live. 'Would love to get it into my lyrics one day. Your challenge is to find a rhyme or reason.'

The sisters settled down into companionable yet reflective silence – the appalling events of what was meant to be a joyous first night overwhelming them despite the attempt at etymological distraction.

Martha hugged a damask cushion with one hand and held a mug of camomile tea in the other. Vikki stuck to the Licenciado Rioja Reserva 2016 – the bottle now finished. Martha, a long-time Naked Wines' Angel, made a mental note to hide the really good stuff before Vikki started on another bottle.

After a long period of silence Vikki woke the elephant in the room. 'What's going to happen? Will the rest of the tour be cancelled?'

'Oh Christ! I really hadn't thought about that.' Martha's emotions flipped. 'It's not up to me. I'm only the star of the show. That's Stanislaw's and the Police's decision. I suppose it depends how ticket sales are affected. Not sure I'm up to performing tonight. But the show must go on.'

'The Police, SOCOs and forensic teams will want exclusive access for a while,' Vikki had slightly more experience dealing with the Police – much more than she wanted to let on to her sister. 'They'll be going through everything with a fine-tooth comb.'

Martha sat in more thoughtful silence for a while.

'Why do teeth need fine combs?' asked Martha lightening the mood.

They giggled at the stupidity of the question.

'You're not having a lot of luck, are you? First the kidnapping and now this.' Vikki brought the conversation back down to earth. For a change, she was the serious one. 'What do you think your fans are going to do? Say you're jinxed maybe?'

'Oh fuck!' Martha shouted loudly in frustration. 'This is a bloody emotional roller-coaster. I suppose we'll know tomorrow how this will play out. I'll speak with Daisy and the PR team. She'll know how to spin it. I expect Stanislaw will call too. He's not good at sharing his thoughts.' *An understatement if ever there was one,* thought Martha.

Vikki hugged Martha. A big sisterly hug. 'Stay positive sis. Think of it this way. You'll probably grab the headlines across the world, more than ever. No such thing as bad news.'

'Let's hope so.' Martha wasn't so sure.

They continued discussing events and the future for a while, *iffing and butting*, but it wasn't long before the nerves slightly soothed, and their eyes began to droop – they took to their beds for a restless night's sleep.

They hugged again and bade each other good night with wishes that they would sleep well. *After all tomorrow is another day, and it's going to be horribly busy*, were Martha's last thoughts before shutting down.

DAY TWO
FRIDAY

10H00 THE MORNING AFTER,
NEW SCOTLAND YARD

THE INCIDENT ROOM AT NEW SCOTLAND YARD WAS packed. Final editions of that morning's newspapers were scattered across the fake-oak side table beside the tea, coffee, jugs of tap water, croissants, and Danish pastries.

'No bloody orange juice due to the bloody cutbacks, I bloody suppose,' harrumphed DCI Harry Bodkin to no one in particular. A sergeant approaching the refreshment station promptly u-turned – his DCI was clearly in a *bloody* mood.

Bodkin hadn't slept well for the three hours he had lain in his bed. He had been woken from his tossing and turning at seven o'clock by Deputy Assistant Commissioner Keith Wallace. Bodkin wasn't surprised that his DAC was taking an interest – he had a reputation for fronting up major enquiries to boost his profile; it was rumoured he was going to retire soon to stand as an MP.

'I assume you have seen the headlines. I want answers. Daily update at a minimum, that's an order. I will e-mail you confirmation.' Wallace offered no opportunity to respond.

Bodkin didn't bother with anything more than a grunt of assent as he thumbed the red button on his phone.

There would be plenty of time for conversations, recriminations, and scape goats. Trumped up half-wit. He threw the phone onto the bed, then stood under a hot and then icy cold shower to try to improve his foul mood.

The headlines did not make comfortable reading for anyone in the police, especially the combined squads of the National Crime Agency and the Major Investigation Team. The Newspapers were *demanding* answers with *a call for* enhanced security at public events – they were all under pressure from their publishers to increase circulation. The mood of many journalists was not helped by the late-night timing of the incident – several reluctantly called back to work to research and write the back story, and to pester their personal contacts in the police. It was all too late for the first and early editions already on their way around the country in a fleet of articulated trailers. The on-line versions, now read far more than their physical cousins, needed constant updating, and amending as the news and rumour filtered out. Celebrity opinion was reported from Twitter or grumpy personal phone-calls despite most not being anywhere near

Martha's concert – *disgust, outrage and sympathy for Martha* put into many of their mouths. *Never let the truth get in the way of a good quote*, the mantra of the less-scrupulous hack in the middle of the night. *They won't remember what they said anyway* their feeble excuse for ignoring the basic rules of journalism.

All the tabloids were jockeying for reader-grabbing headlines using Martha's name and the death of a policeman to sell their sensationalised reportage. Even the broad-sheets and the other so-called serious papers joined the tabloid throng, all hoping to do the bidding of their owners.

"BRUTAL COP MURDER AT MARTHA OPENING NIGHT" *screamed* that morning's headline in 200-point bold block capitals on the front page of one of the red tops, with a full-length picture of Martha from the concert the night before – with a gratuitous display of unsupported side boob. Alongside was a special two-for-one offer for future *Martha Movin' Out* VIP concert tickets.

The Financial Times was more prosaic: "Policeman Shot at Concert" with the sub-header, "The Perils of Promoting Events. Concert Tour Revenue in Question." As frequently quoted, show business is exactly that – the business of show making a profit for its promoters and investors. Or a tax-deductible loss when things didn't go right. Win-win. The talent, on whose tails they affixed, simply cost-of-sales.

It was reported in all the papers, and on breakfast TV and radio news that the Prime Minister, The Right Honourable Phillida Campbell-Horrocks, was going to make a statement in The House. She was briefed at the regular morning meeting that 'she' – AKA her comms team – had already

Tweeted her *personal* heart felt sympathies to friends, family, and colleagues of the dead Police Officer. The Leader of the Opposition, and leaders of the national and minority parties had also shared their *thoughts and prayers* – and then didn't miss the opportunity to criticise the PM for lack of Police resources. It was all a bit half-hearted, going through the motions – the current Parliament had about three months to run. All the party leaders were under pressure to retain their positions. The back-stabbing season was firmly open when political hot air turns into duplicitous spin accompanied by deniable off-the-record briefings – which soon twists and turns into cold-blooded treachery and then to stabbing in the chest. Politics can be a sordid game.

The trolls on social media were having a field day – taking every opportunity to lambast the politicians and each other in increasingly outrageous attacks.

The death of Amelia, Mia the 10-year-old girl had not yet made it to the media or to the politicians – at some point, with the family's permission, a statement would be issued citing the unfortunate circumstances. It was unlikely there would be a prosecution as there was simply no evidence – and the chances of obtaining any were slim or not even appropriate. No-one was sure that a crime had been committed.

A few media outlets had linked the shooting story to Martha's performance in their critiques – generally all positive, some even five stars which, in its own right, was remarkable. The hospitality of the after-show party had no influence on the collective critique – obviously. There was some mild criticism that Martha was not available for a post-show presser – but most reluctantly agreed that due to the unfortunate circumstances this was to be expected. Daisy had given the marauding media a couple of quotes from Martha – or there was more invention in the name of a good story. Normally Daisy would have objected, but on this occasion all news was good news. Good for Martha and for Nowak.

The *cold-blooded murder* of the currently anonymous policeman had consumed the front-page headlines and many of the inside pages of the day's papers, but they had not connected the death of Makarov with Maguire's murder – consigning that story to well inside, taking the line that an unnamed panicking or drunk tourist had tried to catch the departing boat.

There were a few smart phone pictures of Makarov taken by a phalanx of citizen journalists – hastily edited to remove the worst of the gore. Being night-time, with just a few overhead lights, most were grainy, soft focus from camera shake, or poorly exposed – even the most skilful Photoshop operator had been struggling to rescue anything useable.

Few on-line blogs and news-posts mentioned Makarov at all – no one knew who he was, and so he couldn't be famous. He was a no-mark and therefore of no commercial use apart from the titillation value for the more blood thirsty.

The jubilant headlines from just a few weeks ago celebrating Kelly's and the Special Forces' rescue of Martha and Vikki had been forgotten or consigned to rehashed backgrounders, boxouts and padding.

Bill Kelly and Harry Bodkin stood either side of the Clevertouch interactive white board in the internally publicised, newly refurbished, fully integrated meeting room.

Kelly, as the senior officer, began the briefing. 'Detective Chief Inspector Bodkin will be the SIO in the murder of our former colleague Detective Sergeant Michael Maguire. I have assured him that you, my team, will give every assistance we can. My team cannot investigate this ourselves as we are personally involved and witnesses, so must remain arm's length. In due course DCI Bodkin and his team will interview us all. There is nothing to hide and I do not want you comparing notes. Like you all, I want to find the bastard who did this. We work together. But I don't want to see or hear sources close to the police, or any headlines with fake or sensationalised news.'

Kelly held up a couple of the tabloids. 'I am getting increasingly pissed off that an influential slice of the media be it print, TV or radio has decided to insulate its morals in the name of so-called public interest – even when they know it to be distorted, false, or invasive beyond reason. We are not their sales team – all unguarded gossip and unapproved off-the-record briefing does is boost their advertising revenue and affect our investigations. So, no one, I repeat no one talks to them – and immediately tell DCI Bodkin or me if you are approached. Understand?'

Most of the room nodded their agreement. They'd heard it all before.

'DS Maguire's death will deeply affect many of you. It is inevitable that your feelings will be raw for a while. The Met's confidential counselling service will be available to anyone who feels that it might help them. No one, including me, will know that you have taken advantage of this service. Neither will it appear on your records. It's not big or clever to bottle up your emotions. You'll be encouraged to talk confidentially about your feelings and emotions with a trained therapist, who'll listen and support you without judging or criticising. Please use the counsellors if needed.'

Kelly, said no more, nodded to Bodkin, then sat in the chair in the front row.

Twenty-eight investigators, researchers and the inevitable administrators were crammed into the fourth-floor meeting room designed to take twenty-four – four rows of six chairs in front of individual touch-screen workstations, with a few stools acquired from the nearby coffee lounge along the window side overlooking the slowly rotating London Eye and the River Thames bustling with boats and barges.

All were grim faced – the loss of a colleague, a serving Police Officer, is always a serious business.

Bodkin took his cue and stood behind the high-tech lectern – he had recently been on the mandatory day-long course learning how to use the multiple features of all the Met's meeting rooms and huddle spaces. He had inwardly groaned when the geeky, over-excited trainer had put up the first of many text-heavy PowerPoint slides: "How To Make Meeting Rooms The Heart of Your Digital Workplace."

What a waste of my time. What's wrong with what we have always done? He stabbed at the AMX meeting room-controller in revenge – the slatted blackout blinds obeyed, as did the lights. In sympathy, the Sharp NEC projector burst into life with a high-definition picture of the interior of the O2 Arena from the night before – replicated on all the individual touch screens.

'Right then, what do we know? At twenty-two, twenty-two last night at the end of the Martha Moving Out concert'

– Bodkin refused to drop the *g*, from Moving – 'Detective Sergeant Michael Maguire was shot in the head by a sniper in what we currently assume is a deliberate assassination. What must not under any circumstances be shared with anyone outside this room is that the suspected perpetrator was spotted and followed as he made his escape.'

A few in the room were unaware of this development. There was a sotto voce chorus of British swearing.

'Did we get him then?' came a voice from the third row.

'Just wait until I have finished,' Bodkin's very little sleep and the wake-up call from Deputy Assistant Commissioner Keith Wallace was making him much more irritable than usual – combined with a lack of orange juice. 'The suspected perpetrator was spotted as he attempted to make his escape. He was followed by members of military Special Forces who had been invited to attend the concert and were in the audience.'

This time the room was more strident in its ad lib comments. Bodkin raised his voice, 'Will you please shut up and listen.'

The room settled down.

'One of the Special Forces team idiosyncratically spotted what he thought was a muzzle flash. He alerted the rest of his team – one of whom observed the shooter escaping through a doorway from the overhead gantries. The SF team covertly followed him to North Greenwich Pier, where the alleged shooter unsuccessfully attempted to jump onto one of the departing river buses. He missed and fell into the water to be macerated by the craft's propellers. He was pronounced dead at the scene.'

'Good job,' came a voice, this time from the back row.

'Not a good job. We've probably lost the main suspect and our key witness.' countered Bodkin. 'Furthermore, the role of Special Forces will not be discussed further with anyone outside of this team. Understood?'

More much affected arse shuffling and muted mumbled comment.

'I said understood.' Bodkin glared at his audience, who acknowledged the order with more enthusiasm before returning to silent and attentive listening. 'The body, without too much of his legs, was recovered.'

Bodkin clicked the remote control and the screen changed to pictures of the corpse, now removed from the water, with blood from the remains of his legs oozing onto the wooden planks of the North Greenwich Pier pontoon.

'There was no ID or anything to suggest who he was. So, for now, we have lost our main lead. All the labels from his clothes had been carefully removed. Nothing. No clues to his identity. We have taken fingerprints and DNA swabs of course. Nothing so far from our databases. We are trying for facial recognition – his face was unharmed. Does this suggest a professional?'

Bodkin looked at his team all busily making notes.

'However, in his pockets we found a pay-as-you-go Oyster Card and a single front door key with no fob or obvious markings – we need to know which door it fits. Not easy as it came from a Timpson mass-produced blank. But it shouldn't be difficult to find out from where the Oyster Card was purchased. High priority please.'

Bodkin paused to let the information sink in, 'Initial thoughts please?'

DS Culpepper sitting in the second row was first to have a go. 'We could assume that the key won't be for a hotel. Too many people would see him. He would want to avoid potential witnesses, no matter how unlikely. Staying with associates maybe, but I doubt it. Most professional hit men are loners. And I think we all agree he was a professional. So, chances are that the key fits a motel room or accommodation with street access. Or some sort of self-catering apartment. Short term let. Airbnb. Something anonymous that doesn't require interaction with anybody. No concierge, or receptionist, or landlady.'

'Good point,' Bodkin nodded his assent. 'Anyone else?'

DC Evans raised her hand.

'We're not in bloody school, no need to raise your hand.' Bodkin's testiness obviously wasn't going to be abated.

'Sorry Sir,' continued DC Evans.

Bodkin glared at her, 'Get on with it if you have something to say.'

'We know he was trying to catch that river bus,' DC Evans started hesitantly, she had been consulting the screen in front of her whilst Bodkin had been speaking. 'Was this a pre-planned escape route? If it was, the boat – the Monsoon – only continues for two stops. Royal Wharf and Woolwich. That might narrow down the area of search. How did he get to the 02 though? Same route maybe? He would have been carrying some sort of bag with the rifle – some fold down pretty small I am told. We know what he was wearing and what he looks like. Maybe we search the CCTV from before the event using facial recognition?'

'Good thoughts, we might get lucky,' Bodkin was slightly less spiky. 'Well done DC Evans. You take the lead on that.'

'What about if we think about his onward travel.' DS Culpepper wanted some of the approbation, 'If he was planning to travel east as DC Evans suggests. Not a lot of connections that way, unless he was planning to double back. If he wanted to get to the main line train terminals or the airports he would have travelled west and used the tube, DLR, Queen Elizabeth Line, a taxi, or a hire car. Why a river bus? Seems a bit slow for an escape. Maybe he was aiming for a boat pick-up? But he won't want anyone else involved if he is the loner that DC Evans suggests, that probably rules out a boat unless he was skippering himself.'

'That's not likely,' Bodkin suggested, 'but worth chasing up. Seems a lot of faffing?'

'He'll want to avoid live CCTV. Hundreds in the stations and on the trains all constantly monitored.' DC Evans picked it up. 'It would have been too late for a 'plane. City Airport has a night-time curfew.'

'But did he come in that way? If not, how did he get to the 02?' Bodkin was pleased with the way his team was thinking. 'So, who was he?'

The pictures from the SOCOs of the now-dead Makarov scrolled through, taken from various angles. A big close-up of his face followed – with its agonised rictus.

All in the room were, by the necessity of the job, familiar with the dead and violent death – but this was a new one for many.

On cue the screen switched to pictures of the virtually headless Maguire. Bodkin was gentler. 'These images were taken by radio reporter Danny Owen almost immediately after the murder. FYI Mr Owen and Ms Daisy deVilliers have been helping DCS Kelly's team with a separate investigation involving Martha.'

The pictures of their colleague caused an uncomfortable shuffle – several of Kelly's team were visibly and audibly upset seeing their recently dearly departed colleague. Somehow the still images, in silent isolation, seemed more shocking and real.

'As you can see, DS Maguire was knocked back by the round's impact and onto the concert's producer and promoter Stanislaw Nowak. The questions we must answer is why was DS Maguire the target? And who was the shooter—'

'Harry, would you mind if I added a few things?' Kelly interrupted. He was aware that this wasn't his show. He stood anyway.

'Of course, carry on.' Bodkin, despite their friendship, had not a lot of choice with Kelly being the senior officer. Bodkin sat heavily into the chair just vacated by Kelly – having first collected a paper cup of coffee and, on a recyclable plate with a wooden knife, a once-warm Danish pastry. He needed the sugar. A member of Bodkin's team had called catering for orange juice – they didn't want to put up with him in a foul mood all day. None had yet arrived.

'The producer and promoter of Martha's show, Stanislaw Nowak is an evil, dirty, two-faced, lying, criminal shit.' Bodkin's team were shocked by Kelly's outspoken appraisal. 'At the NCA we have been trying to pin something on him for years. Mid-level organised crime. Passports. Forgery. People smuggling. Prostitution. And more. But he has always been one step ahead of us. We learned that this concert tour was intended to be a front for people smuggling and possibly trafficking. No longer happening for reasons we do not wish to discuss here. We also know that Nowak is, or was, an associate of The Vory, Conor O'Murchadha and Ali Baka.'

Bodkin and his team sat up and took notice – these were well-known names. There was much scribbling in notebooks and muted excitement.

'At one-point Conor O'Murchadha was considered to be one of Ireland's wealthiest criminals and leader of an extremely well organised Spanish Irish crime syndicate. Ali Baka is associated with and was thought to lead several people smuggling and trafficking operations. Baka met with Conor O'Murchadha in Spain. I said *was* because we now know that O'Murchadha murdered Baka. Conor O'Murchadha was subsequently successfully prosecuted and *was* awaiting sentence. But he too was nastily offed in the Spanish prison. We suspect on the order of The Vory in a revenge punishment.'

Kelly sipped from his cup. Now cold – made a face of disgust. He looked around the room to assess their level of interest – nothing but rapt attention.

'Or did Nowak order the killings?' Surprised noises greeted this potential bolt from the blue. 'It's all about sending a message to keep everyone else in line. My NCA team are investigating, and we will share any relevant intelligence with you all.'

One of Bodkin's team was appalled, probably speaking for them all. 'You mean Martha's tour is involved with The Vory, the Russian super-mafia, and maybe people smuggling?'

'Unknowingly possibly.' Kelly's tone forestalled further questions. 'She, and a few days later her sister Vikki, were kidnapped by Ali Baka. But we are certain she is not involved in any other way. Special Forces rescued them both as you have seen in the news, which is why they and we were at the concert. My team will prepare a briefing file and it will be circulated by Registry. Each file will be uniquely numbered, and you will be expected to sign for it. You will not copy it or reveal its contents to anyone outside this team. You will lock it away when not needed. You must not take the file outside of Scotland Yard. Is that clearly understood.'

There was mumbled assent from the room.

'Is that clearly understood?' repeated Kelly more vehemently.

A chorus of 'Yes sirs,' reassured Kelly that his instruction had been understood.

From his chair in the front row, Bodkin clarified, 'My team is only investigating the murder of DS Maguire. That is as far as our remit goes. Nothing else.'

Kelly finished. 'Finally, from me for now, you should know that DS Maguire and Nowak had an interesting relationship that I have known about for some time.'

Detective Sergeant Rob Andrews looked shocked, 'How come none of the rest of us, knew about that?'

Kelly ignored the question. *Some things are not going to be shared with everyone no matter what I say,* he mused to himself.

With a nod to each other, Bodkin swapped back places with Kelly.

'Some of what my team does will inevitably overlap with the NCA investigations – and we need to know if and where there are connections. And what those connections are? Why

Maguire? How are Nowak and Maguire connected in their *interesting relationship*?' Bodkin stared askance at Kelly. 'I reiterate – for now everything stays with us, the teams in this room. No leaks. No briefings. No press. Not even upstairs.'

Kelly remained silent.

What does Kelly mean by interesting relationship, Bodkin wondered? 'This is a high-profile investigation. The murder of any police office always attracts attention and public outrage. Need 100% effort from everyone. I've already had the DAC on the phone – the bugger woke me. We need answers and soon.'

The room saw their family and spare time disappear in front of them, but there was also some excitement being involved in what was becoming a very high-profile investigation – with all the focus of attention that comes with it. And potential promotion. *And overtime to boot.*

'The DAC started going on about this being a terrorist incident. I think we can rule that out. To the best of our knowledge, Maguire wasn't involved in terrorist investigations. And also this seems to be a cold, calculated assassination, not some random attack?' Bodkin looked to the room for their confirmation of his assessment.

General nodding followed. There was a pause. Bodkin's body language shifted. 'There is also the death of 10-year-old Amelia Cohen. Her parents are, not surprisingly, distraught. It took three hours to establish who she was in the mayhem. Her parents were searching high and low, they thought she had been abducted. Regrettably, her death we believe was probably an unfortunate accident due to the panic. I have asked North London uniform to go to her home to take a statement from Amelia's parents. Can't see there is a lot more for us.'

The death of a child is always difficult even for hardened officers – no-one is immune. Bodkin looked around the room to see some had been affected by Amelia's death.

'Okay that's it for now. I'll circulate roles and responsibilities in the next hour by secure e-mail.' Bodkin sat, drained – with two daughters of his own, he could not begin to imagine what it must be like for Amelia's parents.

Everyone else stood with noisy chatter and some inappropriate laughter – the now hot and sweaty meeting room emptied.

'Bill, a word before you leave.' Harry Bodkin was attempting to remain calm and civilised. There were just the two of them left in the deserted meeting room. Bodkin stabbed at a button and the blinds opened letting in the mid-morning sunlight. 'What is going on? What else do I need to know?'

Kelly went to the coffee station, poured himself one and motioned with a cup to Bodkin. Bodkin nodded, 'Thanks. Milk and four sugars.'

Kelly raised his eyebrows in surprise. Bodkin responded, 'I need the energy.'

They both sat a couple of chairs apart in the front row and turned to each other.

'This is off the record. I haven't made a note of this anywhere – for which I could be justifiably held guilty of misconduct and disciplined. Probably thrown out of the force.' Kelly realised he had to trust his old colleague and hopefully still a true friend.

'Bloody hell Bill, what have you done?' Harry Bodkin was apprehensive.

'A few weeks ago, I realised we were leaking.' Kelly was hesitant, 'Not serious at first but enough to know that Stanislaw Nowak seemed some of the time to be one step ahead of us. This was confirmed when I put surveillance into Nowak's flat – we heard him talking on the phone to someone or some people clearly in the know. At least one could only have been someone in, or close to my team or someone in the know. I laid a few traps – fed different information to various people including Danny Owen and Daisy deVilliers.'

Kelly did not mention the second set of surveillance found by his team already in place at Nowak's Thames-side apartment.

'Oh Christ, that must have been awful. I'd be beside myself if I thought one of my team was on the take.' Bodkin was sympathetic to his old friend. 'Danny and Daisy? They seem far too close to you guys?'

'Danny was the original link to Nowak's people smuggling. He and Daisy kept me informed from the inside of the Martha concert tour. For a journalist he is straight enough – and delightfully predictable. Keeps his mouth shut most of the time and doesn't go public. Daisy is Martha's PR. Level-headed. Panics at first but settles down usefully. Suggest the four of us meet outside of the office.'

Bodkin nodded, 'Maguire then. Why was he murdered? What was the interesting relationship between him and Nowak?'

Kelly tried to remain professional as he revealed *nearly* all to his old friend. 'Maguire's uncle was Commander Barry Fitzpatrick.'

Bodkin didn't need to have the legend that was Commander Barry Fitzpatrick explained to him, but he was confused. 'Keeping the job in the family then? But what's that got to do with this?'

Kelly continued – he didn't want to be interrupted. 'Maguire and Fitzpatrick were both in the army before joining the police. Same regiment, different times. The 5th Inniskilling Dragoon Guards. Commander Barry Fitzpatrick died a few years ago, having taken unexpected early retirement. I found a photograph of Maguire and Fitzpatrick wearing the same ties. I didn't make the connection at first – but then everything clicked into place. I confronted Maguire.'

Kelly drank some of his coffee.

'Maguire's mother, Fitzpatrick's sister, was terribly ill – she found walking any long distance painful. Most of the time she was fine, but the pain would come on suddenly leaving her totally immobile. Her GP wouldn't sign the application for a disabled badge as he said she didn't fit the parameters. God knows why. Maguire's dad was beside himself, tried everything. One day Maguire's father had a call to say that his wife was stranded at a shopping mall. She'd been there for five hours in the cold and damp.'

Kelly exhaled a long sigh. 'She said she didn't like to make a fuss – you know how they are. She thought she'd be fine in a while.'

Kelly paused – he looked out the window as he collected his thoughts. Bodkin finished his coffee – he didn't want to interrupt. Kelly would tell the clearly emotional story in his own time.

'Maguire's mother didn't have a mobile phone. Didn't hold with them. She eventually persuaded a passer-by to call her husband.' Kelly gave a short ironic laugh. 'Eventually Maguire's father found her – he'd been out looking for over two hours. He drove his car into the pedestrian precinct to take her home. Some bloody local plod decided to book him. Not relevant.'

Bodkin snorted at the antics of some bobbies-on-the-beat. 'Why didn't they offer to help rather than simply book him?'

Kelly continued. 'Anyhow, they got her home somehow. If she hadn't had to walk so far from the public multi-storey car park rather than the nearby disabled spaces, she would not have been in the situation she was. The irony was that the disabled bays were full anyway – delivery lorries, four-by-fours, and posh motors. Some with false disabled badges. The local plod didn't book any of them. Maguire thought then something had to be done about policing disabled parking.'

'We don't really have the manpower. And surely that's a job for Traffic Wardens?' Bodkin had some sympathy for the local hard-pressed police.

'Maguire and his parents went to see their GP – but he wouldn't budge. The doc said his mother wasn't disabled enough to have a Blue Badge. Which was bollocks.' Kelly felt his ire rising.

'What happened?' Bodkin was becoming impatient with the rambling story.

'My team had just started investigating disabled, blue badge fraud – worth over fifty million a year to organised crime. Maguire put in a request to be part of my team which I actioned. Stanislaw Nowak, the producer of Martha's show was running a blue badge scam ten years ago.'

Bodkin began to see the connection.

'Meanwhile, Maguire wasn't prepared to see his mother in that situation again. He gave his father Nowak's contact details, who went and saw him. They were not rich, so no way they could have afforded Nowak's prices. Twenty grand or more. Maguire's dad tried everything, appealing to Nowak's better nature. He got stroppy and threatened Nowak with Maguire and Uncle Commander Barry Fitzpatrick. Nowak wasn't threatened. He simply told Maguire's dad to get Fitzpatrick to contact him.'

'Oh Christ.' Bodkin slumped in his chair. His now empty recyclable coffee cup rolled onto the floor where it remained.

'A few days later Fitzpatrick and Maguire spoke to Nowak face-to-face, just the three of them. Nowak offered them a deal. His mother, unbeknown to her, would get a counterfeit Blue Badge if they occasionally helped Nowak, keep an eye out for him. They resisted at first. But Nowak then went for the carrot and stick, said they had no choice. If they didn't help, Nowak said he would end both their careers. Maguire had only just joined my team.'

'What about Commander Fitzpatrick? What did he say? What did he do?' Bodkin was disappointed that one of the Force's heroes may have been turned.

'Fitzpatrick attempted to scare the shit out of Nowak, which didn't work. In the end Fitzpatrick told his nephew, Maguire to get on with it. Family first. On the way home from that fateful meeting Fitzpatrick told Maguire he was taking early retirement. He didn't say why. But, of course, we now know he was stage four cancer. He died soon after. I asked Maguire why he didn't come straight to me with this? I was bloody angry. Felt very let down. Maguire said that Nowak would break his mum's and dad's legs if he told anyone. Three days after the meeting the Blue Badge arrived at his parents' house – they were both ecstatic, couldn't thank their son enough. They didn't know he'd sold his soul to Nowak.'

Bodkin went over to the side table to get another coffee. Kelly finished his and declined another. Whilst Bodkin stirred in four packets of sugar, Kelly picked up the story. 'To twist the knife, Nowak threatened to ruin his uncle's reputation even after his death. He wasn't having that. Maguire's mother doesn't need the disabled badge anymore – she died a few months ago, two weeks after her husband. Maguire has, had no other family. So, all gone.'

Bodkin retook his seat. 'So, what happened?'

'It was Maguire who put Nowak onto Danny. It was Maguire who removed the evidence from our store. It was Maguire who initially warned Nowak that he was being bugged. It was Maguire who warned Nowak about other things. Only Nowak, no one else he insisted. And not everything, just low-level stuff Maguire said to keep Nowak off his back. I did believe him, but now I know of the extent of information passing to Nowak and it isn't low level.'

'So, he was lying?' interrupted Bodkin.

'Despite everything he is… sorry was, generally straight. I think it was a one off to help his mother.' Kelly was surprised at his sudden emotional turn. A lump materialised in his throat and tears formed in his eyes. He gently levered himself up, then walked over to the side table for more coffee to disguise his emotion from Bodkin. He gave himself a good talking to, *stiff upper lip and all that.* Bodkin kindly ignored Kelly's display of emotion – he would have been the same if one of his had succumbed to a similar fate. Kelly faced Bodkin with a determined look, gesticulating with his still empty mug.

'Here's the thing. I believe that Maguire isn't, wasn't, the only inside informer. Hence the need for secrecy. Confidential information is still getting to Nowak, even after I confronted Maguire and we agreed no more.'

Kelly let it hang there.

Bodkin sat in silent contemplation. Informers within the force weren't new but they were an anathema despised by all good coppers. In 2002 the Metropolitan Police conducted *Operation Tiberius,* investigating the extent organised crime affected their operations. It did not make for happy reading. 'I thought we had dealt with all that years ago. Are you suggesting we still have bastard cunts in the force?'

Kelly was taken aback by Bodkin's vehemence and language. 'It will never go away. We both know that. A backhander here. A drink there. Where does it stop? When does a drink become a bribe? When does a backhander become a substantial incentive to turn a blind eye or even collude? Every organisation has bad apples. What price ignoring the Standards of Professional Behaviour and the Code of Ethics? Family member in trouble? A Blue Disabled Badge? How far up the ladder does, could corruption go?'

Kelly and Bodkin trusted each other. Neither thought the other capable of anything other than total integrity.

'Even in death a reputation can be destroyed?' Bodkin didn't name Commander Barry Fitzpatrick or DS Maguire. Some things left best unsaid. 'Are you suggesting Maguire was murdered because he wasn't prepared to sell his soul? Not going all the way providing inside information?'

The elephant in the room now released.

'It has to be one line of enquiry. Or did he know too much? Or too many of the people involved? After our chat, did he tell Nowak that he had confessed to me?' Kelly accepted that he could have been the catalyst for Maguire's murder.

Bodkin was confused. 'But why target Maguire in such a public manner?'

'Possibly sends a message to other insiders who might not fully engage in passing information. Carrot and stick. Contributes to my theory that there are others. Or a message from The Vory? Seeking revenge for buggering up their smuggling business?' questioned Kelly.

'You say Maguire put Nowak onto Danny,' Bodkin was intrigued 'What has Danny got to do with all this?'

'Danny hasn't always been a radio reporter. He was gaining a reputation as an investigative journalist working on the now defunct *Weekend News*. He is a particularly good investigator – for a journalist. We've known each other off and on for many years – shall we say we have a useful understanding. He would have done well if he had joined our lot. Maybe. He's not a fan of rules and regulations.'

Bodkin noted this was the second or third time that Kelly had used the word *understanding* in less than an hour.

'I trust him,' Kelly concluded.

'You didn't answer my question. How are Danny and Nowak connected?' repeated Bodkin.

'Danny was doing a full exposé of the tossers who had been selling and buying illegal blue badges – many from Nowak. Danny had contacted Maguire as a source to corroborate some of his story. Maguire then told Nowak – who visited Danny at his home with a couple of his heavies and threatened him. One of Nowak's lot smashed Danny's foot with a sledgehammer and threatened Danny's family. As a result Danny spiked the story – told his editor the story wasn't there. He explained his injured foot as a car accident. Let's just say his editor didn't believe him. He sacked Danny on the spot.'

'What happened to the piece that Danny was writing?' Bodkin was fascinated.

'Our friends at Five know we have a shared interest in Nowak. I met with one of their liaison people. It took me a while to work out how they knew we knew. They had built up a large file of information on Nowak. Some of the names in Danny's piece were remarkably high profile. They seemed quite pleased that the exposé wasn't published as it would have embarrassed the Government, senior Civil Servants, City banking types, senior business leaders and I believe some colleagues who are probably now residing on our upper floors. As you know when something is erased on a computer, it doesn't go for good. Whilst Danny was being treated for his foot injury, a team went in and downloaded the hidden data. Danny thought he had wiped his hard drive. My contact at Five thought I'd find the manuscript and photographs useful. Danny was surprised when I said I had a copy.'

'How did Five become involved?' Bodkin wondered where all this was going. 'Disabled badge fraud seems a bit low level for them. And surely people trafficking, and smuggling is Six's remit?'

'Our friends in Five and Six have been trying to understand and insert agents within organised crime for years. They've been tracking high level corruption making some people susceptible to blackmail. It's the people and the routes they want to understand rather than just the crime. Organised crime has its fingers in many pies and connections all over the world. But no-one seems to want to share information. They knew of our leak.' Kelly thought for a while. 'I have always thought though that some of the worker bees don't agree with keeping secrets with the home teams. A file was covertly passed to Yuliet Spooner—'

'Oh bollocks, what has she got to do with it? The Centre for Covert Media Studies has been a thorn in our side for bloody years.' Bodkin was getting annoyed

'My boss has bought all this up with the Joint Intelligence Committee but got nowhere.' Kelly was as frustrated as Bodkin was becoming.

'That's daft. Surely, we are all on the same side? And you didn't answer my question. How did Five get involved?'

'They overheard Nowak speaking on the phone to someone involved in my team's investigations. They didn't know who.' Kelly leant back in his chair. 'We do now. At least one was Maguire.'

The meeting room door opened – an assistant from catering services placed two litres of freshly squeezed orange juice on the sideboard seeming surprised there were only two people in the meeting. As he left, he held the door open for Deputy Assistant Commissioner Keith Wallace – who ignored him.

'What do we know then?' demanded the DAC. 'I asked for daily reports.'

'We've briefed the teams. DCS Kelly and I were just catching up,' Bodkin took the lead. 'Nothing to report yet. We'll know more hopefully at tomorrow's morning meeting when we get back first responses. I'll let you know what we know then.'

'Be sure you do. Everything' The DAC turned and left the room.

Kelly and Bodkin exchanged looks.

'He's one I don't trust,' said Kelly.

Bodkin said no more, knocked back an overly large orange juice and then a second. Each went their separate ways after a firm handshake.

DAY TWO
FRIDAY

10H00 THE MORNING AFTER,
MARTHA PRODUCTION OFFICE

'WHAT THE HELL DO WE DO?' ASKED MARTHA Movin' Out tour manager Jimmy Patrick. 'Nowak is the only person who should make that decision,' responded the Martha Movin´ Out tour PR Director Daisy deVilliers. 'I have tried to call him, no answer. Left several messages. I have also e-mailed and WhatsApp'd him. Nothing. I've just switched off my published phone. I was being swamped. Nowak, Martha, and all you guys have my private e-mail and phone numbers? Please only use WhatsApp.'

Everyone agreed, then checked.

Jimmy had been in early that day – he was tired after the events of the night before. He had agreed to meet DCI Harry Bodkin and one of his Detective Sergeants at eight that morning. The meeting didn't take long as there was little Jimmy could add – he had been stage-side when Maguire was shot. Apart from the messages on his comms pack which made him rush Martha off-stage, he hadn't really seen anything of use. He realised Daisy had continued speaking.

'Until I have a definitive answer, it's going to be difficult keeping on stalling the media. The press conference last night organised by the police was bloody useless for us. Banality and normal bollocks holding messages. They just named Maguire this morning, deliberately too late for the papers. It seems he has few, if any, living relatives. Dedicated policeman and so on. The story has gone global as well. The world wants to know what is going on. I've even had a request for Martha to appear on Good Morning America – Robin Roberts rang me personally. I stalled her for now. But we have no hope until we, not the police, can control the story. So far, I have just put out "Martha's thoughts and prayers are with DS Michael Maguire's colleagues, friends and family at this awful time – please respect their privacy" just the normal holding media release.'

There was a quiet guffaw as everyone recognised the bullshit words, which roughly translated as, *'We are not telling you anything else until we want to. So, stop asking!'*

'Can't have been pleasant having a corpse landing on top of you…' suggested Andy Jackson, the lighting designer, grinning maniacally, '…spurting warm blood?'

'Thanks Andy, extremely helpful. I was beside them both – I was covered in Maguire's brains as well. No, it wasn't pleasant, but I am here,' snapped Daisy. She then realised she had been a bit harsh. 'Sorry Andy, bit stressed.'

Being an old pro, Andy understood that working closely together morning, noon, and night – almost intimately for weeks, sometimes months on end – created inevitable tensions, exacerbated when things weren´t going to plan. *Someone being shot dead fell firmly into the not going to plan category,* he thought. Andy smiled forgiveness – Daisy smiled in return. Drinks would be exchanged sooner or later, for now all forgotten.

But Daisy was bloody angry with Nowak that he couldn't be contacted. 'I spoke to the police last night, and I'm seeing them again later today. They want to speak to Nowak too when he deigns to show up or we can find him.'

The Martha Production Office in the state-of-the-art On-Set twin slide-out Production Vehicle at the edge of the 02 load-in area comfortably held the concert tour's heads of department and travelling management. Rehearsals had finished at Elstree. Everything and everyone that had been at the north London studios had been shut down and pulled out. The production team were *on the road* – and their production offices travelled with them. Sales, marketing, social media, and finance continued in their leased offices on Golden Square in the heart of London's West End luvvie-central.

Danny Owen had rushed straight to the team meeting having come off-air at nine-thirty. He had arrived at the Starshine studios earlier that day at just before five o'clock after less than three hours sleep. He had won the argument with the notoriously penny-pinching overnight news editor – Starshine would pay for a taxi from his home in Balham, south London up to Leicester Square; London's Underground doesn't operate all its lines that early in the morning. Danny had to help produce the packages that were going to be waking up London as part of that morning's extended news bulletins – with re-edited showbizzy versions combined within his reporting of Martha's concert. His earlier live reports had been repeated overnight on the hour during every news bulletin – they had also been syndicated to Starshine's global associates. It was world news – millions of smart phones were displaying BREAKING NEWS accompanied by annoying news jingles. Around the world countless people were inevitably humphing, *what now?* Even the massive video screen banners scrolled the news on Times Square in New York; Piccadilly Circus in London; in Tokyo; Frankfurt and more…

Friday was normally Danny's day off with the studio full of various people eager to promote charitable action, or others plugging their books, records, TV shows, and films – consequently the celebrity fuel tank was customarily full. But this Friday was different. He had bumped several contributors – as they are called – off the running order, much to the chagrin of PRs and egos, to report the sensational exclusive news. He had praised Martha's concert but had also talked about *the terrible shooting,* omitting to mention that he had been sitting just two seats away from the assassinated policeman. He tried to focus on the concert during the main part of the show, leaving the shooting for within the news bulletins.

Danny was one of the regular on-air team that added extra early morning sparkle acting as a foil, or fall guy, to the monstrous ego of the DJ, Gordon. Almost every time Danny thought of Gordon, the words of Graham Fellows' song '*Gordon is a Moron*' entered his psyche as an earworm. A couple of years ago Danny had interviewed Fellows' alter ego Jilted John as a wind-up. Gordon hadn't seen the joke – the relationship between Danny and Gordon had remained frosty ever since. Unless Gordon wanted something.

Danny had been lucky on the Tube in his journey from Starshine's studios to North Greenwich's O2 entertainment complex in the loop of the River Thames. Both the Northern Line and the Jubilee Line underground trains arrived just as he walked briskly onto the platforms – the journey took twenty minutes in relatively empty carriages. As he looked around at the other passengers most were engrossed in the Metro, that morning's free newspaper with pictures of Martha on the front page. Those who didn't have a printed paper were studying their tablets and smart phones.

As he arrived at the 02, the meeting was just starting. He quietly grabbed *a nice cup of tea* as Danny always called it, then sat observing from one of the desks at the rear of the production vehicle. He wasn't involved in the decisions, however as Danny was reluctantly making for the shower from his bed at four that morning after only a couple of hours sleep, Daisy had asked him to support her – before she rolled over, stuck her head under the pillow and within seconds was fast asleep again aided by the organic, natural sleeping tablets. Despite, or maybe because of, the events of the late night before they had both slept remarkably well – aided by some post-traumatic horizontal stress relief.

Daisy and Danny had rekindled a previous relationship and were now virtually living together at Danny's flat in Balham, south London. They mutually agreed at first not to talk shop whilst at Danny's home, but that soon went out the window as the trials and tribulations of Martha's tour developed.

Spooned together, just before she fell asleep, Daisy had asked Danny to chronicle the whole story – *one day it would make a book or a film maybe*, she thought, ever the professional pragmatist. Sleep had evaded Danny – with Daisy's gentle breathing beside him, he lay there wondering and worrying, the past and present tumbling in his active mind. He had only just fallen asleep when his alarm clock had rudely done its job.

Danny, at the rear of the meeting space, jerked back to fully alert as footsteps could be heard on the metal stairway outside the production trailer. The door opened. Johnny Jones, the ticket sales, and finance manager walked in having also journeyed from central London on the Jubilee Underground Line. There was no hello. 'The phone lines and website are overwhelmed. Almost everyone wants to know if tonight's show is still on. If not, will the tickets for tonight's show be refunded or transferred to a new date. We are not responding for now, but a decision about tonight and the future must be taken quickly. What's going on?'

'Hello Johnny, how are you?' Jimmy asked acerbically.

'Fine. What have Martha and Nowak said?' Johnny asked, clearly not in the mood for small talk.

'It's been a tough few weeks for them, what with the kidnapping and so on. Martha is at her home with her close protection team. The press is camped outside – every breakfast TV and radio show claiming they have the inside knowledge. She is not saying anything publicly. But I'd be surprised if she could perform tonight. Or should perform tonight?' Jimmy was pragmatic. 'I suppose that's the decision then.'

Daisy also realised that the decision had been taken for them. *If Martha couldn't, wouldn't or shouldn't perform tonight there was no point in further debate. And it could be usefully the bigger story if she could own the news cycle and agenda for the next few days?*

'What about Nowak?' asked Johnny.

'He's not here. We must move on. My decision. We postpone the second and third show tonight and tomorrow night.' Jimmy was empowered to take responsibility in Stanislaw Nowak's absence. 'Johnny, when can we return here?'

Johnny consulted his iPad. 'There is a four-day window in a month's time. I'll check with the venue to see which work for them.'

'Okay, that's what we'll do.' Jimmy was decisive. 'I'll get onto legal. They can negotiate. Johnny confirm the change of dates and then get your team to move the tickets to the new dates – want to avoid refunds if possible. Nowak's small print covers us. Daisy can you lead on information management, moving the dates and put together statements for our sales, marketing, social media and briefings for the media please.'

Daisy was already on it. But she surprised everyone, 'Let's book an extra night. Three more gigs not just two as planned. In a month's time everyone will have forgotten the death of the policeman, and if we do a job on this, PR and social media will have swamped the news cycle. We'll work up a plan to separate the shooting from Martha and the tour. Get this right and the demand for tickets will be massive. I suggest we book the first three nights of the four-day window, and with a pencil on night four just in case. We'll be rigged so the extra days won't be excessively expensive – just a bit of hire, techs, wages, and venue costs. No extra in-out costs.'

The rest of the team stared in admiration at Daisy. She read from her iPad. 'Here is a draft of what I propose to put out: "Out of respect for DS Michael Maguire, his colleagues, family and friends, Martha is sure that everyone will support and understand her wish to postpone the tour at this difficult time. It will be rescheduled. All tickets will be valid and transferable – no one will lose money. We also realise that many people were disappointed when they could not get tickets for the sold-out events. The great news is that extra dates are being added and this includes a charity benefit night at the O2 with proceeds going to Police Charities."

No one disagreed, but *it was pretty ballsy* several thought. Daisy continued, 'I'll start a charity giving page on our website. I'll also have a go at persuading TV, subscription or streaming to transmit it. I am sure I can sell it in to one of the big distributors.'

Stanislaw Nowak spoke from the back. 'Do it. Confirm the extra charity event. Reschedule the rest of the tour too – we'll make a clean restart after the rescheduled O2 dates. Get on with it Jimmy.'

No one had seen or heard Nowak enter the custom trailer. Everyone turned to look at the ashen-faced wreck that stood there – bluster and confidence departed. He looked frightened. Without another word he simply turned and left.

For a moment everyone sat there, stunned. Then Jimmy chased after him.

'Well at least we know what to do.' Danny spoke for the first time. 'I'll put together something for tomorrow's show as a follow up to this morning. Daisy, I'll need to speak to Martha. Exclusive!'

Daisy smiled her agreement – she loved a crisis. She was one of course director and PR-guru the-late Mike Smith's *flock* on the post-graduate diploma in media relations and public affairs at Cardiff University. Her dissertation was in crisis management – for which she achieved a distinction. Little did she realise then that it would be so influential in her future career.

Jimmy arrived outside just in time to see Nowak's driver, Ray, closing the door on the rear door of the Lexus LS – Nowak was swiftly driven away.

'Bollocks' shouted Jimmy, turning on his heel. He returned to the trailer; everyone was silent. 'Nowak just went without another word.'

'He looked awful,' suggested the front of house sound balancer.

'So, would you if you just had a dead body land on you,' replied the stage-side in-ears monitor technician.

There followed a few moments of quiet brooding.

'Why was the policeman shot?' interrupted everyone's

thoughts. The elephant in the room at last released by Shirley, who ran the tour catering *Starring-Meals-on-Wheels*. 'Are we all safe?'

There was more silence as everyone looked at Jimmy for reassurance.

'This has nothing to do with us or the tour – this is a police matter. It was one of theirs who was shot. It's a one off and not terrorism.' Jimmy paused whilst he considered what he said next. 'The show must go on. What we must do now is to reassure Martha so she can perform. And reassure the fans that they will be safe.'

There was muted agreement.

'Right then derig. Cancel or postpone what you can or have to – let's not allow costs to run away. I'll talk to our insurers, but I don't hold out a lot of hope – that was one of the things we had to economise on at the early stages. Let's be imaginative in making the best out of what we can here – there are lots of opportunities if we are clever. I'll get onto a storage facility – as far as we can we'll keep everything in the trailers or temporarily get off hire. I'll speak with everyone else in thirty minutes backstage to tell them what is going on. This is going to be difficult – many of the team had other gigs. We'll also have to extend the hire on the tech kit. Deal time.'

Jimmy sat down in the private office at the front end of the trailer and started making the calls. This wasn't an occasion for e-mail. He had to call in every vestige of favours. They had been due to stay at the 02 for two more nights – the load out team weren't due until the end of tomorrow night's show, but he hoped to get them in now – if he could. Pictures in the papers of an empty stage set would not play well. Jimmy acknowledged to himself that despite all his experience, every tour is a logistical art form requiring a huge dollop of good luck and a large team of reliable freelancers – each recruited for the minimum period possible but slotting together like the metaphorical well-oiled machine. However, all tours have what Jimmy liked to call it's, *'Oooops moments.'*

Jimmy's back-stage meeting with the entire support, production, and technical team to explain the situation was, at times, vociferous. Overall, it had gone well – most were sympathetic to the plight of the dead policeman and his family, colleagues, and friends. A few, mainly those who had been involved in the rehearsals at Elstree Studios – and some from a previous life – were concerned about Martha's well-being, asking after her. Despite the murder of a policeman, there had been the inevitable gripes from a few hot heads with threats to call in the union. But eventually everyone saw sense and agreed terms.

Jimmy had managed to persuade the derig teams to come in early – and so the well-oiled machine once again swung into action.

He had already rearranged the tour once because the north African and Turkish legs were cancelled by Nowak, without explanation – not that Jimmy objected to these abandonments as they were becoming a customs, tax, and back-hander nightmare even greater than the new EU-imposed laws due to Brexit. Jimmy had told the team that he had been to several all-industry meetings where fears were expressed over the uncertain future that face touring artists due to the UK leaving the EU. In the year before Brexit the value of the UK's live music scene was about £1.1 billion. Martha would be okay as she was a re-established big name and the tour could afford the extra expenses incurred – and had the administrative team that could cope with the added paperwork of visas, taxation, carnets and the transporting of equipment and personnel. It was predicted that life would become completely unviable for new and mid-level artists.

Johnny Jones, the ticket sales, and finance manager was happier too, as pre-sales in north African and the Turkish legs were poor to abysmal, with venue costs mysteriously increasing as extras were suddenly *discovered* – the only people that would suffer were the touts in their unsuccessful black-market operations. Martha, despite being supposedly a global megastar, simply wasn't a big enough name in some countries of the globe. Jimmy ensured that none of the local freelancers were out of pocket – *personal reputation is everything in this business*, his mantra. Jimmy had no idea if he would return in the future with another tour and another client *so best to keep them sweet,* he thought.

Yet again, the tour had to be rearranged with the existing dates needing to be shuffled forward at least four weeks – the added logistics of this could be overwhelming, but Jimmy had an experienced team aided by the great relationships with the many and various sub-contractors, hire companies and venues. Most would understand, with only a few using the delay to attempt to extract more money – generally failing and then falling off Jimmy's preferred supplier list for future gigs. A clean restart with the world's press looking on could be a good thing if handled with aplomb. *It's an ill wind and all that*, thought Jimmy, *over to Daisy. That's her job.*

The cancelled North African and Turkish gigs also gave the opportunity for additional UK dates – especially with the more logical travel schedule reducing unnecessary travel time between venues. Europe could wait. There were no plans to visit the rest of the world just yet. It is not unusual for concert tours to have crews of over 100 people – and Martha's was no different. All of whom had to be moved, fed, and watered, sometimes overnight in sleeper coaches – but in London most were able to enjoy the delights of home.

The *Martha Movin' Out* tour wasn't as large as some of the massive global stadium tours to Jimmy's relief. He had worked on some big stadium concerts – but never the giant ones such as U2's 360-degree tour which contracted over one hundred and twenty trucks to move the stage, the screen, the lights, the two hundred and fifty loudspeakers and more from venue-to-venue. He knew several of the team who had worked on Beyoncé's Formation Tour of Europe which needed seven Boeing 747 cargo planes to transport all the stage equipment across countries – they had needed several weeks off to recover post-tour.

Martha's tour had planned to use just twenty trucks and assorted other vehicles supplied by an old school friend of Nowak's, Pietr Ostrodzko, the owner of Mazury Ostrodzko International. Ostrodzko had rigged several of his trailers with padded walls and nooks to protect the equipment and other *contents*. He had also purchased silent generator units, paid for by Nowak, theoretically for the allegedly less sophisticated or reliable concert halls and stadia in North Africa, Turkey, and Egypt – now on their way back to Wroclaw, unused and unwanted. Nowak had agreed with Ostrodzko he could use them or sell them, keeping the proceeds.

No one could understand why one of Nowak's best, and probably only friends had pulled out at the last minute adding to Jimmy's woes and demanding an urgent need to find a new trucking and logistics company – but at least Jimmy now felt more comfortable with a well-known concert touring specialist he knew and trusted.

Pietr Ostrodzko wasn't that disappointed his contract with Nowak had been cancelled by *mutual consent* after a long and difficult telephone conference between the two – he had become increasingly uncomfortable with what was being asked of him, especially the use for the silent generator trucks with no generators within the lead-lined sides to transport the additional *passengers* demanded by Ali Baka.

Jimmy was unaware that one of his crew was not as billed – the name on her AAA pass, an alias. She had been on the team from halfway through the rehearsals at Elstree. Her arrival initially had been viewed with suspicion by some, apparently the daughter of someone with contacts who knew someone who knew someone – as is the way with the media and entertainment business. Jimmy inevitably agreed to the enforced *nepotism* – soon she became a trusted well-liked member of the team. But he still had some reservations.

DAY TWO
FRIDAY MID-MORNING

NOWAK

STANISLAW NOWAK WAS FRIGHTENED. HE WAS NOT enjoying the luxury normally provided in the rear of his Lexus. He told Ray, his driver, to park up in a random back street about a mile from the 02 Arena – he needed to think what to do next.

He had not slept despite the security systems at his lavish London Docklands penthouse flat, with concierge, manicured gardens, and views over the River Thames; the Barrage; London City Airport; and, away to his right, the dome of the 02 Entertainment Complex – the huge outdoor screens mocking him with full height pictures of Martha.

The unpleasant memory from the previous night of Detective Sergeant Michael Maguire's mutilated corpse writhing in its death throes on top of him was compounded by the unsigned text message he had received earlier that week: *'You owe us a million pounds.'*

He thought he knew who the message was from. His succinct reply at the time had been to the point: *'Fuck off.'*

'You owe me one million pounds. No negotiation,' had been the reply.

The euphoria and arrogance he had enjoyed at *the final rehearsals of my show* had deserted him. He alone thought that the errant bullet should have had his name on it, *but why, how would his death ensure his debt would be paid?*

In some ways Maguire's death removed one of Nowak's potential problems. *Every cloud has a silver lining,* Nowak recalled the last text message from Maguire, *'My boss Bill Kelly knows everything. He knows I am your informer. No more. It ends here.'*

Nowak didn't care about the dead copper – he had another reliable inside source. *And more could be recruited* he thought. Yet again he had got away with it, but he did acknowledge he had been incredibly lucky – the adoring crowd at Martha's concert had been so emotionally infectious that even the normally taciturn Maguire had leapt to his feet as the final few bars of *'Captivity'* reached their crescendo. Maguire's head rising straight into the path of the sniper's bullet.

Ray, who had been checking in the car's mirrors, interrupted his self-pitying solipsism. 'Traffic warden approaching. Can't stay here. Where to Mr Nowak?'

Nowak toyed with his phone. Unless he took prompt action, he was a dead man for more than one reason. He swore under his breath.

'Sorry, Mr Nowak, didn't hear that. Where to?'

'Park up outside your favourite café. Have breakfast on me, whilst I think.' Ray was stunned when Nowak passed over a twenty-pound note.

Ray drove a circuitous route for about twenty minutes, north under the River Thames through the congested Blackwall Tunnel, then back south through Blackwall itself, onto the Isle of Dogs and through Cubitt Town – redeveloped as part of the Port of London in the mid-eighteen-eighties by William Cubitt, then the Lord Mayor of London. Ray was happily chatting to a disinterested Nowak, 'HMS Prince Albert, the first British warship designed to carry her main armament in gun turrets, was launched here Mr Nowak.'

Nowak, distracted, merely grunted. He normally enjoyed his driver's guided tours – it had become a welcome tradition in normal times.

The River Thames was now on their left with an unobstructed view across to the Royal Borough of Greenwich and the O2 Arena, Nowak ignored the views. Ray carefully manoeuvred the car into a space on Saunders Ness Road. Beside them was the tiny Island Gardens Café that, outwardly, had all the appeal of a public toilet.

'Really?' enquired Nowak quizzically.

'The home-made banana cake and the Caribbean hot chocolate are the best in London. Reminds me of home and my mother's cooking,' was Ray's reply. 'Except with great views of the Old Naval College and the Cutty Sark. It's not raining, so I'll sit outside. Call if I am not back when you want me.'

With that, Ray was gone. Nowak looked at his mobile phone again in the hope that it would solve his problems – it remained stoically, stubbornly silent.

He speed-dialled Daisy.

'Good morning Stanislaw, you left quickly,' answered Daisy. 'But we are all on it. Should be able to confirm everything by early-afternoon.'

'Never mind that.' Nowak didn't care, he had more important things to worry about. 'I want to see you and Danny as soon as possible. Very private. Urgent.'

'Okay. I'll speak with Danny. When and where do you suggest?' Daisy was concerned. Nowak sounded more stressed than she had ever known.

'I'm in my car beside the Island Gardens Café on the Isle of Dogs. See you both in thirty minutes.' He rang off before Daisy could answer.

Nowak sat there contemplating his future. 'What bloody future if I don't pay?' His question shouted out loud, remained in the privacy of the car. Then silently he thought, *I will have no problem getting my hands on one million pounds... eventually... but not right now... timing is everything. The bloody postponement due to the shooting has fucked my cashflow... and anyway why should I?* Nowak was between the devil and the deep blue sea – he didn't know it then, but it was about to get a whole lot worse.

He took out his iPad Pro and started crunching the numbers on a password protected Excel spread sheet. After some tapping and typing, he confirmed his gut reaction – the money would be there, but it would be touch and go. The main issue would be transferring one million pounds out of the accounts without raising too much suspicion or attracting unwelcome attention from Johnny Jones, his anally retentive finance director. *The accounts would show some loans incoming so maybe he could show the million as repayment?* It would be difficult, but not insurmountable, repaying to an entirely different entity to the satisfaction of the inevitable auditors, no matter how much he paid them. His first issue would be delaying the timing of the demand for payment so he could raise the funds and then transfer the money to anonymous offshore accounts away from prying eyes.

He took out one of several unused burner phones from the storage box between the seats. He carefully dialled the number from which he had received the threatening text messages – he had stored the number under the name of *Lexus Service* in his normal phone before deleting all the messages. He had reverse looked up the number with, unsurprisingly, no joy. He tried the area code 00 996 312 and was disconcerted to find that the call came from Bishkek, the capital of the mountainous, landlocked Kyrgyzstan in Central Asia. He Googled Bishkek to discover that it is in the north of the country not far from the border with Kazakhstan; with Uzbekistan to the west and southwest; Tajikistan to the southwest; and China to the east.

Up until now all communication had been via text. He wasn't sure that the call would be answered.

'Dobryy den, Mr Stanislaw.' The man on the other end of the phone had a heavy Proto-Balto-Slavic accent. 'You were fortunate. You seem to have, shall we say... police protection.' The wheezing horselaugh at the attempt at wit was chilling.

Nowak tried to keep his emotions and his anger in check. Now was the time for his best negotiating skills. 'Let's get straight to the point. I owe Baka one million pounds. But he is dead? Debt gone.'

There was silence on the other end of the phone.

'Did you hear me?'

'I heard you Mr Stanislaw. Let me help you to understand where we are. Some believe in brute force and retribution; I am a believer in punitive justice. I have now purchased your debt. Its all mine. So now it is just you and me. And you owe me one point two five million pounds. Happy to accept US dollars as well,' laughed the voice yet again.

'My arrangements were with Ali Baka. He is dead. Why should I pay you, and pay you more than I owe?'

'Debt collecting is an expensive business Mr Stanislaw. Because if you don't, it won't be a bullet. Your Martha first and then you. And you will watch as she dies slowly and in agony.' There was a pause whilst the voice wheezed and coughed. 'I will then make your death even longer and more exquisitely lingering. Have you read Rider Haggard's *The Ancient Allan?* I am a great fan. You could call me a disciple of his writing. He has an evocative, descriptive way with words. Death by the boat. Look it up.'

'I need time to raise the money.' Nowak was shaking. The Vory could be evil, but now he did not know with whom he was dealing. 'I need eight weeks. And if Martha dies, I won't have any money.'

'Not my problem. You have four weeks from today or you both die.' The voice on the other end of the phone increased its menace. 'I do not like being kept waiting for what is mine. Eli vy umrete. Or you die. No negotiation.'

There was silence as each considered what the other had said. All that could be heard was laboured breathing.

Finally, Nowak spoke, hoping he sounded convincing 'Okay, I'll do my best. Four weeks from today.' *The money would only be there if the some of the advance sales for the rescheduled concerts are as successful as my team has promised me.* Nowak prayed. He wasn't normally religious.

'Excellent. I knew you would see sense. Eventually. I will send you the bank details. Five banks. Quarter of a million to each. Goodbye Mr Nowak. Please do not be late.' The line went dead. His normal phone pinged five times with five text messages with the details of five bank accounts.

Nowak sat there trembling – he returned the phone to the central storage box between the front seats. More frightened than he had ever been in his life. However only he knew that he had the money. But it was the change of banker that worried him – if he paid up too quickly there would be a demand for more. He had to ensure that whoever it was thought he had no more money to give – he was now dealing with a blackmailer. Nowak knew all about the whys and wherefores of blackmail. How much did *they* know – whoever *they* were?

He took out his iPad and typed into Google "*death boat rider haggard.*" He wished he hadn't:

"You will be laid upon a bed in a little boat upon the river and another boat will be placed over you, for these boats are called the Twins, Egyptian, in such a fashion that your head and your hands will project at one end and your feet at the other. There you will be left, comfortable as a baby in its cradle, and twice every day the best of food and drink will be brought to you. Should your appetite fail, moreover, it will be my duty to revive it by pricking your eyes with the point of a knife until it returns. Also, after each meal I shall wash your face, your hands and your feet with milk and honey, lest the flies that buzz about them should suffer hunger, and to preserve your skin from burning by the sun. Thus, slowly you will grow weaker and at length fall asleep. The last one who went into the boat – he, unlucky man, had by accident wandered into the court of the House of Women and seen some of the ladies there unveiled – only lived for twelve days, but you, being so strong, may hope to last for eighteen."

Nowak felt his stomach tighten and his bowels loosen. He started sweating profusely.

Many months ago, in the drab café in Cairo, he had arranged the loan to top up the seed finance for Martha's tour. There he had idiosyncratically met Ali Baka who, after some verbal circling, confided he needed new routes and safe passage for his illegal people smuggling enterprise – and to money-launder some of his ill-gotten gains.

The deal was simple. Baka lent Nowak the money to seed-fund the Martha Movin' Out tour. The money, when returned to Baka, appeared to come from a legitimate source; and Baka made a profit from the deal. Win-win – for Baka anyway.

Nowak, in exchange, agreed to use Martha's tour vehicles to smuggle into the UK Baka's various *travellers* in relative safety – hence avoiding the treacherous twenty-one-mile journey by ill-equipped boats across the Straits of Dover, the narrowest part of the English Channel, La Manche, from Pas de Calais to the sanctuary allegedly offered by the UK. Baka and his associates didn't care if his *travellers* were genuine refugees fleeing conflict or economic migrants seeking new opportunities. Or both. They were all paying customers – and in Baka's opinion, *desperate suckers ready to be fleeced.*

Far too many had paid all their savings to criminal gangs such as those led by Baka and Conor O'Murchadha to illegally enter the UK. Those who made the journey were lucky to get as far as the UK – but faced an uncertain future that could end in many being deported back to the countries they had left or sent to poorly equipped, overcrowded detention centres. Or to Rwanda.

Baka's issue was also the use of the so-called *McMafia* and other powers by the UK's National Crime Agency to freeze assets and investigate the sources of wealth; as well as the demands on banks to conduct due diligence on wealthy individuals. His business was becoming increasingly difficult by these multifaceted attacks.

Several weeks ago, Nowak had read that Bill Kelly had addressed a Government working party. Some of what he said had been reported in the press, 'At the National Crime Agency we are working hard to go after those who profit from such misery.' Kelly had omitted the finer details of their investigations as some politicians were renowned for leaking. It was reported that the government was working on legislation to overhaul the asylum and immigration system to prevent it being exploited and abused. The report cited Tony Abbott, the Australian former prime minister, who had discussed by Zoom video conference his sovereign borders policy of zero tolerance towards illegal migrants, including blocking their boats and pushing them back into Indonesian territorial waters. 'My policy got the boats down to zero,' later read a sub-headline. Little did Australia's Prime Minister realise that he would have been benefitting Baka's and Nowak's overland enterprises.

Nowak thought he had got away with it – both Conor O'Murchadha and Ali Baka dead and no trace of the route to the money. More importantly for Nowak he didn't have to use the tour to transport illegal migrants. *Home and free,* he thought.

Nowak now realised, with a sinking pit of despair, that O'Murchadha and Baka were both simply fronting up The Vory, the Russian super-Mafia. Pragmatically The Vory had factored the debt to an enforcer, who now wanted his investment plus commission returned or substantially more than a pound of flesh – Nowak's flesh.

The Martha Movin' Out tour was for the first time in Nowak's life both a legal and profitable enterprise – *it had felt so good.* He sat back, shut his eyes, reclined the seat in the rear of his Lexus and selected one of the seven shiatsu massage programmes – not to sleep, but perchance to dream. To think...

The fragrance that had been introduced into the foggers and smoke machines during Martha's concert had been deliberately chosen to remind Nowak of the smell of incense in the cathedral of St John the Baptist in his hometown of Wrocław, Poland.

Nowak missed his old town with its ornate medieval and Eastern Bloc architecture, traditional cobbled main square surrounded by outdoor cafés and bars, with the clock tower keeping watch. He fondly remembered the permanent smell of cooked cabbage and paprika floating through the air; eating Bigos stew, the national dish of Poland made with any kind of meat from pork to rabbit or venison, and always with kiełbasa, spicy Polish sausage. Above all he missed his true friends there, away from the cesspit of his own creation in Britain.

He missed his September visits to the nine-day Zielona Góra Wine Fest – with its drinking, cultural and sporting events, and large crowds. The two-and-a-half-hour journey to the north-west of Wrocław was an attractive proposition for Nowak and his friends – where there were large crowds there was always the opportunity to acquire some złoty.

He had worked reasonably hard at school and achieved respectable enough results, but not good enough to get him into university – he told anyone and everyone he believed in the University of Life. He had been a grafter, not shy of after-hours and weekend physical labour where he could earn a few złoty in pocket money to go drinking with his mates and chat up the girls with considerable success – no relationship lasted more than a few days. *Fuck and forget*, Nowak told his male friends over several local Tyskie beers from one of the oldest breweries in Europe. The labouring had given him a taut, well-honed physique – long gone. At least once a week he got into fights – which, most times, he started and inevitably won. If he were aware of The Queensbury Rules, they wouldn't have applied to him – kicking a man when down always ensured the vanquished didn't arise. On one occasion three drunken louts decided to take him on – a mistake for two of the three. The first was blinded in one eye for the rest of his life; the second suffered a dislocated shoulder before his knees were smashed; the third ran.

Nowak had left Wrocław for the UK aged eighteen, the day before his nineteenth birthday, and had returned only a few times since to see his family and a select group of trusted mates. Trust was important, even in Nowak's shady basement life. Nowak was one of four children who had shared with his mother the cramped two-bedroomed apartment at the top of a six-storey tenement where the lights only worked for a few hours every evening. He didn't know his father. His childhood night-time memories were the sounds of trains shunting, clanking, and whistling from the nearby nineteenth century Wrocław Główny, the largest railway station and sidings in the Lower Silesian Voivodeship – the red-brick castellated building and archaic platforms the centre of many of the main Polish railway routes. He used to sit for hours watching the apparently morose activity as steam shunters chuffed back and forth, stopping for what seemed like ages, the driver doing nothing except quaffing rough potato vodka; eating various stodgy Chłopskie Jadło; and occasionally being visited by 'ladies without a drink.' The shunter returned an hour or two later maybe with a few wagons and a happy driver – stomach full and balls empty. Nothing worked at any speed or with apparent logic – but everything arrived where, not necessarily when, it was meant to.

His arrival into Britain was inauspicious at first. He worked, mainly cash-in-hand, labouring on the building sites of the regeneration of London Docklands, the riverfront and former docks in inner east and southeast London, in the boroughs of Southwark, Tower Hamlets, Lewisham, Newham, and Greenwich. The docks were formerly the world's largest port – but by the 1980s, after the docks closed, the area had become derelict, poverty- and crime-ridden. Their redevelopment created wealth, but also led to some conflict between the new and the old communities in the area. Nowak soon found himself embroiled in discord, settling disputes, and learning ways to extract cash from anyone poor or rich – the only difference being the amount of cash extracted. All would suffer proportionally.

His work-ethic, tough confrontational style, and complete disregard for law and order soon drew him to the attention of the gang-masters – long before the Gangmasters and Labour Abuse Authority had been established. Nowak was sent in to sort out dissent from those in forced labour, trafficking, and other forms of exploitation taking place on the various building sites run by the corrupt many.

All labour agencies were required to hold a licence – it was theoretically illegal for end-users to use the services of an unlicensed agency. In competitive operating environments with little regulation or oversight, the rights and working conditions of workers, particularly those employed on an agency-only basis were generally oppressed. It was here that Nowak became aware of debt bondage and forced labour – and he took pride in putting the squeeze on anyone who fell out of line. There were few safeguards or checks on labour agencies – the inspectorates set up to protect workers were poorly resourced and perceived as largely ineffective. Nowak became adept at working the system with the appropriate application of a little cash here or a big stick there. He soon became a feared adversary and useful associate of many of the Dockland's crime bosses.

It was remembering being a part of the construction team of Limehouse Television Studios that gave him the germ of an idea. Limehouse Studios was a short lived, independently owned, television studio built on the South Quay Import Dock at the eastern end of Canary Wharf in Limehouse – not far from where he was sitting. The original Canary Wharf was built in 1952 for the Mediterranean and Canary Island fruit trade – Nowak had found old crates filled with rotting fruit as he helped clear the site. The studios opened in 1983, and only six years later the innovative building was demolished to make way for the Olympia & York development. The broadcast industry was up in arms at this alleged media travesty. The new studios had quickly become the venue of choice for many of the independent production companies making programmes for the then new Channel 4 – its popularity probably aided by the open-all-hours hospitality boat moored alongside.

But maybe sell-through, TV, live cinema streaming, global was a way of capitalising on the month's delay whilst the tour was being rescheduled. But, more importantly, extracting the cash from his accounts without attracting too much attention would be simpler and easier? Nowak was getting excited. *But is it possible?*

The plan had been to film the whole of Martha's concert on the third night, when everyone had settled down. Maybe with some judicious new filming, editing, and mixing, it could be made to look and sound like the first night – or at least a live concert? The question was how fast could this be turned around and could he find a distributor willing to put up a substantial advance? Martha and the concert were on the front pages – now to capitalise on it.

The tap on the window startled him. Daisy's face looked in, Danny a few paces away – he looked less than happy.

'Come in,' offered Nowak.

Daisy opened the rear door and sat in. Danny took the front passenger's seat, 'Bloody hell Nowak, this car stinks.'

Nowak realised he had been sweating profusely. The windows would not open without the keys – Ray was still out-of-sight enjoying his Caribbean breakfast.

'So, what's the urgency?' demanded Danny. Nowak was silent whilst he considered what to say. When he called Daisy an entirely different conversation had been at the front of his panicked mind.

An uneasy truce, certainly not amicable, had developed between Nowak and Danny after the events of over ten years ago. Danny was there solely to protect Daisy – nothing more. Daisy and Danny had had a casual on-off relationship for many years as their paths crossed in the world of music, celebrity and showbusiness. In recent weeks the relationship had developed from colleagues, through trusted friends, to lovers. Nothing had been agreed or discussed – it just sort of happened, almost by osmosis. Daisy spent more night-times in Danny's south London flat than her own – she had transferred a few of her personal things.

Daisy knew of Danny's past relationship with Martha – she had wondered how Danny and Martha would react when they met again. She needn´t have worried. Danny still cared for Martha as a long-time friend – they had been in school together. Several years later their school days' friendship had turned into a lover's relationship when, almost by accident, they met again at press conference for the release of what was to be Martha's final album. Final album until Nowak had reinvigorated her career. The relationship soured when Martha was dropped by her label and she turned to drink and drugs – she loved him deeply and he, in return, had tried to save her from herself. But she didn't want saving, all she cared about was her next fix and another bottle. The arguments became worse and worse. Then one day Danny had simply walked out never to return. *Love doesn't conquer all*, Martha remembered him screaming at her. He could take no more anger-fuelled histrionics due Martha's drug and alcohol habit. They hadn't seen each other since – until the day Martha had been released from Ali Baka's captivity a few short weeks ago.

Martha had accepted Danny's relationship with Daisy – and reluctantly wished them well. She knew her behaviour had been, in Danny's words at the time, *bloody unacceptable* – she deserved being ditched. Daisy and Danny were two of Martha's very few trusted friends in a showbiz world where duplicity and stabbing each other in the chest were almost the accepted norms.

Danny repeated his question with more force, directed at the windscreen and the road beyond. He couldn't stand to look at Nowak unless he had to. 'You demanded we came here immediately. We did as we were told, like a good boy and girl. So, what is the urgency? What do you bloody want now? What did you have to do with Maguire's death – it was you wasn't it? What are you covering up?'

Still silence from Nowak. Danny, now angry, turned around from the front seat to face Nowak. 'Well?'

'I had nothing to do with Maguire's death.' Nowak answered truthfully but lied by omission. He wasn't sure who wanted him dead – *there could be a long list* his paranoid mind told him.

'Bollocks. Don't give me that. I don't believe you.' Danny turned away.

Nowak couldn't or wouldn't share that he thought he could have been the intended target – no matter how unlikely. *Was it The Vory sending a signal to anyone who dared to double cross them?* Nowak inwardly admitted that Maguire's unfortunate demise had probably served its purpose for The Vory far more effectively than had he been killed – *the word* was out on the streets. But recent events meant Nowak was more frightened of the anonymous voice from Bishkek than The Vory. And what if it wasn't The Vory – what the voice on the phone had said confused him?

'I want to produce a video of Martha's concert – for sale on-line, streaming and as merchandise at future concerts.' Nowak was beginning to regain its bluster. He was good at compartmentalising issues.

Daisy and Danny looked at each other. It was Daisy that answered. 'Why is this so urgent that we had to meet in a car on the Isle of Dogs? What's wrong with the production trailer or the management offices?'

Nowak hesitated. His attempt to smile failed, turning to a snide grimace. 'I trust your judgement. I didn't want to bring this up in front of everyone else.'

Danny turned towards Daisy, they exchanged surprised looks. *Was Nowak telling the truth, or is there an ulterior motive? Another of his scams?*

'But how, we didn't film the first night?' Daisy didn't understand.

'I think we have the video recorded from the cameras sent to the screens. Need to check with Jimmy, but I'm sure it's possible' Nowak was almost getting enthusiastic. 'I watch the movies; anything is possible these days.'

'When do you plan to release it?' Danny was being practical.

'As soon as possible,' Nowak was brusque. 'Daisy, we need a distributor. Good one that has excellent routes to market and can be trusted.'

Nowak was in full flow. 'Find out if we are able to get back into the George Lucas sound stage at Elstree where we rehearsed. Speak to Jimmy too – he has good links with OB trucks and edit houses. He'll know a couple of good TV directors to make it happen.'

George Lucas used Stages 1 and 2 during the filming of the Star Wars and were named after him. At nearly fifteen hundred square metres and fifteen metres high it is one of the tallest studios in Europe and one of the few able to accommodate a full-size stadium tour. Martha's tour was in good company – Take That, Madonna, The Spice Girls, Robbie Williams, Kylie, Rihanna, and One Direction all rehearsed there because the studios could fit a full-size stadium stage and lighting grid. Martha and the production team had been rehearsing there for several weeks.

Daisy was excited by the idea but with reservations. 'Great ideas Stanislaw, happy to help but I am the PR, not a producer. And I'm certainly not technical.'

'You've just been promoted. Recruit a couple more assistants for your PR team to take the load off you, you'll need them – your wages have just been increased by fifty percent to cover the new job.' Nowak really was excited – and one of the few in his position who kept his word when it came to pay – paying well to people who could increase his personal wealth.

He had never made it into *The Sunday Times* Rich List, but that was an unlikely personal goal, as to make it onto the list the wealth has to be known about. The tour had depleted far more of his reserves than he wished. He would never touch, unless absolutely necessary, the cash in his grab bag securely hidden in his apartment. Also in the bag was a passport; four credit cards; a global satellite phone; details of a numbered bank account; and a driver's licence, all in a tested alias – together with a smart suit and couple of changes of clothes with labels removed. He hoped he would never need them.

Daisy, as ever, was the professional PR – and newly appointed producer – who quickly came up with the big idea. 'We could include video from the audience as a competition. Everyone had their phones out. Quality is high resolution these days and we can use image stabilisation and enhancement. They'll be hours we can use. Probably only need five or ten minutes in the whole finished show

– we don't pay, but offer to include name supers on screen of anyone´s footage we do use and give them a couple of tickets. Danny can start a campaign on his radio show to get people to send their stuff in. I'll also speak with Kelvin Edwards – he owes me for giving him exclusive access to Martha and Vikki after their release from Baka's place in the Wye Valley.' Even the normally taciturn Daisy was getting excited. Kelvin Edwards was the showbusiness editor at *The Daily Tribune*, "allegedly the UK's leading celebrity daily newspaper and on-line blog spot" – repeated anywhere and everywhere at every opportunity.

It was Danny who put a damper on it. 'Great ideas, but how do we deal with the issue of the little girl who was killed, and the shooting of Maguire? We can't just ignore that?'

There was silence in the car.

Nowak, Danny, and Daisy were interrupted by the return of Ray, the driver, at first smiling from the enforced sugar rush. He was surprised to see two more occupants in the car. He occasionally had to go beyond the role of driver to become Nowak's personal bodyguard. Ray was an imposing figure, not to be underestimated. He had learned some unarmed tricks of the trade as a younger man with the Jamaica Defence Force – and more unorthodox, but equally effective techniques on the back streets of the east end of London. On high alert he opened the door, 'Everything all right Mr Nowak?'

'Fine thanks Ray. These are my friends Daisy and Danny.' No one shook hands.

Nowak passed Ray another twenty-pound note, 'Bring back three coffees for us. And something for yourself.'

No please or thank you. Nowak was back on original form. Ray shut the driver's door and scuttled off to get the coffees – he didn't complain. Nowak paid him considerably more than the going rate for a driver – convinced that loyalty could be bought.

Daisy's post-grad crisis training kicked in. 'Right, we need a two-pronged solution. We say the charity video has been specially recorded. We donate a percentage of profit from the video across several Police Charities. Martha shoots a piece to camera at the top – carefully scripted. Maybe include a few pieces to camera and weepy police family interviews with suitably melancholic music in the breaks as the show goes along. We treat this like any fund-raising telethon. You know, in light of the terrible atrocity on the first night its only right we support charities for serving and veteran police officers and staff, volunteers, and their families who have suffered any physical or psychological harm as a result of doing their job in difficult circumstances. We include links to the charities scrolling across the screen at points throughout the concert. Maximum social media and PR. Need to get Martha talking about it on TV and radio shows, features in the media – no request turned down.'

Danny and Nowak were stunned at Daisy's unemotional cynical suggestion.

'And the other prong, I assume the little girl who died? What was her name?' *All this altruism and we can't even remember her name*, thought Danny.

Daisy consulted the multi-page notebook, her bible. 'Amelia Cohen. Aged 10. From Camden Town. Mia to her parents and friends.'

Daisy had already thought it through. 'This needs to be handled more sensitively. My first thoughts are we need to give it a couple of weeks, then Martha personally telephones Mia's parents and asks if she can drop round. Preferably before the funeral. Martha only lives two hundred metres from Mia's house. Martha visits alone, looking upset, no make-up, no minders, no obvious press. It's got to look genuine and not a showbiz scam. Assuming they say yes, which I am sure they will, Martha says she would like to help Mia's parent set up a Foundation in Mia's memory. Maybe help with Mia's school. Martha can play the local neighbour card.'

'Wonderful,' Nowak was at his sardonic worst. 'But how do I make any money out of that?'

'Oh, for fucks sake Nowak, have you no bloody heart? Do you really only care about money?' Danny was pissed off.

Daisy wasn't put off. 'In six months' or so, to kick start the Foundation, we put on a show at The Round House on Chalk Farm Road – which is near to both Mia's parents' and Martha's homes. It will hold over three thousand people. We give free tickets to Mia's school, friends, and family – and then sell VIP tickets, corporate hospitality, TV rights and sponsorship. Martha headlining, with other top names – all donating their time. Not the full touring show, but closer to Martha Unplugged. Keep it raw and genuine.'

Daisy faced Nowak. 'And yes, it will make money. Everyone will be scrabbling to take part if we sell it well. Don't see a problem with sponsorship packages either, especially after Martha's sell-out concert tour – it'll be the hottest ticket in town.'

Nowak looked happier, he would be making money – and would have more than enough money streams through pre-sales to be able to easily take out the one point two five million without attracting too much suspicion or raiding his private secure stashes. He was back in business. And he had kept the secret.

Daisy hadn't finished. 'Now this part remains strictly between us. When Martha meets Mia's parents, she carefully asks if she can privately attend the funeral as a mark of respect. She will assure Mia's parents no press, this will be a private visit that is kept confidential. But I will have a word with Kelvin Edwards – and tell him he'll never get another story from us if he breaks his word. He's a two-faced shit but has his uses. He gets one of his freelance snappers to pap Martha going into and coming out of Mia's parents' house, also Martha attending the funeral. Really long-range covert stuff. Martha grieving. We anonymously start the rumour about the Foundation and the launch concert – if asked, we all deny everything saying this was Martha acting privately. The more we deny, the more we'll stoke the flames of the story – especially if we have a few unnamed sources helping us along the way.'

'I never knew you could be so duplicitous.' Danny wasn't sure what he thought about it all.

Nowak was thrilled. 'I knew I was doing the right thing when I employed you. Genius. Works at so many levels.'

Danny's phone interrupted their discussions, 'Sorry, have to take this.'

'Give me two,' Danny said into the phone. He left the car and walked thirty metres away to the footpath alongside the river. He did not want his conversation with DCS Bill Kelly to be overheard by Nowak.

'Okay. I am on my own.'

'So how are you after last night's fracas?' Kelly was straight to the point.

'Fine.' Danny's answer was equally succinct.

'We need to meet.' Kelly paused, 'Very privately. Bring Daisy, tell no one else.'

'Okay. Why, where and when?'

'I'll WhatsApp you.'

Kelly disconnected. Danny walked back to Nowak's car deep in thought.

DAY TWO
FRIDAY AFTERNOON

NEW SCOTLAND YARD

'So, what more do we know?' Bodkin was under pressure from above and from the red top newspapers, not that he cared about them. *Let Virginia Stephani and her PR sisters deal with them,* he scoffed inwardly. *What do bloody PR, and the lawyers for that matter, know about the day-to-day pressures of this job*?

He had called the twice daily meetings to keep everyone in the loop. Kelly's team from the National Crime Agency had not been invited. Some of the team had spent most of the morning interviewing witnesses – those that had stayed at the Yard ate their lunch *al desko*. No one had dared to be seen to leave other than on official business. Most arrived in the incident room for the second meeting of the day with mugs of afternoon tea and note pads. No side-table catering at this meeting. There was an uncomfortable silence.

'Oh, come on. We must know something.' Bodkin challenged his team. 'What about our alleged sniper? Have we found him on CCTV yet? What about the door key? Has the weapon been found yet?'

More time passed. Looks were exchanged. Eventually Detective Constable Toby Pawlek, eyes red from most of the day spent in a darkened room spooling back and forth, spoke. The rest of the room visibly relaxed – someone had, at last, opened the batting. 'We obtained almost all the CCTV. Over two hundred cameras in and around the area. I have a team of seven still going through it all. There are more to get hold of. Some people are being bit tardy, so we had to remind them of their civic duty.'

Muted amusement from the room.

'I started at the North Greenwich pier and working backwards. Our John Doe was clearly in a hurry to leave – not a pretty end. I have got some good facial shots which, with the pictures taken of the corpse, we're putting through facial recognition. So far nothing to ID him. I'm also trying to find our John Doe arriving. So far, I've gone back three hours before the start of the concert. Nothing. But we are searching.'

'Have you passed the pictures to our liaisons at Five and Six?' Bodkin was double checking everything. 'Our shooter was almost certainly a professional.'

'Sent them through a couple of hours ago. No response

yet,' Pawlek wanted to assure his boss he was up to speed. 'I assume I can authorise overtime?'

Bodkin found the financial constraints tiresome. He couldn't expect his team to work long hours for no reward. 'No more than fifteen hours per person per week. But we can also offer double time off in lieu when this is over. Some people might prefer that or a combination. But don't let it be a blank cheque. And keep good logs.'

'I am sure that the team will be incredibly grateful Sir,' answered Pawlek. Bodkin wasn't sure if he was taking the piss but ignored it for now.

'What has Kelly's team said?' Bodkin questioned the room. 'And the other witnesses nearby?'

'Nothing much to add so far.' Detective Constable Sharon Spears spoke for her four colleagues who had spent the day speaking with a long list of people. Kelly's team had not added much – except for their investigations into some of Nowak's shady operations. 'So far we haven't come up with any reason for Maguire's killing. Some of the VIPs and celebrities are bloody prima donnas. One told me to make an appointment via their agent. Twat.'

Laughter.

Bodkin had kept to himself the conversation with Kelly about Maguire's potential involvement and links to Nowak. But he was becoming increasingly uncomfortable withholding what was important information. He realised that DC Spears was still talking. 'Bloody actors. One had a minor part in some shitty police drama years ago. He told me he knew his rights and how to investigate a murder.'

More laughter.

'And Amelia Cohen? Mia?' Bodkin's question calmed the room down. The death of a child affected even the most hardened member of any police force.

'The parents don't want a Family Liaison Officer, FLO, permanently at their house. Not surprisingly they are devastated. The media hasn't picked up on this yet – hopefully, we can keep it that way.' Detective Constable Amanda Turner had been assigned the task of lead FLO. 'It seems that Mia and her parents lost contact in the panic – she was a small girl.'

The FLO took a moment to compose herself. 'She was trampled to death. The mortuary is trying to tidy her up before we ask the parents for a formal identification. We are still waiting for the CCTV where she was killed.'

The picture on the screen showed a forlorn picture of Mia's bruised body on the mortuary slab – most looked away. DC Amanda Turner didn't always enjoy her job, but it did give her a lot of job satisfaction at what was an awful time for any family – someone had to do it, and a professional compassionate response often helped to solve difficult cases. Her role was to gather evidence and information from the family to contribute to the investigation and preserve its integrity by securing the confidence and trust of the families. It was also her job to keep the family updated with information in accordance with the needs of any investigation and before they read about it in the papers.

'So, who is the shooter?' Bodkin raised his voice. 'Someone must know something. Who has spoken with Nowak?'

'We haven't been able to find Nowak,' said a Detective Constable from the back.

'What do you mean you haven't been able to find him. That's bollocks,' shouted Bodkin.

'As you know we spoke to Martha's tour manager, Jimmy Patrick, earlier. He said that Nowak had briefly been seen at this morning's production meeting. He then left in a hurry. I've been trying to track his whereabouts since then using ANPR and CCTV,' continued the DC. 'No luck so far. The traffic is very heavy and number plates often obscured.'

'I insisted that tonight's and tomorrow's concerts were postponed. They didn't seem so happy about that.' The room laughed – Bodkin consulted his notes 'Forensics are going over the roof space and technical areas. Nothing so far. What about the two sitting next to Nowak? Kelly's mates, Daisy deVilliers and Danny Owen?'

'deVilliers was at the press conference last night and they were both at the production meeting this morning too. Then they disappeared. Not seen since.' One of the team consulted their notes.

'You say they were sitting next to Nowak at the concert. Do we think they are connected somehow?' Asked another.

Bodkin took that one. 'DCS Kelly and his team know more about all this than they are letting on. They have been investigating Nowak and his business interest for bloody years but hasn't been able to pin anything on him. He seems to have a guardian angel protecting him.'

Bodkin's phone interrupted what was about to become a diatribe. He looked at the screen and then at his team. 'One moment, please.'

After normal hellos, Bodkin said no more. He listened and after one hundred and four seconds simply said, 'Thank you.'

Bodkin turned back to the room. 'The weapon has been found hidden in the ductwork above the 02 auditorium. This information does not go out of this room – is that clearly understood?'

The response was half-hearted. Bodkin repeated the order, 'No details of the weapon are to leak. This must remain confidential. This team only. Is that clear?'

Pause.

'I said is that clear?'

Unanimous agreement from the team.

'The weapon is a Russian Vintorez sniper rifle issued mainly for covert operations to Spetsnaz units. No prints of course, anywhere. The rifle can be dismantled into three main components carried in a special briefcase measuring 450 by 370 by 140 millimetres. So, could also be a large tote bag or a backpack.'

'So is our guy Russian then?' asked DS Culpepper.

'Could be, but we cannot assume anything.' Bodkin answered. 'A professional could have acquired the weapon from anywhere. But at least this narrows down the search on CCTV a little. DC Pawlek, please go back over the CCTV you have already examined to check for anyone carrying bags and back packs. The shooter might have used a courier. But I doubt it.'

DC Pawlek gave a resigned nod. Several colleagues around him did the same – it was going to be an even longer day for which even the overtime would not be compensation.

'Right, that's it for today. We'll meet here again same time tomorrow. Please have updates for me.'

Everyone stood to leave. The meeting room door opened; the team remained standing as Deputy Assistant Commissioner Keith Wallace walked in.

'Well?' was all he said. 'Report.'

Bodkin yet again took the lead. 'Nothing really to report yet. We have the CCTV. We've passed the pictures of the alleged shooter to various facial recognition teams. We should know more in a day or two.'

Bodkin deliberately kept some of the information to himself.

'I'll await your update. Keep the pressure on Bodkin.' The DAC turned and left the room ignoring everyone else, who exchanged looks. Extra pressure from on high was an unwelcome addition to an already complex investigation.

DAY TWO
FRIDAY EARLY EVENING

MARTHA'S TOUR PRODUCTION OFFICE

MARTHA MOVIN' OUT TOUR MANAGER, JIMMY
Patrick had spent most of the day on the phone calling in
every favour. He sat back after a solid six hours' work. *At last,
a sense of normality in the crazy world of showbusiness and
concert touring,* he thought as he sipped his eighth coffee that
had gone cold on his ever-disorganised desk with the Post-It
Notes littered on every available surface.

Heads of departments from lighting, sound, video
playback, rigging and screens – all friends from days, weeks,
and months on the road together on many tours, now sat
with Jimmy enjoying an early evening cup of tea – a couple
had a chilled lager – before returning to their homes for

some unexpected days and nights off. Some had already called partners, or potential girl or boy friends, to suggest date nights.

'We're completely out. Staging, truss, rigging, bespoke kit loaded onto the trailers and off to the storage facility. Tech off hire and rebooked.' Andy Jackson summarised for them all. 'Just the production vehicles, wardrobe and catering to go.'

'Hard day,' everyone agreed.

'Not as hard as an overnight get out,' suggested Jimmy.

They all snorted in agreement.

'And at least we are working with a transport and logistics team we all know,' continued Andy, 'one of the drivers owed me twenty quid from a previous gig!'

More chortled nods all round.

Jimmy's phone rang. He exhaled a long sigh and asked rhetorically. 'Bollocks. Now what?'

His shoulders dropped. He looked at the caller display and saw it was Daisy. He perked up a bit. 'Hiya. I was just about to go home. Everyone has finished – arena's empty. Everything else will be out of here later this evening. All off hire or going to storage.'

'Ah! Right. Good. Erm...' Daisy was hesitant. *Nothing for it* she thought, *no point is prevaricating.*

'Nowak wants to arrange a video shoot,' Daisy heard the almost silent lament from the other end of the phone. She was sitting in Danny's flat with an exceptionally large glass of chilled prosecco laced with some *Wye Valley Blackberry Liqueur.*

'You're fucking joking,' was Jimmy's almost despondent reply. 'Why, when, how, where? Oh! Bloody hell.'

Jimmy gesticulated to the others to stay where they were. Looks were exchanged. Andy stood and put the kettle on – he thought they were all going to need another cuppa.

'And I've been sort of promoted. I am now Producer and PR.' Daisy was worried that Jimmy wouldn't take the news well – if anyone deserved to be promoted it was Jimmy.

'Congratulations.' Jimmy sounded genuinely delighted for Daisy.

'Thank you. But producer should be your job, not mine.' Daisy offered an olive branch.

'That's good of you to say. Nowak pays me a fair wage. And I've got enough on my hands managing the tour, the crew, everything else. More than happy for you to take the extra shit.' Jimmy laughed.

'I will need your help. This'll have to be a partnership.' Daisy explained the details of the proposed video shoot to Jimmy. It would give his team some unexpected extra work. 'Cheers m'dear. The department heads were about to go home. I'll give them the good news. We can knock out some budgets tomorrow. I'll get onto it.'

They arranged where and when to meet before disconnecting.

'What was all that about?' Andy Jackson, the lighting designer was intrigued.

'Looks like we're going back to Elstree if I can get a slot. Soon too. Nowak wants to shoot a video of the concert for sell-through. Some of the proceeds to Police Charities.' Jimmy explained.

There was excitement around the production office. A video shoot without an audience enabled the opportunity for retakes to ensure everything was perfect and meant they weren't temporarily laid off – the life of a freelancer.

'What are the deadlines?' asked the front of house sound balancer.

'We shoot as soon as possible and have everything through editing, post-production, duplication and on-line ready a couple of days before we next get back here. Music downloads as well through all the normal outlets, plus a souvenir CD. So tight – four weeks from today. Must look something like the first night. A campaign is being launched for last night's audience to contribute smart phone footage.' Jimmy was on a roll. 'Right then, let's have tonight off. As soon as I have details, I'll e-mail you all. Looks like we'll be getting everything back out again.'

The rest of the team stood and trooped off together to North Greenwich underground station, chattering happily. Jimmy took to the phone again. Although late, TV was a twenty-four-seven business – Jimmy had home and mobile phone numbers of the key contacts in the bookings departments of most suppliers. Within half an hour he had pencilled dates in ten days' time for Elstree's largest studio. He had also contacted a couple of UHD OB facilities truck companies. There was nothing more he could do for now, but the ball was rolling. He WhatsApp'd the immediate team with the provisional dates.

He packed up his laptop, collected his notes and put them all in his backpack, looked around one last time to check there was nothing of importance left in the production office and headed for the door. He didn't get far – as he opened the door, coming up the steps were DCS Bill Kelly and DS Anastasia Spencer-Hatt.

'Can I help you? I was just going home.' Jimmy didn't know these two, but instinctively guessed they were police. Confirmed a couple of seconds later when Kelly and Spencer-Hatt introduced themselves showing their badges.

'I spoke to you lot last night and again early this morning. I'm knackered. Didn't really sleep much last night and it's been a busy day. Can this wait?' Jimmy asked pleasantly enough

'This won't take long,' said Kelly.

Jimmy shrugged, turned around and switched the power and then the lights back on again. He realised he needed caffeine. 'Tea? Coffee? Beer?' he offered.

'Two coffees would be good. Ta.' Kelly spoke for them both. 'Milk. No sugar.'

'We've had a long day and night as well. Murder tends to do that.' DS Anastasia Spencer-Hatt was prickly. She absent-mindedly helped herself to the remaining custard cream from a plate on the central meeting table.

Jimmy reached under the side counter and brought out a *Nestlé Big Assorted Mixed Biscuit Box* that Shirley had supplied from 'Starring-Meals-on-Wheels,' the tour's catering company. Without further asking Anastasia picked a Toffee Crisp; Bill Kelly a Yorkie bar; Jimmy a KitKat. Jimmy served the strong hot coffee in Martha Movin' Out mugs, 'You can keep the mugs if you like.'

'You trying to bribe us?' Bill Kelly asked through a shower of chocolate. It was a friendly dig – he would take his mug home or use in the office.

'Who did you see this morning?' asked Anastasia finishing off the custard cream, before unwrapping the Toffee Crisp.

'I didn't really get their names; they weren't here long. Tall guy called Bodkin I think and a woman he kept calling Sergeant. Seemed very formal.' Jimmy pointed at the chairs around the table. They all sat. 'How can I help?'

Kelly took a slug of coffee before carefully replying. 'DS Rob Andrews says you can be trusted. Is that true?'

Kelly's stare was hard.

'What do you want me to say? I suppose so. I deal in millions of pounds and am responsible for many people. Complex logistics. I think I have a good reputation.' Jimmy didn't really know how to answer. *Bloody silly question,* his thought unsaid.

'Detective Chief Inspector Harry Bodkin runs the Major Investigation Team – he oversees the specialised homicide squad investigating the murder of the late Michael Maguire, my detective Sergeant. We must keep arms-length as we are actively involved. We will offer every assistance, but DCI Bodkin leads that investigation.' Kelly carefully considered his next move. 'That's not why we are here. And I'd rather DCI Bodkin didn't know about this conversation.'

Jimmy was surprised. 'Don't you all work for the same police force?'

Coffees were sipped and biscuits munched.

'I lead the covert serious organised crime investigation team at the National Crime Agency. My team is responsible for national and international investigations into serious and organised crime, international financial fraud, people smuggling, human trafficking, arms dealing and drug running.'

'Do I need a lawyer?' Jimmy was worried, although he couldn't think what he had done to attract this sort of attention.

'I don't know. Do you?' DS Anastasia Spencer-Hatt was assertive – before helping herself to another treat from the biscuit box. Both Jimmy and Kelly stared at her.

'What?! I missed lunch. Bloody starving.' Anastasia Spencer-Hatt was one of those annoying people who could eat-and-eat and never put-on weight. One of those people who looked good in whatever clothes they were wearing – today black trousers, black jacket, white blouse, and black shoes. Her blonde hair was tied in a scraped back ponytail. She wore little makeup. A simple gold chain was the only jewellery. Her voice was upmarket, but not annoyingly aristocratic, which betrayed her post-graduate entry into the Police directly from Newnham College, Cambridge.

Although neither had agreed before the meeting, Kelly fell automatically into the good cop role whilst Spencer-Hatt naturally gravitated towards the role of bad cop.

'What's all this got to do with me?' Jimmy was becoming uncomfortable, not through guilt, but the unknown.

'We want to talk about your boss Stanislaw Nowak.' Kelly announced.

'What about him?' replied Jimmy.

'How much do you know about him?' Kelly thought Jimmy was being deliberately difficult.

'He is as good or bad as any promoter. Really only cares about the cash. Goes off on one frequently – shout and bluster. Not sure he means anything by it. I haven't known him that long really.' Jimmy was hesitant. He wasn't sure where this was leading.

'How did you meet? Why did you get the gig?' Anastasia Spencer-Hatt's turn.

'Martha introduced me to Nowak via my agent. I've worked with Martha several times before and she trusts me. Despite her, er, past difficulties I trust her. Trust goes a long way.'

Kelly snorted, 'Does everyone have an agent in this business?'

Jimmy was getting a bit annoyed about the direction the interview was taking. 'I spend my life on the road managing tours. Trying to keep on top of everything is both time consuming and counterproductive. My agent ensures I get paid. Manages my personal and professional accounts. My future diary. She sifts the serious offers from the time wasters and advises me on which projects best not to be associated with.'

'What do you mean? Not associated with?' The flipflopping between Spencer-Hatt and Kelly continued.

'Some in this industry hide behind shell companies set up for one-off projects or tours. When they have extracted their cash, they shut it down and many of the freelancers and suppliers don't see a penny, or maybe only a few pennies in the pound.'

'Nowak financially underwrites this tour?' Kelly's smile belied where the conversation was going. 'And is legitimate and trustworthy then?'

'Seems to be. He leaves almost everything to me. There is always money in the bank, so I authorise payment to everyone I am responsible for. I have a company credit card for petty cash and small items. But I have my budgets and individual limits, which I pretty much stick to. Never had a problem. Johnny Jones, the ticket sales and finance manager is the final sign off on the bank transfers and larger payments; I send him a list every week. He also runs the company's finances, HMRC, VAT and so on. I don't want anything to do with that.' Jimmy was curious. 'What's all this about? Has someone had their hand in the till?'

'Have they?' Spencer-Hatt again.

'Not as far as I know.' Jimmy stood. 'Look I am tired. It's been a long day after a long night. I'm not sure I can add any more. Can we carry on some other time?'

'So, you didn't know the tour vehicles were going to be used for people smuggling then?' Kelly dropped the question quietly. Both Spencer-Hatt and Kelly watched Jimmy's reaction.

Jimmy's reaction wasn't immediate. He was confused. The tiny arrector pili muscles on the back of his neck tried to raise his non-existent fur pelt. He started rubbing the area in response.

'What?' Jimmy dropped back into his chair. 'What are you talking about? Of course, they're not.'

Spencer-Hatt and Kelly remained silent, watching him carefully. After a while Jimmy continued. 'Okay, on past tours we've had the odd stowaway that we haven't reported. But any trucker crossing the channel has encountered that issue. They do their best... but sometimes... oh, you know. With the best will in the world some of the stowaways are very clever and have learned to hide. Even the Customs' heat scanners, radar things and searches miss them. But we haven't got on the road yet.'

'This isn't about the odd one or two stowaways. Nowak was planning to use the tour to transport dozens, if not hundreds,' spat Spencer-Hatt. 'So, don't give me that one or two bollocks.'

'I said I knew nothing about this.' Jimmy stood angrily. 'I think you had better leave now.'

The two police officers ignored Jimmy's request.

'Nowak is in a whole load of shit because he can't deliver on the people smuggling deal. Various very unpleasant people want their money back. And maybe even revenge.' Kelly was attempting to be conciliatory, but equally determined to find out if Jimmy Patrick was a very good actor or really knew nothing. 'What can you tell me about the transport and the tour schedule?'

Jimmy thought awhile, not because he was going to lie, but he wanted to ensure he was going to be accurate. He sat back down, 'In the last week everything suddenly changed. Nowak's mate Pietr Ostrodzko pulled out of the transport contract. No reason given. Perhaps he found out about your people smuggling thing?'

'Not mine. Nowak's,' countered Kelly.

Jimmy continued, 'Left us in the shit. I wasn't disappointed. Ostrodzko didn't have the expertise or experience, but Nowak insisted. He doesn't insist or stick his oar in often. Luckily one of my regular large event and music transportation companies, Stage Truck, had availability. Freight forwarders are normally given three to six months to organise concert tour transportation. We were able to use the same labelling technologies and then simply transfer the schedule. We don't need as many vehicles, so I've saved on the budget. At least I now know the reason why. To be fair Pietr Ostrodzko transported to Stage Truck all their custom-made steel cases for the delicate specials.'

Spencer-Hatt was getting bored with the excruciating transportation details and coughed loudly. Kelly took his cue. 'And the tour schedule?'

'North Africa, Turkey, and Egypt have been cancelled by Nowak. We won't need incredibly complex customs carnets now for those. They're even more difficult than the bloody Brexit paperwork – plus maybe cash for bribes and backhanders. Probably shouldn't have told you that?' Jimmy admitted. 'I'm told by the finance team that ticket sales weren't going well either. But it's an ill wind and all that, gives us the opportunity to add more UK and European gigs. Still have the masses of additional European paperwork and visas to deal with because of the bloody Brexit fiasco though.'

Jimmy finished his coffee.

'So, I take it you are a Remainer then?' mocked Spencer-Hatt.

'Too bloody right. It's a fucking mess for far too many businesses.' Jimmy stood, hoping the two police officers would get the message he wanted to go home. He was disappointed. 'Are we totally legit now do you think?'

'I don't know, are you?' Kelly looked directly into Jimmy's eyes. 'You don't know how Nowak obtained the money to seed fund Martha's tour I suppose either?'

Again, a long pause whilst Jimmy thought. As he answered, he looked up and to the left, 'It accumulates.

Starts with Nowak's personal cash and a few angel investors that he probably knows. Then the venture capitalists and the banks jump aboard. Once established, advance ticket sales, together with the sponsorship deals arranged by Daisy deVilliers really get the show on the road. But not my job.'

'So, what about Ali Baka then?' Spencer-Hatt's turn to interrogate.

'Who is she, this Ali Baka?' asked Jimmy – he thought Ali was short for Alison. Neither of the police reacted. There was another long silence.

Jimmy picked it up. 'What I don't understand is why your man was shot. What has he got to do with it all?'

'Not our case. Detective Chief Inspector Bodkin's team is investigating the murder of my sergeant – we are too close,' explained Kelly. 'Matter of protocol—.'

'—thank you, Mr Patrick for your help,' interrupted Spencer-Hatt. 'We'll probably be back in touch.'

'What about Nowak? Are we in danger?' Jimmy needed to be sure his crew was safe.

'You'll have to take that up with him.' Spencer-Hatt mocked Jimmy.

With that, at last, they got up to leave – on their way each taking another favourite from the rapidly emptying *Nestlé Big Assorted Mixed Biscuit Box*. Jimmy made a note to ask Shirley for another.

He sat there awhile planning how he was going to bring all this up with Nowak. Jimmy's anger demanded a full-frontal attack. His head told him to be careful.

Danny or Daisy would be wise counsel.

10

DAY THREE
SATURDAY AFTERNOON

FRANCISCO'S, LEICESTER SQUARE

DETECTIVE CHIEF SUPERINTENDENT BILL KELLY, Detective Sergeant Rob Andrews, Danny Owen, and Daisy deVilliers sat facing each other in Francisco's Café, just off Leicester Square in the heart of London's theatre land. The lunch time rush had run its course – the afternoon tea-takers dispersed. The staff were clearing and cleaning the laminated tables before going home. There were no other customers.

Outside it was bright and sunny with vibrant blue skies bringing out the tourists all keen to take in the varied delights and opportunities that Soho made available to them. A constant stream of 'planes left vapour trails in the sky as they made their final descents into Heathrow Airport. A Police helicopter hovered overhead, seemingly biding its time waiting for a call to immediate action. On the edge of the grassy square, alongside the seated statue of Mr Bean, "Silver Steve" Hobart, the human statue covered in silver paint spent hours perched perfectly still, seemingly sitting on thin air until he suddenly moved to the delighted shrieks of young children who ran to hide behind the legs of their parents. The long queue hoping for reduced price tickets at the Society of London Theatre 'tkts' box office watched in fascination – and then communally laughed, a catalyst for nattering with those around them.

Danny ordered a large cappuccino, with an extra shot, together with a fist-sized Cannoli Siciliani. Francisco, the café owner, and Danny knew each other too well from too many post-radio show breakfasts which Danny always called lunch as, by then, he had normally been up and awake for five hours Monday to Thursday – and, this week, Friday as well.

Kelly and Andrews ordered strong tea. Daisy, a decaffeinated latte. The three also ordered the Cannoli Siciliani.

'So, you like my mother's recipe from Piana degli Albanesi.' Francisco as usual ostentatiously crossed himself in memory of his late Sicilian mother. Kelly, Andrews, and Daisy had only recently been introduced to the addictive tube-shaped shells of fried pastry dough filled with the sweet, creamy filling of figs, honey, and ricotta.

On the wall between them was a grainy, slightly stained black and white photograph of the *Arandora Star*, the converted cruise liner – Kelly had been staring at it.

Francisco was in an expansive mood, 'More than eight hundred men were killed including my grandfather. Two of my uncles survived after spending a very long time in the water. They rarely discussed the sinking. They came from a generation that did not discuss difficult personal experiences. After the war ended many of them were busy rebuilding their businesses and lives rather than living in the past. My father, also named Francisco, started this place – he was lucky to be able to buy the freehold after the war, otherwise I could not afford to stay here. Many of us, come from Bardi in the upper Ceno valley. We go back to there in Agosto si tiene "La festa dell'emigrante", occasione per molte famiglie emigrate nel Regno Unito di ritornare nei luoghi natali – to visit the cemetery of our families.' Francisco returned to his native language when emotional – mainly family and football. 'Every year we celebrate in a great reunion. Crazy times. Too much eating and drinking and games.'

He flamboyantly gesticulated around the empty café at many other black and white photographs including one of a younger, machismo, Francisco halfway up, or down, a greasy pole being admired by a gaggle of attractive slim young women – one of whom later became his wife, and no longer slim.

The four smiled but remained silent. Francisco scuttled off, realising he had talked too much, and transferred his attention to the Gaggia coffee machine.

'Why are we meeting here?' asked Danny. 'Have you run out of meeting rooms at the Yard, or are you both in need of sugary sustenance?'

Neither Kelly nor Andrews reacted. Kelly simply took out his iPhone, selected a file and hit play.

Nowak's voice was instantly recognisable. *'Let's get straight to the point. I owe Baka one million pounds. But he is dead? Debt gone.'*

Pause.

'Did you hear me?'

A slightly longer pause

'My arrangements were with Ali Baka. He is dead. Why should I pay you, and pay you more than I owe?'

Danny shot a glance at Kelly and was about to speak. Kelly put his finger to his lips.

'I need time to raise the money.'

'I need eight weeks. And if Martha dies, I won't have any money.'

'Okay, I'll do my best. Four weeks from today.'

They heard Nowak's phone ping five times.

'We assume those messages are the details of five bank accounts. So that's probably quarter of a mill a time.' Kelly concluded. 'We are going to put a track and trace on Nowak's bank accounts, the ones we know of anyway, but I suspect that's not going to help us much. The UK doesn't technically have a set limit on how much you can send overseas, but both the FCA and HMRC will monitor transfers for illegal activity. He'll only run into a barrier if there are reasonable grounds for concern that the transfers are in aid of money laundering or tax avoidance.'

'As we have bugged Nowak's car...' Andrews stated the obvious, '...we also know about the plans for the Police Charities concert—'

'Very commendable by the way,' interrupted Kelly.

Daisy blushed. She realised that they had also heard her plans for Martha. Neither of the policemen said anything.

Francisco arrived with the teas and coffees, and a large plate covered with the afternoon's calorific treats. 'The café is closed now. I'll be well out your way in the back office entering information for my tax return. You won't be disturbed.'

This time he left promptly, via turning the sign on the front door around to read closed and pulling down the window blinds. The four were alone.

'What's the bloody purpose of decaffeinated coffee?' Kelly demanded. 'Utterly pointless.'

He popped a piece of the Cannoli Siciliani in his mouth. He didn't have to wait long for the sugar-buzz. His tea was strong, dark brown and tannin rich.

'You didn't answer my question,' Danny was like a dog with a bone. 'Why are we meeting here?'

Kelly had already decided he had to trust Danny and Daisy – they might be able to learn the information that the police couldn't. *Illegally*, *off-the-books* unsaid. 'Nowak was receiving tip offs from DS Maguire.'

'Surely that can't be why Maguire was killed?' Danny was confused.

'Maybe. Maybe not, but it's too much of a coincidence. I don't like coincidences.' Kelly finished the remnants of his Cannoli in one bite, wiped his mouth and then explained how and why he had confronted Maguire.

Andrews had heard the story a couple of times and was still angry from being let down by who he thought was a trusted colleague – albeit, at times, a grumpy one. *Maybe the grumpiness was due to the stress,* he mused to himself by way of mitigation.

Danny and Daisy listened to Kelly's candour with increasing exasperation.

'That must have been awful, one of your own letting you down like that.' Daisy was sympathetic.

There was an awkward silence as Kelly considered what he was going to say next. *Just out with it,* he told himself. *No way of dressing this up.*

'Maguire admitted it was him who put Nowak onto you, Danny.' Kelly said it quickly and then watched Danny for a response.

Danny didn't know how to react. Initially anger. 'So, Maguire was the ultimate cause of my bloody foot being smashed then? Good fucking job he's dead, otherwise I would have fucking killed him myself.'

Danny was furious. His foot greeted him with a massive painful throb in salute.

Daisy tenderly reached over to hold Danny's hand. She gave it a light squeeze. 'He's dead now. He's paid the price.'

Danny realised he'd probably gone too far. 'Sorry. That was out of order.'

They all sat quietly, allowing a few moments for Danny's emotion to subside. He carefully considered what he should say next by way of explanation. 'I had contacted Maguire to get some inside information for my bloody disabled badges story – I didn't really know him. Only spoke to him on the phone. A colleague in the newsroom suggested he might be a person to speak to. If it's any help I don't recall him giving anything away. When we all met at the Yard to discuss Martha's disappearance, I didn't really put two and two together – it was ten years ago. Tried to forget all about that period.'

Danny's foot again throbbed in compliance.

'It was Maguire who removed the evidence from our store. It was Maguire who initially warned Nowak that he was being bugged.' Kelly gave Danny a look; he knew that Danny had also told Nowak about being bugged. 'It was Maguire who warned Nowak about other things. Only Nowak. And not everything, but only low-level stuff Maguire insisted. I did believe him. I didn't have any sympathy for Maguire. He should have come to me immediately. But I did sort of understand his predicament – that's why I didn't take it any further.'

Daisy's turn to press the point. 'You could have said all this at the Yard. You haven't explained why we are meeting here.'

Kelly and Andrews looked to each other. An imperceptible look passed between them. Although Kelly was the boss, he needed the support of his trusted DS – this was going miles outside Police regulations.

'Even after Maguire confessed with the promise there would be no more, information continued to leak to Nowak. I don't think… no let's rephrase that… I am certain it wasn't Maguire. I now believe that Maguire wasn't, isn't the only inside informer – hence the need for secrecy. Confidential information is still getting to Nowak, even after I confronted Maguire. We don't know the extent of what other information is leaking.'

'How do you know?' Daisy was intrigued.

'We still have the listening devices in place at his flat and as you know in his car. We recorded him talking to someone on his mobile phone. Someone who could only have had inside knowledge,' Kelly hesitated, 'Nowak is canny, he knows his flat is bugged – he didn't give anything away.'

'Can't you intercept his calls?' Danny was intrigued to know.

'That man has more mobile phones than Carphone Warehouse and changes them more often than a tart changes her knickers.' Kelly was exasperated.

Rob Andrews picked up the diatribe. 'With Maguire gone we need to see what happens next. We've laid a few traps.'

'We want Nowak and whoever is pulling his strings, but we also want the inside shit who is pissing on us. What's the connection? Surely it can't just be the disabled badges, that's old news now – but could be, must be connected somehow? He might have something on someone. Is it the people smuggling? With Baka and Conor dead we thought that was all over.' Kelly realised he was thinking out loud. *Had he said too much to Danny and Daisy, the outsiders?*

'And who has he been talking to on the phones in the car?' Kelly paused. He looked straight at Danny and then at Daisy. 'I need you to get hold of those phones. I suspect he keeps separate phones for separate conversations?'

Danny and Daisy couldn't believe what they had just been asked to do.

'How the hell do you expect us to do that? And what

happens if we get caught?' Daisy was angry. 'Totally unfair of you to even ask. You are the police, not us.'

There was an uncomfortable silence. It was Danny who broke the contemplation. 'I'll do it.'

'You can't. Mustn't. It would put you in danger.' Daisy pulled away the hand that had up until now been reassuring Danny.

'I'm the one who Nowak assaulted. I want this shit. I also want the story – it could be my break back into mainstream investigative journalism. I'm fed up with the overinflated egos of some bloody celebrities and, worse still, their fucking people.' Danny's harangue surprised them all – including Danny himself.

The door from the back office opened. Francisco's head stuck out, 'Is everyone okay? I heard shouting.'

'Four more please Francisco. Same again.' Kelly responded pointing at the empty cups.

Francisco came over, collected the used crockery and cutlery, then busied himself with more teas and coffees. The four around the table sat in contemplative silence.

After a few minutes Francisco returned and placed the fresh cups on the table with a plate of cantucci; traditional almond biscuits. 'I'll need to lock up and go home in about twenty minutes. I've had enough paperwork and accounting. I am an honest citizen who pays his taxes.'

Kelly passed over four twenty-pound notes in more-than payment – as he did so, he winked. 'Here you go Francisco. We'll be gone soon. Thanks for this, appreciate it. Don't need a receipt.'

The five of them laughed at the irony.

'Grazie Signore.' Francisco carefully folded the notes which vanished into his back pocket before he disappeared out the back again, carefully shutting the door behind him.

'Nowak is being bugged.' Kelly restarted the conversation.

Danny was confused. 'No shit Sherlock. You just played a recording from the car – and you told us his apartment was covered.'

'We weren't the first to get into Nowak's place. Our team reported someone got there before us. And with some sophisticated apparatus connected to the mains, with frequency hopping timed burst transmissions. One hour of recording can be sent in less than five seconds on several different frequencies, meaning sweeps are unlikely to find them. We were lucky. One of the lads chose the same location and was shocked to find another device. He didn't say anything but did have the sense to take a photo on his iPhone. Hopefully, they don't know we know.'

'Whose are they?' Danny asked more in hope than expecting an answer.

'That's just it, we don't know. But from their sophisticated nature we can only assume must be a state – or state sponsored. Could be anyone. The pictures are with our TSU, sorry, Technical Surveillance Unit, they might be able to help. The serial numbers and all markings had been erased so we can't check official UK logs. The Home Office insist we keep a record of all covert surveillance operations. The trouble is that where there is a record, it's possible to access the information if you know how. But the lack of ID makes that impossible.' Danny's investigative journalism antennae could tell that Kelly wasn't telling them the whole story.

'I spoke to Jimmy Patrick yesterday evening. He says he didn't know anything about the people smuggling plans?' Kelly aimed the question at Daisy and Danny. 'Can't believe he didn't realise anything was unusual at all? He seemed genuinely shocked when I told him about the covert plans for the tour's vehicles.'

'He is a good guy,' said Danny. Daisy nodded her agreement.

'Okay, let's leave Francisco to his paperwork.' Kelly wound up the meeting. 'This could be dangerous. We know Baka and Conor worked with The Vory. We must assume Nowak as well. We don't know what we are getting into.'

They finished their drinks. Rob Andrews polished off the couple of remaining biscuits.

As he stood up, Kelly looked down at Daisy and Danny. 'You have Rob's and my mobile numbers. We are the only people you speak to. Good luck.'

With that the two policemen left leaving Daisy and Danny at the table.

'What just happened?' Daisy was overwhelmed.

'I think I just agreed to go undercover.' Danny was excited and apprehensive in equal measure. *What the fuck have I done?* Danny thought. Then realised this is his journalistic calling, *not schmoozing with self-important, self-styled celebrities and artistes with egos the size of planets together with their agents, managers, publicists and their other people who thought they were even more important than those they handled but lived on their tails.*

'I thought I heard the front door?' Francisco came out from the back office. He gazed at Daisy and Danny, 'You two okay?'

'Yeah. Couldn't be better,' Danny was obviously distracted. 'Thanks for today, we'll be off.'

They both shook Francisco's hand as he held the front door open for them. 'Alla Prossima!'

They walked together past where Danny had been attacked a few short weeks ago – he hardly noticed. In the distance they saw Kelly and Andrews deep in conversation across the other side of Charing Cross Road walking towards Trafalgar Square.

'Wonder what they are up to?' Daisy asked.

'Bet it's something they haven't told us,' suggested Danny.

Kelly hadn't mentioned that the photographs of the listening devices had also been sent to the specialist training and communications facility at Fort Monckton – a Napoleonic-era fortress surrounded by barbed wire, high reinforced steel fences, formidable walls and accessible only through a heavy-duty, ram-proof barrier followed by a massive green, round-topped, double steel door across a single drawbridge. The Fort overlooked the Solent on the eastern end of Stokes Bay, near Gosport, Hampshire, now referred to as No. 1 Military Training Establishment by the British Army, it was officially occupied by the Ministry of Defence – but all SIS, MI5 and MI6 officers got extensive training there before allowed out on to the streets. The SAS, SBS, covert police and other special forces were often there too, training for joint ops. Security was extremely high and unusually protected by armed private contractors, generally ex-special forces, and not the military or police. Few people knew what went on behind the massive dual layer stone fortifications.

What Kelly didn't know – yet – was that his actions had set off a cascade of communications all the way up to the JIC – the UK's Joint Intelligence Committee. Phones were ringing across Whitehall, the heart of the UK Government.

11
DAY TEN
SATURDAY MORNING

DANNY'S FLAT

TEN DAYS AFTER THE SHOOTING OF DETECTIVE Sergeant Maguire, Danny and Daisy were in bed enjoying a relative lie-in. Daisy's tea and Danny's coffee both finished – Danny had made the wake-up drinks at just before seven o'clock before crawling back into bed. Toast jointly forbidden due to a recent exploding crumbs-in-the-bedclothes episode.

It was now eight – the weekend breakfast TV rolled on from the screen on the far wall, neither really watching nor listening, engrossed in the newspapers on their iPads. Danny: *The Times*. Daisy: *The Mail*. Then they would both plough through the celebrity pages of all the other on-line newspapers, occasionally reading a piece of juicy gossip to the other – sardonically adding the word *allegedly* at every opportunity. When something caught their eye that they knew to be fake or grossly exaggerated they shared out loud an outraged, 'Never let the truth get in the way of a good story', then jointly cackled with derision.

Some of their ire was directed at Kelvin Edwards, the showbiz and gossip columnist from *The Saturday Tribune* who was still plugging the request for video footage from Martha's first night – alongside special offers for future concert tickets; several pictures of Martha from *that* night; and various paparazzi shots. Edwards criticised the lack of progress by the police to stir up a social media eruption for his personal promotion, to satisfy his ego and build up followers. Daisy wasn't that unhappy as Martha was still being talked about – which led to more ticket sales.

'Christ. I despise that man. Hate every moment I have to suck up to him.' Daisy humphed, 'but he is useful.'

'Yes dear,' was Danny's absent-minded reply, earning him a playful twisted nipple.

The shooting and the concert no longer made the lead item on the television news, consigned to nine minutes past the hour and just forty-five seconds in duration. Both vaguely watched with indifference – they knew the details better than any.

The presenter voiced-over a few wall-paper pictures from the post-show chaos: '*Moving on to the death of the police officer ten days ago at the opening night of Martha's concert tour. Investigators are no nearer to identifying the sniper responsible for the murder of Detective Sergeant Maguire. Last night Deputy Assistant Commissioner Keith Wallace made this statement.*'

The picture cut to a pre-recorded VT of the DAC is his best uniform outside New Scotland Yard. *'The investigation continues into the appalling murder of Detective Sergeant Maguire. We are following a number of leads but have yet to identify the shooter.'* The sound inelegantly chopped out as the barrage of reporters' questions continued unheard.

The picture cut back to the presenter sitting on the red sofa, *'We'll be speaking live to Deputy Assistant Commissioner Wallace later in the programme. Sergeant Maguire's funeral will be held later this week at New Southgate Crematorium in North London. Right, time now for the weather, here's…'*

'Still no mention of poor Mia then?' Daisy mused muting the TV's sound – this Saturday it was her turn for the remote control. 'Good news for the family, but it will break soon surely? Someone will leak it.'

'Her family requested that it was kept private,' Danny was distracted by something, *he wasn't sure what it was.* 'But when the news does break there'll be a shit storm.'

Daisy and Danny both procrastinated, not wanting to leave the comfy bed, but there was work to be done. In two days the Martha production team would begin the build at Elstree Studios to film what had become known within the team as *Nowak's video.*

Daisy's PR campaign picked up by most of the media, supported by daily appeals from Danny during the Starshine Breakfast Show, had done its job. Over three hundred video clips had already arrived from the first night audience to be possibly dropped into the final edit.

'I'm amazed. The response has been fantastic.' Daisy was playing for time. She snuggled down into her pillow.

'Too fantastic really. We now have over one hundred and twenty hours of footage to trawl through. Why didn't you simply agree the video editor could review it all?' Danny wasn't cross, but he certainly wasn't relishing the thought of reviewing hours and hours of amateur video. 'And bloody Kelvin's piece this morning will generate more. We'll have to shut it down.'

'I had a quick spin through some of it. We'll easily be able to whittle it down to a couple of hours. Lots of useless selfies and wobbly cam. I sometimes wonder if people watch what they see on TV. But there is some really good crowd footage singing along to Missing You.' Daisy was trying to encourage Danny. 'Should make for a great multi-screen montage.'

'Oh good,' was all that Danny could manage, still thinking distractedly. Daisy gave him a sharp poke in the ribs, which precipitated more horizontal delaying activities which distracted Danny from his distracted thinking.

An hour later, having dozed awhile in satisfied post-coital bliss and then a mutual shower, they both sat at Danny's computer in his spare-bedroom-come-office. They both wore over-sized monogrammed bathrobes. Daisy was gently caressing the soft, thick, white towelling.

'I acquired these from the Hôtel Barrière Le Majestican in Cannes whilst I was there for one of the Film Festivals. The view across the Boulevard de la Croisette to the Mediterranean was breath-taking. A bit like the room rate. Luckily, I wasn't paying. I was the guest of a film company now gone bust. Can't even remember what I was meant to be reviewing,' explained Danny. 'I thought I had got away with stealing them until my credit card bill had arrived showing four-hundred Euros in extras. There were two in the bathroom. Thought I might as well have both. One for the occasional visitor. But the film company said they only covered the cost of bed and breakfast at the hotel.'

Daisy sniggered, 'I feel guilty if I walk away with a teeny-weeny plastic bottle of shampoo.'

Daisy had downloaded the massive crop of video footage to a portable hard drive. They now started harvesting, separating the wheat from the chaff. One of her newly appointed team had earlier undertaken the mind-numbing task of uniquely renaming the files to match a database of contact details, so they could caption every clip used with the name of the *citizen videographer*. They had also decided to give away two Golden Circle tickets to everyone whose video clips were used.

Two hours later they had managed to copy into carefully labelled sub-folders fifteen minutes of useful material from the thirty hours considered – they had become adept at spooling through the rushes discarding obviously useless material, occasionally pausing to go back to re-review and then either saving or ignoring.

Daisy stretched, 'I'm going to get dressed and make some breakfast.'

Thirty minutes later she arrived back in Danny's office, smelling freshly showered – with coffee, and bacon and egg butties, to find Danny spooling the same segment back and forward, then in slow motion, eventually freezing a frame.

'Look,' demanded Danny.

'At what?' Daisy didn't understand what she was seeing. 'Great crowd shot. But we already have lots of those.'

'Up there.' Danny had opened the video in Adobe Premiere Pro, his personal edit software. He zoomed in to the top right of the frame, motion stabilised and enhanced the picture as much as he could – it was a little pixelated but obvious enough. He slowly shuttled the image back and forth. 'That's a muzzle flash.' He looked at the timecode in hours, minutes, seconds, and frames – 22:22:20:16. He grabbed the frame, saved it, and hit print. He then edited the video, first in full frame and then added a slow-motion circled close-up. 'That should make the TV headlines?'

'Can we release this?' asked Daisy.

'We'll have to credit the person who supplied the footage – and have to check when they ticked the T&Cs box that they gave their permission, so we are copyright cleared.' Danny thought for a while. 'The Police know where the shooter was located, so we are not revealing evidence. I'll send a copy to Bodkin and Bill. Maybe later, after you have sent it out to your media contacts list.'

'That should stir it up. Maybe move us up the news agenda again.' Daisy was ever the pragmatist. 'Might even give us back the headlines rather than the end of the bulletins.'

Danny suddenly leapt to his feet, knocking over the coffee. He grabbed the remote control of his smart TV and selected BBC iPlayer, and then that morning's Breakfast News.

'What are you doing?' demanded Daisy.

Danny said nothing – he pressed fast forward until he saw the trailed live interview with Deputy Assistant Commissioner Keith Wallace. He watched in fascination – the sound muted.

'What?' Daisy questioned.

Danny returned to his laptop and opened BBC iPlayer, selected the Breakfast News, and spooled to the same point as on his TV. He frame-grabbed the still and printed it out – he sat there looking at the picture for a good three minutes. Daisy said nothing.

Eventually Danny spoke, 'I know that face.'

Daisy was perplexed. 'Yes, you've seen him on TV for the last week pontificating. Taking a long time to say nothing.'

'No. From a while ago.' Danny put his face in his hands and continued probing his memory. He suddenly sat up straight, picked up his phone and dialled Detective Chief Superintendent Bill Kelly on the private number he had been given earlier in the week.

'Danny, how are you?' Bill Kelly didn't hang about with small talk. 'Got Nowak's phone yet?'

No small talk for Danny either. 'Bill, you know you managed somehow to acquire my original Blue Badge story from my laptop. Did you get the accompanying pictures as well?'

'Where's this suddenly come from?'

'Answer the bloody question.'

'Not sure. Why?' Bill Kelly was uncertain.

'Please can you check and get back to me ASAP. If you find them, send the pictures over please. Something just triggered me which might explain a lot about what we are dealing with.' Without waiting for a response Danny pressed the red button.

Daisy looked directly at Danny, 'What's going on?'

Danny took a while to answer. 'I'm not sure. Just something tickling my memory. With Wallace just then on the TV.'

He ate his bacon and egg sandwich, finished the coffee that Daisy had remade after clearing up the spillage, and mopped his mouth.

'It'll come to you if you don't think about it,' offered Daisy. 'Now we've got work to do. Stop delaying.'

For the next two hours they both continued the frustrating task of sifting the hours-and-hours of video footage extracting just six minutes of *potentials* from the latest batch. They had now selected a total of twenty-one possible minutes from nearly forty hours of submitted video shots. 'Bloody hell, a shooting ratio of one hundred and fifteen to one – we'd be bankrupt if this were a proper shoot,' Danny's and Daisy's eyes were sore. 'Let's take a break. A walk on the common?'

Before she could answer, Daisy's and Danny's phones both played a breaking news jingle. Together they exhaled a long, 'Now what?'

Daisy's work phone gave the answer – it went wild with texts, WhatsApps and calls. The news of Mia's death, the little girl trampled to death at the concert, had just broken on social media. Everyone demanding corroboration, answers, statements, and interview requests.

Using her other phone, she called Virginia Stephani, the Met Police's PR and Comms team leader who answered almost immediately. No greetings – Stephani's Saturday had just been ruined as well. 'I thought we'd agreed not to release that news of Mia until the family gave the say-so?'

'It wasn't us.' Daisy replied.

'If it wasn't you, who was it then?' asked Virginia Stephani not believing a word the tour's PR said.

'I assumed it was you. So not either of us. Who was it and why?' Daisy thought for a moment. 'Did Bodkin or one of his lot leak it?'

'Very unlikely. Bodkin is a good copper who sticks by the rules. He wouldn't have let that information out without the family's and my agreement.' Stephani was defensive.

'What about his team?' Daisy was on the attack.

'Unlikely, as they follow Bodkins orders to the letter.' Stephani couldn't be certain, but she was as certain as she could be.

'What about Bill Kelly. He plays fast and loose.' Daisy was trying to control her frustration turning to anger.

'Wouldn't know. We don't have anything to do with the NCA. But I can't see why he should.'

They disconnected without fond farewells. They both had work to do.

Danny called Kelly. 'Was that you?'

Kelly was confused, 'Was that you… what?'

'Released the information about the death of Mia?'

'No! Oh Christ. Is it out there?' Kelly consulted the screen on the phone to see the breaking news alert. 'Yeah. Just seen it too.'

'Daisy's phone has just gone mad.'

'Wasn't us.'

'Are you sure? Bodkin, and his PR person, said the same. So, who leaked it?'

'No idea. Leave it with me.' Danny believed Kelly. 'I'll find out.'

Daisy worried about Mia's family. 'The Family Liaison Officer, Amanda Turner had better get round to the parents' house. With Stephani as well to handle the media – who will, very shortly be rushing to the house. The breaking news gave enough information to find them with a bit of basic research. What a fuck up?'

Daisy didn't have to wait, her private phone pinged with a message from Amanda, the FLO. 'On my way. But someone is going to hang for this.'

'If Bodkin and Kelly haven't leaked the information, then who did and why now?' said Danny.

Daisy hesitated, then asked, 'Could it have been Nowak himself?'

'What does he have to gain? Can't see it was him.' Danny thought carefully. 'Pretty certain it wouldn't have been one of the crew – they wouldn't have known.'

'Who was it then? Normally a newspaper would break this as an exclusive and then all the other media would try to play catch up.' Daisy was frustrated. 'We'd almost certainly have had advance notice by being asked to comment an hour or so before going online and to print. But this seems to have come from everywhere.'

Danny looked at his phone again and clicked on the breaking news banner. 'I can't find a source. It looks like one of the broadcaster's Breaking News logos, but it's not. It's fake. This has come from an anonymous account. It's already all over Twitter, Facebook and more.'

'Sky, the BBC, and ITN haven't reported it yet. I suspect they are waiting for independent corroboration from Stephani, not just reporting a rumour. At least they still have some journalistic standards.' Daisy scrolled through her news feeds. 'But Stephani won't be able to deny it.'

'You'd better warn Martha and Vikki – do they know? And the rest of the team too,' said Danny.

'On it,' responded Daisy. But it was too late, Daisy's private phone was ringing – the caller ID, Martha's new number.

'Martha, I was about to call you.' Daisy put her finger to her lips for Danny to remain silent. After a pause, Daisy responded, 'Yes, it's true.'

Danny couldn't hear what Martha was saying. But from Daisy's expression Martha was not happy.

'It was a terrible accident. On an awful night.' Daisy was placating her. 'The parents asked for, insisted on privacy. They didn't want to be a part of the media shit-storm whilst they grieved.'

Daisy continued to listen. Occasionally uh-huhing.

'If you are seen to get involved the media will be all over it,' Daisy continued without mentioning the PR plan already hatched. 'With Nowak we have been developing a strategy, but for now, I'll put out a personal statement. From you and Vikki. As with the policeman, you won't be taking questions.'

Daisy and Martha continued for another few minutes – Daisy took the opportunity to tell Martha about the gruesome death of Aleksandr Makarov. 'It was in some of the papers. But none had made the connection with the events at your gig.'

Daisy realised she was perspiring – the thought of the awful night affected her more than she realised. She hadn't really been concentrating on what Martha had been saying but picked the story up. 'It is thought that the shooter was running away, jumped for the boat and slipped. They have no idea who he was. They are not certain that he killed Sergeant Maguire. But strongly suspect.'

Daisy was about to continue, but the line was silent. Martha had disconnected without saying goodbye.

'You didn't mention the charity concert for Mia,' Danny was surprised.

'She hung up on me. Wasn't the right time anyway. Let's be honest' Daisy scoffed at the irony, 'We haven't exactly been candid with her. Martha is very fragile. And Vikki will wind her up.'

'Not surprising really. Career resurrected, kidnapped, the shooting, tour postponed. A bit of a roller-coaster.'

'Do you suppose,' Daisy hesitated, the next question was huge and complex, 'she'll revert to her, er, old ways?'

Daisy exchanged knowing looks with Danny.

'I hope not. I don't think so.' Danny wasn't as sure as he sounded. 'Do you think I should go and see her and Vikki?'

'Might help. You should go on your own.' Daisy suggested. 'I'm not sure I'm in her good books.'

'Does she know why the original tour schedule was changed? Cancelling the gigs in North Africa and Turkey?'

'Oh fuck! No! That would be the final straw…' Daisy went pale, '…she really doesn't need to know about Nowak's transport plans.'

Danny's phone pinged with a WhatsApp message. It was from Bill Kelly. The message was simple. *'Francisco's 17:00.'*

Danny responded with a thumb's up emoji; he turned to Daisy. 'He must have the photographs I asked him for.'

DAY TEN
SATURDAY

MARTHA AND VIKKI

MARTHA AND VIKKI WERE UNAWARE OF THE ACTION going on elsewhere safe in the luxury of Martha's apartment. The first few days after the concert had been difficult for both of them. Neither had witnessed at first hand the post-show carnage from either the bloody effects of the bullet or the panicking audience – due to the swift action of the tour manager Jimmy Patrick escorting Martha off the stage, then collecting Vikki, to whisk them both away from the 02 before the ensuing pandemonium.

Neither had known of the death of Amelia Cohen – but that was about to change.

The media had not made the connection between

Aleksandr Makarov's *unfortunate accident* and Maguire's assassination – yet.

The fall-out and reportage on TV, radio, and the press had been supportive of the colleagues, friends, and family of the *assassinated brave copper* as the popularist media would have it. Daisy and her PR team had turned down all requests for Martha to be interviewed or to appear on TV or radio – she was not important or relevant in the investigation into the murder of a policeman and didn't want to become the story. Daisy had insisted that the simple statement expressing condolences sufficed.

Many media outlets had also reinvigorated the background of Martha's and Vikki's relatively recent kidnapping, captivity, and incident-free rescue by Special Forces – with an excuse to rehash pictures featuring *our brave boys* in balaclavas or face protection. This was all associated with statistics of Martha's sensational journey to the top of the music charts in record time. One of the red-tops had excelled itself with a total of sixty-three pages over the week devoted to Martha, her music, and the events of *that* first night concert.

The reaction on social media had also been immense – uninformed opinion, outrage, indignation, and at first a demand for increased police presence – but then the blame game started. The trolls took up the cudgel, from initially simply unkind comments to, as the momentum took over, the posts turning hostile, vicious, and vitriolic. The *incompetence of the police* was a recurring theme. *Terrorism and islamophobia* were cited. Calls for *increased security at public events* were met with demands *for more freedom and increased civil liberties.*

Inevitably Martha then became the target. *Unaffordable ticket prices. Her semi-revealing dress sense. Too many new songs. Too many songs from her back-catalogue.* Suggestions that *her and her sister's kidnapping was staged. Vikki arranged the kidnapping. Martha was sleeping with one of the special forces team that rescued her.* Pictures of Martha and Danny were dredged up from long ago under the headline, *'the mysterious new man in Martha's life'.* Martha had become accustomed to the vileness and absurdities of trolls – she had learned to live with it and generally ignored the half-wits. She sometimes fantasised about sending in *the boys* with baseball bats and electric drills for the kneecaps. *How would they react if someone had personally bad-mouthed them or questioned their integrity, if they had any?* She wondered. *They are covert bullies masquerading behind absurd identities – fantasists who would probably be unable to survive in the real world.*

At first neither Vikki nor Martha could leave the apartment without being hounded by the press who had been camped outside within hours, if not minutes, of the terrible events. They were effectively prisoners living, once again, in the lap of luxury.

Their house landline and mobile phones hadn't stopped ringing. How the press had obtained the supposedly ex-directory numbers was a mystery – generally solved by a few bungs to people who know someone. Martha's *people* had arranged for the land-line number to be changed; new mobile phones and essential groceries to be delivered, together with various toiletries, alongside a case of 2013 Chilean Cabernet Sauvignon from The Maipo Valley, allegedly one of the red wines that has the most beneficial effect on health. Not that Vikki and Martha were drinking it for their health.

Together in captivity, whilst they were not collaborating in creating music and lyrics, Vikki and Martha had discussed at length, the ups and downs of celebrity – it had brought them closer than they had been for years. They had eventually reached agreement that stardom and being permanently in the public eye couldn't be switched on and off at will. Their discussions drove their most successful song, 'Captivity' – an allegorical muse examining the virtual chains that prevented them from being free. The song resonated with many who yearned for a relationship, yet for one reason of another were unable to fulfil their wishes, their dreams, their desires.

I found peace in captivity
Whom I'm supposed to be in captivity
A brand new me in captivity
And finally I'm free

Vikki was more annoyed than Martha by being disturbed on nights out by the selfie-takers and autograph-hunters who all felt they owned a part of Martha – although, on more than one occasion, not everyone was sure who was who – a game played by the identical Vikki and Martha. Martha was stoic, *I will worry the day I am not disturbed, the fans are my bread-and-butter.*

They both missed the intimacy of someone with whom to share their innermost thoughts and their beds. Neither currently had partners of either a permanent or temporary nature. It was simply too complicated. Both had decided and discussed that they were generally heterosexual after brief experimental forays into same sex relationships – sometimes successful, others turned into one-night stands. They had both agreed that dating a celebrity, or former celebrity, or identical twin of a celebrity, came with a whole host of baggage not enjoyed by *normal* people. *Whatever normal is.* Martha had played 'Star Fucker' by the Rolling Stones on her studio grade music system at extremely high volume after one terrible night that, after some initial fumbling, didn't even make it to the definition of a one-night stand. Amazingly good looks and witty repartee didn't overcome halitosis and intimate body odour.

A week after the concert the media storm had mainly died down. No-one had been interested any more – there were other things to discuss; people, innocent or guilty, to lambast; celebrities to out; marriages to ruin; and salacious scandals to expose. Even social media had calmed down – no more trolls accusing Martha of a conspiracy to drum up supporters and publicity; wildly absurd news had largely been eradicated, the death of the policeman was faked according to some; no more offensive suggestions, sexual innuendo, or Photoshopped naked or compromising pictures.

On Friday night, at the end of a long week, Vikki and Martha had been able to enjoy going out with a few mates, without most of the intrusive hassle. They enjoyed their relative freedom. Life was gradually improving. There was a quiet joint cry of *'Smeeee,'* followed by a giggle, when *Captivity* was played, as it inevitably would, on the music system of whichever bar they had chosen.

Suddenly, almost at the flick of a switch it all changed. The news of Mia's death, the little girl trampled to death at the concert, had unexpectedly broken across social media. Vikki's and Martha's phone blared out annoying news jingles, bongs, dings, and pings as the news broke – and was then reposted around the world

Martha was front page again with every media outlet demanding answers, statements, and interview requests.

Martha carefully peered out through the window – she didn't want to be seen or photographed. The TV trucks were setting up outside once again – none went live until the news had been corroborated by the police, the family or Daisy. The death of a child was generally treated with respect by the mainstream media.

Martha was fuming that she learned of Mia's death from social media rather than being told personally. She called Daisy in high dudgeon.

'Martha, I was about to call you,' responded Daisy before Martha could say anything.

'Is it true? A little girl trampled to death at *my* concert?' Martha emphasised the word *my*.

Daisy reluctantly admitted, 'Yes, it's true.'

'Why the fuck wasn't I told? I look like an uncaring bitch. How are the parents and the rest of the family?' Martha was not happy.

'It was a terrible accident. On an awful night.' Daisy was trying to placate her. 'The parents asked for, insisted on privacy. They didn't want to be a part of the media shitstorm whilst they grieved.

Martha hesitated before a not very convincing, 'Okay.'

'But I want to pay my respects to, what's her name, Mia's parents.' Martha sort of understood, 'in private.'

'If you are seen to get involved the media will be all over it,' Daisy continued without mentioning the PR plan already hatched. 'With Nowak we have been developing a strategy, but for now, I'll put out a personal statement. From you and Vikki. As with the policeman, you won't be taking questions.'

'I suppose that's for the best. But I am not happy. I should have been told.' Martha conceded.

'We were told by the police that it should be kept confidential.' Daisy was defensive. Then thought this was a good opportunity to get all the bad news out of the way. 'You ought to know that the incident with the man slipping into the propellers of the water taxi may also be connected. The police think that the dead man was the shooter, but they are not releasing that for now. Must remain strictly between us. All they are saying it was an unfortunate accident.'

'What man?' Martha demanded. 'I don't know about that either.'

'It was in some of the papers. But none had made the connection with the events at your gig.'

'What happened? I have ignored the news since last Saturday.'

'It is thought that the shooter was running away, jumped for the boat and slipped. They have no idea who he was. They are not certain that he killed Sergeant Maguire. But strongly suspect.'

Martha hung up without saying goodbye, just a grunt.

Martha was beside herself. She threw down the phone onto the sofa and burst into tears. Despite being the star of the show, she was not really in charge of her own destiny. She was merely a puppet when it came to her audience, PR, and messaging – with Nowak and Daisy the arch-puppeteers.

'Are you okay sis?' asked Vikki.

'Not really. Everything seems to conspire against me. It's a bloody roller coaster.' Martha was all over the place. 'Career reinvigorated. Awesome set and staging. Brilliant band and dancers. Then our captivity and rescue. First number one I've had in years. Global too. Amazing first night concert. Fantastic reviews. And then this. What am I to do? Mia's parents and her friends must be devastated. How can I help?'

The two sisters hugged. Martha sobbed.

'Did you hear Daisy say about the bloke who was killed by a boat's propellers?' asked Martha into Vikki's back. 'Daisy said it might have been who killed the policeman.'

Vikki pulled a little away, so she could see Martha's tear-stained face. 'I had seen that on the news. But I didn't know he was connected. They assumed it was a drunk fan. They weren't even sure he had been to the concert.'

'What!' exclaimed Martha in jest. 'Not been to my concert. How very dare they!'

'Well, if it was the killer, it's good he's dead.' Vikki's turn for some pragmatism. She then laughed out loud, 'Look on the bright side. It has kept you in the news.'

Martha lightened up and gave Vikki a sisterly, none-too-gentle punch in the arm.

'Too soon?' responded Vikki.

'Too soon,' Martha moaned out loud at the enormity of what had happened. 'This will never leave me. My concerts will forever be associated with the death of the policeman and of Mia. It'll never, ever go away – never forgotten.'

The two sisters hugged for a minute or so more, before breaking apart.

'I'll make some tea,' suggested Vikki.

A few minutes later Vikki returned to the lounge with two steaming mugs. No biscuits as Martha had to retain her figure and fitness. After taking a few sips Martha delicately put the cup down on the table beside her – using the placemat branded with some other artiste's recent music release. It was difficult to see who due to the red and brown rings from the tea, coffee, and wine stains.

'Everything leads back to Stanislaw.' Martha was thoughtful. 'When you dance with the devil... I know he isn't totally legit. But who is? He offered me the chance to get back in. And I grabbed at it. I needed the fix of being back in the limelight.'

Vikki remained silent, allowing her sister to let go.

'Am I naïve? Is it all worth it?' Martha scoffed ironically, looking into her sister's eyes. Despite their on-off sibling relationship, there was no-one else in the world with whom she could have these sorts of conversations.

'You can't live without it. Performing is in your blood.' Vikki knew her sister better than anyone else.

'Maybe.' Martha was pensive, 'But perhaps not other people's blood?'

DAY TEN
SATURDAY 17H00

FRANCISCO'S, LEICESTER SQUARE

'THEY'VE DISAPPEARED. EVERYTHING.' BILL Kelly was beyond reason. 'All the files corrupted or irretrievably inaccessible.'

He sagged in the chair, picked up his coffee – he sipped without enthusiasm. 'This is getting beyond anything I have known. Your piece. The photographs. Other evidence. All gone.'

'How could they have all disappeared from within the Yard?' Danny was dumbstruck. 'So much for your security.'

'Nothing on the computers – server files deep erased to security service standards. No hope of restoring. My hard copy disappeared from my office. Someone on the inside is protecting someone – or themselves.' Kelly was dispirited rather than angry. 'We have a bad 'un somewhere.'

Danny and Kelly were alone in the corner. Francisco was out the back getting ready for the Sunday rush the following day. He was now accustomed to his café being used as an unofficial meeting house.

'Where's Daisy?' asked Kelly. 'You two seem to have been inseparable lately?'

'Working with Jimmy Patrick at the Soho offices teeing up the forthcoming video shoot. Contracts. Distribution rights. Pre-payments. Not my bag. You normally have Rob Andrews or another Sergeant with you?' responded Danny.

'It's helpful it's just the two of us.' Kelly was hesitant, 'off-the-record?'

Danny nodded – he frowned.

'We have a big problem. I really don't know who to trust anymore. I trust you. Fuck knows why. I was knocked back, disappointed, when I discovered Maguire's duplicity. I hoped that was the end of it. But clearly, it's not.' Kelly paused whilst he collected his thoughts. 'We are being played. I'm not altogether sure that Nowak is at the heart of all of this. He might be the catalyst or the starting point. That second set of listening devices at his flat. No one is admitting to installing them. And then this…'

Kelly reached inside his jacket pocket and brought out a small circuit board with a high-capacity memory card attached. 'I removed this from my office.'

'What is it?' asked Danny, although he thought he knew the answer.

'It's a listening device.' Kelly was exasperated, not with Danny but by the whole situation he now found himself in. 'No transmit. Record only. So, two things. Firstly, normal sweeps won't find it because there is no RF. Not even timed burst. Secondly it can only have been planted by someone on the inside who has access to my office both to fit it and to change the memory card. And then wipe my computer and remove the hard copies of your disabled badge piece with its photos.'

Danny was concerned. 'Won't they know you know that you have removed it?'

'I'll put it back later today, once I have filled the memory card with noise and garbage, so it won't record anymore. Hopefully, they, whoever *they* are, will assume the device was faulty. I am going to install a concealed camera in my office to catch the bugger with any luck.'

'This all starts with my story.' Danny rubbed his face with his hands – but his investigative hackles were now up. 'What about your original source. Surely they have a copy?'

'I haven't been able to get hold of my source. All I have been told is that they are *unable to help at this time.*' The shutters had been firmly pulled down on Kelly. 'It's almost feels that I am under suspicion, investigation.'

'Isn't there a process?' asked Danny, perhaps naively.

Kelly ignored the question, 'And you are sure you don't have a copy. Or access to a copy of the file?'

'I wish I did. It would be a massive story, even today.' Danny was frustrated. He made no mention of Yuliet.

The pair of them sat awhile contemplating the potential enormity of the situation.

Danny stirred. 'I think I know who it is. Or could be. And there may be more than one person.'

Kelly was acerbic. 'Oh good. A conspiracy theory.'

'Do you want to hear what I think or not?' demanded Danny.

Kelly put down his cup and looked directly at Danny. 'Okay. Sorry. Go on.'

'Deputy Assistant Commissioner Keith Wallace.' Danny responded sotto voce, despite being in the deserted café.

'He might be a self-serving arrogant shit with an eye on his future, but I didn't think he was bent.' Kelly was shocked into disbelief. 'Why do you think?'

'I was watching breakfast news this morning, the funeral, and a camera angle made him look younger – and that triggered a memory from over ten years ago.' Danny looked straight into Kelly's eyes to gauge the reaction.

Kelly's face was passive. 'Is that why you wanted the photographs?'

'Yes. But it also reminded me of some of the other people we have on camera. This might go right to the heart of Government too.' Before Danny could continue his phone rang. The caller ID read Yuliet. Kelly nodded that Danny should answer the call – he put the call on loudspeaker. 'Hi Yuliet. Right in the middle of something with Bill Kelly. Can I call you back later please?'

'My office has been broken into – and my safe opened. Professional job.' Yuliet didn't give Danny the chance to end the call.

'Where are you now?' Kelly butted in.

'Still in my office,' she replied.

'Have you called our lot?' asked Kelly.

'No, not yet. Called Danny first considering some of what was stolen.'

'Stay there. Don't call anyone else.' Kelly answered for them both. 'Don't touch anything, we'll be there in half an hour.'

Danny rang off, left ten pounds on the table and together they quietly left Francisco's café.

14

DAY TEN
SATURDAY 18H15

CENTRE FOR COVERT MEDIA STUDIES

Yuliet Spooner's Chubb Trident Euro Grade Six safe was open wide. Some of its former contents now spread across the floor. There was no obvious sign of forced entry – to the safe; to her office; or to the locked and alarmed building.

'When did you discover this?' asked Kelly, taking out his notebook – and then putting it away again. He was in two minds whether he should call in local CID. Danny's earlier theory had left him concerned.

'I came in to finish off a bit of work about five o'clock. Made a coffee in the kitchen and then came up here. So, I suppose five fifteen.' Yuliet was hesitant, 'I called Danny rather than the police due to the nature of what I do. There is stuff in here that is highly confidential. Details of my sources and so on.'

'What did you expect Danny to do?' Kelly was curious.

Yuliet laughed. *Gallows' humour*, she thought. 'Speak to you!'

Kelly ignored her. 'How did they get in?'

'I thought it strange when I unlocked the building. The alarm didn't give me the normal ten seconds to deactivate. I was going to send a bollocking e-mail to the team. I thought whoever was the last person to leave, after work last night, hadn't set the alarm. Doesn't happen often. If at all.' Yuliet thought. 'One of the interior doors was open, latched on the fire door magnet. We shut all the doors as we leave. We have to be careful.'

'A professional job then. And whoever opened this was clearly a skilled Peterman,' observed Kelly bending down to examine the various keyholes and handles. 'This model has relocking devices and anti-drilling plates. Explosives and hi-tech cutting tools would have been impotent too. Suggests to me someone in the know. Who else has the keys?'

Yuliet Spooner, head of the Centre for Covert Media Studies was not happy, 'To the safe? Only one other person – and I trust them implicitly.'

'We'll have to talk to them. Give me their contact details.' Yuliet scribbled on a piece of paper.

'What's missing?' asked Danny. 'What's so important?'

'The file.' Yuliet admitted quietly.

'File?' challenged Kelly. 'What file?'

'The file I was handed by the anonymous woman. The Vory, Conor O'Murchadha, Ali Baka and Stanislaw Nowak. Press cuttings and redacted intelligence. Danny's story and photographs.' Yuliet had a long-term professional relationship with Kelly, and they trusted each other with off-the-books conversations of mutual benefit.

'Is this the file we discussed?' Kelly demanded of Danny.

Danny was a little sheepish. 'Yes.'

'The one I asked you to get a copy of?'

'Yes,' replied Danny.

Yuliet gave Danny a hard stare. 'The file I told you about in strictest confidence.'

Danny nodded.

'Did you make copies?' Kelly asked Yuliet more in hope than expectation.

'No!' answered Yuliet a little too quickly. She tried unsuccessfully to stop her eyes looking up and right.

Kelly stared at her, remaining silent – he could easily read unintended body language. There was a long pause in the room.

'Okay. Yes. I have a copy.' Yuliet eventually admitted under Kelly's intense stare. She avoided, just, saying *copies*. 'In my house, in a secret compartment under the kitchen cabinet.'

She did not mention the other copy stored with her trusted friend, not a colleague – whose name she never spoke. Yuliet insisted to all her team that in the world of investigative journalism *'who might be listening'* and *'need to know'* were as essential considerations as in the security services. *'A secret is a secret, and it only stays that way if no one is told'* she hammered home during the in-house training sessions.

From the file Yuliet, more than anyone in the room, knew the full extent of Stanislaw Nowak's past and present – and his dubious relationships not only with the criminal underworld; but also, those across society and government devoid of morals; together inevitably with the less fastidious rich and famous. It was the list of the great and the good who had taken advantage of Nowak's forged disabled badges from ten years ago that was of most interest – some with accompanying incriminating photographs. Even Danny did not know that within the missing file she had a copy of the original Blue Badge story with all his photographs from the time – plus others more recently acquired.

'What else is missing?' Danny intervened.

'Apart from the file, about a thousand pounds. Ten thousand Euros. Same again in US dollars and various amounts of Iraqi dinar, Iranian rial, and some Russian rouble. I guess the equivalent of fifteen grand in all.'

Kelly raised a questioning eyebrow.

Yuliet responded. 'For informers and sources.'

'But no other paperwork, photographs or files?'

'I don't think so.' Yuliet knelt on the floor. She looked up to Kelly for permission to touch what should have been protected for forensic examination.

Kelly nodded his assent. *Unlikely that professionals would leave any marks or evidence anyway,* he thought.

'I suppose I had better report this formally to your lot?' Yuliet mused rhetorically.

'I don't think any of us wants this to go further. No need to disturb other people's Saturday.' Kelly was sanguine. 'How are you going to explain the missing currency to your colleagues?'

'Very few people knew it was here. Not a big problem.' Yuliet also omitted to mention that much of the currency *had been acquired.*

'Do you have CCTV?'

Yuliet shook her head. 'No. We actually don't want to record some of the people who come in here.'

Whilst Yuliet examined the remaining contents of the safe, the other two looked around the room. The furnishings and decoration were minimal – but had a certain sophistication melding old with new. A dark green carpet extended wall-to-wall. LED downlighters provided even daylight-balanced lighting with three focussed spots picking out the original Georgian alcoves with their *objets d'art* – mainly sprayed resin reproductions left behind by the office's previous incumbent. An antique copper light sat on the oversize mahogany partners desk inlaid with tooled embossed green leather and light oak marquetry. Her chair, in contrast, was a SIHOO Ergonomic Office Chair with lumbar support, high back and breathable mesh fabric. Two black leather four-seater sofas sat either side of a large table – the top constructed from a single piece of polished green resin-inlaid beech. In the centre the spider shape of a conferencing telephone. Mains power, USB sockets, TV and projector connections had been dropped into the top giving the whole thing a business-like yet informal look. On one wall a glass cabinet housed eight trophies of one shape or another for *outstanding investigative journalism* – each, as the years passed, trendier or more *en pointe* as their designers tried to out-do each other. *There should be an award for awards trophy designers,* humphed Yuliet one day at a team meeting the morning after another absurdly priced alcohol-fuelled late-night post-ceremony celebration. On the wall there hung seven *outstanding contribution* awards certificates – mainly from charities who couldn't afford or justify bespoke trophies – and a dozen or so press cuttings mounted symmetrically in simple black frames, and a couple of non-touristy souvenirs from trips abroad. There were few clues to Yuliet's private life – this was a professional office.

'Looks like there's no other damage. Put everything back in the safe.' Kelly ordered. 'Let's check around the rest of the offices, lock up and get out of here.'

Thirty minutes later the three of them had relocked the safe, closed all the doors, turned out the lights, set the alarm and left as if nothing had happened. They turned left, walking south towards the West End of London.

'Pint?' suggested Kelly.

'Just the one,' smiled Danny.

Yuliet nodded.

The watchers watched.

'We're being followed.' Kelly affectedly laughed to conceal what he had just said – and to not give away that he knew.

'Hope they like beer.' Yuliet was in a better mood.

'And pork scratchings,' suggested Danny, who sent a WhatsApp to Daisy telling her where they were going.

Ten minutes later they settled into the saloon bar of The Calthorpe Arms, admiring the traditional 1820s splendour on the corner of Wren Street and Gray's Inn Road. Danny nodded at a couple of ITN and Channel 4 news colleagues from long ago – their studio a few metres away. Glasses were raised to him, but by mutual non-verbal consent no further contact was required or expected.

Daisy had just arrived too. 'I'd just finished, so walked up here from Soho. Needed some exercise and a drink.' she explained.

Danny and Daisy exchanged kisses. Yuliet air kissed. Kelly wasn't sure what to do, so smiled and just sat down.

Yuliet insisted on buying the first round by way of a thank you – she delivered three pints of Wainwrights and a Wye Valley gin – the tonic from the house pump. Daisy wrinkled her nose. 'Why ruin a good gin with crap tonic?'

Four bags of *Burts Hand-Cooked Sea Salt Chips* dropped onto the table from under Yuliet's chin. 'No scratchings, sorry. And we're not American, they're bloody crisps not chips.'

They chinked glasses, making a show of amiable bonhomie.

'Who is following us?' asked Yuliet through her smile.

'Bloody hell, not again,' Daisy was exasperated.

Kelly didn't answer, stood up walked towards the gent's toilet, swerving at the last second to sit with another pair of watchers, a man, and a woman, who had been tasked with following them into the pub. He took out his warrant card. 'Good evening. I'm Detective Chief Superintendent Bill Kelly of the National Crime Agency. Who are you?'

No answer.

'As you probably know the National Crime Agency is the UK's lead agency against organised crime; human, weapon and drug trafficking; cybercrime; and economic crime that goes across regional and international borders but can be tasked to investigate any crime. To do this we work closely with regional organised crime units, the Serious Fraud Office, as well as individual police forces.' Kelly pulled out his phone. 'My next call will be to my colleagues at the Met to take you into custody as I suspect you are, oh I don't know, let's say planning to sell drugs in this pub.'

Still no answer. Before he could make the call, another man joined them at the table. 'I really don't think that will be necessary.'

'Not your call. And who are you anyway?' Kelly wasn't flustered by this arrival.

'Call me John.'

'You didn't answer my question.' Kelly dialled his contact at Scotland Yard.

John attempted to take the phone from Kelly. 'I said I really don't think that will be necessary.'

Kelly's grip was firm – he carefully twisted *John's* fingers. *John* let go, making a show of massaging his hand.

'I do hope you are not intending to assault a Police Officer. You have seen my Warrant Card, so you cannot deny you did not know who I am.'

Kelly spoke into his phone. After identifying himself he continued, 'I'm in The Calthorpe Arms, corner of Gray's Inn Road and Wren Street. Please supply urgent backup to arrest three people. Two men and a woman.'

The other end acknowledged.

Bill Kelly turned to them, who by now were beginning to look uncomfortable. 'I repeat who are you?'

All three remained silent.

'Okay then. I have properly identified myself as Detective Chief Superintendent Bill Kelly of the National Crime Agency. I have reason to believe you are carrying something which could be used to commit a crime. I have requested that you provide me with your identity on three occasions, which you have refused to do. I therefore am arresting you. You do not have to say anything. But it may harm your defence if you do not mention when questioned something which you later rely on in court. Anything you do say may be given in evidence. Do you understand?'

John spoke. 'You are making a big mistake. Maybe even career limiting.'

'Do you understand?' repeated Kelly.

'Yes. We fucking understand,' *John* spoke for the three of them.

'Then tell me who you are.'

There remained a silent stand-off.

'That'll be all,' said Deputy Assistant Commissioner Keith Wallace standing over the table. No greeting. No one saw him enter.

Kelly looked up at him with a satisfied smile – he refused to act surprised. Wallace was not in uniform – wearing beige chinos, a checked open necked shirt, and a beige windcheater. 'You three leave,' he said looking at *John* and his two unnamed companions.

'Kelly, a word please.' Deputy Assistant Commissioner Wallace pulled across a spare chair from a nearby table and sat down facing Kelly. He looked hot and flustered.

Kelly ignored him.

The intense rotating blue lights shone through the leaded windows – they stopped outside the pub. Everyone heard the doors slamming – the happy burble of early-evening conversation dropped and then rose more excitedly as six uniformed Police Officers walked into the bar and across to the increasingly crowded table.

'Handcuff those three and place them in custody,' ordered Kelly.

'I said that'll be all.' Wallace stood. He turned to the six Police Officers. 'You know who I am, stand down please. You are not required.'

Kelly was adamant. 'I am the arresting officer. Carry on and take them into custody.'

The six Police Officers were in a dilemma. *Who to obey?*

With that, Danny arrived. 'Well, well. DAC Keith Wallace. Parked anywhere illegally lately. A disabled bay for example?'

The DAC did not need to be introduced to Danny Owen, former investigative reporter at *The Weekend News*. Wallace knew he would have been named and shamed in the original exposé – he also *thought* he knew the piece would never see the light of day ever again. He believed he had ensured the disappearance of the original and all its copies. He was not the only one who thought they were now safe – as a senior police officer he had been informally tasked to protect the group of co-conspirators. *Now Danny had re-emerged and was obviously baying for blood, but did he have proof? How much had he told Kelly?*

Wallace reluctantly nodded to the Police Officers. 'Carry on. Do what DCS Kelly requires.'

'Handcuff them,' ordered Kelly. 'Take them to the high security cells at the Yard.'

John, with his face less than ten centimetres from Kelly's face, was apparently not contrite. 'We'll meet again.'

'That will be a certainty,' said Kelly.

Across the pub Danny saw Yuliet answer her phone, listen for a few seconds, and explode to her feet. Daisy grabbed her gin and one of the beers, saving them from imminent free fall to the floor.

The whole pub heard Yuliet's, 'Fucking bastards.'

She rushed outside followed by Daisy. Danny and Kelly joined them a few seconds later, leaving Wallace alone at the table.

Yuliet was incensed. 'That was my home alarm monitoring service. Apparently, the phone line system went offline half an hour ago – and the GSM back-up also failed. A patrol has just been there to find the place trashed – two people were seen leaving. The home alarm monitoring service have called the police who say they may be on their way.'

Daisy and Yuliet hailed a taxi.

Danny and Kelly returned inside The Calthorpe Arms to confront Wallace, who was sitting at the table recently vacated by the three arrested watchers. He had a fresh pint of bitter making no offer to buy a drink for the returning duo.

'I didn't know if you were coming back. Nothing is better than a proper pint in a traditional London pub is there?' he sneered.

Danny went back over to his original table and collected Kelly's and his beers – or what was left of them due to Yuliet's vertical eruption. He sat back at the table, deliberately sipped his beer, and faced Wallace.

'You have a counterfeit disabled badge supplied by Stanislaw Nowak?' demanded Danny.

Wallace remained silent – his face inscrutable.

No point in delaying the obvious or inevitable, thought Danny. So, he pushed further. 'I have the photographic evidence. What did you trade for it? Your honesty? Your integrity? Your soul?'

Wallace said nothing – he wasn't aware that Danny had been trying it on. Fishing. He sipped his beer. The pub had returned to its amiable chatter – some glanced over to the three of them, clearly still the topic of conversation and supposition.

After a long silence Wallace turned to Bill Kelly, 'We don't need this bloody journalist here. Tell him to go home and leave this to the big boys.'

Danny started to get up – his intention to beat the crap out of Wallace, rather than to go home. Kelly put a hand on Danny's arm. 'Sit down Danny. That won't get us anywhere.'

Bill Kelly turned to Wallace, 'He stays. Now explain why you bought a counterfeit blue badge from Nowak and why Danny has pictures of you, and several others, using it.'

'That was a long time ago.' Wallace sipped his pint and wiped his mouth. 'I was part of the investigation. Collecting evidence.'

So, he did have a disabled badge, thought Danny. No wonder he wants to see if he is named in my story and seen in the accompanying photographs.

Bill Kelly had to admire Wallace's chutzpah. 'Bollocks. No, you weren't part of any investigation, or I would have known.'

'Look at the files,' responded Wallace.

Kelly was incensed. 'You know I can't. They have disappeared.'

'What a shame. Too many files and evidence bags go unaccountably missing. More than a thousand pieces of evidence lost or misplaced by the Met last year alone – it's a worrying trend. We are bringing in sanctions for officers who are not careful enough or break the SOPs.' Wallace mocked Kelly.

'You shit.' Kelly's outburst was tempered with not wanting to attract the attention of the rest of the pub. 'Too many criminals are walking free and victims going without justice because of people like you. You make me sick.'

'Remember who you are talking to DCS Kelly.' Wallace sat up straight.

'I know who I am talking to. A bent copper. A two-faced shit.' Some of Bill Kelly's beer laden saliva landed on Wallace's beige wind cheater leaving a pearl drop shaped stain. Wallace made a flamboyant show of wiping it clean.

'I hope you can substantiate that. That is a profoundly serious allegation, which of course I refute.' Wallace continued smugly, 'We have set up several new infiltration exercises because of the awful results of the last one. Worryingly lax security. Eighty-five per cent of buildings able to be breached. My team conducting the exercise was able to stroll into so-called secure areas of police stations and buildings and access confidential files; computer systems;

steal weapons; walk away with illegal drugs; and remove sensitive evidence. I mean seriously, just imagine these being taken and used to commit crimes, or to breach the security of other organisations. Members of the public too walked into buildings without being asked for identification. Doesn't bear thinking about does it?'

Wallace was naturally verbose and absurdly pompous, not just in front of the cameras. He took a long draught of his beer, finishing it before carefully returning the glass to the soggy beer mat on the chipped table. Then made a show considering what he was going to say.

'I'm going to forgive and forget your disrespectful, insubordinate outburst DCS Kelly. I'll put it down to over zealousness. As for you Mr Owen, be incredibly careful. My friends have deep pockets. A private citizen defending libel and slander accusations can find it awfully expensive. Could even bankrupt them.' Wallace picked up his empty glass. 'Good evening gentlemen.'

With that he stood up, adjusted his windcheater, returned the empty glass to the bar, and walked out into the night air.

Kelly walked briskly to the bar. Collected Wallace's glass before the bar staff could wash it and carefully deposited it into an evidence bag that he had magicked from an inside pocket. He returned to Danny.

'Cocky bastard. I'm going to have him.' Kelly was infuriated. 'Another one?'

'No. We ought to get up to Yuliet's place – see what the damage is and what has been stolen,' said Danny, shaking his head.

15

DAY TEN
SATURDAY EVENING

YULIET'S FLAT

YULIET'S KITCHEN WAS WRECKED. SHE SAT AT THE kitchen table with a paper notepad and biro. Daisy sat the other side stirring the tea that she had just made for them both.

Yuliet hadn't needed her front door key. Whoever had entered had left it slightly ajar – there was no sign of forced entry. They had both made a brief circuit of Yuliet's home – the kitchen had borne the brunt of the attack.

'I suppose I better start making a list of what is missing.' Yuliet wasn't in tears, but she was angry – furious. 'I'll start in the lounge. They didn't take my CDs. Some are very precious. They took about fifty quid from the vase. I put my charity money there.'

Yuliet turned the notepad around to face Daisy. There was no list. Yuliet put her finger to her lips as Daisy read.

Not a random burglary. Vindictive shits as well. Must be listening devices in the office. Maybe here too.

Daisy mouthed, 'How do you know?'

Yuliet frowned and passed Daisy the pen. She repeated the question on the note pad.

'Seems someone might have disturbed them, only the kitchen seems to have been completely trashed,' said Daisy out loud. *The show must go on*, she thought.

Yuliet scribbled her reply. *At office. Only time ever spoke about file under kitchen cabinet. No one else knows.*

Only was underlined three times.

'What about the bedrooms?' asked Daisy out loud. She wrote, *are you sure?*

There was no need for Yuliet to write an answer, as this time Daisy could read her lips. The forthright, magnificent, mute swearing was crystal clear.

'The arseholes emptied my Rive Gauche perfume all over my bed. Why did the fuckers do that? Bloody evil bastards.' Yuliet theatrically raised her voice, 'If, when, I catch the them, I'll castrate them – man or woman.'

Daisy couldn't help it – she barely stifled a chortle. Yuliet carefully walked over to the 'fridge avoiding the detritus on the floor.

'Well at least they didn't touch the fizz. Nothing for it. The police don't react quickly to burglary anymore if at all. Sod the tea, might as well have a drink.' Yuliet pointed at one of the gloss white fronted cupboard doors hanging off its hinges. She knelt. 'I'll just get the glasses. If I can find any that aren't smashed.'

Yuliet knelt in front of the lower kitchen cabinet to the right of the double width Fulgor Milano Induction Range cooker. She turned to Daisy shaking her head. *'Gone'* she mouthed.

'Here we are.' She clinked the glasses for effect. Yuliet was a fan of radio drama.

There was a pop as the bottle was opened – no drama.

Danny and Kelly walked into the kitchen and surveyed the chaos.

'You don't hang about do you?' mocked Danny, looking at the opened bottle.

'What a bloody mess.' Kelly shook his head in bewilderment – he'd seen it too many times before.

Before any more could be said, Yuliet held up her earlier note, *'Must be listening devices in the office. Maybe here too.'*

She turned the page

'At office. Only time ever spoke about file under kitchen cabinet. No one else knows.'

Danny mouthed, *'what?'*

Kelly was matter of fact. 'You can't stay here tonight. Forensics will want to go through everything.'

'As if,' Yuliet scoffed. 'Your lot said they would try and get here today, if not, in the morning.'

Kelly took out his mobile phone, pulled rank and stirred it up. 'They'll be here in ten minutes. Where are you going to stay tonight?'

Yuliet simply shook her head and then winked, 'I thought I'd go to the Savoy. Always wanted to stay there.'

Daisy, Danny, and Kelly suppressed a collective guffaw – despite the mess and effect on Yuliet.

'I'll give you a lift,' offered Kelly

'Let me go and pack a few things.' Yuliet had had worse days. *No one has died. No one tortured. No one gone missing. No children molested.* She thought pragmatically.

There was a knock on the front door. 'Trampled all over our evidence I see.' The white-suited scene of crime forensics team leader entered carrying her large black suitcase with her tools of the trade.

'I suppose you'll want to know everything yesterday. I'm a forensic scientist, not a bloody miracle worker,' she answered herself.

Kelly held up a piece of paper on which he had written, *'Check for covert surveillance equipment.'*

The SOCO's eyes widened. She nodded as she passed the note to the rest of her team – who were equally surprised but remained silent.

Kelly's phone rang. After a couple of okays, he hung up and with his thumb indicated that they were all leaving to let the SOCOs get on with their job.

'Lock the door on your way out. Let me know when you leave,' was all that Kelly said. Yuliet handed over a spare set of door keys – one for the Yale BS3 maximum security nightlatch, the other for the Chubb five-lever deadlock with concealed microswitch that should have triggered the intruder alarm after a short delay.

Daisy and Yuliet had taken the tube to the flat. Now all four of them piled into Kelly's police issued car – an unmarked, dark blue, high-powered Ford Mondeo Estate with a range of specialist modifications. To the untrained eye it would not be discernible as anything but normal.

Kelly could have had a driver, but for routine work he elected to drive himself. The car had been randomly assigned. All police vehicles have trackers, but no-one knew that Kelly had taken this vehicle – he planned to do the on-line logging in the morning.

'To the Savoy then?' suggested Kelly, breaking the silence. 'It has the only road in London where you can legally drive on the right.'

'So, you did start as a traffic cop then?' Danny teased Kelly, who started the engine, looked in his mirror, indicated and drove off. Kelly disregarded Danny.

Yuliet admitted, 'I can't actually afford to stay at the Savoy. I'm more of a Premier Inn girl.'

'Prefer Travel Lodge,' said Daisy. 'Unless someone else is paying.'

'Hilton man m'self,' offered Danny.

'When you have all finished writing your hotel guides.' Kelly was thoughtful. 'I would suggest a Police safe house, but I don't trust anyone or anywhere right now.'

'Premier Inn it is then.' Yuliet took out her phone and was about to select the booking app.

Danny stopped her. 'We simply do not know who we are dealing with. They could be tracking our phones even if switched off.'

'Not mine.' Kelly said. 'It has several layers of specialist encryption.'

Danny was sceptical, he repeated. 'You don't know who you are dealing with.'

'Are we all getting a bit paranoid?' suggested Daisy.

Danny was forthright. 'Maybe I am a paranoid conspiracy

theorist? But someone is behind all this. Someone who has access and influence.'

'What the fuck is going on?' demanded Yuliet. 'First my office and then my flat. One thing is for certain they, whoever *they* are, they don't care that we know what they are after. And they're bloody vindictive too—'

'Who are they then?' Danny. 'What is in that file that is so important?'

'I hadn't had time to go through it all. Mainly about Nowak. His people smuggling and other activities. Your disabled badge piece together with the photographs was in it. The Vory. Ali Baka. Lots of background. Heaps of black pen redaction as well. The file was almost two centimetres thick. Massive amount to go through. Whoever compiled the file was good, no original documents obviously. Copies made after redaction so it's not possible to reveal the original words even with the cleverest digital technology.' Yuliet was annoyed with herself for not paying more attention when she received the file. 'I've only sped-read it, but realised it is dynamite. But as with many stories on which I'm working they all vie for my attention. One, maybe a couple of your pictures keeps popping up in my mind. Can't think who it is, or they are. I'm sure it'll pop back when I'm least expecting it.'

Yuliet made no mention of the third copy she had made – trust was still in short supply especially with Kelly. She didn't want anyone to know.

Yuliet, sitting in the front seat of the Mondeo, gazed at the array or non-standard controls and switches. 'It might not be one person who is after the file. How do we know? Easy to start thinking of conspiracies and cover ups.'

'Indeed. Just because I'm paranoid doesn't mean there is or isn't someone, or several someone's, trying to shit on us,' said Danny. 'When I was an investigative reporter, I quickly learned the bigger the story, the more people tried to silence me – using the courts or physical methods.'

Yuliet turned to face Danny. 'You are still an investigative reporter at heart. Bit like riding a bike.'

'Maybe. But it still hurts when you fall off.' The four of them contemplated Danny on a bike.

'Take the SIMs out of your phones, then switch them off. It's not guaranteed but it's a start,' instructed Kelly, passing his phone to Yuliet whilst keeping his other hand on the wheel. 'I have a steel lock box in the back where the spare tyre should be. Its normally reserved for firearms. But it should act as a Faraday cage and block any signals.'

Kelly turned left into St John's Wood Road and then right into Oak Tree Road opposite Lord's Cricket Ground, the home of the MCC. He pulled over in front of some white doored lock-up garages. The not-that-distant roar of London traffic never abated – but all seemed as serene as it should be. He looked around, opened the tailgate, lifted the flap, and put the phones in the steel box.

As Kelly carefully manoeuvred through the Saturday evening traffic the four of them sat in silence, absorbed in their own thoughts. They passed along the top of The Regent's Park, then turned right – back toward the West End. They stopped at a twenty-four-seven corner shop where Danny bought four pay-as-you go phones with data plans.

Kelly found a spot to park just opposite Mornington Crescent Underground Station and led them into the

Lyttleton Arms. They found a quiet table in the corner and sat down on the burgundy buttoned leather banquette sofas.

'We seem to spend our lives meeting in pubs and cafes. I remember the days when we used to use offices and meeting rooms.' Daisy sipped her lime and soda. None of them were tempted with alcohol.

Danny unwrapped the four phones, carefully stored the number of each into the memories using false names – Barney, McGrew, Cuthbert, and Dibble.

'I want to be McGrew,' demanded Daisy.

'I'm Barney,' said Yuliet.

'Oh, for Christ's sake, that makes me Officer Dibble' said Kelly reminiscing about *Top Cat*, the TV cartoon from his childhood.

'Excellent, I'm Cuthbert,' said Danny finishing typing the last of the names. He then set up a WhatsApp group, calling it Trumpton.

Each took their phone.

Yuliet collected hers. 'Time for bed—'

'—said Zebedee.' Interrupted Danny.

All were tired – it had been a long day.

'You'd better pick up your phones from the car, except you Yuliet. I'll keep yours. I'm going to have one of my specialists check it over. I'll return it to you tomorrow.' Kelly was adamant. 'Where are you going to stay tonight?'

'There's a Premier Inn near Euston Station, one stop on the tube.' Yuliet yawned.

They finished their drinks, Daisy and Danny collected their personal phones.

'Don't insert the SIMs or switch back on until you are nearly home,' instructed Kelly. 'I'll restart mine at the Yard.'

Yuliet disappeared into Morning Crescent Underground Station. Thirty minutes later she was safely in bed – she sent a message to the Trumpton group. 'Good night all.'

'See you all tomorrow,' was Daisy's reply from Danny's flat.

Kelly, back at Scotland Yard, racked his brain – he was missing something. Or someone.

Although late he decided to take the elevator down to the custody suite – the earlier phone call whilst at Yuliet's flat had intrigued him. The watchers had been released – he knew no more.

The duty custody Sergeant was engrossed in the westernmost province of the Kingdom of the Isles, upon the world of Midkemia. At first, he didn't see DCS Kelly approaching.

'Wes, what are you reading?' said Kelly extending his hand to a colleague whom he had known for over twenty years.

Wes took the outstretched hand and shook it warmly. He held up the book with the jailer's keys on the front cover. 'Raymond E. Feist's Magician. First of the Rift War Saga.'

Kelly raised an eyebrow, 'More of a Lee Child man m'self.'

'Long time and all that. You don't normally get involved with the hoi polloi down here.'

'You are welcome to the scrotes. If I had my way I'd lock 'em up and throw away the keys.' Kelly engaged in normal banter.

'Tea?' offered Wes.

'Why not. Thanks. It's been a long day.' Kelly realised he was knackered. He sat in one of the battered armchairs that had been purloined by the custody staff to while away the long nights when the cells were empty. 'NATO please Wes.'

Wes added milk and two sugars. He handed the Met Police branded mug over. Kelly took a sip of the hot restorative liquid – he placed the mug on the Met Police branded table mat.

'Bad job about your Mike Maguire. Can't say I really knew him that well. But he is still one of ours.' Wes was thoughtful. 'Any ideas yet on what happened or who did it?'

'Harry Bodkin is keeping the investigation close to his chest. We can't be involved. But there's not a lot to go on so far I understand.' Kelly consulted his iPhone, 'The formal police service and cremation is next week at New Southgate Crematorium. The details will be on the e-notice board. Timings. Pall bearers. Honour Guard. Seating plan. Media arrangements. Top brass wanting to be seen. Full dress uniform with medals. The normal bloody circus. There's a commemoration and interment in his hometown of Enniskillen later – can't see anyone other than close colleagues, friends and family going to that. Not that Maguire seemed to have any family.'

Kelly felt invigorated by the strong sweet tea. 'So then, my prisoners. Who authorised their release?'

'They weren't released, they were transferred.' Wes could see that Kelly was bloody annoyed. 'A couple of Home Office FLUBs turned up unannounced. They had all the right IDs, papers, and authorisations. I checked upstairs and was told to do as I was told. I had no choice.'

Kelly inwardly laughed at one of the old police acronyms. FLUB: Fucking Lazy Useless Bastard. In an earlier life, as a sergeant himself, Kelly had used the term out of earshot for a very disagreeable and inept senior officer, who was also probably corrupt. Allegedly.

'Who did you speak to upstairs?' Kelly thought he already knew the answer.

'Deputy Assistant Commissioner Keith Wallace, called him on his mobile. Saturday night. He told me not to contact you. So, I didn't!' Wes winked theatrically.

'Very grateful Wes. Very grateful. Between us then.' Kelly paused, sipped his tea. 'Did you get their names and department?'

'They had Home Office photo ID. They brought all the right paperwork with them and took it all away too. Said it was a security issue and they didn't want to leave evidence that could prejudice their internal investigations.'

'Why did you call the DAC? Surely there was a Duty Officer?' Kelly needed to understand the connection.

'The FLUBs told me only the DAC had the right clearance. Couldn't really argue.' Wes sipped his tea. Clearly there was something bothering him. 'What's going on Bill? What have you done?'

It wasn't an accusation – simply an old friend asking another friend if he needed help, as often friends do.

'Not me Wes.' Kelly contemplated. 'Something is not right. Think there is some tidying up from the past going on. Someone's sins coming back to haunt them?'

They finished their tea in silence, stood, shook hands – Kelly made to leave. 'Thanks for the tea. Good to see you. Next week maybe?'

Wes smiled his agreement.

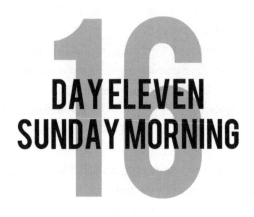

DAY ELEVEN
SUNDAY MORNING

NOWAK

Nowak found the days post Martha's opening night an emotional roller-coaster. He had just about recovered from the grisly shock of a dying body writhing on top of him.

During waking hours, he could see light at the end of the tunnel in extracting himself from the grips of The Vory and their associates – *it was going to take money, but it was only money*, he told himself. Due to the success of Martha and the concerts, money was something he would probably have plenty of – maybe more money than at any time in his varied and wide-ranging past. *Easy, buy my way out of trouble, not for the first time, almost certainly not the last*, he thought, *simple. As long as the ticket sales come through. Is it a big ask? Are they bullshitting me?*

A shiver went through his body.

The words of the archbishop in the cathedral of St John the Baptist in Wroclaw once again haunted him: *"No matter how safe you think you are, if you are a sinner, your sins will find you out."*

In the sweaty, sleepless periods just before dawn he replayed the phone call to Bishkek in Kyrgyzstan. The heavy Proto-Balto-Slavic accent. *'You were fortunate... You won't be so lucky next time.... I am a believer in retributive justice... I will make your death long and lingering. Death by the boat.... you owe me one point two five million pounds.... Happy to accept US dollars as well... You have four weeks from today or Martha dies.'*

He wasn't sleeping well.

Nowak had become enthralled with legality to his surprise – life was simpler. He had even been gentler with his paid-for sexual entertainment – and had found the encounters surprisingly more pleasurable for it.

He couldn't erase his past, no matter how hard he tried or what he did. Some of his 'business' interests were easy to shut down or hand over, he chastised himself, *hand-over? Sell! I'm not a charity, I worked hard to build up those businesses. I'm not going to give them away.*

Nowak's lonely thoughts over early-morning coffee in his apartment overlooking the Thames turned to how to remove the threat. It was a double-edged sword – on the one hand he wanted legality, yet on the other, he had to remove the threat of his past transgressions if revealed. *But how?*

His other worry was the disabled badge business – not so much the business itself, but the people with whom he had dealt and its history. He couldn't remember them all – and he kept no written records. *That policeman Wallace is the only certainty. His snitching days are numbered. How do I remove the threat,* pondered Nowak?

There was a tatty postcard photocopy of a sign attached to his 'fridge door by a souvenir magnet – he couldn't remember from where it came: *If you think, don't say. If you say, don't write. If you write, don't sign. If you sign, don't be surprised.* He laughed to himself *It's not as if I'm going to be completing a tax return on that particular enterprise.*

Fake Blue Badges were no longer viable due to the digital economy and cyber-checks. Some of his badge customers had risen to the top of society, government, and the authorities – they all knew too much. He regretted not having kept a list – he remembered some of the people, not all, *but that could be evidence if the list fell into the wrong hands. Shame. Might have been able to persuade them to help me,* he laughed to himself, *the informers, insider intelligence and people in high places, too much to lose? If only I hadn't destroyed that fucking journalist's story.*

There was no way any of them wanted their past disabled badge purchases to be exposed – he thought again of the day he wrecked Danny's foot, *what of that bloody journalist Danny whatshisname. Is he a risk? Too close to those bloody coppers. He certainly knows everything – it was nothing but bad luck that he has come back to haunt me?*

Nowak didn't know if his apartment was still bugged – he only knew of the one set of listening apparatus. He felt his life wasn't his own. He had taken to using *the safety of his car* for the more sensitive conversations – keeping conversations at home banal, anodyne, and occasionally outrageous, to keep everyone amused.

His team were all over making the complex arrangements for the video shoot at Elstree on Wednesday – and by all projections the legitimate source of even more income. He had begun to trust his highly experienced production team, unlike the workers in many of his other less-legal enterprises which had been taking a back seat. *Need to get a grip there*, he thought.

He decided to take a walk to clear his head – and to consider the issues. He had given Ray, his driver, the day off. It wasn't warm, so he selected a windproof red and white sailing anorak. Before long he arrived at the Thames Barrier Park, the redeveloped urban oasis and wildflower meadow. He sat on a bench just upstream of the gleaming metal-clad arches and yellow cantilevers of the largest movable flood barriers in the world. He admired the incredible engineering feat of the ten 3,300 tonne steel gates across five hundred and twenty metres of the river that protects one hundred and twenty five square kilometres of central London from flooding caused by possible tidal surges. Nowak liked facts – they were incontrovertible and somehow reliable.

He took out of his pocket the mobile phone that had only ever been used to contact one person – caller line identity had been inactivated. From his small notepad he looked up the number – carefully coded. GCHQ wouldn't have a problem decrypting, but the casual observer or 'plod' would have more of an issue.

He dialled and patiently waited for the call to be answered – he knew that the answerphone function had been disabled. *Precautions. Always take precautions,* Nowak thought.

17

DAY ELEVEN
SUNDAY MORNING

WALLACE'S RESIDENCE

THE RINGING TELEPHONE DISTURBED DEPUTY Assistant Commissioner Keith Wallace's Sunday morning routine.

Earlier he had walked the mile or so to the corner shop with Bella, his dog, a white pedigree Bichon Frise of Mediterranean origins. He collected his pre-ordered *Sunday Telegraph*, together with *The Mail on Sunday* for his wife. Some smoked thick cut bacon took his fancy as did *The Sunday People* – despite being a died-in-the-wool right-winger *it is sometimes useful to read the opposing views from the left-leaning, communist rag – no matter how wrong they are.* Wallace mused. All went into a Waitrose hessian bag-for-life – along with the scented, sealed bag containing Bella's warm organic discharge recently collected from the grass verge.

The walk gave Wallace an opportunity to consider his future without Margaret, his obedient long-suffering wife of thirty years, nagging him about what *other people* would say. She was immensely proud of her husband's position in the Police and had always assumed one day he would make it to the top. 'Of course, when *my* Keith is promoted, we'll have a driver and must attend many important social events, meet important people, even the Prime Minister,' she had told anyone at the local WI meeting who would listen. Not that many did anymore.

When Wallace announced his plan to his wife that he was going to take early retirement and accept the nomination for prospective parliamentary candidate for the constituency where they lived, she was at first not happy, 'What am I going to tell people?'

She didn't know how to back-track on her Police boasts. After a while, and considerable scheming, she decided that her position in society would be considerably enhanced as the wife of an MP – consequently after a few days, she had talked herself into *dear Keith* being elected and then accepting a ministerial position. *Hyacinth Bucket eat your heart out* – if only she knew what people called her behind her back. Now she told anyone who would listen, the list getting shorter and shorter, that, 'It was my idea for Keith to stand. He was reluctant at first, but I persuaded him. Such a clever man, too clever for the police, of course.'

The current sitting MP had announced his retirement the previous week due to ill health – with the election probably only three months or so away, it would have to be a high-speed campaign with a local man. It hadn't occurred to the middle- to late-aged white men of the local association that a woman could or should be considered. Wallace would stand on the double platform – a former policeman demanding increased resources, and being local, he knew the issues in *his* constituency.

His selection was just a matter of a formal vote at the Association Meeting the following week. He played golf with several on the selection committee and was the Worshipful Master, the highest-ranking official of his Masonic Lodge. Members of Parliament are not required to declare if they are Freemasons but may choose to disclose this information in the Register of Members' Financial Interests if they wish. Wallace saw no point in declaring this interest *when* he was elected.

The newspapers were full of stories about the leaky duplicitous Cabinet – 'sources close to Downing Street' suggested that the current Prime Minister, The Right Honourable Phillida Campbell-Horrocks no longer commanded their, or her party's respect. Several stalking horses had thrown their hat into the ring – but Wallace was confident that when *his friend* the current Minister of State for Crime and Policing, the Right Honourable Michael Ramsey formally announced his candidacy, he would be supported by a majority to become the next party leader and Prime Minister – and a formidable personal ally.

With a skip in his step, Wallace continued his walk. Poor Bella could hardly keep up and was frequently pulled away from lampposts and trees where her doggy friends had left unreturned messages.

Back home, he had just taken the first few mouthfuls of the traditional Sunday breakfast demanded by Wallace and always cooked by Margaret. The newly purchased bacon, fried eggs, tomatoes, mushrooms, black pudding, and thick cut white toast, with unsalted butter, accompanied by Lapsang Souchong tea, without milk, the water at exactly 88°C to give a milder, fruitier flavour. Wallace never realised that Margaret ignored the strict temperature instructions – she just waved a thermometer around for effect. 'The temperature exactly how you like it dear,' she always said. The thermometer hadn't worked for years.

The words, *thank you* rarely passed Wallace's lips. *She's my wife, no need to praise her for doing her wifely duty.* The same was true in the bedroom.

'That isn't your normal phone ringing,' said Margaret, who eschewed the full English in favour of a simple fruit salad with pine nuts. 'It's the mobile in your study. It will be *that* man.'

Wallace carefully placed in perfect parallel his knife and fork on his side plate, rolled his white linen *serviette* and inserted it into the monogrammed *serviette* ring. 'Keep my plate and tea warm will you. I might be some time.' It was an order.

He left the breakfast table, walked across the hall with its oak herring bone parquet floor to sit in his desk chair, having slammed the study door. Only one person had this number. 'What do you want. Its Sunday.'

'Good morning to you too, Keith,' said Nowak.

'Yes. Good morning. What now?' replied Wallace. 'I thought we'd agreed no more.'

'How is the investigation going into Maguire's death?'

'Proceeding slowly. We still have no idea who the shooter was or why Maguire was targeted.'

'You will keep me informed, won't you?' Nowak's friendly response had sinister undertones.

'Why do you care?'

'We should all be concerned about our fellow man – especially an officer of the law.'

'As if you mind?' responded Wallace. Nowak ignored the barbed response.

'On another matter, are you sure that no-one can get hold of that journalist's story about the disabled badges? It wouldn't do any of you any good if it emerged?'

'It's all in hand,' was Wallace's curt reply. 'But you are not immune either. It would ruin you.'

'Then we have a mutual interest, don't we?'

'Don't play that game with me, Nowak. I could get you arrested in a heartbeat.'

'Oh please, Keith,' only Nowak could make the use of Wallace's given name with such menace, 'we really don't want to hurt each other, do we? Don't forget I know where many, many skeletons are buried. And whose remains they could be.'

Nowak rang off without the normal social unpleasantries.

Wallace threw the phone onto his desk. Got up. Walked back to the kitchen where his tea remained resolutely cooling on the kitchen table. The fat on the bacon gently congealing.

'I thought I bloody-well told you to keep those warm,' he shouted at his wife.

Margaret, ignoring her husband's petulance, wiped her lips on her white linen *napkin* before returning it to her monogrammed *napkin* ring. Margaret was a devotee of Nancy Mitford who wrote in her 1954 essay on *The English Aristocracy* that to say serviette was *non-U* and *infra dig, the correct term is napkin.* She left the room with her morning tea – in a fine white translucent porcelain teacup, part of an extensive matching dinner service. She settled herself in the conservatory to read avidly her *Mail on Sunday* – the newspaper of record that informed her opinion. The world cruise supplement fell out of the paper and on to the floor – as she picked it up a bright light shone. *I wonder how long it will take him to notice I've gone.*

DAY TWELVE
MONDAY

ELSTREE STUDIOS

THE PRODUCTION, TECHNICAL AND RIGGING TEAMS had the rare luxury of two full days to load-in and build the tonnes and tonnes of set and staging – without having to work overnight. They would be rehearse-recording all day Wednesday – rehearse a song or a link, roll-to-record, then move on to the next. 'Roll-to-record' being a hangover from the days of video tape machines, now obsolete – just a term everyone understood.

Wednesday's schedule summoned the main crew and the band to be ready to rehearse at 11h00. Martha, the dancers, make-up, and wardrobe had been called for 09h30. Shirley and her catering team would be ready with bacon or halloumi rolls at 08h30 for those with last minute faffing. The wrap was scheduled for 21h00 – with a contingency of one hour that few knew about. The acronym 'Wrap' another hangover term from the earliest days of breathtakingly expensive film – only good takes were developed and printed – *Wrap that take*: Wind Roll and Print. They would be derigged and out by noon on Thursday – casual observers were stunned how quickly everything was safely packed away and loaded-out.

The multi-page schedule, marked *strictly confidential*, contains every piece of information anyone working on the project would need – from phone numbers to meal breaks; local doctors to job numbers for invoices; and the ubiquitous *tech reqs*. But the schedule was always the source of irritation for the technical, location and production managers – and amusement for everyone else as they deliberately asked wind-up questions that elicited the answer, *'Read the bloody schedule.'*

The rigging team had suspended the various quad- and tri-trusses from the slinging points high in the support girders across the ceiling of the massive George Lucas stage at Elstree. When everything was rigged at ground level, the massive motors would incrementally lift the complex kit into the air. First lights and some of the loudspeakers; then the video screens, moving scenery, follow spots, foggers, fans and mirror balls until everything was at the right height. Once completed and effectively out of the way, the steeldeck staging and other ground supported kit could be manoeuvred into position using built-in retractable wheels. It was a well-rehearsed process with which everyone was familiar.

Essentially the set and staging had to look on camera like the first night of Martha's sell out concert tour. This time there was no audience to get in the way. The front of house team didn't have to be situated seventy-five metres from the stage. Massive green drapes, illuminated by even green-gelled cyclorama-lights, had been slung around the 'front of house' where the audience would have been 'on-the-night' – to be composited later in post-production. Green tape had been applied in crosses and long lines – easily seen by Martha and the other on-stage performers to give them defined eye-lines, but invisible once the edit team had adjusted and applied Avid's ChromaKey edit software. The effect would be seamless – no-one, not even some of the team who worked on the opening night, would be able to tell the difference between the Elstree recording and the first gig. As Jimmy would often muse, *'whoever said the camera doesn't lie, is a liar.'*

Tomorrow, seven ultra-high-resolution Sony UHC-8300 cameras with Canon CJ14 or UJ111 lenses would be mounted on rolling pedestals and Jimmy Jib Triangle Pro cranes – some with arms extending out to twelve metres for the exciting sweeping shots. Red triax and SMPTE fibre cables snaked out to the massive expanding-sides, most technologically advanced 8K OB transmission and production vehicle. One more radio linked camera was mounted on a Steadicam M-2. It would be used to dance with and around Martha – the camera operator had started their career as a ballet dancer.

Jimmy had told Nowak, he had 'done a great deal' – an understatement if ever there was one. Several high-end television and broadcast manufacturers and integrators were using the Martha recording as an 8K testbed – in exchange

Jimmy only had to recruit the additional freelance crew, saving tens of thousands of pounds by not having to pay for the technical kit and an engineering guarantee team. It was contractually agreed that photographs and video from the day could be used freely for their publicity, PR, sales, and marketing. The technical, production, broadcast and cinema magazines were already slavering at the thought. It had also been agreed that Martha would be available for carefully set-up photoshoots and an on-set press conference. It was a two-way street that worked for everyone.

Once the above-head civil engineering was complete, the backstage and front-of-house rigging crew were safely able to wheel in the myriad of flight cases – so the technical team were able to connect everything together. Fibre optic; CAT6; audio; video; DMX; and power snaked everywhere in a random rainbow of colour. IP, 5G, RF, and normal WiFi had been securely mapped in conjunction with the other studios on Elstree's massive site – long gone the old analogue days of taxis breaking into the sound systems of West End shows. The team in the sound recording truck added a whole new layer of complexity not normally seen on tour – taking individual feeds via a splitter or Dante from every microphone, playback device, sampler, and instrument in lossless 32-bit 192 kHz for recording and mixing later into 5.1 surround sound.

Jimmy Patrick surveyed the scene. He was a past master at the art and science of big events – but this was an exciting technological first for all and a testament to the position Martha had regained in celebrity currency. There was a calm concentration – everyone knew what they were doing and what was expected of their teams.

Jimmy sat just inside the huge stage door sipping his *nice cup of tea*. Shirley, the sterling catering magician, who owned 'Starring Meals of Meals' delivered a bacon sandwich for Jimmy and one for herself. Everyone else was busy, the morning coffee break was an hour away. Shirley took the opportunity to put her feet up for fifteen minutes – the schedule said she could.

'Why do your bacon sandwiches always taste the best in the business?' asked Jimmy.

'Trade secret,' laughed Shirley. 'But as it's you… I make my own bread and know the farmer who produces the bacon and the dairy that churns the butter. No mass-catering shit here.'

With that a large gobbet of butter dribbled down Jimmy's chin.

'Here take this,' said Shirley passing Jimmy a paper towel. They sat in silence a while. It was Shirley who broke the peace. 'Can I ask you something?'

Jimmy nodded. He couldn't speak with his mouth full – his late-mother would have remonstrated with him from far above.

'So, Stanislaw Nowak then. How well do you know him?'

Jimmy finished his mouthful and wiped his mouth.

'Martha introduced me to him. Nowak had contacted her people about taking her back on the road.' He hesitated. 'Why?'

'Well, it's been bugging me for a while now – I didn't know what to do or say. I've been sort of storing it up since not far off the beginning of rehearsals. I spoke to my hubby about whether or not I should tell you. He said I should.'

Jimmy smiled encouragingly but said nothing. Shirley continued hesitatingly at first. 'I sort of… accidently… you know… overheard Stanislaw on the phone behind my catering truck. He obviously didn't know I was there. But *never heard such a thing.*' Shirley's turn to hesitate. 'Oh. I don't know. I'm not really sure I should be telling you.'

Jimmy nodded for Shirley to continue.

'Well, you know the rules. We all keep secrets when on the road. On tour. You know, what goes on tour, stays on tour.' Shirley was in a dilemma – she gave a little embarrassed laugh. 'He was talking to someone about removing a threat. He kept on talking about blue disabled badges. He was threatening them if they didn't do as he said. He mentioned Danny.'

Jimmy listened in silence. Clearly Shirley had more to say – he gently encouraged her with one of his best heart-melting smiles.

Shirley was encouraged, 'The bit that really worried me was he threatened to ruin the careers of whoever he was talking to if they didn't comply. Made all sorts of horrid threats. *Never heard such a thing.*'

Shirley's mantra, *never heard such a thing*, was a source of great amusement and, at the same time, genuine affection by both the cast and crew. Her location catering was legendary within the industry.

'Did you hear a name?' Jimmy asked, 'Who he was talking to?'

'Not sure, but I think he said Angie.' Shirley was hesitant. 'No. Think it was Angela? Sorry…'

Jimmy was worried. Nowak's now defunct people smuggling enterprise had been a well-kept secret. He had wondered about resigning – and possibly telling everyone, but that would almost certainly end the whole tour and affect many people's livelihood. Touring and events were under huge pressure – there simply weren't the number of jobs around for so many exceptionally talented freelancers.

Shirley, now on a roll, continued, 'He said Danny's foot would be nothing compared to what he would do to them. Didn't understand what Danny's foot had to do with it. I thought he had hurt it in a car accident.'

Jimmy was as confused as Shirley. Jimmy shared Shirley's thought that Danny's foot injury was due to a car accident.

'By the way, later he asked me to buy in basic catering for an additional seventy-five people. Mainly vegetarian. But I was to bill him personally, not to go through your books. Thought it very odd.' Shirley was worried that Jimmy might be angry. 'But he cancelled all that well before the first night. Never heard such a thing.'

'Not needed now.' Jimmy's calm response surprised her. 'So, no harm. No foul. It was a plan that was cancelled.'

'Thanks Jimmy. Better get back to work – help the team prepare for morning coffee and cut up some of my special banana cake. Do this lot ever stop eating?' Shirley laughed. She stood, collected their plates and mugs – and returned to her bespoke catering truck.

Jimmy wondered what he should do. What Shirley had told him could be serious – he was beginning to understand the extent of Nowak's *business interests*. None of them made Jimmy feel comfortable – even the tour, now with its almost guaranteed success, left him feeling ill at ease with Nowak's original intention of using it for people smuggling. *What don't I know?* He walked away from the studio to call Daisy – the only person he thought he could trust. She answered at the second ring. 'Hi Jimmy. How is the load in and rig going?'

'Pretty good. We are a little behind schedule, but nothing to worry about. One of the winch motors failed – wouldn't go up or down. Everything was stuck in mid-air for nearly an hour. Then the cherry picker blew a gasket – so the poor old studio floor received another dosing of hydraulic fluid.' Jimmy was referring to a staging lift failure in the early days of rehearsals in the same studio. 'So, we had to move the cherry picker by hand – they are bloody heavy – before we could get another one in so we could replace the winch. We are not doubling up as we are in the studio and not on a tight tour schedule. Anyway, all cleared up and working now.'

Daisy was busy trying to negotiate distribution and PR for the yet to be made Martha video. 'You called me?'

'Yeah. Look I've just had a sit down over a coffee with Shirley. She told me she overheard a conversation that Nowak was having with someone on the phone...' Jimmy told Daisy what Shirley had told him.

When he had finished Daisy wasn't sure what to say. 'I'll have a word with Danny.'

'Thought you should know.' Jimmy hoped for more.

'Thanks Jimmy.' Daisy disconnected.

DAY THIRTEEN
TUESDAY

NEW SOUTHGATE CREMATORIUM
AND THE WAKE

New Southgate Crematorium in North London was packed – standing room only. The many burial sections around the central building reflecting the broad range of people who live and die in the surrounding neighbourhoods – with individual areas for Christians, Greek Orthodox, Roman Catholic, Caribbean, agnostic, and other communities. There was even a charming, wooded area for those who wished to rest in peace in more natural surroundings. None would be required for Maguire's ashes – after the cremation they would be transported to Saint

Macartan's Cathedral in his hometown of Enniskillen in Northern Ireland for burial.

The service for the late Detective Sergeant Michael Maguire had become a national event – stoked by social media, the press, TV, radio, and angst-ridden politicians.

In the warmly furnished funeral space, officers in full dress uniform from the National Crime Agency; representatives from The Met and Police Forces across the UK; and members from the emergency services who attended the post-shooting pandemonium were all there to pay their respects, mourning the loss of a colleague.

The inevitable civic dignitaries were also there, wanting to be seen to be seen paying their respects.

Outside was bedlam, as hundreds of the public crowded into the grounds and car parks. They would listen to the service from hastily arranged loudspeakers – the assassination of a serving police officer always raises high dudgeon, moral outrage, and a forest of flowers from well-wishers.

Within the tranquil walls of the crematorium itself the press and media had agreed a pool who would later share their photographs, video, audio, and stories – the Celebrant did not want an unseemly media scrum within the already packed space. Outside the media chaos built – red faced crematorium staff attempted in vain to move the TV satellite trucks off the grass verges of the gardens of remembrance – all needed to find a clear path to the southern hemisphere for their satellite signals. As far as the media were concerned this was a media event – not a sombre funeral.

At a suitable distance, keen observers watched the assembled masses for any sign of guilt, pleasure, or an over-developed unwelcome interest. Around the corner, out-of-sight, two well-concealed vans were parked – each with six armed officers within. Overhead three drones with high-definition gyro-stabilised cameras live-linked to the police control position. Against the grey sky, with their battery-powered motors, they were imperceptible. Media drones and their larger siblings, proper helicopters, were prohibited for a radius of three miles. Everyone and everything were recorded for later analysis using concealed video cameras in addition to the crematorium's own CCTV and web-streams.

The precautionary principle was being applied by the Police. No-one had yet been able to establish why Detective Sergeant Michael Maguire had been so brutally murdered. Despite the alleged assassin now dead, one train of thought was that those associated with Maguire's murder might attend the funeral. The police also had their own Senior Officers and a government minister to protect from the massive crowd growing by the minute.

The Right Honourable Michael Ramsey, Minister of State for Crime and Policing in Her Majesty's UK Government made a show of trying not to make a show of taking his *rightful* place in the front row. His seat carefully chosen by his SpAD – politically appointed special adviser – to be perfectly positioned for the TV cameras in a two-shot incorporating the coffin and the *grieving* minister. He had chosen – advised by another of his SpADs, a PR and communications specialist – to save any words to the press until outside when the service had concluded.

Detective Chief Inspector Harry Bodkin, with two of his Detective Sergeants, together with police PR Virginia

Stephani sat three quarters of the way back from the altar. None of them had met Maguire, except as a bloody corpse. The detectives were frustrated – their investigations had simply stalled. Nothing – nothing that Bodkin was sharing. He was certain that someone knew something more both from inside the police and within the security services – despite frequent requests for information.

As the service began, the coffin was carried by six uniformed officers to the catafalque, accompanied by the simple yet haunting *Canon for Strings and Continuo* by Johann Pachelbel. Deputy Assistant Commissioner Keith Wallace and Detective Chief Superintendent Bill Kelly followed the coffin, in best dress uniforms with hats under arms. There were no family.

Kelly took his seat in the third row next to Maguire's former colleagues. Wallace sat beside the Minister in the front row – they greeted each other with curt nods and an informal handshake.

Once the coffin was settled and everyone was in their seats, the service took the traditional course – a clichéd greeting by the freelance Celebrant, a portly former bit part actor of indeterminate age in a dark suit; white shirt with stiffened collars; and a black tie. Slicked-back greasy, Brylcreemed grey-hair accompanied by a dusting of dandruff on his shoulders made him look like an out-of-work arms dealer. In an affected deep sing-song voice he welcomed colleagues, friends, and family of Detective Sergeant Michael Maguire – no one had briefed the Celebrant that there was no immediate family, just a solitary distant cousin who sat unnoticed at the back. Together most then sang half-heartedly or mouthed to a pre-recorded organ, the hymn *Jerusalem*. The folded A4 service sheet, with the Metropolitan Police Crest and a formal police photograph of Maguire on the front cover, informed everyone Lyrics: William Blake, 1804. Music: Hubert Parry, 1916. The Celebrant was completely unembarrassed by his enthusiastic variable key basso-profundo rendition. He then read from Ecclesiastes 3:1-4 *There is a time for everything, and a season for every activity under the heavens: a time to be born and a time to die, a time to plant and a time to uproot, a time to kill...*

Most managed to feign interest, their minds wandering as they considered why it was Maguire's time to be killed and by whom.

The Celebrant invited Deputy Assistant Commissioner Keith Wallace to say a few words. Knowing he would be on that evening's news bulletins, Wallace gave a short eulogy rehearsed and rehearsed in front of the mirror before leaving home – he had written it himself with the unwanted intervention of Virginia Stephani, mostly ignored. He had ordered that he was to be the only serving officer to speak: 'Today we mourn an exceptional man and even as we do, we give thanks to each and every one here and around the UK. You selflessly serve our society, the thin blue line which runs through our community. You continue to inspire us. Some might say Sergeant Maguire was an ordinary man with an ordinary job. I do not agree. He represented policing at its best. He was everything you wanted in a police officer. Authentic, brave, genuine, and kind...'

Wallace continued for another couple of minutes, at one point claiming to be a close friend of Sergeant Maguire. Kelly sitting in the third row was incensed at the DAC's duplicity – he was certain that Wallace had no idea who Maguire was.

'… and so, together, we give grateful thanks to Sergeant *Martin* Maguire in giving his life in the service of the Metropolitan Police. As Albert Einstein said, the world is a dangerous place, not because of those who do evil, but because of those who look on and do nothing. Sergeant Maguire did not look on. He did something to protect us all. For that we must all be eternally grateful.'

With that Wallace left the lectern, saluted the coffin, and sat down with a self-satisfied po-face beside the government minister, who nodded his approbation.

Michael Maguire's colleagues exchanged shakes of heads and silent, mouthed euphemisms not normally suitable for a funeral.

The *pause for thought* was accompanied by Samuel Barber's *Adagio for Strings*. There were few if any tears.

The Celebrant invited everyone to pray if they wished – after several paragraphs from the Catholic book of Funeral Prayers, together they recited the Lord's Prayer. There was a skirmish as the modern and ancient versions verbally conflicted – followed by a barrage of mistimed, patchy 'Amens.' When the congregation looked up, the curtains had surreptitiously closed, hiding the coffin from view before removal to its fiery fate.

After the inevitable final parting tidings, it was all over – the spirits lifted by *Fare Thee Well Inniskilling*, the quick march of Maguire's former army regiment, The Royal Dragoon Guards. All soldiers never leave the family of their original regiment wherever they end up in life – or death.

The emotion after the service was mainly relief. The awkward tension as everyone assembled before the funeral service had lifted as the congregation filed out mingling around the flowers. The floral tribute area set slightly away from the chapel, offered a quiet spot to gather after the service – paparazzi with long lens hoped for saleable pictures. Occasional muted laughter could be heard as inappropriate stories were told about their former colleague – as police officers are wont to do by way of diversion.

The Right Honourable Michael Ramsey, and Deputy Assistant Commissioner Keith Wallace took the opportunity to hold forth on any TV or radio channel that would have them – in advance, they had privately agreed what each would say. Their words of political rhetoric and policing praise were broadcast repeatedly on almost an hourly basis for several days until the media lost interest – or another scandal knocked the story out of the collective conscience.

Margaret, DAC Wallace's wife, was thrilled – she had already told all and sundry how, when, and why to watch *her Keith*. She had invited a few close friends to coffee so they could coo together watching the BBC's red button live news broadcast – the mourning totally ignored in favour of watching *her Keith* on the television set, *never TV* and certainly not *the box* she espoused to her acquaintances. None of them had noticed her husband's appalling faux pas in calling the deceased Michael, Martin. A few days later the front page of *Private Eye* had a field day with pictures of Wallace in four boxes – calling Keith Wallace: Kevin, Kendrick, Kenton, and Kermit. His wife had never seen, nor would even see, what Wallace called, *'that tawdry little rag.'*

Photocopiers in Police Stations across the UK had been busy in ensuring no Officer missed the front-page news – the new internal sport became more-and-more absurd as colleagues dreamt up new names for each other.

Kelly conferred with his team. Nothing out of the ordinary had been observed by any of the watchers. No suspicious people. No one acting strangely. No one taking an unhealthy interest in any of the mourners.

'Always a bad day when we have to give one of ours a seeing off,' suggested Harry Bodkin to Bill Kelly – who hadn't heard him sidle up. They shook hands. Bodkin gently guided Kelly out of earshot of the other mourners.

'Always,' replied Kelly. After a pause, 'How are you getting on?'

'Nothing.' Bodkin shook his head. 'We're certain that the IC1 male who wrapped himself around the boat's propellers was the assailant. We found the rifle he used and matched it to residue on his clothes. Russian Vintorez sniper rifle manufactured during the late 1980s by the gloriously named Central Scientific Research Institute for Precision Machine Engineering. Issued primarily to Spetsnaz units for covert operations. No prints of course.'

'Not even on the trigger?' Kelly had some experience with firearms.

'I'm told by our firearms support that the trigger loop is large enough to fit a gloved hand. Apparently designed as an important consideration when supplying special forces.' Bodkin had already been there. 'We found the gloves in the IC1's pocket. They'd been treated on the inside not to retain fingerprints. We have DNA, of course, but no matches yet.'

'A professional job then?' Kelly raised an eyebrow.

'Has to be.' Bodkin nodded. He hesitated. 'Probably.'

'That's one hell of a rifle otherwise.' Kelly said. 'Not the normal gangland weapon.'

The pair of them looked around at the floral tributes – occasionally smiling or briefly lifting a hand to wave at a long-forgotten colleague, but not welcoming enough for them to come over.

Bodkin broke the silence. 'So, what has Maguire got to do with the Russians then?'

The way Bodkin phrased it was as close to an accusation as he could get. Kelly said nothing.

'Oh, for fuck's sake Bill. What else do you know? What aren't you telling me?' Bodkin held back his voice and temper, nevertheless some of the mourners looked around at the two senior detectives.

Kelly was formulating an answer when the silence was interrupted by DAC Keith Wallace, 'Still failing to come up with any answers Bodkin?'

'Afternoon Sir.' Kelly tried to divert Wallace's attention from Bodkin. 'Good service. Your eulogy needed to be said.'

Kelly didn't think this was the moment to raise the DAC's name *confusion.* Or mention their last acrimonious encounter at The Calthorpe Arms. *Keep the powder dry,* thought Kelly.

'Yes, thank you DCS Kelly.' Wallace gave a bravura performance – he wasn't going to be seen to be diverted or covertly threatened. He turned to Bodkin, 'Well?'

'Not a lot closer to identifying the shooter. We presume, maybe, that he could be Russian from the weapon he was using. But nothing more, sir. We're not getting any help from our colleagues in the security services. Its one-way traffic. We feed them information but get nothing back in return. I was just discussing with DCS Kelly whether or not Detective Sergeant *Michael* Maguire could have had any connection with the Russians.'

Wallace did not notice Bodkin's barb in emphasising Maguire's given name, Michael.

'Well Kelly?' Wallace demanded. 'Connection?'

'Not that we know of Sir. But it would help if our colleagues in five and six cooperated.' Kelly looked straight into Wallace's eyes to gauge a reaction. There was none.

Bodkin picked it up. 'We sent the pictures of our shooter ages ago. Nothing. Rien. Nyet.'

'I'll do what I can at our next liaison meeting.' Wallace seemed to be cautious.

'And when is that, please Sir?' asked Bodkin

'I'll let you know.' Wallace turned and stalked off.

'He's a cold fish?' Kelly working at the NCA didn't directly report to Wallace, but nevertheless he was a senior officer – albeit with some serious allegations against him yet to be thoroughly investigated and reported to Professional Standards. 'Seems to be taking a lot of interest in this.'

'It's very public. He wants to raise his profile.' Bodkin hesitated, rubbing the toe of his shoe in the gravel. He was thoughtful.

Kelly picked up the clue. 'Go on. What?'

'I've been going over the crime scene time and again. Thinking about where everyone was seated – or standing.'

Kelly looked around at the throng of mourners – he recognised many. He waited for Bodkin to continue. 'What if Maguire wasn't the target? We know where the shooter was. We know where Maguire was when he was killed'

Kelly wondered where this was going. 'No shit Sherlock. We know where everyone was.'

'Indeed, we do. Maguire was seated immediately in the row in front of Nowak. If he hadn't stood exactly when he did, Nowak would have taken the bullet... and he does have a big connection with the Russians,' Bodkin surmised. 'I have requested the forensic animation and analysis of the bullet trajectory to establish the relative positions of shooter and victim. It might help us one way or the other. Will take a few days despite me kicking their arses. Apparently shooting is very popular!'

Kelly was silent as he assessed what Bodkin had said. Eventually he asked, 'You're saying Maguire was unlucky?'

Bodkin nodded, 'Maybe. Maybe not. But on the balance of probability, yes. Very bad day for Maguire.'

'Then why didn't the shooter take a second shot?' Kelly grimaced at his friend's assessment. 'If Nowak were the target, surely he would have ensured he completed his task?'

Bodkin was thoughtful. 'Or maybe he hadn't realised he missed his target. I went up to where the shooter positioned themselves. With the dazzling bright lights followed by darkness—'

'Minister, I would like to introduce to the two senior detectives leading the enquiry into the death of Sergeant, M... Maguire.' Wallace had returned with the Minister in tow, interrupting Bodkin's hypothesis. Neither had seen them approach.

After the traditional handshakes. The Minister pontificated, 'Bad business. Are you making any progress with the investigation? The PM is demanding answers.'

The PM wasn't demanding answers – Ramsey was using the age-old political trick of trying to emphasise his closeness to the Prime Minister and therefore his own importance.

Before either could answer, Kelly spotted a photographer snapping away in what Wallace had arranged as a meaningful four shot. He realised they had been set up – he nudged Bodkin and gesticulated in the photographer's direction with his head.

'Good to meet you Minister. Sorry, must go. Our transport awaits.' Kelly gave Wallace the cold shoulder as he and Bodkin departed leaving the Minister and Wallace standing there.

As they left, they heard Wallace quietly say, 'Thought you should meet them. See you tomorrow, Minister. Think we said eleven.'

The Minister replied. 'Hope we can get this bloody mess sorted once and for all, Keith.'

Kelly and Bodkin raised eyebrows but continued walking.

Several cars and minibuses had been arranged to take everyone to the wake at *The Great Northern Railway Tavern* a couple of miles away in Hornsey, N8 – chosen for the twenty-four craft beer taps on the bar and a spectacular selection of Scottish single malt whiskies. The upstairs private room had been booked and a traditional post funeral buffet spread had been laid out. A wag was heard to say, *'the Met has pushed the boat out as the buffet includes cod goujons. Only get goujons on special occasions.'*

The room soon became noisy as alcohol spurred the conversations – for many it was a time to let their hair down and catch up with the gossip. Old war stories were repeated and exaggerated as the afternoon would progress into evening. Losing a colleague was a serious business which required serious drinking.

Bodkin chose a pint of Frontier in a tankard whilst Kelly went for a London Pride Unfiltered in a branded straight glass. They chose to take their pints down to the peace of the outside space not far from where the legendary Scottish hero, William Wallace, was savagely executed in 1305.

'Incompetence is often highly regarded in governmental circles,' said Bodkin.

'What?' Kelly's pint stopped on its way to his mouth.

'Attributed to William Wallace,' Bodkin's degree had been in British History. 'I watched that film *Braveheart* the other night. Mel Gibson cried *"freedom"* just before he was beheaded. Highly unlikely as Wallace probably had other things on his mind – the executioner had already sliced off his genitals, removed his intestines and then burned them, making sure Wallace witnessed the act.'

Bodkin took a long pull of his beer. 'The mark of a truly exceptional executioner was that they could not only pull the heart out of a criminal's chest, but they could also keep it beating the whole time. There's no record of Wallace's executioner's success, but we know he did have his heart removed following his entrails and genitals. The hangman declared, *"Behold the heart of a traitor,"* as he held it up for the crowd to see.'

Kelly was appalled by Bodkin's soliloquy. 'So, you are in favour of capital punishment then?'

'Come on, some of the things we have seen humans do to each other is beyond imagination. Too brutal for the public according to the popular media who insist on toning the story down with banal euphemisms.' Bodkin was on a roll. 'Punishment should fit the crime. And both crime and punishment should be made fully public. Then we might dissuade a few of these bloody traitors.'

'That's a bit harsh,' said Kelly ever the pragmatist. 'But talking of traitors, *our* Wallace and that bloody minister. They seem close?'

Kelly looked out towards the street.

'I don't trust either of them. Something is going on.' Bodkin realised he had nearly finished his pint. 'Ramsey is tipped for the next Prime Minister, God help us. It is said, according to his colleagues, he will do anything to get to the top. Stop at nothing. He'll shaft anyone who gets in his way, the man doesn't seem to have a conscience. He is well on the ASPD spectrum.'

'ASPD?' Kelly knew the term, but the spectrum is wide. 'That's one hell of an accusation?'

'Not sure if he is a sociopath or a psychopath. He tries to hide it well by being outwardly amiable. Not always law-abiding for an elected law maker. He'll break rules or make impulsive decisions without feeling guilty. A two-faced shit is a better description.' suggested Bodkin. 'Wallace is rumoured to be resigning soon to stand as an MP for where he lives, supported by Ramsey. Wallace is taking an unhealthy interest in this case too. He normally leaves me alone to get on with it.'

'Never met Ramsey before all this. I don't know Wallace that well. Heard rumours on the grape vine of course.' Kelly pointed at Bodkin's now empty glass. 'Another one?'

'Go on then.' Bodkin handed his jug over.

A few minutes later Kelly returned with two more pints, and some sandwiches from the buffet. 'There's going to be some sore heads tomorrow. Looks like several have got their eye well in.'

They knocked glasses and exchanged, 'Cheers.'

'So, what do we know? Full disclosure.' Bodkin demanded of his old friend and colleague. He took a cheese and pickle sandwich. 'You first.'

Kelly smacked his lips. A third of his straight glass already downed. 'Nowak has to be at the centre of all this. Must be. He's not alone. But he has always been one step ahead of us. I know that someone on the inside is protecting him. Maguire was foolish – didn't want to let his family down. I don't believe anything more sinister than that. Not saying it's right. But this is more serious than I thought. I didn't tell you that we found a second set of surveillance equipment in Nowak's apartment.'

'What!' Bodkin was exasperated. 'Why the bloody hell didn't you tell me? Whose is it?'

'I didn't think it was relevant to Maguire's murder. I am not accusing you, or suggesting anything, but I don't want this to leak. No one is admitting to installing them. I was told, not too gently, to leave it alone.' Bodkin was about to interrupt. Kelly held up his hand, now relying on his long-time friend. 'And then I found a listening device in my office.'

Kelly air-dropped Bodkin the picture to his personal iPhone, avoiding trackable e-mail. 'It can only have been planted by someone on the inside who has access to my office. And now vital evidence has disappeared. They, whoever they are, wiped some of my computer files both locally and on the server. And removed the hard copies of Danny's disabled badge piece, with its photos too.'

Kelly drank deeply from his pint. 'Evidence and intelligence about Nowak's attempted people smuggling activities using the concert tour have gone missing too. TSU is trying to recover the computer files, but don't hold out a lot of hope.'

'This is getting profoundly serious. What have we got ourselves mixed up in? The bigger question is who and why?' Bodkin considered his thoughts. 'This isn't just about Maguire, is it?'

'We know Nowak is an evil, dirty, two-faced, lying, criminal shit. And you and I know Maguire was feeding him some information,' agreed Kelly.

'My team thought it a bit over the top when you said you were distributing numbered, signed-for files.' Bodkin took another swig from his pint. 'What's the connection then? The connection to your Danny's disabled badge piece or the people smuggling? Or something else? Or both?'

'Not my Danny.' Kelly insisted. 'But I am beginning to think you are right. There must be some connection. But what?'

'Okay. Let's assume that Nowak was the target. I can't see why anyone would want to take him out for the disabled badges.' Bodkin considered his thoughts. 'Unless it's an inside job. Someone trying to protect themselves. Then surely Danny would have been the target. Unless it was a message?'

'True, Danny had been doing a full exposé of the tossers who had been selling and buying illegal blue badges – many from Nowak.' Kelly spoke quietly, 'Paralleling my team's investigation. All that was a very long time ago. But why now?'

'I thought the article and photographs was spiked by Danny?' Bodkin was fascinated, 'you said Nowak threatened him and his family. Did his foot in?'

Kelly was reticent. 'Long, long time ago. Novak and Danny haven't set eyes on each other until Daisy called Danny to interview Martha. So the story has just resurfaced. Then disappeared again. I was given a copy – but that was one of the things stolen from my office and wiped from my computer. A while ago a file was covertly passed to Yuliet Spooner—'

'Oh bollocks, what has she got to do with it? The Centre for Covert Media Studies has been a thorn in our side for bloody years.' Bodkin realised that this was getting complex.

Kelly ignored the question. 'The file contained much of the information I had. Her office was burgled. Yuliet's evidence and research about Nowak, Danny's stories and more has also gone. When we talked at her office, Yuliet thought that Nowak's people smuggling was the bigger story, bigger than the disabled badges. I'm not so sure. There is something we are missing. But before she got home, her flat was also burgled where she kept duplicates. Her office was also bugged we discovered later. Her home too.'

'Where are all these intercepts going?' Bodkin questioned. 'If it's not us, who is it?'

'Our friends at Five and Six know we have a shared interest in Nowak. I met with one of their liaison people,' said Kelly. 'It took me a while to work out how they knew we knew – they had built up a large file of information on Nowak. Allegedly some of the names in Danny's piece were remarkably high profile – they seemed quite pleased that the piece wasn't published as it would have embarrassed the Government, senior Civil Servants, City banking types and I believe some of our colleagues who are probably now residing on the upper floors.'

'How did they get the copy of Danny's piece?' Kelly had already told Bodkin that Nowak had wiped Danny's computer.

'As you know when something is erased on a computer, it doesn't go for good – whilst Danny was being treated for his foot injury, a team went in and downloaded the deleted data. Danny thought Nowak had wiped his hard drive and destroyed the back-ups. As had I.' Kelly looked around. He wondered if he was getting paranoid. 'Apparently instead of completely wiping a file, only the tiny bit of information that points to the location of that file on the hard drive is erased. So, if the computer hasn't been used since a file was deleted, chances are it will still be there. Anyone can recover the data using off-the-shelf software. Obviously, our lot are a little more sophisticated.'

'No wonder Danny was surprised when you had a copy.' Bodkin joined Kelly in his surveillance of their surrounds.

'The question is why now?' Kelly expressed the thoughts

he had been keeping private. 'What has happened, or is happening, that has caused the story to be resurrected?'

'Or who?' suggested Bodkin.

'Our friends in Five and Six have been trying to understand and insert agents within organised crime for years. It's the people and the trafficking routes they want to understand rather than just the crime – organised crime has its fingers in many pies and connections all over the world. But no-one seems to want to share information. They knew of our leak or should I say leaks.' Kelly thought for a while. 'I have always thought though that some of the worker bees don't agree with keeping secrets with the home teams. My boss has bought all this up with the Joint Intelligence Committee but got nowhere.'

'That's daft. Surely, we are all on the same side? And you didn't answer my question. How did Five get involved?' Bodkin was becoming as frustrated as Kelly.

'They overheard Nowak speaking on the phone to someone involved in my team's investigations. They didn't know who.' Kelly leant back in his chair. 'We do now. At least we thought we knew it was Maguire. But could it have been someone else as well?'

They both drank more of their beer.

Bodkin didn't push Kelly. 'Maguire's death could have been an unlucky accident as you say. But it could be the catalyst for reopening investigations into Nowak. Is that what you are saying?'

Bodkin had finished his pint. Kelly had barely touched his – but Bodkin's rapid despatch of the glorious honey brown liquid prompted him to knock back his in one draught.

'One more?' Kelly didn't wait for the answer. It wasn't his round, *but who was counting?*

When Kelly returned Bodkin was just finishing a conversation on his phone, '… okay. Thanks. Call me when you know something. Appreciate this. I owe you.'

Kelly said nothing. They toasted each other – Bodkin had a foamy moustache superimposed upon his real one.

'That was a mate at the Army's Seventy-Seventh Brigade,' explained Bodkin.

Kelly raised an inquisitive eyebrow.

'Created in 2015 to specialise in information and cyberwarfare. They recruit part time reservists from the City, hackers and elsewhere with skills in online analysis, marketing, social media and so on,' Bodkin was paraphrasing from their website, 'Supporting partners across Government upstream.'

'And we are upstream Government I suppose?' questioned Kelly.

Bodkin simply nodded. 'I sent them the picture of the listening device in your office. They recognised it instantly. Only could have come from one of us.'

Kelly was impressed. He'd failed using his contacts to confirm any identification.

'Our chums in Five and Six have their own agenda sometimes. They are particularly good at protecting their own interests. And they have long memories. I think the question is who and not what. That file, or at least Danny's piece and photographs, will probably answer that question. But you know the old rule – never let your enemy know what you know, or how you know it.'

Kelly then dropped the bombshell.

'I said Nowak could have been talking to someone else.' Kelly paused, not for dramatic reasons, but to ensure he wasn't overheard. 'Danny thinks it's your Deputy Assistant Commissioner Keith Wallace.'

Before Bodkin could react, they were noisily interrupted by the arrival of DS Rob Andrews and DS Anastasia Spencer-Hatt – who had half a dozen other colleagues in tow.

'There you both are,' Anastasia Spencer-Hatt was clearly very well refreshed. 'Party poopers.'

There was nothing for it – the mob had arrived. Bodkin and Kelly silently acknowledged by the raising of eyebrows that their conversation would have to wait.

'Sit down Rob, Anastasia. You know Detective Chief Inspector Harry Bodkin, don't you? We were in college together...' Hands were shaken. Introductions made to those unfamiliar with each other – they pulled up benches and chairs. Glasses were clinked in a toast to Maguire.

After suitably pretentious drinking and lip licking, there was a short hiatus whilst everyone was waiting for the other to speak.

'Are you planning to go to Enniskillen for the interment?' asked Bodkin, filling the silence. 'When is it?'

'Thursday week. I thought I should. After all he was a colleague,' Kelly hesitated, 'Thought I'd take Rob and Anastasia with me. There are not going to be many there. I doubt whether the media will be taking an interest. They've had their day out.'

DS Rob Andrews and DS Anastasia Spencer-Hatt looked slightly taken aback – it was the first they had heard of their unexpected journey.

'I've cleared the expenses. Flights to Belfast. Hire car. Three rooms at The Enniskillen Hotel for two nights plus standard subsistence.' The two DSs nodded their approval, not that they had a lot of choice – a couple of nights away would make a pleasant change from London.

'We might see something or someone. Not that we noticed anyone obvious today.' Kelly didn't say that he had already recruited a Belfast surveillance team and an armed response unit to be secreted around Saint Macartan's Cathedral. 'Danny and Daisy will be going as well – paying for themselves.'

Bodkin nodded – he had considered going, but with Kelly and his team already there he couldn't justify the budget.

The rest of the day disappeared into a haze of oft-told inappropriate police stories and more beer. The kitty was depleted and restocked with more twenty-pound notes.

Beer soon turned to whisky.

Maguire's death was well-and-truly commemorated.

DAY FOURTEEN
WEDNESDAY

ELSTREE STUDIOS

EVERYONE WAS SURPRISINGLY EXCITED. THE STUDIO floor was buzzing. Organised chaos and multiple radio talkback channels. VIP seats were the hottest tickets in town. Personal invitation only, for a tax-deductible charitable contribution of one thousand pounds – anybody and everybody wanted to be seen helping Police Charities after the terrible event. Few turned down the opportunity. A 'free' lunch; post-show champagne; meeting Martha; appearing in the celeb and gossip pages of many magazines and newspapers; and to be seen on the video helped their altruism.

Few of the production team had been involved in a 33-million-pixel 8K Ultra HD shoot before. It did present its own set of challenges as every detail was clearly seen in amazing resolution designed to be superior to the human visual system, so that no pixels are visible to the eye – and shoots at twice the rate of normal video so that movement is smooth and realistic. Long gone the days of 16mm film and standard definition television where a covered plywood flat and a bit of painted masking tape could hide a multitude of sins. Gone too, many years ago, fixed luminaires and analogue dimmer racks consuming tens of thousands of kilowatts with many kilometres of thick, heavy electric cable.

Martha's concert tour used hundreds of intelligent low-power LED moving lights – relatively lightweight and flexible, with results in the right experienced hands, that were uber-spectacular. *Creative Technology* were suppling many Flyer 18 and MiTrix LED displays – even the stair treads were enhanced using MiStrips, elevating and enriching the beautiful stage set. Ten high brightness Barco FLM projectors were used to project and map images onto various elements and surfaces of the stage set. The intense visuals had been programmed to match every nuance, step, beat and concept of each song and to complement Martha's and her dancers' choreography.

Over the last few days, the production team had watched most of the video from Martha's first night – both their own professional footage, and from audience members' smart phones selected by Daisy and Danny. The planning ensured that the shots would match – many cutaways, b-roll, audience shots, GVs and interviews were already *in the can* from the first night, but they all wanted more. Eye-lines were being plotted and marked. Later in editing, compositing, and grading, would be where the magic would happen – seamlessly integrating everything.

The sound team were doing their own thing as well, with each microphone and instrument recorded separately. They needed a clean multi-track audio recording – *nothing wrong with on the night, but it could be improved,* said the sound supervisor. The sound also had to match *on the night* with subtle colouration as if recorded in the massive 02 Arena – with added crowd effects.

The technical crew had plenty of time to rig, test and even set up several *specials* – hidden cameras that might only be used for a few unusual shots. One miniature camera had been attached to the beater of the kick drum; another on the head stock of the electric bass guitar; and one fixed on a 'lazy arm' aiming at the hi-hat, cymbals, and snare.

Daisy's PR team was shepherding around the studio in four groups the specially invited guests, journalists, photographers, and TV crews. Later they would all be given goodie bags with a media pack, a selection of Martha merchandise, together with freebies from the key sponsors. Also included was a certificate of valuation so everyone could include the benefit-in-kind on their tax return – probably. Maybe?

Kelvin Edwards sat at one of the catering tables drinking coffee served to him by one of Shirley's Martha-uniformed waiting staff especially brought in for the day. Kelvin had decided he was too important to traipse around with the hoi polloi and deserved special treatment. Daisy managed to avoid him. Kelvin hadn't noticed that the tables were laid with Martha-branded cloths and themed flower arrangements.

Starring-Meals-on-Wheels had a massive additional catering workload – not only the additional crew but also a high-end hospitality buffet lunch for the VIPs, journalists, celebrities and from the Police and their charities – together with the after-show party. Shirley was stressed but coping – even managing to satisfy one guest who had just announced that they were a fruitarian. *'Never heard such a thing'* could be heard being muttered as Shirley prepared a special plate at the back of one of the additional catering trucks brought in for the occasion.

In the corner of the studio an exclusive, pre-lit film set had been constructed for Martha to record her pieces-to-camera for the appeal on behalf of the Police Charities – and to record multiple TV interviews. Each interviewer had been allocated strictly ten minutes – to be fitted in between shooting Martha on the main stage. On a separate highly branded film set, representatives from the various charities, invited celebrities and other VIPs would also be interviewed. Everything ready to go each time in less than a minute by interviewer and cameraman. Production assistants with clipboards, lists and timers ruled the roosts – no arguments. Everyone had received briefing notes in advance – with specific exclusions that were not permitted to be discussed with Martha on pain of being thrown out.

To stage left, camera right were banks of raised audience seating where VIPs and celebrities would be seated, matched to the first night celebrity seating at the 02 – no-one would spot that they had been edited in or not even been at the first night.

Make-up and wardrobe had set up in the dressing rooms and quick-change areas. Anyone seen on camera would be offered *personal enhancement* that would take care of facial wrinkles, lines, and bags under the eyes more likely to be seen on the new super high-resolution pictures. Their clothes would be immaculately pressed and prepared. Everybody was given newly designed Martha Police Charity pins or brooches to unashamedly demonstrate their support.

Production Assistants raced around ensuring everyone who would appear in shot, even subliminally, had signed Artiste Release Agreements – no fee, unlimited global use. *'After all it is for charity,'* they kept saying.

Walkie-talkie equipped runners, or in cinematic terms fourth assistant directors, had been briskly walking back and forth between the studio and the main gate, signing in guests, issuing photo ID, and ushering them to holding areas depending on their pre-determined category and importance. Several minor celebrities and reality show no-marks had arrived at the main gate who were not on the guest list but were chancing their luck. One of Daisy's team was on hand to either sign-in the uninvited ligger after a suitable charitable donation or, with a discreet nod, have security eject them. As the hopefuls waited, they posed for the ever-increasing raucous crowds assembling outside – backing up to the roundabout on Shenley Road. The police were trying, unsuccessfully, to manage the crowds and had called for back-up. As Daisy had briefed her team, 'To be exclusive, you have to exclude.'

The studio's close protection and security teams were jumpy and on edge – no one was permitted to bring in their own minders, for security reasons. Elstree studios was familiar with global A-lister celebrities and their foibles –

and the attempts determined fans would make to gain access. As a result, there were no watchers watching the watchers – security on the Elstree site was too locked down.

Bodkin and Kelly had insisted that they had their own teams at the studios – they didn't know what or whom they were seeking, but anything could happen.

Only a very few Gold AAA – Access All Areas – passes had been issued, all with photographs and holographic security imprints. For this day there were two levels of AAA – Silver and Gold. The silvers were not aware of the golds – so no fragile egos would be potentially bruised.

Stanislaw Nowak sat in a traditional canvas and wood director's chair with his name stencilled on the seat back. Nobody dared admit to him that they were taking the piss. He quietly watched the action evolving around him. Nowak preened with pride – he had almost forgotten the demand for one point two five million pounds. Almost.

Ray, Nowak's driver had parked the car behind the main gate out of sight. Knowing he would not be needed for a while he locked the car with the key fob, then walked up to the catering area for a cup of tea, the paper, a piece of cake, and to watch what was going on.

Keyless car theft is exactly what it sounds like – achieved by cloning the signal from a car's remote key fob. Nowak's Lexus was normally immune to such attack – unless you are supported by Kelly's Technical Services Unit.

Danny sat in an office overlooking where Ray had been told to park the car by an anonymous security guard – one of Kelly's team. Danny intercepted the digital signal from the wireless key fob onto his illicit device. He watched Ray walk up the central avenue towards the George Lucas Stage where Martha was about to start performing. Danny was, not surprisingly, apprehensive. Earlier in the day he and Kelly had discussed what he was about to do.

'Why can't one of your lot get hold of Nowak's phones?' asked Danny.

'We would need all sorts of special permissions for what is, essentially, burglary. If we obtained a search warrant, Nowak would know what we are up to. And we don't want Nowak to know.' Kelly replied, adding quietly, 'Or others for that matter.'

'You managed to bug the car. How did you do that?' Danny was confused.

Kelly smiled, 'Different department. Nothing to do with us. The Home Secretary also gave permission.'

'What happens if I am caught?' Danny demanded.

Kelly wasn't helpful, 'Don't get caught.'

Danny picked up on what Kelly had said, 'Others?'

Kelly said nothing more.

Earlier in the day Danny had also carefully examined the running order – around midday Martha's nineteen-minute song set would be performed, just before the lunch break. Allowing for run-to-record and ending the take that probably gave him twenty minutes – the fifteen or so 'no entry' revolving red lights around the exterior of the studio would be illuminated. The bells would clamour for five seconds. All the doors would be shut and protected by high-viz clad runners who would not allow entry or exit. When the take finished, the red lights would be switched off and two short bells sounded. Danny wouldn't be able to see the lights, but he could hear the bells.

True to form he heard the bells ring for five seconds. As he walked around the corner to Nowak's car, he donned a pair of thin latex gloves. He held his breath and pressed the single button on his device. There was a satisfying clunk as the car unlocked. He checked no-one else was around.

He gingerly opened the driver's door half expecting alarms to sound. Silence. He remembered to breath.

He was about to reach in when he heard two short bells from the studio. He froze in panic. Closed the door and pressed the button to relock the car.

Nothing. No clunk.

He tried again.

Still nothing.

He walked briskly back to his hiding place. If Ray returned to the car, he hoped he wouldn't notice the car was unlocked.

He realised he was shaking. *'Bloody hell, I'm no good at this,'* he said to himself. He found a bottle of water and took a hefty swig.

He heard the long bell again, took a deep breath and walked back outside. The long central avenue up to the studio was empty. He returned to Nowak's car and opened the driver's door still half expecting the alarm to sound – glorious silence.

In the central pocket between the driver's seat and the passenger's seat were three phones. He took a picture on his iPhone so he could return them to their exact position later. From his jacket pocket he took a small laptop and a selection of connecting leads that would fit any mobile phone. He was in luck – he connected the laptop's USB to the charging port of the first phone. Within seconds the contents were copying.

He was frustrated to see that the estimated time was seven minutes. Nothing to do but wait patiently. He left the devices on the driver's seat and walked around the corner to check no-one was approaching. His heart was pounding – he didn't want to be surprised by the imposing figure of Ray, or Nowak for that matter.

Six minutes later he returned to the car. *One percent to go.* Suddenly the display changed to *'file transfer complete.'* He relaxed, slightly.

He connected the second phone. This time the data transferred in less than a minute.

The third phone had a different connector. He fumbled in his pocket to find the right one. He looked at his watch – this had already taken twelve minutes from the red light and bells sounding. He had about eight minutes to complete the task.

Eventually he connected the laptop to the third phone and hit the transfer button. He was horrified to see the message: *'Ten minutes remaining.'*

'Fuck. Fuck. Fuck.' He muttered under his breath.

Eight minutes later he heard the double bell signifying the end of recording.

He reprised his earlier, *'Fuck. Fuck. Fuck.'* As he looked down at the display.

'Four minutes remaining.'

'Can't these bloody things add up' he asked himself, willing the annoying transfer bar to rush to the right. It remained obstinately passive.

He walked back out to look up the central avenue to the studio – people were spilling out of the studio doors into the fresh air. Danny could hear the excited chatter. Clearly Martha had been on song. But no one coming down towards him.

He dashed back to Nowak's car. *Two minutes remaining.*

He felt his body begin to sweat and his heart race.

'One minute remaining.'

'Are you Mr Nowak's driver?' The voice came from just out of sight around the corner.

Danny heard Ray's unmistakably voice reply, 'Yes. That's me.'

'You are not displaying a parking badge. Please can you accompany me down to the security desk to collect one.' Asked the other voice.

'What now?' responded Ray. 'I only came back to the car to collect a phone for Mr Nowak.'

'It won't take a minute. I'm going off duty soon and the afternoon team won't know who the car belongs to. Security is tight today.' The other voice was insistent.

Danny was terrified. He didn't want to be caught – and the plan was to transfer the contents of the phones without being discovered. He made to pull the plug.

'Thirty seconds remaining,' tormented the laptop's screen.

'Okay,' said Ray. 'I only have a minute. Mr Nowak gets very irritable if he is kept waiting.'

Danny heard footsteps retreating down to the security cabin.

'Transfer complete.'

'*At bloody last,*' Danny muttered, sweating even more. His heart was racing. He disconnected the final phone and carefully returned all three to the centre storage box, taking care to replace them in exactly the same positions, checking with the picture he had taken earlier. He pocketed the small laptop and the leads, checked around that he had not left any incriminating evidence and quietly shut the door. He pressed the button on the cloning device – the car remained resolutely unlocked. He had to get out of there. He removed his latex gloves and walked back out to the central avenue, colliding with the incoming Ray brandishing a piece of paper.

'Hi Ray,' Danny was chirpy despite his banging heart.

'Bloody security demanded we put a poxy bit of paper on the dashboard. Don't they know who Mr Nowak is?' Ray replied.

'You'd think so with all the fuss here today.' Danny was at his best, considering the circumstances. The small laptop felt as if it was burning a hole in his jacket pocket. He walked with Ray back towards Nowak's car in the hope of diverting his attention from the car not unlocking. 'Have you seen any of the show yet?'

They reached the car. Ray took out his key.

'It's bloody amazing,' replied Ray, pressing the key fob. Danny coughed whilst metaphorically crossing everything.

Ray opened the door, without noticing anything amiss. He reached into the centre pocket and took out one of the phones before locking the door with a satisfying clunk and two beeps. Together they walked back out to the central avenue.

'Are you going back up,' asked Ray.

'Will do in a few minutes. Have a couple of things to do. See you for lunch?' Danny replied. Ray walked away back up the hill.

The security guard saw the ashen-faced perspiring Danny. 'You okay?'

'Thank you,' replied Danny. 'That was quick thinking.'

'Thank you, Sir.' The security guard gave Danny one of his best smiles, confused – he had no idea what Danny was talking about. 'Important that we have all the right paperwork especially for a day like today with all these celebs on site.'

Danny saw Kelly's DC waiting in the warm near the entrance to the bar – he couldn't get rid of the mini-laptop with the phone data quick enough. There was a brief exchange of thanks and Danny was free – he bounded up Elstree's central avenue with the weight of the world no longer on his shoulders. The tension release transferred to his stomach – he realised he was starving.

He joined the queue for the crew catering up the metal steps to the normal *Starring-Meals-on-Wheel's* catering truck. The crew member behind him talked whilst they waited. 'Don't you qualify for the VIP lunch?' She asked.

'I don't know how you do it, the thought of pandering to all those monstrous egos is just dreadful.' Danny shook his head.

'I ignore them all. They ignore me. I am invisible.' The crew member responded.

'Wish I was at times.' Danny's introspection surprised him.

'You're lucky. They need you. Without you they, and their mates, wouldn't be a celebrity. It's you that puts them on the pedestal.' Was the crew member's thoughtful response.

'You are bloody right. I can't do this any longer. This celebrity bollocks.' Danny vehemence startled them both. 'I'm going back to what I love when all this is over.'

'What's that?' asked the crew member.

'Investigative journalism,' was Danny's response.

Shirley interrupted his thoughts. 'Eating with the hoi polloi today?'

'Not you as well,' said Danny sharing the joke with the crew member. 'What's good?'

'It's all good of course.' was Shirley's good-humoured reply. 'But I made the lamb hot pot and the celeriac mash.

'Well, that's it then, no choice,' Danny laughed.

'Me too please Shirley.' The crew member and Danny walked over with their trays to a spare table.

They continued chatting for half an hour before going their separate ways. Danny to find Daisy. The crew member to make a phone call.

DAY FOURTEEN
WEDNESDAY

85 ALBERT EMBANKMENT

85 ALBERT EMBANKMENT IN THE SOUTH WESTERN part of central London, on the bank of the River Thames beside Vauxhall Bridge, had been the headquarters of MI6, the Secret Intelligence Service since 1994, when it moved from the *"irredeemably insecure"* Century House – the 22-storey office block not far from Waterloo main-line railway station described as *"London's worst-kept secret, known to every taxi driver, tourist guide, and KGB agent"*. The new building, much more secure but also as well-known, is rumoured to include a tunnel under the Thames to Whitehall – one of many tunnels that criss-cross the Government's estates.

Nothing is left to chance – the SIS's meeting rooms are swept and searched before every meeting by personnel from GCHQ.

The green tinted windows around the exterior of the building and those overlooking the River Thames, are triple- or quadruple-layered to provide some reduction from the sun's intensity when it appears in London – but by no means the main reason. The randomly angled middle layer or layers of glass have transducers attached, diffusing variable velocity and amplitude ramping pink and white noise, inaudible to the occupants of the room, but designed to confuse and prevent out-of-visible-spectrum bounced laser beams from decoding the conversations going on within – effectively preventing the glass from acting as a microphone.

On the fifth of March one year, Joseph Stalin's birthday, one joker had replaced the white and pink noise with Wolfgang Amadeus Mozart's Piano Concerto number twenty-three in A major, *Köchel Verzeichnis 488* – the concerto for piano and orchestra – reportedly to which Stalin repeatedly listened after his wife had committed suicide. The head of the SIS was confused when he received from the London Head of Russia's FSB – apparently for no reason – a gift-wrapped CD of the piece together with a bottle of Mamont Siberian Vodka. Cyber security and scientific officers could find nothing wrong with either. "*An idiosyncratic gift*" was reported in the log.

A security anachronism meant that only the name of the chair is recorded in the meeting room log – the other participants are not named. Which was just as well considering what was being discussed and by whom.

At exactly eleven o'clock Angela Fitzpatrick cleared her throat. 'Right then, we ought to make a start.'

Cups of tea and coffee were returned to their saucers. Rich Tea biscuits were finished – dropped crumbs brushed off clothes. The room wasn't exactly alive to the nuances of bonhomie – but it nevertheless settled.

As everyone was on her turf, she fulfilled the role as chair – known as Angie to her friends, part of her role was MI6's Senior Verification Officer managing the relationship between MI6 and the government, responsible for validating any intelligence received. She also had a wider confidential remit seeking out corruption in high places – coordinating a small team that few, even within the SIS building, knew about. 'As a reminder nothing leaves this room. All notes, if you make any, to be shredded before departing.'

Around the table the others nodded in agreement – earlier they had all stored their phones, tablets, laptops, briefcases, and other impedimenta in secure lockers just off the magnificent, marbled reception area. This was as secure as they thought they were ever going to be – but none were happy to be there, to have the past raked over.

Deputy Assistant Commissioner Keith Wallace was in his everyday uniform – it was not unusual for him to attend security meetings at the home of the SIS. Today, in uniform, he was shown in the Metropolitan Police log as off-site all morning.

The Right Honourable Michael Ramsey, Minister of State for Crime and Policing in Her Majesty's UK Government wore a dark pin-striped suit, white shirt, and sober checked tie. He had to deliver the closing statement later in the debating chamber of The House, as the UK Parliament is colloquially known. The Government was attempting to increase Police spending but didn't want to be seen to be too extravagant with public funds. His speech writers had included some political point-scoring, *'It's too easy to spend money we don't have as the party opposite has demonstrated to the country's cost on too many occasions.'* When he concluded, with a carefully rehearsed flourish, he would commend the proposal to The House – supported by back-benchers waving their order papers. The Speaker of the House would call for a vote by acclamation – the volume of 'ayes' and 'noes' often indistinguishable which inevitably lead to a division. The annunciator video screens declared 'Division.' Three hundred and eighty-four bells within the Parliamentary estate, and one hundred and seventy-two outside it, including several in private homes, would sound giving MPs just eight minutes to dash to their chosen lobby to vote for or against the resolution. Party Whips were on standby to ensure that there were no navigation errors.

The Minister hoped he would have time after this current meeting to speak with his political supporter, Eddy, the owner of *The Daily Tribune* – he needed his media support for future prime-ministerial aspirations and to shaft *the current PM, that bloody woman Mrs Campbell-Horrocks.*

Edwin 'Eddy' Porterhouse was allegedly the hands-off owner of *The Daily Tribune* – the current editor had christened him Eddy as he couldn't keep his hands-off editing and politically positioning *his baby* – the pejorative nick-name pun was not lost on anyone except Edwin himself. Today in black jeans and a pink polo shirt he sprawled across two chairs, his feet – clad in brown leather deck shoes with no socks – on a third chair. He was Kelvin Edwards' boss, the showbiz and gossip columnist from, which Eddy had self-styled in one of his oft-repeated *hands-off* moments, *the UK's leading celebrity daily news-paper and on-line blog spot.*

Pelham DeCourcy was probably the most nervous. Despite being thoroughly accustomed to confidential discussions, the location of the meeting had spooked him. He aspired, in a few years, to become one of the Deputy Governors of the Bank of England – if he kept his nose clean. He was a typical banker who was never seen without his gold-and-red-striped Marylebone Cricket Club tie – except on the day before the Christmas holidays when he'd push the boat out with a daring tie which incorporated eight reindeer. Any hint of financial impropriety or scandal would put paid to his hopes and dreams.

The sixth person around the table was deliberately the least memorable. An off-the-peg dark-grey suit, white shirt, a Brigade of Guards burgundy and dark blue diagonally striped silk tie with matching pocket square, black socks, and black brogues. *Never brown in town,* he would tell any man joining his department. Everyone knew him simply as Sefton – not his real name, but an alias he had given himself in tribute to Sefton Delmer, one of Churchill's *camoufleurs* or deception wizards from World War Two. Sefton's office was not in the SIS building, but he was certainly familiar with it and its super-secure spaces.

What several of them had in common was a relationship with Stanislaw Nowak that had begun over ten years ago – which they wished, in hindsight, that they hadn't initiated.

All hoped their sins would remain forever hidden – they craved to learn from today's meeting that the thorough cover-up would once and for all allow them to continue their professional lives without the counterfeit disabled badges, their Sword of Damocles, hanging over them.

Michael Ramsey was first to speak, even in closed meetings he liked the sound of his own voice. 'So, where are we? Have we at last got *all* the copies of that bloody journalist's outrageous poisonous piece and photographs? All the computer files deleted. The alleged evidence lost. This was meant to have been sorted out years ago – bloody incompetence.' He glared at everyone around the table, 'I know I can rely on you Edwin. But really, can I? I don't want to see a picture of me from ten years ago in your competitors' newspapers either – or anywhere else for that matter.'

Around the table there were enthusiastic nods of agreement – hiding the private thought, *'pompous twat.'* They might have a collective interest but that didn't mean they were friends or even had to like each other.

Ramsey's face was red. Perspiration dribbled down his forehead. 'And what about that bloody man, Nowak? We need to ensure he remains silent… for ever too... He knows where the skeletons are buried… And I don't want to be one of them... Bloody shame *that bullet* didn't hit him… He could still fuck us all over. No-one will miss the shite.'

Ramsey rarely used profanities in public. His speech was littered with pauses to allow him to get air into his hyperventilating system.

Sefton and Angela Fitzpatrick exchanged glances – the way Ramsey spoke of *that bullet* caught their attention.

DAC Wallace made a mental note as well. This was the first time he had heard *his colleague, his unlikely ally, his associate, his political sponsor or whatever*, speak so vehemently.

'Thank you Minister. I spoke to Nowak a few weeks ago, before the tragic first night. He was at Elstree overseeing rehearsals of that Martha concert he is producing.' Angela chose her words carefully, 'He is as concerned as anyone about all this getting out. He reminded me about the injury to Danny Owen's foot – I think he thought he was frightening me. He threatened to ruin my career if I didn't comply. Made all sorts of vile medieval threats. He said Danny's foot would be nothing compared to what he would do me. He didn't like me laughing at him.'

'Are we all in danger?' Pelham DeCourcy was naively nervous. 'Is the shooting of the policeman connected with Nowak, do you suppose?'

Eddy interrupted, 'Bloody great for sales though. Nothing like the random assassination of a policeman to increase circulation.'

Angela firmly held Wallace's arm – holding him back from physically attacking the newspaper owner. Emotions were already running high.

'Gentlemen, please. Bickering won't get us anywhere.' Angela Fitzpatrick's calm voice belied her private opinion of these white middle-aged men (mostly) in suits at testosterone-fuelled occasions. *If only God had put men's brains in their hearts rather than between their legs*, she had once said at an Oxford Union debate to thunderous applause.

'Sefton, perhaps you'd like to bring us up to speed please?' Angela was a believer that no meeting should last longer than one hour – they had already wasted ten minutes.

'Thank you, Ms Fitzpatrick,' Sefton began formally. 'Let me start at the beginning.'

'Oh! Please do,' interrupted Michael Ramsey. Angela gave him a stern look. Sefton wasn't deterred in the slightest.

Sefton continued. 'As we all know, Stanislaw Nowak's offer of free or easier parking, no congestion zone payments and so on by using the blue badge, disabled parking scheme was very tempting – his enterprise's blue badges were excellent forgeries for which not inconsiderable sums of money were paid by many people.'

Eddy Porterhouse was about to interject – Angela's look restrained him.

'Regrettably, the investigative journalist Danny Owen, then of the now defunct *The Weekend News*, found out about the scheme – we know not how – and wrote a potentially damaging feature with accompanying photographs. Mr Owen's detailed assessment and insider information is alarmingly accurate – he did write, that using an alter ego, he negotiated with Mr Nowak for the purchase of a badge for twenty thousand pounds. He did also interview, or attempt to interview, many potential and actual purchasers including several around this table. *The Weekend News* would have ruined many peoples' Sunday morning breakfasts – and almost certainly several careers.'

This time Porterhouse couldn't be restrained. 'Weekend News. Bloody awful rag. Deserved to go bust.'

'Thank you, Mr Porterhouse for your considered opinion.

I will continue. Some might say that by good fortune Mr Owen's article came to the attention of Mr Nowak just before it was published. With some persuasion from Mr Nowak and his associates, involving a sledgehammer and threats to members of Mr Owen's family, the piece was…' Sefton look at Porterhouse, '…I believe the expression is, err, spiked?'

Eddy simply nodded.

'If the piece had reached publication those around this table – and several, maybe many others – might not be in the positions they are today. As we all know it is a criminal offence to misuse a disabled badge and doing so can lead to a £1,000 fine. However, the knowing use of a counterfeit badge is a more serious offence with a considerably larger fine followed by, almost certainly, a period of incarceration. The adverse publicity and disqualification from certain private, public and professional offices would also be a career limiting serious issue. DCS Kelly's team has been investigating Mr Nowak's activities for some years. Frustratingly he has yet to deliver evidence that would satisfy the Crown Prosecution Service. Several witnesses contracted severe bouts of amnesia due to intimidation similar to that delivered to Mr Owen, with equally long-term effects. The CPS offered therapeutic help necessary both to assist their recovery and to give their best evidence in criminal proceedings, but regrettably with little success. Witness protection was declined.'

Sefton did not need notes.

Wallace was about to interrupt but was silenced by Angela. 'You'll have your turn DAC Wallace.'

'The blue badge scheme began to be reformed in 2011 with the changeover to secure printing, supply and distribution.

Central to the reforms was the desire to crack down on drivers who abuse the scheme. The most obvious change was the new badge design, which made it much more durable and far harder to counterfeit, together with a common database of badge holders to enable verification checks to be made quickly and easily. A web-based management information system was created for local authorities which the police and traffic wardens could easily access.'

Even the normally benign Pelham DeCourcy was getting frustrated by the plodding assessment. 'With the greatest of respect Sefton, how does all this affect us? Are we out of the woods so to speak? We know most of this.'

'Thank you, Mr DeCourcy. We might, but I do believe that context is important in all matters. Although a few years ago, and Mr Nowak's badges now not able to be utilised for reasons just highlighted, the adverse events if their use by those around this table and others was revealed, as I have discussed, would still be potentially catastrophic.'

There was shared discomfort as the change to life and livelihoods was reconsidered.

'It was thought that Mr Owen's writings and accompanying photographs from ten years ago had gone for good. Regrettably, this is not the case as they appear to have re-emerged through two routes. Firstly, via journalist Yuliet Spooner of the Centre for Covert Media Studies who was furnished with a file by a woman, identity unknown. Ms Spooner and Mr Owen are known to each other and have in the past collaborated on several front-page investigative pieces of journalism. Secondly, through Detective Chief Superintendent Kelly's team's investigations into Mr

Nowak's potential people smuggling operations utilising the vehicles of the Martha concert tour. Also being investigated by Ms Spooner and Mr Owen.'

'What people smuggling operation?' The Minister interrupted, 'Did anyone of us know about this? Is this something we can use against Nowak?'

Sefton coughed, took a sip of water.

'I'll come onto that later if I may. Nowak has been a person-of-interest for several years by many UK, European, US and Soviet policing and security agencies. He appears as if he is trying to regularise his affairs.

Sefton prepared himself for the big reveal.

'Ten years ago, DS Maguire – and now we understand with the help of his uncle, a senior serving police officer – obtained a counterfeit Blue Badge for his parents free of charge… in exchange for Maguire providing intelligence that would be of benefit to Mr Nowak. Furthermore, we know that not long before he was killed DS Maguire admitted to DCS Kelly that he had been liaising with Mr Nowak, passing on to him what should have been confidential internal intelligence. We also know that a more senior officer must have also been supplying Mr Nowak with information too. Don't we DAC Wallace?'

Wallace was about to say something again, Sefton beckoned him to remain silent. Wallace felt the room become uncomfortably hot, whilst keeping his counsel. *Was that an accusation or merely a request for confirmation?*

'I understand that DCS Kelly's evidence has disappeared?' quizzed Wallace with a smug smile belying his angst.

'Yes indeed. A good piece of work there DAC Wallace.'

If the room was shocked, that was nothing compared to how Wallace was feeling. *How the hell did Sefton know that?* Wallace asked himself.

'It's a shame DCS Kelly knows about the surveillance equipment you installed. He sent a picture of the unmarked equipment to Fort Monckton for identification and tracking.'

Wallace was now feeling distressingly uncomfortable – the room even hotter.

'The Fort sent the request up the chain to the JIC, who contacted me. They were concerned a senior police officer was the subject of surveillance without their knowledge.' Sefton was enjoying Wallace's discomfort. 'Luckily, I already had some fiction in place – and was able to produce a couple of Minutes from various meetings. All false of course. But the paper trail never lies, does it? Internal investigation branch. Bent coppers. Connections with serious crime. Bad apples. Suspicion of informers. Other nationals. An excellent smoke-screen.'

There was a mixture of pleasure and relief in the room. Wallace was still agitated.

Sefton was beginning to enjoy himself, though was careful not to let it show. 'What we do not know is who passed the large file to Ms Spooner. Not just containing Mr Owen's article and photographs, but considerably more information about Mr Nowak's activities. I can confirm that the file has been retrieved from Ms Spooner's safe at her office and, additionally, a duplicate from her home.'

Angela Fitzpatrick was accomplished in the art of deception, so remained impassive. *Just because something is spoken, it doesn't make it true*, she thought. She snorted out loud with suppressed laughter. *If only everyone else knew of Sefton's and my plans. Or realised it was me who gave Yuliet the edited file.*

'So, we're in the clear?' challenged the Right Honourable Michael Ramsey, ignoring Angela's suppressed snigger. He had remained uncharacteristically silent during Sefton's briefing. 'Evidence destroyed? Only Nowak and that journalist to go.'

Angela and Sefton exchanged glances – Ramsey's comment about *Nowak and that journalist* raised their already heightened suspicions. How to prove them another matter.

'Maybe. Of immediate interest is the close relationship between DCS Kelly, Ms Spooner and Mr Owen. They, Kelly's team, and their associates have been meeting discreetly in locations around London. Upon discovering the break-in at Ms Spooner's house, DCS Kelly himself attended. They then all departed for an unknown location. They know they are still being watched; they do not know by whom. They did take several successful precautions to prevent surveillance by both HumInt and SigInt which is why and how we lost them.' Sefton made no mention of the surveillance devices in Yuliet Spooner's office and home.

'Still being watched?' picked up Wallace. 'Still? I thought that my surveillance team had been arrested by Kelly. Are there others?'

'Indeed *still*, DAC Wallace. Going back in time, it appears that there was interest in several groups by various intelligence organisations not just our own. For a while Russia's FSB were taking an unhealthy interest in our gallant gang. At one point they tried to abduct Mr Owen, whom we now discover that the FSB thought was in cahoots with Mr Nowak, The Vory, Conor O'Murchadha and Ali Baka. Luckily, our chaps were on hand to save him.' Sefton revealed some of what he and Angela knew as a sop to add candour and veracity. 'No harm apart from a headache, a few bruises and a broken phone.'

Eddy interrupted, 'I know about The Vory, but who the hell are Conor O'Murchadha and Ali Baka. And what have they got to do with us?'

Sefton's answer was patronisingly suave, 'Regrettably they only had an interest in Mr Nowak. I was hoping that Messrs O'Murchadha and Baka were going to take care of Mr Nowak on our behalf. Unfortunately, they are both deceased. Victims of The Vory. The FSB interest has now also dispersed as they were only interested in bringing to heel The Vory, Russia's super Mafia. They have no interest in domestic people smuggling activities or in Mr Nowak.'

'More's the pity,' interrupted Ramsey. 'Nowak has to go.'

Sefton ignored the comment but made a mental note of Ramsey's almost morbid fascination with Nowak. 'With the disappearance of the FSB, our home teams were exposed. However, DCS Kelly did put surveillance on Nowak – in his investigation of Nowak's smuggling and other activities. He doesn't know that we know his team discovered our surveillance in Nowak's apartment. However, our home team has not been as circumspect as they should have been. This will be reflected in their annual appraisals. Luckily, DAC Wallace was at hand to defuse what could have been several difficult situations. Surveillance equipment has been installed at various locations that have provided us with useful intelligence that might help to protect those that might need protecting.'

'So, what the fuck are you saying?' demanded Eddy Porterhouse. 'Are we safe? Are you saying that our past indiscretions won't come back to bite us on the arse?'

'Not entirely. I am saying the physical evidence has more than likely disappeared. But there are several who might be party to anecdotal evidence and who may be the author of our potential downfall.' Sefton was circumspect.

There was silence around the table. Angela Fitzpatrick was about to speak when Wallace unleashed the elephant in the room. 'Does anyone have any idea why Detective Sergeant Michael Maguire was shot? And is there a connection to what we have been discussing? Nowak must be the link.'

The Minister interjected looking directly at Wallace, 'Can we also rely on Detective Chief Inspector Bodkin not to go off-piste and delve into Nowak and his other affairs? Can you guarantee that Bodkin will concentrate solely on the, er, unfortunate death of DS Maguire?'

'Nothing in life is certain,' Sefton was suave. 'Except taxes and death, of course.'

DAC Wallace interrupted, 'I have made it clear to DCI Bodkin that his interest should only be in the unfortunate demise of Maguire. Anything or anyone else is outside his remit. DCS Kelly is National Crime Agency and does not report to me, so I have less sway with his investigations. Kelly and Bodkin do seem close though. I understand they were in police college together. I have insisted Bodkin keeps me fully briefed.'

Michael Ramsey banged the table in anger, 'So Kelly's a bloody loose cannon, is he? Can't you do anything?'

'Michael, we are all in this together.' Wallace was at his smarmy best.

'Don't you fucking-well *Michael* me. I'm a Minister of State. You will address me as Minister,' demanded Ramsey pompously.

'Not in here I don't. We are all in this together. Brothers-in-arms…' Wallace showed some unexpected backbone. He looked at Angela Fitzpatrick, '… and sisters. We are in this shit together *Michael*.'

Sefton and Angela Fitzpatrick yet again exchanged imperceptible looks. The meeting was going exactly as they hoped.

Wallace then spoke quietly. 'That journalist Danny Owen recognised me on the television, on the news, after Maguire's funeral. He accused me of purchasing a blue badge from Nowak. He said he has photographic evidence. Kelly was there as well when he made the allegations. I told them I was a covert part of the investigation. Collecting evidence. I told them to look at the files. Kelly didn't believe me, made all sorts of disrespectful insubordinate suggestions. Mr Danny Owen is a danger to us all.'

'And Nowak,' reminded Ramsey.

Before anyone could comment Angela Fitzpatrick interrupted. 'Right, we've had an hour. I suggest we leave it there for now. Sefton thank you for that excellent summary. And thank you for your work behind the scenes. Nothing more any of you can do for now. I will contact you all in the normal way with further developments.' She stood. 'I'll escort you all back to reception where you can collect your things.'

'We can't just leave it there.' Wallace interrupted, 'What

about me? That bloody journo and Kelly know about me. Who else do they know about?'

'We'll discuss that at our next meeting. For today time is up.' Angela Fitzpatrick insisted. Despite working for the SIS, she could be remarkably adept at applying Civil Service standard operating procedures: *Meetings never overrun. Outstanding items adjourned until the next meeting.*

As they took their leave from the building Michael Ramsey grabbed Eddy Porterhouse firmly by the arm out of earshot from the rest. 'There's this saying that bandies about Washington: *"it's not the crime, but the cover-up"*. My belief is that only idiots subscribe to that. It's always about the crime. The whole point of a cover-up is that full disclosure of the original sin is not survivable. The cover-up is simply another crime. The only answer is for everything to go away once and for all. Nowak and Danny Owen are the threats.'

'Don't forget Yuliet Spooner knows as well,' offered Eddy.

With that Ramsey walked off along the River Thames at a brisk pace in the direction of Parliament. Porterhouse hailed a cab – he did not offer to share it with DeCourcy or Wallace.

Angela Fitzpatrick stood beside Sefton who had lingered in reception. 'Shall we continue upstairs?'

'Why not?' replied Sefton.

Ten minutes later they were in Angela Fitzpatrick's office. Sefton removed his jacket arranging it carefully using one of the hangers on the coat hooks. They settled into two armchairs around an informal table; each had a vibrant red mug of coffee poured from the Thermos jug on the side table.

No fresh milk, just a selection of sachets of various creamers, sugars, and sweeteners.

'You've been promoted since we last met?' suggested Sefton.

Angela smiled but said nothing.

Sefton looked around the modern office. A large world map dominated one wall – with no extra marking revealing potential places of interest. There were some personal effects – no pictures of partners, Angela hadn't been successful at longer term relationships mainly due to the secrecy of her work. There were half a dozen sporting trophies; a photograph of her parents on the beach in El Cotillo, towards the north-west coast of Fuerteventura in the Canary Islands – she had enjoyed many a Christmas in the warm sunshine at her parent's villa. Alongside the photo of her late parents was a picture of her grandparents, obviously taken several years ago by the professional photographer at a formal dinner – her grandmother in a long black three-quarter sleeved A-line chiffon evening gown set off by a single row of pearls; her grandfather, the recently discussed Commander Barry Fitzpatrick, was in full dress uniform.

'Well, what do you think?' asked Angela. 'Where are we?'

Sefton took a sip of his coffee before carefully returning the mug to the mat on the table beside him. He disliked mugs, preferring the more traditional fine china cup and saucer. He adjusted the mat and mug several times until they were in perfect alignment with the side of the table. 'Bodkin continues to investigate the assassination of your cousin, DS Michael Maguire. Did you know him well?'

'Not really. Not a close cousin. Normal weddings, funerals, and large family gatherings. Of course, it was incredibly sad, but I haven't really been in mourning. We spoke. Friendly enough but didn't seem to have a lot in common especially since his parents, my parents and my grandfather all died. He didn't know what I do for a living – he thought I was *a girlie* in the administrative section of the Civil Service. We sort of lost touch as some families do. Michael Maguire was close to my grandfather – his uncle. As was I – probably loved my grandfather more than my parents. I went to the funeral yesterday but didn't go on to the wake – all those police people telling inappropriate war stories, over too many pints of beer wasn't for me.'

They both laughed in mutual disrespect for their New Scotland Yard colleagues.

'Yuliet Spooner didn't attend, so there was no question of me being recognised. No-one but you and I know that she has hidden a third copy of the file I passed to her whilst she was sitting on the bench eating her lunch. Or the copy I have here in my safe.' Angela's personal document safe was inset into the ferro concrete outer wall of her office. 'It might be time for an edited copy to get back to Mr Owen. Maybe we redact a few names. We know that Mr Owen recognised DAC Wallace. I was surprised that Wallace admitted it. That raised the tension a bit.' They both shared a smile. Angela had the intellect and cunning to interpret multiple threats and threads. 'Not sure Mr Owen has put two-and-two together with Minister Ramsey. We have to decide what our end game is here?'

'Off the record, we need to understand the role of your

grand-father – we want to ensure he is not seen to become involved.' Sefton smiled for what might have been the first time.

Angela acknowledged Sefton's kindness. Both Angela Fitzpatrick and Sefton were adept liars and dissemblers in the service of their country. Both subscribed to Adolf Hitler's school of thought: *If you tell a big enough lie and tell it frequently enough, it will be believed.*

'Wallace and Ramsey have been in cahoots for some time. Both Freemasons. And both shit-scared that their indiscretions will affect their career progression.' Sefton was naturally duplicitous, 'What with Wallace hypothetically becoming an MP and Ramsey potentially, probably PM, our decision is whether we let them run and, at some time in the future, recruit them for our mutual benefit whatever their crimes. And of course, for the benefit of our great country. Or, do we *persuade* them, no more talk of budget cuts, or regrettable investigations into this department's past activities, for example? We could own them.'

Angela, nodded in agreement. 'Interesting thinking.'

Sefton ignored Angela. He was in full flight, 'Wallace, of course, is disposable. Ramsey will be much more useful. But I think it's time we investigated Wallace and Ramsey further – I don't trust either of them. They both have political ambitions and I get the sense at any cost… at any cost.'

Sefton amused himself by the thought of costing political ambition.

'The higher they climb, the easier it is to knock them off…' he paused, smiled sardonically, '… or do we offer them a life-line? One they would find difficult to refuse.'

'Is our cover watertight?' asked Angela. Sefton and Angela had both been given the budget and authorisation from on-high to purchase counterfeit blue badges. They had both used new working aliases – in-house Special Resources had created legends, phoney bank statements, utilities bills and more just in case.

'The cover story should be watertight. The legends were designed to look good, but deliberately wouldn't stand up to the scrutiny if Nowak delved deeply.' Sefton was the acknowledged master of duplicity. 'We couldn't look too good. Many people use false names. I doubt whether any of our select group have seen our badges, or our chosen names. And I doubt whether Nowak can remember what he sold and to whom. It was over ten years ago. I doubt whether he kept written records. I suggest that Nowak himself isn't actually a source of concern to any of them, but it helped us to stoke that particular fire.'

Sefton was also the king of the allegories.

Angela suddenly had a bout of realisation, 'The danger is that journalist's article and photographs? That means that Danny Owen might well be vulnerable, possibly more so that Nowak?'

'Indeed.' Sefton mused.

'What about DeCourcy and Porterhouse? There are many others as well not in our…' she contemplated before continuing, '… immediate circle who may or may not appear in Danny Owens's original exposé?'

'I think we can rely on Eddy Porterhouse's rag to toe the line in the future – he might ruck up for a while whilst we have the discussion, but he has nowhere to hide. DeCourcy is a bumbling idiot who has reached his own level of incompetence. He won't be a loss to the bank.'

'And Nowak?'

'He knows that we know he knows that someone has surveillance in his apartment. But he doesn't know about his car or the additional crew member on the concert tour,' reported Sefton. 'She hasn't provided any grade one intelligence. She has managed to get herself liked by most people, especially Jimmy Patrick, the tour manager. She had an on-set lunch with Danny Owen but it wasn't that useful apart from initiating a relationship that she might be able to leverage. She reported that he was fed up with celebrity and showbusiness, and I don't blame him for that, she said he wanted to get back to investigative journalism. But nothing really of use to us... yet. I'm going to leave her in place for the rest of Martha's concert tour. Might be useful long term. It's not costing us any budget, as she is being paid by Nowak. Perfect irony. We'll offer her a small bonus when the task is completed. And will help her with future employment. I can't see her being of further general use to us. Maybe only surveillance?'

'Agreed. We were lucky to find her. She had just completed several rigging qualifications. She's the daughter of one of my researchers, who told me about her over coffee in the canteen. She was very proud. Apparently, her daughter passed all the courses with distinction.' Angela looked down and read from her always-with-her non-confidential notebook, 'UK Rigging are one of only two PLASA-approved centres chosen to deliver the National Rigging Certificate Qualification.'

'PLASA?' asked Sefton.

'No idea,' replied Angela. 'But fortuitous for us. It was easy enough to get her a working apprenticeship with the Martha tour.'

Angela opened her confidential notebook, which never left her office and was locked away when she was not there – *safer than any digital device,* she told the geeks. She added an item to her things-to-do-list. 'If our Mr Owen does return to investigative journalism, and even if he doesn't, he could become extremely useful to us. It's in his psyche to investigate. A journalist hides in plain sight as well – many a journalist has batted for our team.'

Sefton agreed. He liked cricketing metaphors – he was considered to be the fastest and most aggressive swing bowler to have ever played for his village cricket team. 'Maybe it's time we had a word with him? Kelly seems to rate him. If you are correct, he could become a useful asset in the future?'

'Agreed. I'll start unobtrusively vetting him. Let's thoroughly check him out before we tap him on the shoulder.' Angela added to her note.

Sefton stood, took a small notebook and a digital recorder from his jacket pocket. He ensured that the jacket was perfectly returned to its hanger then sat back down – giving the jacket a sharp brush with the back of his hand to remove an invisible fragment of nothingness. He also made a note on the tiny pad using his Parker Duofold fountain pen.

Angela waited whilst Sefton carefully screwed the top back on the pen.

'Do you know how Bodkin is getting on?' Angela concealed her laugh at her colleague's prissiness.

'Not officially.' Sefton handed Angela a sheet of glossy

photographic paper. 'Bodkin has received this information suggesting the bullet was intended for Nowak. The trajectory animation implies that Maguire's death was an unfortunate accident – he stood up at exactly the wrong moment, taking the round instead of Nowak.'

'How did you get this?' asked Angela.

Sefton didn't answer, merely shook his head, indicating *need to know* – and Angela didn't need to know. 'That's awful. Do you think Nowak realises?'

'Oh yes, he knows all right. GCHQ traced a conversation he had with a telephone number in Bishkek. Persons unknown.'

'Where's Bishkek?' Angela had an idea it was vaguely somewhere in central Asia.

'Kyrgyzstan. Landlocked. Almost bang in the centre of Asia.' Sefton stood again and pointed at the map on the wall. He sat, drank some coffee, then carefully returned the mug to take up perfect symmetry once more on the table. 'Bill Kelly also knows – we piggy backed on the surveillance equipment his team had installed in Nowak's car.'

Sefton pressed play on his small Olympus digital recorder. Nowak's voice was clear but stressed.

'Let's get straight to the point. I owe Baka one million pounds. But he is dead? Debt gone.'

'Did you hear me?'

'My arrangements were with Ali Baka. He is dead. Why should I pay you, and pay you more than I owe?'

'I need time to raise the money.'

'I need eight weeks. And if Martha dies, I won't have any money.'

'Okay, I'll do my best. Four weeks from today.'

'Nowak's being blackmailed then?' asked Angela. 'With Ali Baka dead I presumed The Vory have directly taken on the debt?'

'That's what we thought initially.' Sefton stood.

'GCHQ time matched the phone call – we know that Nowak was speaking with a Vory freelance enforcer and debt collector. The Enforcer takes twenty five percent of any debt recovered, so he will return three quarters of a million to The Vory and keeps the rest. The Vory won't know he added his, let's call it a finder's fee. So, stands to collect half a million pounds less expenses.' Sefton was precise and unemotional.

'This still doesn't make sense. Why attempt to kill Nowak?' Angela was confused.

'Certainly, a conundrum. Why indeed?' Sefton drank more coffee, carefully wiped his lips with a paper serviette and once more returned the mug to its symmetrical resting place.

'Let's assume then that as you say the target was Nowak, and Maguire was an unfortunate accident. But as you say this would leave us with a puzzle...' Angela stood and looked out her window overlooking the Thames, 'and we can agree that we are both fascinated by the things we don't really understand, or comprehend, or challenge us. Like Marc Breman's fiendish crossword.' Both Sefton and Angela had been working on solving it for over a year.

Angela turned away from the window to face Sefton. 'Why would The Vory or their enforcer want Nowak dead as the chances of recovering their debt would almost certainly spiral down to zero.'

Sefton was quizzical. 'So, who else would benefit from Nowak's death? Who could afford to recruit an assassin? Or who couldn't afford not to? Was The Vory's enforcer simply lucky that someone else had decided Nowak's time had come, and used that luck to leverage his position with Nowak? Who stands to benefit from Nowak's death? Maybe they don't even know about the money he owes? Maybe it's time to rattle a few cages?'

'What are you suggesting?' Angela was intrigued.

'Some of Danny Owen's photographs and a redacted and edited version of his piece from ten years ago probably needs to reach our Eddy?' contemplated Sefton.

'Do we include Wallace in the redaction or not?' Angela was deep in thought. 'His name would certainly pepper up the story. Maybe we should include a few lesser mortals not in our select group just to stir the shit and so we don't draw attention to the source of this information?'

There were a few moments silence as they both contemplated.

'Maybe Pelham DeCourcy as well? Definitely not our Minister.' Sefton suggested, sneering when he mentioned *our Minister*. 'He is too useful. But we will have him by the balls. We'll keep Eddy faeces-free for the moment too. He remains useful if he does as he is told.'

'We know Yuliet Spooner has a third copy of the file hidden somewhere.' Sefton revealed. 'Maybe time to bring her back into play.'

'How do we protect the Minister?' Angela wondered, 'if we want to own him?'

'He wasn't in the files you passed to Yuliet. We had

already fashioned some judiciously edited and redacted data before we supplied the copies.' Sefton was smug. 'And I think we can rely on honour amongst journalists to keep Eddy out of the story, especially if we persuade him to pay Yuliet and Danny over the top for the, let's call it scoop.'

'You are a tricky one, aren't you? Angela was not surprised. 'But that still doesn't answer the question who recruited the shooter?'

From her top floor office, Angela once again turned to look directly across the burgundy and ochre iron spans of Vauxhall Bridge, to St George Wharf Pier where two Thames Clippers languidly waited just upstream to take their turn to disgorge and collect their passengers. Other water traffic passed to-and-fro mid-stream – London's rubbish, pleasure boats, work boats, a police RIB, and a single scull. There was something calming about their passage. Nothing seemed to be in a rush, yet there was a certain deliberate intent. In the far distance she could see the four towers of the iconic Grade II* listed former-Battersea Power Station, surrounded by cranes helping to bring the area back to life. She had read that it was to be *one of the most exciting and innovative mixed-use neighbourhoods in the world. A legendary landmark that's a symbol of hope and positivity.*

With great deliberation, Angela turned from the window and faced Sefton. 'You know, don't you?'

Sefton's smile was enigmatic.

22

DAY FOURTEEN
WEDNESDAY LATE EVENING

ELSTREE STUDIOS

DANNY AND DAISY SAT EXHAUSTED IN THE RUSHES Bar of Elstree Studios – It had been a long but very satisfying day.

'Its bloody hard work being nice to people all the time,' said Daisy sipping her third double house gin and tonic. The first two had disappeared too quickly. Danny leaned across and squeezed her hand.

'I have just about stopped shaking. I don't know what would have happened if I had been caught.' Danny had explained his adventures burgling Nowak's car. 'One of Kelly's team collected the laptop almost straight away. Couldn't get rid of it fast enough.'

Daisy squeezed Danny's hand in return.

They sat in amiable silence watching out of the window the last of the celebrities, VIPs and other invited guests leaving along the roadway outside – occasionally some waved and smiled hoping for an invitation to continue drinking in the bar. If anyone attempted entry, two security guards at the main door explained that *regrettably everything is now shut* – not quite true, but good enough for the hopeful drinker to save face. The official after-show party up in the studio had finished at eleven – it had taken until eleven thirty to persuade the last to leave allegedly for health and safety reasons as the crew had wanted to start the derig. Not true either – unusually the load out would be started the following day. Only a few in the know knew of the after-work back door to the private studio bar which would stay open until the early hours. This was a place to wind down without the hassle of *other people*.

'Martha was fantastic. How she managed to perform so well and pander to the wilder excesses of some of the guests is beyond me. We tried to protect her – but she just seemed to be happy to mingle between takes rather than rush off to her dressing room.' Daisy was genuinely impressed. 'Do you know she did over twenty-five TV and radio interviews and sounded fresh for each one. `Bloody amazing. Kelvin was his normal prick-ish self. He demanded thirty minutes with Martha on his own. He had ten, plus the main media event, which is more than anyone else from the press.'

'Where are Martha and Vikki now?' Danny was equally impressed with Martha's professionalism. 'Vikki was really helpful keeping an eye out for her sister. She seems to be growing into the role of personal assistant and emotional protection. Maybe a bit of purpose in her life?'

'Going home for long baths she told me.' Daisy snuggled down into the soft sofa with her shoeless feet folded under her.

'Nowak?' asked Danny.

'Ray took him home an hour ago. I think even he got fed up with wall-to-wall luvviedom.' Daisy was delighted that she didn't have to see him – she needed to chill.

'When do you start editing?' Danny asked.

'The DIT has already uploaded everything to the editor and backed up most of today's rushes. The files are massive.' Daisy was showing off.

'DIT?' Danny was bemused at the speed that Daisy was picking up the jargon.

'Digital Imaging Technician,' Daisy was smug. She didn't let on that she only found out about the DIT that morning. 'They ensure data backups and quality control. The original camera data and metadata is backed up at least twice daily, ensuring data integrity with checksum verification. Replaces one of the camera assistants. No more film rushes and hands-in-the-bag according to Greg, whatever that means. Did you meet him? He has the wonderful title of data wrangler and spent ten minutes explaining what he did. Luckily one of my team rescued me otherwise I might have been stuck there for days.'

'DIT you,' Danny prodded Daisy. 'Suddenly a cyber-geek. Kelly might have found a DIT useful with his missing files?'

'Editing proper starts tomorrow morning.' Daisy ignored Danny's jibe. 'Most of it was cut live, so after a bit of tidying up from the ISOs, it's mainly compositing with the actual concert itself. We should have a first very rough cut by the end of tomorrow. Sound have started as well, they are going down to Cranc, a studio in Cardiff, to start mixing, but can't do a lot until they have the edited pictures against which to sync and marry up. For now, we're getting it out as soon as we can at 4K UHD for streaming and download. BluRay and DVDs will take a week more but before we resume the tour. The 8K stuff will be conformed later and probably only shown at broadcast and trade industry events. Probably the first showing at the ISE in June. Maybe NAB and IBC as well I am told.'

Daisy had clearly embraced her new role as producer with alacrity.

'We sent out video news releases of Martha's first sequence to all the broadcasters mid-afternoon, together with interviews of her talking about supporting police charities for the evening news shows. We made the headlines of every broadcaster in the UK and thirty or more across Europe. Future ticket sales have already significantly spiked.' Despite all the good news Daisy's enthusiasm and excitement was now waning – tiredness and the gin beginning to win the remains of the day.

'Oh fuck,' Danny sighed. 'There's Kelly and Rob arguing with security. I suppose I'd better let them in. Why are they here so late? I'm sure it could have waited until the morning.'

Danny stood and wearily walked across to the main door.

A few minutes later they were seated at the table. Daisy with her fourth gin and tonic was becoming even more immune to everything going on around her.

'Why didn't you simply show the guys on the door your badges?' asked Danny.

'Didn't want to attract attention, this is simply an off-duty social visit to say thank you.' Danny didn't believe Rob Andrews' not-so-innocent answer.

'Gold dust,' Kelly, returning from the bar, picked up the conversation. 'Thanks to you, we've made a massive leap forward in the investigations.'

Kelly took the drinks from the tray and carefully laid them out on the table. Danny noticed that Kelly had asked for a receipt at the bar, so it wasn't completely off-duty.

'Brilliant job. It might be the phone data itself cannot be used in court as we didn't acquire it legitimately,' Rob Andrews looked exhausted but happy, 'but what it has led us to is one hundred percent admissible. No one must know what you did. We would deny any knowledge. Fair enough?'

'Deal. But don't ever ask me to do anything like that again. If it weren't for your security guard I would have been caught.' Although a bit surly, Danny appreciated Kelly's and Rob's thanks.

'What security guard?' Kelly appeared to be puzzled.

'The one that distracted Ray, Kelly's driver.' Danny didn't like being teased. Despite watching Martha perform for the rest of the day he was still shaky.

Kelly didn't know what Danny was talking about. 'Seriously Danny. Once our guy directed Ray where to park the car, he changed back into police uniform and returned to his station. What happened?'

Danny explained what had transpired.

'Someone must have been on your side,' Kelly shook his head. 'Not one of ours. Genuinely part of Elstree's security team who had no idea what you were up to – *audentes Fortuna adiuvat.*'

Rob Andrews translated to the astonishment of both Kelly and Danny, 'Virgil in his Aeneid has the phrase shouted by Turnus, the King of the Rutuli and chief antagonist of the hero Aeneas. Fortune aids those daring. Or as we would say today fortune favours the brave.'

Danny started shaking again. 'I didn't feel brave or daring. I was shit scared.'

'That's not how we see it. It was a bold and courageous thing you did for us. You should be proud.' Kelly was trying to placate Danny.

Daisy gave a huge snorty snore – she was sound asleep in a world of her own.

Kelly sipped his beer and looked directly at Danny, 'We think you and Yuliet are in significant danger.'

'No more than usual. That's par for the course for an investigative reporter.' Danny was facetious, but realised he liked the thought of returning to his journalistic roots.

'This is serious Danny.' Rob Andrews was stony faced.

'What has happened to suddenly make you decide this?' asked Danny with increasing concern.

Kelly looked across at Daisy's sleeping form and decided to continue.

'This is in strictest confidence. Whilst you've been here enjoying yourself, we analysed the three phones and their contents. With professional help it didn't take long to crack the security. Since then, we've been in meetings and video conferences.' Kelly didn't say with whom. 'We've shared these data with our friends in Six and others. To be fair they have also shared important intelligence back to us.'

Daisy stirred, snorted, wriggled, and returned to deep sleep.

'It seems we may have been barking up the wrong tree. Despite what I said, this probably does all start with your blue badge article – it seems there are some people in high places that want to ensure your story never ever sees the light of day. Ten years later people were on the bottom rung. Now after years of climbing up the ladder of power, they are not far from the very, very top. They don't want the rug pulled from under them.'

Danny was about to interrupt Kelly's string of mixed metaphors and allegories – Andrews silenced him with a look.

'You are absolutely right about DAC Keith Wallace's duplicity. We have strong evidence that he is feeding information to Nowak. Maybe others we have yet to find. We have traced calls between one of Nowak's phones you downloaded, and a burner phone located at Wallace's house. We couldn't access that conversation, but we could triangulate the locations to within a few metres. Due to the sensitive nature, we agreed that this would remain confidential on a need-to-know basis. But thanks to you we have all Nowak's numbers. This morning I was given permission by the Commissioner herself to instigate telephone surveillance on Wallace. We also will be putting full surveillance on all Wallace's phones including his office, registered mobiles, and the burner. I shouldn't be telling you this—'

Kelly hesitated just enough to allow Danny to interrupt. 'So, you've got the fucker?'

'It's not that simple,' continued Kelly. 'We don't just want Wallace for providing Nowak with information. Whilst you were nicking phone data this morning, he met with several others to discuss covering up their illegality surrounding the acquisition of counterfeit disabled badges. Like an idiot you told Wallace that you knew and have evidence he had acquired one as well. Wallace has passed this information on to the others.'

'I was angry. Sorry.' Danny did look a little contrite.

'We both were. I seem to remember calling him a bent copper and a two-faced shit.' Kelly was unrepentant. 'Some of those at this morning's meeting you would have named and shamed had your piece ever seen the light of day. Obviously, they don't want it all to come out now.'

Kelly sipped his pint and returned it to the table, 'We suspect we have evidence that suggests the assassin's bullet was targeted at Nowak. Maguire's death was an unfortunate, terrible accident. So, the question is if true, was the assassin who accidently killed Maguire employed by The Vory as we originally suspected, or by someone wanting to ensure Nowak would never have any hold against them.'

'And to ensure anyone who knows about the sale of the counterfeit disabled badges and to whom, wouldn't be able to name names.' Rob Andrews had begun to like Danny – not a true friendship yet. 'We have a chief suspect but are still compiling a list of other possibilities who would be severely compromised if their behaviour from ten years ago was outed.

Someone who would want Nowak dead. Of course, they also would need to ensure your story would never be published.'

Danny was beginning to understand. 'So why not shoot me as well, whilst I was so near Nowak? Or Yuliet for that matter?'

Danny's brutal question surprised both Kelly and Rob Andrews.

'They have to be—' began Kelly.

'Come on. They?' interjected Danny. 'Who are they? You keep on talking about they and others. Who?'

'Not for now.' Kelly picked up, 'They need to be certain that all the evidence has been destroyed and you and Yuliet do not have copies. But even then, you still might not be safe. I don't know where that leaves me?'

For some reason Kelly and Andrews thought this was funny. *Black Police humour* thought Danny, who certainly didn't find this in the slightest bit amusing.

'The people behind the burglary at Yuliet's office and her home are linked to all this then?' challenged Danny.

'I would think so.' Kelly realised his beer remained three quarters full. He swiftly attended to that issue. Rob Andrews remained silent – watching and listening.

'Someone planted listening devices in Yuliet's offices, her home and probably my home too.' Danny's investigative juices were combined with adrenalin. 'You said Wallace met with several others. Who?'

'That's confidential for now. Sorry.' Kelly stood to leave. 'But please take care.'

'How am I to take care if I don't know who I am looking out for?' Danny was beginning to get riled.

'Don't worry,' said Rob, 'You will recognise some of those tailing you.'

'So, I'm to be the bloody target, am I?' He leapt to his feet and faced Kelly. 'A sitting duck? How many more people do you want dead? What about Yuliet? Does she know?'

'Sit down Danny. Have another drink.' Kelly changed his mind about leaving, returned to the bar and bought three more drinks. Daisy was still fast asleep. Rob and Danny sat in silence. Rob looked around the bar in the hope of celeb-spotting from some of the other shows and films being produced at the studios. He wasn't disappointed. He reluctantly adhered to the house rules – no photographs, no autographs, no soliciting.

Kelly placed the fresh drinks on the table. 'Daisy is out for the count?'

Danny looked at his sleeping girlfriend with affection. *Girlfriend?* He realised that his feelings for Daisy were growing. *Maybe this is what love feels like? He was never sure he actually loved his first wife... Which was maybe why he didn't miss her. He didn't hate her either. He had no feelings one way or the other. Probably worse. But he did miss his children, because they were of him. An unconditional bond had developed.*

His mind returned to the matter at hand.

'We can run and hide, or we can come out fighting. Another way to ensure our safety is to publish. Get enough evidence for you to lock them up?' Danny was feeling the first frisson of excitement. This could be a massive scoop. 'If we publish before you arrest them then we won't be hampered by sub judice? Other witnesses and information might reveal themselves?'

Kelly and Andrews smiled. They wondered how long it would take Danny to get it.

Daisy stirred, her eyes opened and in a hoarse voice asked, 'Can we go home please?'

Danny was thrilled that Daisy considered his flat to be home.

Daisy turned to Kelly and Andrews, 'What have you been talking about then?'

Danny ignored the question. He turned to the two policemen. 'Tomorrow. What time and where?'

Four large gins had taken their effect on Daisy. 'Tomorrow is another day.'

DAY FIFTEEN
THURSDAY MORNING

NEW SCOTLAND YARD

'DID HE TAKE THE BAIT?' ANASTASIA SPENCER-HATT enquired.

'What bait?' asked Bodkin He was the only member of his team at the meeting. The two teams were meant to remain professionally at arms' length. There was inevitably some overlap

'I think so,' responded Rob Andrews. 'Don't like doing this to Danny though, but he might rattle more cages than we can.'

'Hopefully Yuliet Spooner will get involved as well,' offered Bill Kelly. 'I trust them both. And they have noses like truffle pigs.'

For Bill Kelly, Harry Bodkin, Rob Andrews and Anastasia Spencer-Hatt this was the first of what was to be several informal liaison meetings. Rob Andrews had booked one of New Scotland Yard's huddle spaces. The basement room had just four chairs, with room for no more; a round table festooned with power, network, and video screen sockets; a digital white board; and various communications equipment. It was blandly decorated with no windows and highly efficient sound proofing. There was a persistent low hum of air conditioning. The only feature that disturbed the insipidness was an on-brand Foamex sign that read: *'Please adhere to your booked times. Leave the room empty and clean. Bins are not to be used for the disposal of secure waste.'* This was the first time any of them had huddled.

'What do we do about Wallace? We are going to have to go to the Commissioner with this, who will have to call in professional standards.' Anastasia Spencer-Hatt thought Wallace was a nasty slime-ball. 'There is evidence clearly demonstrating he purchased an illegal disabled badge for his personal use. We know he is feeding confidential information to Nowak and maybe to others as well. He has destroyed evidence. He has ordered unauthorised surveillance. Probably have him for conspiring to pervert the course of justice as well.'

'My decision. We hold fire whilst we collect evidence. Harry, you are going to have to tread very carefully though,' said Bill Kelly to his friend. 'If you suddenly stop briefing him, he will get suspicious.'

'That's why I am here without anyone else from my team – they don't even know I am meeting with you. Thought it best to prevent information accidentally getting to Wallace. He has a habit of visiting the incident room unannounced.' Like any decent copper Bodkin hated the idea of a bent officer, especially his boss. 'For now, it looks to an observer like the team are following up leads and making slow progress finding Maguire's killer. Let Wallace shout and posture if he doesn't like it. He'll soon get his comeuppance.'

'Are you actually making any progress with finding the shooter?' Kelly enquired.

'We know how, what, where and when, but we don't know who. And we can only guess at why. From CCTV, we have traced our John Doe's arrival at the O2. Not that it was that helpful – we know he was carrying a bag that would take the stripped-down rifle. We haven't been able to find the bag yet. He didn't leave with it. The rifle itself has not been a lot of help other than we know it is devoid of any markings. We have agreed with the O2 that we will continue searching only when the auditorium is clear of the public. Facial recognition has revealed nothing yet of his identity. We've sent video and stills to all our colleagues in the various security services.'

Bodkin cleared his throat; the air-conditioning made the room very dry.

'We have had some luck finding his digs. A worker, employed to clean an Airbnb studio flat after guest check out, found what we now know to be John Doe's change of clothes. She didn't know what to do, so she called the owner, who called their local nick, who called us, so there was a delay. The key we found in John Doe's pocket fitted the door. We now understand why he was trying to board the river taxi – his digs were just two hundred metres from the Royal Wharf pierhead and then one stop on the Docklands Light Railway to London City Airport. When we searched the property, we found a leather briefcase; inside a passport, a thousand Euros in cash give or take, a credit card and a self-printed boarding pass to Zurich for the first flight of the day after the shooting. He would have been indistinguishable from anyone else on the plane. Dark pinned striped suit, white shirt, black brogues, and old school tie. Forensics have not been able to find any fingerprints but have recovered some DNA in the bathroom that matches the corpse. We have already passed on the DNA far and wide. Nothing so far. We tracked the credit card to the purchase of an Oyster card at Paddington station. We have the CCTV but learned nothing new. The credit card was purchased via the dark web with anonymous cryptocurrency. Same card was used to buy the plane ticket and pay for the accommodation.'

'Did you find a computer or laptop? Or phone?' Andrews enquired.

'Nothing like that. We have been able to recover the contents of the iPhone on the body. It appears that Apple's guarantee is good, no damage. Waterproof to six metres for up to thirty minutes they say. Contract paid for by the credit card. No stored numbers. No calls in the log. We have asked the airtime provider to send us a list of calls and any texts. No WhatsApp, just Apps that come with the phone. Tracking switched off. Nothing in the phone's wallet.'

'So definitely a pro then. Does Wallace know about this yet?' Kelly probed.

'I'm going to brief him later at this afternoon's team meeting.' Bodkin was hesitant, 'but it's going to be difficult not strangling that bastard.'

'Think of the long game.' Anastasia as ever was down-to-earth. 'Don't get mad, get even.'

The room laughed.

'It's pretty clear our John Doe was a gun for hire, a professional. Someone somewhere must know how he was contacted. If you can't be contacted, you cannot be employed. GCHQ are on the case.' Bodkin sat back in his chair. 'If he hasn't been arrested in the past by friendly police allies, it's unlikely we'll get a DNA match. Professional hitmen try not to have photographs anywhere either. A ghost.'

'You're getting somewhere, but it must be bloody frustrating,' suggested Kelly.

'Tell me about it. So, what about your side of the investigation. Anything to add?' Bodkin was inquisitive both personally and professionally. 'Motive for the shooting seems ambiguous?'

'Some progress. But it opened a can of worms on a couple of fronts. We acquired the contents of Nowak's three phones he left in his car yesterday whilst he was sat in the studio watching Martha's video shoot. Don't ask me how – and the data itself we captured won't be admissible as evidence, but it has given us some extremely helpful leads.'

'Useful I assume for both our investigations?' Bodkin knew when not to ask too many questions. 'But surely didn't Nowak have a phone on his person as well, won't that have further information?'

'No. Daisy deVilliers ensured the no-phones-in-the-studio rule was strictly applied. I had a word with Jimmy. Jimmy and Daisy said that Martha's tech team had set up talkback and comms circuits using carefully allocated and scanned radio frequencies. Daisy convinced everyone that, never mind the disturbance of ringers and people shouting into their phones, they couldn't risk interference with the various RF channels that the concert was using. Nowak as well. Some of the journos kicked up apparently but were given the choice of store your phone out of the studio or go home. Bit like Downing Street.' Kelly was always annoyed that whenever he went to Downing Street, even a serving police office couldn't take a phone beyond the entrance hall.

'Clever.' Bodkin was impressed. 'Can of worms?'

'The phones were a rich seam of gold. We have passed the information mined around to various other teams who have been investigating organised crime. Seems we are owed a lot of beer. More importantly we now know the phones confirm our surveillance that Nowak is being blackmailed to hand over one point two five million pounds. The Vory have passed the debt to an enforcement collector who takes a cut and a mark-up. The enforcer suggested that Nowak...' Kelly referred to his notebook, '... won't be so lucky next time. So, we assumed at first that the shooter was employed by The Vory.'

Rob Andrews picked up, 'But of course if Nowak was dead, The Vory or their enforcer would be very unlikely to see the return of their money.'

'Indeed. Also, yesterday whilst all that was going on, another meeting was being held at Six – apparently off-the-books. Several persons now of interest who all purchased counterfeit disabled blue badges and are concerned their illegality is about to come to light, including your friend DAC Wallace.' Kelly continued explaining Danny's role ten years ago, his suspicions and how the story has resurfaced. 'My sources tell me there were some interesting people around the table.'

'Sources?' Bodkin leant forward. He sensed that the meeting was going to become even more revealing. 'What sources?' Kelly ignored the question. 'In addition to DAC Wallace, there was Edwin 'Eddy' Porterhouse the owner of *The Daily Tribune,* Pelham DeCourcy from the Bank of England, allegedly destined for stardom, a couple of people from six and last, but not least…' Kelly paused dramatically, '…The Right Honourable Michael Ramsey, Minister of State for Crime and Policing in Her Majesty's UK Government.'

'Bloody hell,' was all that Bodkin could manage. 'Are you saying Ramsey bought a counterfeit badge? If that came out, it would take him down. If there was enough evidence he would almost certainly end up in court.'

'We do have evidence that Wallace, DeCourcy and Porterhouse might have bought fake badges, together with at least sixty other people. We had all this information in the files that went missing. It seems that those who have the most to lose have gathered together, led by senior officers from Six. But then the trail goes cold. Danny's story from years ago we suspect had been edited before it was mysteriously returned to me.' Kelly smiled. 'Danny says there were so many people involved he cannot remember them all.'

'What the hell are Six up to?' wondered Anastasia Spencer-Hatt. 'Whatever it is, it won't be entirely legal?'

'Indeed,' said Kelly.

24

DAY FIFTEEN
THURSDAY MORNING

THE CEMETERY

MARTHA KNEW THAT TODAY WOULD BE DIFFICULT after the highs and absurdities of showbusiness from the video shoot the day before. This day could not have been any more different.

The graveside funeral service for ten-year-old Camden Town native Amelia Cohen, Mia to her friends and family, was meant to be private for family only. But since the news of her death was deliberately leaked by persons unknown, the details of the funeral had also become public knowledge.

Family Liaison Officer, Amanda Turner had tried to help, but Mia's parents had assumed it was the Police who had been careless – or someone from within the police who wanted to make a few pounds from an unscrupulous journalist – consequently the parents refused further help. The official police statement, forced to be released post the frenzy on social media, simply said Amelia's death had been a terrible accident; asking anyone who had been at the concert who might have information to call the investigation's hot line – anonymously if wished. The statement made no mention of the funeral arrangements.

A few days earlier Martha had personally telephoned Mia's parents to ask if she could call on them to express her condolences and to propose establishing a foundation in Mia's name. She said she would visit alone. Mia's parents graciously accepted the offer – they believed a lasting memorial to their only daughter would help them to grieve. Martha surprised herself – this wasn't something she wanted to do in name only. By agreement, Martha arrived at Mia's parents' house – looking as little like a celebrity megastar as possible. She was genuinely upset; no make-up; no minders; no press – except, unbeknown to Martha, for Kelvin Edwards' photographer with the two-thousand-millimetre lens mounted on a very heavy tripod, which due to its five-figure cost, was hired especially for the day.

Martha was welcomed to the family's home. Mia's mother began to say, 'If only Mia had been here, she would have loved to meet...' before dissolving into racking sobs. Martha sat down beside Mia's mother cradling her gently in her arms. The sobbing subsided. Martha was determined to really help by getting stuck in and, as far as it was possible, anonymously. She was seeing for herself the dignified, yet overwhelming sorrow shown by Mia's parents. Sorrow that would last with them for the remainder of their lives. Sorrow and guilt, *'could they have done more to protect their daughter?'*

After coffee and home-made fruit cake which normally Martha would have rejected, but today seemed churlish to refuse, she explained, 'As I said on the phone, I would like to help you set up a Foundation in Mia's memory. Maybe in partnership with Mia's school.'

Mia's parents could not have been more pleased as Martha outlined the details. 'In six months' or so, to kick start the Foundation, we will put on a show at The Round House on Chalk Farm Road. We will give free tickets to Mia's school, friends, and family – and then sell VIP tickets, corporate hospitality, TV rights and sponsorship. All the profits donated to Mia's Foundation. I will not be taking a fee and I have persuaded my band to do the same. I can't say who yet, but several well-known friends have also agreed to perform – all donating their time.'

They continued discussing the arrangements for another twenty minutes or so. Martha explained that this would mean the parents would be in the spotlight for a while – with everything that entailed. 'But hopefully in six months-time your sorrow and emotions will be less raw – but it will still be a challenge.'

Mia's parents looked at each other – and with silent nods agreed. Martha felt she had achieved a little to help Mia's parents at an impossible moment in their shattered lives. She asked about the funeral arrangements. Mia's father explained that they had decided to keep the funeral as simple as possible – a graveside service within the Children's

Memorial Garden of the one-hundred-and-ninety-acres of the Islington and St Pancras Cemetery.

'Would you mind if I attended?' asked Martha. 'I will come alone and hopefully remain incognito.'

'Of course. Please do,' replied Mia's mother.

This morning as Martha looked around the burial ground, the sun was shining; the sky was blue; the air had the promise of a warm spring. White snowdrops; bluebells; purple, white, and gold crocuses; single and double yellow daffodils; and an array of red, pink, dark purple and variegated tulips provided cheerful colour – the Cemetery's dedicated gardeners with their greenhouses did their best to always display a mass of colour whatever time of the year – forced and held back when needed.

There were about two hundred uninvited guests gathered at a respectful distance from the graveside and away from the family – many with floral tributes; a few cards; some with small teddy bears and dolls that would be placed on the grave after the service.

Further away a single photographer.

Martha, dressed in black and dark grey, with a stylish hood, wore dark glasses – the bright sunlight meant they didn't look out of place. She marvelled at the peaceful, beautifully laid out lawn area with magnificent silver birch trees whose leaves were softly whispering in the gentle breeze.

Mia's parents were clearly trying to hold it together with as much dignity as they could muster. There are no words that could be spoken to console parents after the death of a child – the tickets for Martha's opening night concert were meant to have been a special birthday treat for Mia from her parents.

The service lasted about ten minutes – no hymns nor music. A simple prayer was said as the coffin was lowered into the ground before everyone spoke the Lord's Prayer with extraordinary feeling.

The celebrant finished with an amended line from Shakespeare's Hamlet: 'Good night, sweet princess: and flights of angels sing thee to thy rest.'

Mia's parents and close family scattered peat and wildflower seeds into and around the grave – later in the year there would be a riot of colour. Later in the year Mia's parents would tend to the grave – and meet other grieving parents who share a common awful bond.

The gentle sound of crying could be heard from all around.

'Hello Martha,' the voice from behind startled her. She began to turn. 'Don't turn around, stay exactly where you are.'

Instinct or reflex meant she continued to turn. A rough hand prevented further movement. The voice was rich and sonorous, clearly eastern European. 'I said don't turn around.'

'Who are you? What do you want?' Martha wished she had accepted the offer of her close protection.

'We want a message passed to your Stanislaw Nowak,' spat the voice.

'Why can't you do it yourself,' she said trying to claw back some of her fear.

'It would be much, much better coming from you.' The voice had a menace that Martha had never known.

'What's the message?' she asked.

'Tell Stanislaw two weeks to pay up or you die.' The reply was to the point. 'Got that?'

Martha nodded. Scared. *Did the man mean by "you", Stanislaw, or me?* raced around her petrified overloaded brain. Her synapses fired and misfired as she tried to make sense.

'Now count to thirty, keep looking forward or you'll never sing again.' Martha heard the footsteps walk briskly away on the gravel path. She felt her legs buckling.

'Are you okay?' asked a woman in a black coat – one of the uninvited mourners. 'Oh my God, it's you.' Her manner changed as she beckoned to her husband, 'Malcom, Malcom, over here. It's Martha!'

The mood in the cemetery changed from mawkish sadness and grieving to excited chatter as the uninvited guests decided that meeting Martha was more interesting than burying a child. Mobile phones were extracted from pockets and handbags, as everyone wanted a selfie. Martha reacted as an automaton – fear consuming her. Few noticed or cared. *This was Martha.*

For Kelvin's snapper, this was going to be gold dust.

Suddenly another voice was heard loud and brutally shouting – Mia's father. 'For God's sake leave her alone. This is our daughter's funeral.' He grabbed Martha and hustled her to the waiting limousine.

Martha was horrified. Everything had gone wrong. Who was that man? What did he mean? What should she do? She allowed herself to be led into the back of the long wheelbase, black, beautifully polished funeral car. Bottles of water were arranged in holders around the rear seating area – she drank one in a single go. It settled her a little – she apologised profusely. 'I am so sorry. That wasn't meant to happen. I tried to keep a low profile.'

She made no mention of the man or the message.

'Don't worry,' said Mia's mum now sitting beside her – eyes red from crying. 'I could see you were trying to be discreet. We didn't want all those people there anyway. Are you okay? Come back to ours with the family. We have some sandwiches and a drink, and you can meet everyone else and tell them about plans for Mia's foundation.'

Clearly this kept Mia's mum going on a challenging day.

Martha didn't have a lot of choice. At the first opportunity she would call Danny – he'd know what to do.

She eventually was able to escape just after five that afternoon – exhausted. It had been a testing few hours listening to tales of Mia; her love of music; her hobbies; her school successes; and meeting a few more of Mia's friends who had not attended the graveside but had been invited to the house. Martha was able to discuss her plans for the foundation in Mia's name – followed by more tears and lots of hugging. After some initial concerns Martha found the day surprisingly cathartic being in the company of real people in unfortunate circumstances. It was not long before Martha's celebrity status was forgotten as she blended in with family and friends.

Martha walked straight home without being accosted – she was a local, so most people simply ignored her. Vikki was out somewhere. She removed the clothes she had worn for the funeral and lay on her bed – her eyes inexorably closed.

Next thing she knew it was dark outside – she was woken by her bedroom door opening.

'Are you okay, Sis?' asked Vikki.

'Yeah, fine thanks.' Martha was groggy. Too much tea and sympathy had taken its toll. For now, she had also forgotten about the man at the graveside. 'Where have you been?'

'Daisy invited me to the edit to see the first cuts of yesterday. It really is looking fabulous.' Vikki was excited, 'It's going to be amazing.'

But Martha had already returned to sleep. Vikki pulled the duvet over her and quietly closed the bedroom door.

DAY SIXTEEN
FRIDAY MORNING

THE MESSAGE

MARTHA WOKE WITH A START – THE DAYLIGHT
streaming through her open curtains announced the new
day. It was just after seven. She had slept better than for
ages – she wondered why? The video shoot had gone well –
and the funeral yesterday had been what is euphemistically
considered to be *a success*. She liked Mia's parents, family,
and her friends. All was well with the world – until she
remembered the rich and sonorous, eastern European voice.
How could I have forgotten, she asked herself, *maybe some
sort of primitive defence mechanism.*

'*Tell Stanislaw two weeks to pay up or you die.*'

Her day disintegrated. She picked up her phone and called Danny.

'Hello,' said a semi-comatose Danny. 'It's my day off, Martha. Please tell me this is important.'

'It's important,' was all that Martha said before bursting into tears.

Danny transformed from somnambulant to fully awake. Daisy, beside him, sat up aware that something wasn't right.

'It's okay, Martha. Calm down.' Danny was as gentle as he could be having been rudely awoken. 'Tell me what's happened.'

Martha explained the message and how she had received it. 'Tell Stanislaw two weeks to pay up or you die.'

'Have you told him?' asked Danny.

'Not yet, I thought I'd call you first,' was all that Martha could manage before the breathless sobs returned.

Daisy could just about hear what was being said, she whispered. 'Ask her if she would like us to go round? Is Vikki there?'

'Daisy is on her way over to you now,' Danny responded without bothering to ask the question, before leaping out of bed. 'I'm going to see Nowak face-to-face and pass on the message. We need to find out what is going on.'

Both departed Danny's home within fifteen minutes – they walked briskly to the tube station. Danny was heading east to Nowak's apartment. Daisy north to Martha. At Waterloo they quickly pecked each other on the cheek before going their separate ways down the escalators, each engrossed in what they were about to encounter.

Nowak was woken by the sound of his door entry system being repeatedly pressed. He looked at the small screen and was surprised to see Danny Owen glaring back at him. 'What do you want?'

'To see you,' was Danny's terse reply.

'Give me time to put clothes on,' Nowak didn't wait for a response

Five minutes later the outer door buzzed. Danny entered, walked up the stairs, he disliked lifts. Nowak was waiting at his open door in an ill-fitting tracksuit.

'I'd like to say this is a pleasure, but it's not. I won't offer you anything to drink, as I'm sure you are not staying long.' Nowak's greeting wasn't friendly. 'Don't bloody stand there. Come in.'

Danny couldn't help but admire the view from the lounge windows. Nowak slurped an orange juice. 'Well. What did you come to say?'

'Came to pass a message that was given to Martha yesterday,' responded Danny.

'What couldn't be said on the phone?' demanded Nowak.

'I wanted to be certain our conversation was overheard and recorded,' Danny gesticulated to where he imagined the surveillance equipment had been installed. 'For both our sakes and my safety.'

The irony was not lost on Nowak. 'Well say what you have to say then.'

'Martha was given a message at Mia's funeral. Remember Mia, the little girl who was trampled to death in the chaos at the end of Martha's concert?' Danny was laying it on thick. He didn't care what Nowak thought of him. 'Or don't you give a shit?'

'Get on with it I said.' Nowak let out a long impressive polyphonic fart, with a pleased expression. 'I have things to do.'

Danny ignored the not-so-passive aggressiveness.

'Martha was given the message, tell Stanislaw two weeks to pay up or you die.' Danny watched Nowak for a reaction – and got it.

Nowak slumped in a chair.

'Well, what does it mean?' interrogated Danny. 'Why are you going to die? Or is that a threat to Martha because of you?'

Nowak sat there; *this is all getting out of hand*. What he hoped would remain private was now out in the open. However, his bluster returned. 'I borrowed money to finance Martha's tour. The lender was a short-term theatrical angel, a specialist backer, but with strings attached. Once I had repaid, they had no further involvement or profit share. I was meant to repay the debt after the first three nights, but because of the shooting and postponement I couldn't make the repayments. The lenders weren't sympathetic to my plight.'

'Death threats don't sound like an angel to me,' Danny's response was brutal. 'What strings?'

Nowak ignored Danny's question.

Danny remained impassive as he took out his iPhone and pressed play on a media file.

Nowak's voice was instantly recognisable. *'Let's get straight to the point. I owe Baka one million pounds. But he is dead? Debt gone.'*

Pause.

'Did you hear me?'

A slightly longer pause

'My arrangements were with Ali Baka. He is dead. Why should I pay you, and pay you more than I owe?'

'I need time to raise the money.'

'I need eight weeks. And if Martha dies, I won't have any money.'

Pause

'Okay, I'll do my best. Four weeks from today.'

Then the sound of Nowak's phone pinging five times.

'Who is Ali Baka' Danny demanded. 'And to whom are you paying more?'

'How did you get that?' Nowak leapt to his feet angrily. He lunged at Danny, who stepped back leaving Nowak to steady himself on the wall.

'Remember walls have ears,' Danny taunted. 'And cars do as well.'

Nowak was breathing heavily, trying to control his temper.

'And while we are about it, what happened to your plans for using the tour for people smuggling? Jimmy is not at all happy with you about that when he found out. He nearly resigned and that would have left you with a massive problem.' Danny pronounced massive, ma-who-sieve. 'And your mate Pietr Ostrodzko pulling out, leaving your team in the lurch for transport? Martha was in a terrible state being asked to pass on the death threat. She might not be able to perform. Suddenly everyone is deserting you.'

Nowak remained silent. His mind racing.

'And the Angela you were speaking to on the phone, you threatening to ruin their career. Suddenly my fake blue disabled badge story about your illegal enterprises and the people who bought them comes back to life. Apparently, my foot would be nothing compared to what you would do to Angela. Who is she?' Danny was spitting out the words, goading him. 'You are a shit. Nothing but a grubby little conman with an over inflated sense of your own importance in low level crime. And now your sins are finding you out for what and who you are.'

Nowak unfolded his body from the chair and took two paces towards Danny. The animal like body odour was revealing itself – his eyes were wild. His fists clenched and unclenched. He stood with his face ten centimetres from Danny's. 'Fuck off. Get out of here. Before I do you. You shit. You know nothing of what it is like to be in business. Proper business. Creating employment. Paying people. Families relying on you. You are just a nasty peddler of gossip, never happier than ruining people's lives with your snide innuendo. Now get out.'

'Not until you guarantee me that Martha is safe. No more grubby activity with the tour. It's one hundred percent legit?' Danny stood there. 'You repay the money you owe. Two weeks Nowak. Two weeks and then you might die if you don't. Message delivered.'

Nowak simply nodded. 'The tour is straight. No-one needs worry. I have the money and I will make the repayment of the loan in plenty of time.'

'Let me make it clear. You step out of line. I find you are involved in anything that gets close to illegal. From now on you are squeaky clean. Otherwise I will ensure the keys are thrown away.' Danny was angry. 'I'm not doing this for you. This is for Daisy and for Martha. The Vory will be the least of your worries.'

Nowak was shocked into silence. *How did Danny know about The Vory?*

'I'm not putting you on every front page – yet. But I have everything. Even those fake blue badges and who you sold them to from ten years ago. You put a foot wrong, and I will haunt every waking hour you remain living. You will become the most reviled man in Europe. Your time in prison will be a living torture. You won't be killed but you will wish you had been.' Danny left the room slamming the door. He walked back down the stairs into the fresh morning air. Using his iPhone, he speed-dialled, 'Did you get all that?'

Danny had phoned Kelly on his way to Nowak's to alert him to what he was doing.

'Every word,' replied Kelly. 'You pushed him. I thought too hard at one point.'

'He's a bullying slob. In some ways I wish he had had a go. Then I would have had an excuse to deck him.' Danny wasn't contrite.

'Don't get mad get even,' Kelly tried to calm Danny. 'We're nearly there. Stay with it.'

Sefton smiled as he listened to every word – unbeknown to Kelly or Danny.

Meanwhile across London, Daisy and Vikki were attempting to console a distraught Martha. 'What have I got myself into?'

'It's not about you. Its Nowak.' Vikki hugged her sister.

'But the man said pay up or *you* die,' sobbed Martha.

'That was the message you were being asked to pass on,' reassured Daisy. 'You. Nowak. Not you, you.'

'But it's still horrible. Death threats.' Martha managed the words between crying. 'Are you sure?'

'Bloody trolls. They do the same on social media. This has nothing to do with you. This is Nowak's problem. They probably don't mean it. Just jealous of his success.' Vikki was trying to calm her sister down.

'Danny has delivered the message to Nowak. So, you've done as you were asked.' Daisy tried a reassuring smile but wasn't sure she was successful.

'Tea, toast and honey?' suggested Vikki.

Martha and Daisy nodded their acceptance of the universal cure all.

'I don't know if I can go on,' Martha looked tiny and afraid sitting on her kitchen chair.

It was Vikki who took control. 'Stop being such a bloody prima donna. Performing is what you live for. Deep down you always knew that Nowak was a shit, but you accepted it because you were desperate to get back to the top. Its within you. Now suck it up. Let's work out what we are going to do and stop feeling so fucking sorry for yourself. You have millions of adoring fans. Don't forget that first night. Twenty thousand people chanting your name. You loved it. Every moment of it. And it wouldn't have happened without Nowak. Love him or loathe him.'

Daisy was astonished at Vikki's assertiveness. She had never seen her like that. *But it is what Martha needs,* thought Daisy. *Performers can be fragile introverted people despite their on-stage and public persona.* Her respect for Vikki notched up significantly, *maybe the last few weeks have done her good. She's grown up at last.*

Martha sat quietly contemplating. She spread the honey on the unsalted buttered thick brown toast and took a bite, savouring the Fortnum and Mason French Lavender Honey from Mont Ventoux. She drank the strong tea with a dash of milk added second, selected from the Fortnum's Famous and Classic World Wooden Restaurant Box – all taken from a massive hamper, a gift from a record company trying to woo her.

Daisy and Vikki sat quietly with their tea watching Martha.

At last, the contemplative silence was broken by Martha, 'How do we get Nowak out of my hair? Out of the tour? Who owns the tour if Nowak dies?'

Martha did not realise how prescient she was…

DAY NINETEEN TO TWENTY-TWO MONDAY TO THURSDAY

THE INTERMENT

THE JOURNEY TO ENNISKILLEN FOR MAGUIRE'S interment had been uneventful, apart from some uncomfortable buffeting as the Ryanair Boeing 737 crossed the Irish Sea. Kelly, Rob Andrews and Anastasia Spencer-Hatt had landed a few minutes behind schedule but, with hand baggage only, were out of the airport by four pm. From Belfast International Airport they drove in their Avis rental Seat Ateca west along the M1, passing Lisburn and bypassing Dungannon. They stopped for a break at Cabragh before continuing their journey along the A4 to the police-approved-budget of The Enniskillen Hotel – arriving in time for dinner. The funeral was scheduled for Thursday, the following day. They planned to return to London on Friday afternoon, leaving enough time for recovery from the post service wake.

Daisy and Danny had decided to make a trip of it and left a few days before the small police contingent – it was their first time away together. Danny had taken the week off from the Starshine Breakfast Show – it was an opportunity to consider his professional options. He had already decided his personal plans, much to his surprise.

Daisy's team could handle the day-to-day PR of Martha's tour. The tedious finalising and post-production of Nowak's video could carry on without her. There were few creative or artistic decisions to be made as everything was scripted and story-boarded – and there was still ten days until the first night of the sell-out four days at the 02. After the awful shenanigans of the past couple of weeks they both needed some personal R&R.

On the Monday, they had travelled by hire car from London to Holyhead catching the just gone two o'clock sailing on the MV Ulysses – the largest car ferry in the world that can carry well over a thousand cars and double that number of passengers. They watched Ynys Môn disappear behind them in the afternoon sunshine before finding a couple of comfy chairs in the Club Lounge. The three-and-a-half hours crossing to Dublin was smooth, allowing them both to read, doze and drink tea.

Danny had reserved a suite at The Shelbourne on St Stephen's Green so they could explore Dublin's fair city.

Both were amazed how easy they had become in each other's company away from the pressures of Martha's tour, Nowak, and *helping the police with their enquiries*. Conversation flowed – or there were periods of blissful companionable silence. Enjoyment of Dublin blossomed with the tender love for each other – the glorious weather helped.

Danny discussed whether or not he should stay on at Starshine or return to his roots. 'Newspapers simply aren't recruiting anymore especially investigative journalists. Most newsrooms are being culled as social media takes over and sales decline,' he told Daisy. 'I talked to Yuliet about joining their team. She wasn't optimistic.'

Daisy remained silent, knowing that Danny's introspection was rhetorical.

'I suppose I could try freelancing, but it's a precarious life,' Danny continued.

'The unexpected always happens unexpectedly. Something will come up. Have you spoken with any other radio stations or media outlets?' asked Daisy.

'I don't want to put the word out just yet. This industry is too incestuous,' Danny mused. 'Keep my powder dry for now. And I don't fancy TV.'

'You'd look good in front of the cameras,' Daisy reckoned his smile and easy manner would win over millions of viewers.

Their sight-seeing ambition was too much to fit into a couple of days, but they did their best visiting the castle, Kilmainham Gaol, Christ Church Cathedral and wandering around Temple Bar with its quirky boutiques, aided by their Lonely Planet Guide. And, of course, refreshed by the mandatory visit to the Guinness Brewery.

The second night they dined on the contemporary Irish menu with French classical roots at Restaurant Patrick Guilbaud, the two Michelin star restaurant in Dublin city centre. Daisy chose Flaggy Shore Dainty Oysters followed by Lacquered Challans Duck Breast whilst Danny went for Butter Roast Castletownbere Scallops followed by Kilmore Quay Turbot. Danny had selected one of his favourite white wine grapes, viognier, originating in present day Croatia – but had never tried the Domaine Michel & Stéphane Ogier La Combe de Malleval Condrieu 2019. Neither of them was disappointed.

They shared a Grand Marnier Soufflé which arrived with a bottle of Veuve Clicquot 'La Grande Dame Rosé' 2006 champagne.

'You're pushing the boat out,' exclaimed Daisy, with a huge smile, 'I love pink fizz.'

They waited until the sommelier had poured the rose nectar into Patrick Guilbaud's specially designed champagne flutes.

'Go on, what is it?' asked Daisy holding up her glass ready to clink with Danny's. 'You've been on edge most of the evening.'

Danny stood, and did up the single button of his Gucci navy blazer. And then undid it again. Daisy wondered what was going on – her anxiety soon changed to an entirely different emotion as Danny took a small box out of his pocket and went down on one knee beside Daisy.

By now Danny had the attention of all the other diners. There was an expectant hush. 'Daisy, these last few weeks have been a joy, despite one or two tiny issues.'

Daisy couldn't help a nervous laugh. His hands were clammy. He felt his face flush. He continued, determined to deliver the speech he had rehearsed in his mind for the past couple of days. Words were not normally a problem for the experienced journalist – now trying to write his own story. 'For some time have realised I want to spend the rest of my life with you, if you'll have me.'

Daisy felt a tear of joy welling up from within her – she wasn't normally an emotional person. She knew what was coming – but was determined to make Danny work for it. *This will only happen once in my life, hopefully. Let's savour and remember every moment. So maybe I am a romantic after all?* She surprised herself. She realised Danny was still speaking.

'Daisy, please will you make my dreams come true and do me the honour of marrying me?'

Silence. The waiters ceased their service. The other diners had returned their knives and forks to their plates. Even the distant traffic outside seemed to have stopped.

Daisy took Danny's free hand and kissed it gently. 'I've waited over five years for you to ask that question. I've loved you from the first day we met. Absolutely yes. Of course. Now take that ring out of the box and put it on my finger before either of us changes our minds.'

The Tiffany engagement ring with a single diamond stone and platinum diamond encrusted band fitted perfectly.

They kissed passionately – awkwardly as Daisy was still sitting.

The dining room erupted into cheers and applause that soon turned to joyous chatter. One of the diners on the far side of the room stood, 'Ladies and gentlemen please be upstanding as we all toast the happy couple. I've no idea of your names but you've made this a memorable evening for my wife and me on our fortieth wedding anniversary. Congratulations. Cheers to…'

Danny helped the man out, '…the future Mr and Mrs Owen.'

The room joined in the happy toast to the future Mr and Mrs Owen. From another table a woman joined the celebrations, 'My husband would be thrilled to gift you that champagne, on condition that if there is any left the bottle comes over here.'

More laughter and clapping. The room settled back to convivial decorous chatter – it had become a memorable evening.

Daisy and Danny finished the soufflé. They each had half a glass more of champagne before asking the waiter to take the rest of the bottle over to their benefactors.

Celebratory bed beckoned. It wasn't long before 'the day' closed their eyes.

The following morning after a leisurely light breakfast in their room of smoked salmon and scrambled eggs with tea, further delaying activities, and a shared shower they departed for Enniskillen.

'It'll certainly be a memorable funeral,' suggested Daisy.

'It's your inappropriate sense of humour that drew me to you.' Danny was looking forward to the journey north.

'I reckon two to three hours if we go straight there,' Daisy examined the map. The hire car was equipped with sat nav, but they decided to take the country route avoiding the M3 and N3. 'I'll drive for the first hour.'

Danny was happy to be chauffeured, looking out over the Irish scenery in quiet contemplation.

'Go on, penny for them?' Daisy asked.

'I was thinking how many children we should have...' Danny answered. Then after a short pause, '...and whether Maguire's internment will be incident free? I'm fed up with all this intrigue. Kelly and his team said they would be on the look-out and had drafted in local surveillance teams just in case.'

'I don't want to think about it,' shuddered Daisy at the thought of Maguire's organic detritus covering her. She had thrown away the clothes she had worn that night.

They parked up a short distance from the shore of Lough Oughter within the Killykeen Forest Park in the picturesque heart of County Cavan. The sunshine and smell of pine persuaded them to take a short stroll. They crossed the footbridge over to Gartanoul and then sat awhile watching an angler fail to catch anything.

The Shelbourne Hotel had provided them with a carefully packed lunch in a hessian bag. They had declined wine – instead, they opted for a lemon fruit cup and some sparkling water.

Danny took over the driving and headed north to the five-star Lough Erne Resort in Enniskillen. The view from their room towards the Fermanagh Lakelands and The Faldo Course was spectacular – not that either of them played golf.

The following morning the sunshine had been replaced by dark grey clouds and a dank, gusty drizzle – a *ceobhrán* or *brádán* according to the concierge who offered them umbrellas.

The taxi-ride to Enniskillen's Saint Macartan's Cathedral didn't take long – they decided not to drive in case *the aftershow party* got out of hand. They had deliberately left early so they could meet with Kelly and his team. They exchanged greetings, 'Nothing unusual so far,' reported Kelly. 'But you never know. Standby to standby!'

The stringer from the local newspaper, *The Impartial Reporter* approached Kelly, he was straight to the point, 'Why was Michael Maguire murdered? Was there an IRA connection?'

'I have no comment to make. Please speak with the Met Police's PR team.' Kelly turned away from the reporter, who realised he wasn't going to get any more. He nodded at his photographer who had been at work from a few metres away. There was enough for the front page of both the print and on-line editions. The murder of a London based police officer, originally from County Fermanagh, at a high-profile event ensured there would be public interest – and subsequent sales and sign-ups with further work guaranteed for the freelance journalist.

The drizzle continued – everyone took shelter near the main door. There was obligatory shaking of hands as the various mourners arrived. Self-introductions were made, names exchanged and mainly promptly forgotten. Rob Andrews and Anastasia Spencer-Hatt made notes of anyone who might be able to help but weren't hopeful. There were very few local family, mainly cousins; not many friends from school and growing up; two officers from the Royal Dragoon Guards in dark suits and regimental ties; and a couple of the deceased's former colleagues from around the United

Kingdom of Great Britain and Northern Ireland who had worked with Maguire in the past before he joined the NCA – for them it was a couple of days sanctioned absence away from the grind of police work, rather than any love for their former colleague.

Maguire's ashes in a simple council urn, sat in lonely isolation on a small table covered with a plain violet pall between the empty choir stalls at the foot of the wooden altar table. There were no wreaths. The only flowers were those that the Cathedral's floral committee had dutifully arranged a few days earlier according to their regular weekly roster.

The sound of the solitary tenor bell was muffled within the nave. Outside on Townhall Street a few locals crossed themselves in anonymous respect for someone they didn't know – it was just something they did when funerals were heard in the distance at the top of the hill.

Eventually the mourners mutually decided, unasked, that it was time to take their places on the Hopsack Terracotta cushioned hardwood pews. The truncated service continued according to tradition, there was no Holy Communion due to the poor Catholic turn out. A short welcome address was followed by prayers and a couple of hymns – *Abide with Me* and controversially for some in Northern Ireland, *I Vow to Thee my Country*. Reverend Patrick Quigley, the Dean of Clogher invited Kelly to say a few 'Words in Remembrance.' He spoke for just over four minutes – generic, bland, and non-controversial.

None, except those in the know, spotted the surveillance teams sitting in the gallery high above the nave; or concealed outside around the perimeter; or the heavily armed teams in body armour hidden in nondescript vans parked on the roads leading to and from the cathedral.

The service for the late Detective Sergeant Michael Maguire's ashes concluded – huddled under umbrellas outside, the mourners watched as the urn was lowered into a small grave in line with the Catholic Church's recommendation of burying the ashes of the deceased.

'How long do we have to stay here? I'm soaked to the bloody skin,' demanded Danny.

'I'm working, so have to stay until everyone has gone.' Bill Kelly surreptitiously put his finger to his ear, listening to a message from one of the watchers via his concealed walkie-talkie. He clicked the switch in his pocket twice to silently transmit he had received and understood. 'And if I'm here you can bloody well stay too.'

The Level Seven Bar within Blakes of 'The Hollow,' just down the road from Saint Macartan's Cathedral was already doing brisk business – and was beckoning to the few remaining at the cathedral.

'Okay, let's call it a day. Stand down.' Bill Kelly spoke into his concealed microphone – those in immediate earshot ostentatiously heaved a sigh of relief. He turned to Danny and Daisy – she had been hopping from foot-to-foot trying to keep her feet warm despite the boots, 'Looks like there is nothing to see here. I'll see you at the wake in twenty minutes or so. I'll just clear up here.'

Without further asking the newly engaged pair walked away from the cathedral hand-in-hand down the stone slabbed path and through the recently restored lych-gate. Danny mansplained, 'This used to be called the corpse gate.

The coffin might be kept here while the introductory part of the burial service was read.'

They turned left onto the road. Daisy cwtched her arm around Danny's, 'I don't know what I'd do without you. Good job you asked me to marry you otherwise just think what I would be missing out on.'

Danny was about to suitably respond when a boy's voice shouted out, 'Here, mister. A bloke told me to give you this.'

The boy, without dismounting from his mountain bike, held out a white DL envelope with the name Stanislaw Nowak written in thick black felt pen on the front. 'He said you'd give me five pounds.'

'What man?' asked Daisy.

'Over there,' replied the boy turning around to point. The road was empty. Not even a car in sight.

Daisy fumbled in her handbag for a five-pound note – she'd claim it back when she did her expenses. The crisp note was exchanged for the envelope, which she stuffed in her already packed handbag. The boy cycled away – his legs pushing hard. The video surveillance would be analysed later.

'Don't you want to open it,' asked Danny.

'Not addressed to me,' replied Daisy. 'And anyway, a large gin and tonic is beckoning.'

Daisy was famed for her encyclopaedic knowledge of the world's gins – and disdain for house tonic *dispensed from some hideous CO_2 contraption.*

Meanwhile Detective Chief Superintendent Bill Kelly was frustrated – he still needed to understand why his former colleague, Detective Sergeant Michael Maguire was so publicly assassinated. Was it an unfortunate accident as Bodkin and the forensic animation might have suggested? Or was there a connection to the case he and his team from the National Crime Agency had been investigating for months, if not years? He had hoped that someone – or something – would stand out. Nothing had appeared unusual at the recent cremation either. After three weeks of intensive investigations, they were no closer to learning the truth. *If there was a truth to be had in this sodding mess*, he thought.

For Kelly, the bigger question that kept revolving in his mind, is *who would want Nowak dead? It just doesn't make any sense. Who? Why? Motive?*

'This is very irritating.' Kelly said out loud to no one in particular.

The frustration was getting on top of him – unusual for the normally calm senior detective. He thought back to what was meant to be a joyous celebration – the return of Martha and her fabulous first night.

The more he replayed the final moments of Maguire's life the more certain he was that Bodkin's hypothesis might be right – *maybe Maguire wasn't the intended target?* He closed his eyes and reconstructed the scene. *Where everyone was seated. Their reaction to the shooting.* In his mind he spooled back and forward. *What was he missing?* It came to him in a flash – *why wasn't Nowak behaving in his normal flamboyant self? He had been publicly acclaimed from the stage by Martha, but he barely acknowledged the plaudits. It was as if he was in semi-hiding – half-heartedly, reluctantly, responding to the applause.* Then Kelly's seminal thought. *No sniper, not even the most skilled and experienced, could possibly have targeted Maguire at the moment of his death – it was virtually impossible to shoot someone in the head whilst they were rising from their seat. The sniper's round would have already left the barrel of the Vintorez rifle before travelling at 263 metres per second across the arena. Maguire could not have been fully standing – he might not even have started standing – and certainly the sniper could not have predicted Maguire's movement.*

But if this was true, that still left the massive question, *why would anyone want Nowak dead? It simply didn't make sense. He owed money to The Vory, albeit through the newly appointed enforcer. It was in the enforcer's interest to keep Nowak alive. So, who else would benefit from Nowak's death?*

Kelly realised the time had been passing and he was expected down the road at Blakes for the wake. He had prepared a few notes for the benefit of his former colleagues – the proper, much-anticipated tribute to Maguire, his life and career. He was happy that no immediate family would be there as some of the salacious stories would even have Maguire's ashes glowing red in embarrassment yet be the cause of uproarious hilarity fuelled by an excess of *the black stuff* with *Irish Whiskey* chasers.

Before he departed, he e-mailed Bodkin: 'Monday morning catch up. Book a huddle room please. 09h30. Just us.'

27
DAY TWENTY-SIX
MONDAY 09H30

NEW SCOTLAND YARD

'HOW WAS MAGUIRE'S INTERMENT?' HARRY Bodkin asked Bill Kelly in one of the Yard's huddle rooms at almost exactly 09h30.

'Fine. All the normal tributes and banal praise. He was everyone's best friend and could do no wrong,' responded Kelly.

They both laughed. They sipped at their coffees in disposable reinforced paper cups collected from the canteen. Bodkin was clearly relaxed.

'Friday morning was a bit of a struggle. I am told I left at two and walked back to the hotel although it's a bit hazy. Rob Andrews did the decent thing and held back on the booze so he could drive us to the airport.' Kelly was not a fan of post-session analysis. 'Maguire was properly sent off. But flying home with a hangover isn't to be recommended.'

'Good turn out?' Bodkin was engaging in small talk before the real purpose of their meeting began – a delaying tactic for the inevitable.

'Not bad, I suppose about twenty-five. Only the three of us from the NCA. Caught up with a couple of old hands from around the force. Met a couple of his old army colleagues. Normal stuff.' Kelly paused, sipped more coffee, but could not prevaricate any longer. 'Well?' What news?'

Bodkin considered his answer before he spoke. 'I've just had the forensic trajectory analysis back. No one else has seen it yet, just you. It is almost certain that your Maguire was not the target.'

Kelly leant back whilst he absorbed the information.

'But we really are no closer to identifying the shooter. We have the means. We have the opportunity. But we do not have a motive. All we can assume, and that's the problem it is an assumption, is that our dead John Doe was paid by someone to kill Nowak and Maguire got in the way.' Bodkin was frustrated.

'We agree. There is no way that Maguire was the target, it would have been an impossible shot.' Kelly had been considering his thinking. 'Terrible misfortune, bad luck that Maguire stood just as the round left the rifle. So now we proceed on the basis that Nowak was definitely the intended recipient. And he knew he was being targeted – I remember now thinking how he was trying to keep a low profile. He hated it when Martha thanked him from the stage. He could barely sit down fast enough.'

'So now we have the question who did want Nowak dead?' Bodkin was contemplative. 'Who would benefit from his death? We know he owed The Vory, via the now deceased Ali Baka and Conor O'Murchadha a million quid, but if he was dead, they would be unlikely to be paid.'

Kelly picked up, 'We know that Nowak has been receiving reminder messages from The Vory's enforcer that the debt is now one and a quarter mill and that he now has less than four days to pay up. First message to Martha at Amelia Cohen's funeral. And then Daisy and Danny received a note after the interment given to them by a young boy on a bike. Unfortunately, our surveillance didn't see who gave the boy the envelope. And the gobby shite isn't helping us. And we can't do a lot due to his age. Nowak told Danny that Ali Baka's loan was vaguely legitimate but couldn't be repaid on time because the remaining three concerts were postponed due to the shooting. The trouble is that I am not sure we can prove criminality. With Baka and O'Murchadha dead we're not even sure the people smuggling will stand up in court.'

'Are you saying Nowak could get away with it?' asked Bodkin. 'That man is Teflon coated. Other polytetrafluoroethylenes are available.'

'What?' Kelly was sometimes bemused by Bodkin's humour. He reluctantly nodded, 'This is a marathon not a sprint. We'll get him one day.'

Coffees were finished and the empty paper cups thrown into the secure waste bin in a fit of rebellion.

'You say you are not any closer to identifying our shooter, John Doe?' Kelly asked, 'Surely that now is central to it all?'

'Nothing.' Bodkin was frustrated. 'Our dear friends in Five and Six have no idea. No match. Nothing in their files.'

'Do you believe them?' Kelly knew the extent of their duplicity.

'Don't think we have a lot of choice. I've tried every back door and contact. Nothing. Shutters pulled firmly down.' Bodkin realised he would be unlikely to get further. 'And here's the funny thing. The Deputy Commissioner herself called me up to her office on Friday afternoon. We had a weird conversation. She said that they had to start making budget cuts and were looking at senior officers approaching retirement. I only have two years to go. As a thank you for my excellent service, rather than make me redundant she suggested I take immediate early retirement on full pension with a golden goodbye of four years' salary as a lump sum.'

Kelly was astonished. 'Wow. That's amazing. Surely you couldn't refuse?'

'I asked about current cases and timescales. She told me not to worry, my cases would be passed on,' Bodkin reported.

'Timescale?' Kelly raised an eyebrow.

'Well, that's the other thing. This is my last week as I have seven weeks' leave accrued.' Bodkin was actually smiling. 'Finish on Friday.'

'You utter, utter lucky bastard. Congratulations.' Kelly stood and in an unexpected moment of emotion gave his old mate a big hug, realised that this wasn't the sort of thing that chaps of his age were meant to do, pulled back and warmly shook Harry Bodkin's hand.

They sat back down.

'What did Sheila say?' Kelly knew Bodkin's wife for almost as long as Bodkin himself.

'She said she had a long list of jobs around the house that have been waiting for this day,' Bodkin sounded happy, 'And she has already ordered the world cruise brochures.'

Not many marriages had survived the twenty-four seven intense nature of police work especially in the murder squads. Mr and Mrs Bodkin were a delightful exception. 'Mrs B knows Friday night could get messy after work and has said she will come to pick me up as long as it's before midnight.'

They both laughed. Genuine happy laughter. The mood subsided. 'I don't think we might ever find out who was responsible for accidentally killing Maguire. And I suspect that there are attempts to quietly drop the investigation,' Bodkin was reluctant. 'I got the distinct feeling that there is a will for this case to forever remain unsolved?'

Bodkin reached down to his briefcase and took out a two-centimetre thick manilla folder. 'I haven't given you this. It's a photocopy of everything. No-one knows I made copies. I made them over a weekend off-site at a back street copy shop down on the south coast. No receipt. No CCTV. Paid cash.'

Neither acknowledged that they both knew that dark forces were at work.

DAY TWENTY-SIX
MONDAY 09H30

CLAVERTON STREET, PIMLICO

'WHERE ARE THE OTHERS?' DEMANDED MICHAEL Ramsey, 'I thought this was an update meeting. Why so early? And why aren't we meeting at your normal offices?'

'Seeing someone as important as you might well be noticed and remembered,' explained Angela Fitzpatrick.

'A safe house is better for us all,' picked up Sefton, 'more comfortable. More anonymous. Part of my department. No logbook to come back to bite us.'

'Right. Good thinking. Well done.' Ramsey liked the thought of being important. He hung his British Warm overcoat on one of the curved walnut coat hooks. Ramsey was rarely seen – whatever the weather – without his black, double-breasted coat made from a 100% Melton wool cloth. Its military style first appeared around 1914 for British officers and was made famous by his hero, Winston Churchill. He believed it gave him the appearance of authority – which befitted his position.

Ramsey looked around the back room of the anonymous traditional white stucco terraced house with pillars either side of the steps leading up to the black front door. As he sat into the pine wheelback chair at what once must have been the kitchen table, he nodded to Sefton who smiled benignly. The thick bullet proof glass to the rear and the additional sound proofing created an eerie silence not normal for this busy part of London.

Ramsey ignored Angela Fitzpatrick.

Sefton, ever gracious, went across to the small kitchenette area equipped with a Nespresso coffee machine, brightly coloured kettle, and a small refrigerator – earlier in the day one of the full-time staff, who doubled as security, had bought fresh milk and biscuits.

He turned, 'Tea, coffee?'

Angela nodded, 'Tea please Sefton.'

'Me too,' grunted Ramsey. 'Milk. Two sugars. Where is everyone I asked?'

Under the worktops were three concealed buttons – one to begin audio recording; one for video recording; and a much larger button to summon armed help. Only the audio record function was in use today.

As Sefton boiled the kettle, he spoke towards the wall, 'It'll just be the three of us this morning. And this is for your ears and eyes only. And exclusively about you.'

There was silence as Sefton completed his tea making duties. He turned to stare straight into Ramsey's face, walked over with the tea and without shifting his gaze carefully poured the scalding liquid into Ramsey's lap. Sefton had pre-loaded the Minister's mug with an additional twenty spoons of sugar.

For a moment Ramsey couldn't believe what had just happened – he tried to leap to his feet. Sefton demonstrated his considerable latent strength holding him down.

'What the fuck are you doing? I'm a Minister of the Crown. I'll end your career for that,' screamed the Minister of the Crown successfully testing the sound-proofing of the room.

It was Angela who serenely picked up, 'I am so sorry Minister. Sefton that was very careless.'

'Terrible accident.' Sefton clearly wasn't sorry. 'Apologies, of course. Shall I get you another one Minister?'

'No, I bloody well don't want another one.' Ramsey's bluster was tested as the sticky liquid began to cool, 'I need to go home and clear up this mess.'

'All in good time. Please remain seated,' ordered Sefton. 'We don't want to get a mess on the carpet.'

'What the... But...' began Ramsey. 'You can't order me about—'

'From now on, you will only speak when answering a question.' Sefton was cold. His face impassive. 'You will remain seated. Do not attempt to get up.'

'I'm not taking orders from you. What's going on?' Ramsey shouted, 'This is false imprisonment.'

Sefton's quiet intimation was unnerving. 'We only want a little chat. No need to get upset.'

'Let me go, I demand to see my lawyer,' was the best Ramsey could do.

'Why do you need a lawyer over something like spilled tea?' Angela asked. 'Sorry I'm confused. That was an unfortunate accident.'

'You bloody well know that was deliberate. I want to leave right now.' Ramsey repeated.

'What don't you understand about, from now on you will only speak when answering a question?' Sefton reiterated. 'Stay seated and remain silent. Believe me, the last person you want here is your lawyer.'

Ramsey made the mistake of trying to stand – Sefton deftly pushed him back into his chair.

'From this moment on, you are about to start making some significant career decisions. It is up to you how you respond.' Sefton's quiet determination even spooked Angela, who up until now had watched proceedings with a mixture of contempt and fascination. She had never seen Sefton in full spate before.

'First question and think carefully before you answer,' Sefton smiled. Not a smile of warmth, but a sinister cold contortion, 'Who is Aleksandr Makarov?'

After a few seconds Ramsey replied, 'Who?'

'You heard me, Aleksandr Makarov.' Sefton spat out the name.

'I've no idea. I meet a lot of people. Who is he?' Ramsey's response was mixed with anger. 'I'm leaving now, and I will have both your careers. You'll never work again. I'll ensure the keys are thrown away. I'm calling the police.'

Ramsey attempted to lever himself up – the wet patch turning uncomfortably cold and sticky on the front of his shirt and trousers. He removed his phone from his inside suit jacket pocket.

Yet again Sefton pushed him back down onto the now cold, sticky, wet cushion. He snatched Ramsey's mobile phone from him, dropped it onto the floor and ground his heel into the screen. 'We'll come back to Aleksandr Makarov, don't worry about it for now. I'll try another question. Who is Limehouse Prestige Motors?'

Ramsey stared down at his wrecked phone. The silence in the room was overpowering. Just Ramsey's laboured breathing.

Sefton continued, 'And what did you buy from them for twenty-five thousand pounds?'

'I'm not answering any more of your questions. I'm leaving.' Ramsey attempted to stand for a third time. This time Sefton grabbed both Ramsey's ears and twisted – Ramsey had played rugby in the front row of the scrum at school, the pain had never matched what Sefton was now inflicting.

'You are not leaving until you have satisfactorily answered our questions.' Angela was equally steely. 'Answer Sefton's question. What did you buy from Limehouse Prestige Motors for twenty-five thousand pounds?'

'How do you know? That's a private matter.' Ramsey contemplated his answer, 'A surprise present for my wife.'

'What you bought her a car?' Angela turn. 'What a lovely present. How kind of you. She must have been thrilled.'

'I don't have to answer that. What's going on. Let me out of here,' Ramsey's resolve was wavering.

Sefton sat opposite Ramsey at the table. Angela and Sefton opened their files.

Angela powered up the meeting room's video screen connected to her iPad, 'I suggest you hear us out.'

The bile rose in Ramsey's stomach – he thought he was going to be sick. *What did they know?*

Sefton continued. 'At this moment, the only people who know what we are about to say are in this room. Cooperate and it will remain that way. If you lie that will change. Answer dishonestly or by omission, that will change. Dissemble or in any way be less than honest, if you understand the meaning of honesty, and we will personally ensure you will be on the front page of every newspaper in the land for the wrong reasons. And probably the world where they care about shits like you. Do you understand?'

Ramsey knew when he was beaten, reluctantly nodded.

'Do you understand?' repeated Angela.

'Yes,' whispered Ramsey.

'Do you understand?' repeated Sefton louder.

'Yes,' shouted Ramsey.

Angela swiped right on her iPad. A picture of what once purported to be a used car dealership appeared on the screen. Its graffiti covered metal roller shutter door recessed within the bricked-up archway – a metal clad service door was located just to the right.

A faded graffiti-overpainted sign was on the left wall – Limehouse Prestige Motors. Nothing about the faded glory was prestigious.

Angela swiped again – a video started playing. The cameraman walked inside; the fluorescent lights flickered into some sort of action, to reveal a smooth concrete floor and a vaulted painted brick ceiling. Along each side wall were recessed arched alcoves – one had been converted into an office, one a kitchen, and one once was the lavatory – a dead rat could just be seen on the floor at its entrance. No cars. No sign of business. The sound revealed the rumble of a train from the tracks above the arches.

'Do you want to tell us about Limehouse Prestige Motors?' asked Angela.

Ramsey recovered some of his confidence. *Did these two think this is all about cash payment for a car?* 'I never visited them. I did everything online. I paid them twenty-five thousand pounds for a car – a Mercedes convertible.'

'Surely you must have examined the car before you bought it. What happened?' Angela questioned.

'I met the salesman with the car. Personal service, they came to me.' Ramsey was struggling.

Sefton. 'Really. Where did you meet?'

Angela. 'Who did you meet?'

Sefton. 'What did he look like?'

Angela. 'What was his name?'

Sefton. 'Did you haggle?'

Angela. 'What colour was the car?'

'I can't remember,' replied Ramsey to the barrage of questions.

'You can't remember the colour of the car, or from whom you purchased it, or anything at all about a twenty-five-thousand-pound purchase?' scoffed Sefton.

'I was busy with parliamentary work,' Ramsey was sweating.

'Your wife must have been thrilled with her present. I would have been thrilled if my husband bought me a car.' Angela hesitated, 'Except I don't have a husband and I don't drive.

Sefton turned to Angela with vaudeville extravagance, then back to Ramsey. 'Your wife doesn't drive either. She can't. She has two years of her ban remaining. Speeding and dangerous driving. Allegedly. Some wonder if she was actually behind the wheel at the time?'

'Where is the car, Mr Ramsey? Where is it parked or garaged?' Angela was enjoying herself. 'And to whom is it registered?'

There was silence in the room before Ramsey answered, 'I was conned. It was never delivered.'

'Did you report this to the Police?' asked Sefton with an exaggerated frown.

Ramsey replied quietly 'No. I didn't.'

'Why not?' Angela's voice was soft.

'Because the papers would get hold of it and make a fool of me.' Ramsey admitted.

Angela and Sefton nodded at Ramsey, it looked like sympathy for the travails of a hard-done-by politician.

Sefton thumped the table, the deep noted reverberance bounced around the room. Hard. Vicious.

Angela jumped.

Ramsey jumped. His emotions on the metaphorical knife edge.

'Okay let's stop this nonsense, now, shall we? Limehouse Prestige Motors is a front for a group of contract killers. One of whom is Aleksandr Makarov. You paid twenty-five-thousand-pounds to assassinate Stanislaw Nowak.' Sefton shouted into Ramsey's face, his spittle showering Ramsey's chin. 'We have proof you paid them. There is no record of any car, anywhere.'

Ramsey threw up onto the table – Angela just managed to retrieve their files before the effluent engulfed them. Ramsey's disgusting mess was now mixed with the sticky solidifying tea on his shirt and trousers. Sefton was impassive.

Angela poured a glass of water – which Ramsey gratefully accepted.

No-one spoke. Silence yet again the great inquisitor.

It was pointless Ramsey denying the inevitable, 'How did you find out? How long have you known?'

Sefton expelled air from his nose. The stench in the room was overpowering. 'Because we are the secret intelligence service. What do you think we do? We have known who the shooter was – a contract killer, former FSB – from the day following Maguire's death but chose not to share that information. What we didn't know was who contracted him to kill Nowak. It didn't make sense at first. We always knew Maguire wasn't the intended target.'

'Thanks to DCS Kelly, DCI Bodkin and their teams they have helped us enormously. We learned that Nowak owed The Vory a million pounds.' Ramsey was about to interrupt Angela, but her look silenced him. 'A debt collector purchased the debt from The Vory and added a bit for his troubles. What we then realised was that Nowak's death would not have benefited them, especially the debt collector. So, we asked ourselves the question, who would benefit from Nowak's death and why?'

Sefton picked up the story. 'Despite his best-efforts, DCI Bodkin's team would have found it next to impossible to identify Maguire's killer. It was simply bad luck for Nowak and for you that the journalist Danny Owen knows Nowak's

PR, Daisy de Villiers. The re-emergence of Danny Owen's disabled badge piece rekindled our interest in Nowak, someone with whom we have been trying to get to grips with for many years. Suddenly the pieces started falling into place.'

Angela and Sefton flip-flopped filling in the gaps. Angela's turn. 'We don't give a damn about who bought disabled badges and from whom. Low level crime from many years ago. But someone did care for several reasons. We know Wallace obtained a copy of Danny Owen's spiked disabled badge piece where he named names. Yours and his included. Wallace contacted a few people on Danny's list to conspire against Mr Owen. What no one knew was that Wallace had been feeding information to Nowak for several years. This could have been the evidence to set him free. We know that Nowak was threatening Wallace.'

'Despite the newspapers continuing the misinformation that burner phones cannot be hacked, our colleagues at GCHQ were able to intercept many of Nowak's and his associate's conversations, as the former French President Nicolas Sarkozy found to his cost. French Police intercepted a dozen conversations between Sarkozy and his lawyer on burner phones that they thought could not be traced to them.' Sefton's clandestine relationships throughout the UK's security service ran deep. 'GCHQ and the French DGSI, General Directorate for Internal Security, Direction Générale de la Sécurité Intérieure have been collaborating for years.'

'What concerned us was police corruption at high level. We learned that Nowak was being fed information by inside sources.' Angela felt there was no need to mention her grandfather, Commander Barry Fitzpatrick, and his relationship to DS Maguire. 'We didn't know how deep and who was involved. Danny Owen kindly assisted DCS Kelly in obtaining three phones belonging to Nowak, two of which we had no knowledge. The data from these phones were not legally able to be given in evidence per se, but the conversations and data we discovered as a result are admissible.'

'So, what do we know?' Sefton showed no emotion as he revealed some of the background. 'Ten years ago, you and several others purchased counterfeit disabled parking badges. At the time it was simply a convenience to help your bloody ego. You weren't aware that Danny Owen was on to you and was drafting a story that could make headlines for weeks. That would have destroyed your career and that of several others. You had no idea, even with your massively inflated ego that you would end up possibly becoming Prime Minister. But you didn't know that Nowak had accidently helped you by ensuring that Danny's piece would never see the light of day. We had been investigating Nowak for many years. We followed Nowak and his henchmen to Danny Owen's flat but couldn't reveal our hand. When Danny and his now ex-wife left the flat in the ambulance, we went in and downloaded the contents of Danny's computer. Neither of us were involved then, so the files languished in the for-follow-up pile, that was never followed up until Nowak started becoming a person of interest again. DCS Kelly and his team had been following Nowak's career for years, trying to establish the depth and breadth of Nowak's let's call them business interests. No one could understand why Nowak had decided to get involved with concert touring and the singer Martha. We started putting two and two together.'

'The more we looked the more complex it became,' continued Angela. 'We soon discovered that Nowak was planning to use the concert tour for smuggling people as you know. What we couldn't understand was how he seemed to be one step ahead of us all. We knew about Wallace before we found out about Maguire. Wallace had personally obtained a disabled blue badge many years ago, before Maguire had obtained one for his parents. It meant that both could be blackmailed by Nowak. Our investigations kept hitting a brick wall. And we didn't know who to trust. So, I anonymously gave a file with an edited, redacted version of Danny Owen's story and information about Nowak's people smuggling activities to Yuliet Spooner, of the Centre for Covert Media Studies knowing she would realise that she had gold dust and was not restrained by legal niceties. Sefton here suggested that we should remove you from Danny's story, at first because he felt it was his duty to protect a minister of the crown. But then our plans changed when it became clear you were standing for Prime Minister and we might be able to it to our advantage.'

Ramsey sat quietly. He was overwhelmed by his own vomit, cold sticky tea, and the certainty his life was about to change.

Angela continued. 'In common parlance, the act of soliciting to murder may be thought of as hiring a hitman, though the word hiring is used loosely, and the act requires no financial transaction to qualify as such. Merely the intent to engage another in an act of murder qualifies as soliciting. Encouraging or assisting a crime is itself a crime in English law, by virtue of the Serious Crime Act 2007. It is one of the inchoate offences of English law.'

'Aid, abet, counsel or procure. Conspiracy to murder. Soliciting an offence of perverting the course of justice,' Sefton referred to his file. 'Murder is a specific offence with intent but if the sniper misses and hits someone else by accident that is still murder. If you intend only to wound but the victim has a weak heart that no one knew about and dies of shock, then that is still murder. Law is a delight of confusions. Those sitting near to Maguire and affected by his gruesome death also have civil claims against you. Although not pulling the trigger, the procurer could also be guilty of the full offence, if carried to conclusion. Murder is peculiar as it is contrary to Common Law, not to a statute.'

Sefton and Angela remained silent. All that could be heard was Ramsey's laboured breathing as he tried to control his heart rate.

'You do as we require or your engagement of the assassin to remove Nowak, and killing a policeman, will emerge in every newspaper in the land.' Sefton's sickly smile emerged again as he recited the law, 'Whosoever shall solicit, encourage, persuade, or endeavour to persuade, or shall propose to any person, to murder any other person, whether he be a subject of Her Majesty or not, and whether he be within the Queen's dominions or not, shall be guilty of a misdemeanour, and being convicted thereof shall be liable to imprisonment for life.'

Angela and Sefton had laid it on thick – the barrage of law leaving Ramsey in no doubt he was facing the end of his freedom.

'To discredit you further, your indiscretions with fake disabled badges will hit every headline too. You will be both reviled and a laughingstock.' Angela closed her file. 'Murder for a disabled badge. Outrageous?'

Ramsey sat still, contemplating his future. His body sagged. His face pale. *Is this the end of my career and aspirations to become PM?* he thought. He worried more about that than prison – *several colleagues had been guests of Her Majesty and survived.*

Ramsey remained silent for at least a minute deep in thought. Angela and Sefton waited patiently.

'So now we all have a dilemma?' Sefton eventually stood and leant his back against the kitchen worktop. 'Do we throw you to the wolves or do we assist you?'

'I'm not sure he deserves to be helped.' Angela answered Sefton's question in their carefully rehearsed playbook.

'We'd want something in exchange, wouldn't we?' Sefton's turn next on the script.

Ramsey saw a tiny chink of light. Despite his dire situation, his shrewd political antennae were twitching. 'What are you suggesting?'

Sefton enlightened him, 'Well, the way I see it is this. We subtly assist your campaign to become the next Prime Minister of this great country. Then let's say the purchase of your wife's car remains hidden whilst you cooperate.'

Ramsey perked up. 'So, blackmail? What you seem to have forgotten is you also purchased fake disabled badges.'

'Yes, we did,' Angela was commanding, 'Our badges were purchased with the full knowledge and approval of our superiors. Secondly disabled badges versus murder? Do you really think that's a trade? You are on a murder charge. About the most serious crime, next to treason maybe, that anyone can commit. What we are offering you is a route to salvation. We are your saviours. It all comes out and you go to prison probably for the rest of your life and you would become the most reviled former politician in history. Or you help us, and you will become Prime Minister with our help. But we own you. No police or security budget cuts. Far from it. One of the first things you will do is to announce your one hundred percent commitment to the security of this great country of ours. You increase police budgets by ten percent at first, with more to come. Security service budgets are secret, but you will increase our budgets as well by ten percent. Both ramp up by ten percent for the next five years whilst you are in power.'

'That's not too difficult, is it?' Sefton quizzed. 'Well not too difficult compared to the rest of your life being buggered in the showers by nasty tattooed villains with sexually communicable diseases. Because believe me, we'd put the word out. No soft cushy open prison for a murderer. Maximum security. Twenty-three hours a day locked down. We'd make your life more miserable than you could imagine. If you last more than a few months.'

Ramsey contemplated. What he was considering was conspiring with the devil or considering a very deep blue sea.

'Just to ginger up the deal, when you become PM, we'd feed you useful intelligence about the behaviour and peccadillos of your colleagues and opposition. You'd be the most powerful Prime Minister in history. Nobody could touch you,' offered Angela.

Ramsey made to stand up. He normally paced when he had difficult decisions to make. 'Remain seated. I didn't give you permission to stand.' Sefton snarled. 'Remember, we own you.'

'Who else knows about this?' Ramsey tried to understand the depth of his problems.

'Just the three of us. By the way, if you think returning to Limehouse Prestige Motors to commission anyone else to deal with either of us, we have arranged for our evidence to be sent to every newspaper in the world. You would be signing your own conviction.'

Ramsey was thinking hard, 'What happens about the disabled badge story?

'Your name won't appear. The only copy that exists with your name and picture I have safely locked away. Oh, and a spare back up,' Angela didn't mention her third copy. 'The copy of the file I personally gave to Yuliet Spooner was carefully edited to remove your name.'

'I thought at the last meeting Wallace said that all her copies had been destroyed?' Ramsey frowned.

'Surely you have learned that Wallace can't be trusted to do a job properly.' Angela was sardonic. 'Ms Spooner still has at least one other copy. And my two copies of the masters have your name big and bold.'

Sefton filled in the gaps, 'What's going to happen about your co-conspirators you might ask. Pelham DeCourcy and DCI Wallace are going to take early retirement on ill health grounds. Wallace will withdraw his candidacy as an MP. Edwin Porterhouse, the owner of *The Daily Tribune* is going to nail his colours firmly to the mast supporting your bid to become the next PM. He has also agreed to make Danny Owen an outrageous offer to become their next chief reporter and lead a new specialist team of investigative journalists. One of their first stories will reveal some distasteful details about our outgoing PM, Mrs Campbell-Horrocks, that will make her position untenable. Mr Owen's future will be assured with an information flow that will be the envy of many. Yuliet Spooner will also have first dibs at any juicy morsel we can throw her way as well. In exchange any mention of counterfeit disabled badges will remain forever on the back burner – unless someone is tempted to err from our version of the events. Yuliet Spooner's third file that she thinks no one knows about has no mention of you, *Michael.*'

The Minister had already had one outburst being addressed by his first name in a professional capacity but thought now wasn't the time to complain.

'Mr Nowak remains firmly in both our sights and those of DCS Kelly's team. Kelly has agreed not to pursue enquiries about the disabled badges to protect the reputation of several officers in the Metropolitan Police. It wouldn't be in the public interest, would it?' Angela stood. '*Michael*, there is a bathroom next door so you can clean yourself off a bit. Then I suggest *Michael* you put on your coat and go home. We'll be in contact.'

DAY TWENTY-NINE
THURSDAY

THE O2

THE HOUSE LIGHTS DIMMED, THE AUDIENCE STARTED to cheer and applaud. In the dark the band took their places.

Nowak paced backstage – Jimmy gave him the thumbs up with an immense smile.

Nowak had received acknowledgement that five times two hundred and fifty thousand pounds had been safely transferred one day ahead of the deadline.

'Deadline,' he snorted aloud – the irony was not lost on him.

'Sorry, did you say something,' asked Jimmy.

'No worries Jimmy. Great looking show thanks to you and your crew.' Nowak was genuinely ecstatic.

His euphoria and misplaced arrogance convinced him that he had got away with it. *All of it. I am a free man. Debts paid.* The thoughts overwhelmed him.

He made his way up to the VIP seats with a bounce in his step. As much of a bounce as his corpulent bulk would allow.

Danny squeezed Daisy's hand. Alongside them the soon to be Danny's employer Eddy and his partner; Yuliet; Bill Kelly, Harry and Sheila Bodkin, and their teams.

Around them celebrities and significant contributors to Martha's Police Charities. This was the first of four rescheduled nights at the O2 – all sold out. The fourth night would be a special where all proceeds went to Police Charities – in the audience would be thousands of serving police officers and their families from all over the UK who had been offered free tickets. The optics had been overwhelmingly excellent.

No Gordon with an over-made-up girlfriend this time. *'I am free of that wanker,'* thought Danny remembering the last first night and the sometimes-excruciating mornings he had to endure on Starshine's Breakfast Show. No more before dawn alarm clocks. No more post-show Cannoli Siciliani from Francisco – he had promised Daisy who had poked fun at his expanding waste line. He would miss the addictive tube-shaped shells of fried pastry dough filled with the sweet, creamy filling of figs, honey, and ricotta. But it was worth it.

Nowak sat heavily into the vacant aisle seat beside Daisy – the seating creaked ominously but held. There was nothing more he or any of them could do. The show would be a fabulous success.

Deep-blue lights circled – the audience ramped up the excitement drowned by the heart-stopping ultra-bass. The brass kicked in with a tower-of-power rock fanfare. A single guitarist spot lit up-stage-right joined in with an E minor 9 funky vamp. The risers either side of the stage, with the rest of the musicians on board, smoothly lifted and rotated into position, the ultra-bass joined by an ostentatious tympani player up-stage-left building the tension. Fog and dry ice poured on and around the stage. The Vari-Lites circled.

The ten banks of 5x5 Par30 light matrixes illuminated the audience at full brightness, 'blinding' them so they couldn't see the stage. Suddenly dead black out, synchronised with the snare roll. More colossal cheering.

In perfect synchronicity, the massive Mitrix screens displayed a glorious cascade of gold discs behind bulging prison bars. As the words 'Martha Returns' resolved, Alan Dedicoat's pre-recorded voice-over boomed out in a rising cadence, 'It's time. It's time. It's time for the return of… Martha.' The bars broke under the pressure from the gold discs.

The O2 once again had never heard anything like it – the audience reached new levels of excitement that surpassed the previous first night.

Stage centre, there she was wearing a long, gold evening dress – the gold discs sewn into the fabric sparkled like personal mirror balls from the six follow spots illuminating her from back, front and sides.

The massive O2 danced to the reflected sparkling gold. The ten-metre ultra-high-resolution video screens showed Martha's laughing face in ultra-close-up – in glorious high resolution. The music kicked into the opening of one of her most high-energy songs, the perfect show-starter.

'Hello London. I... have... returned!' Ear-shattering cheer. 'And it's great to be back.'

EPILOGUE

THREE MONTHS LATER

BREATHLESS REPORTERS AND BORED CAMERA CREWS standing opposite Buckingham Palace, near the flower beds paying tribute to the NHS, awaited the arrival of the soon to be Prime Minister, The Honourable Michael Ramsey MP.

His Majesty King William V, inside the Palace, privately shuddered at the thought of inviting the slimy, newly elevated politician to form a government in his name.

Later that day the King and new Prime Minister would be at a ceremony where two cheques would be presented. One for over half million pounds to the Amelia Cohen Foundation from the proceeds raised through the sale of

Martha's video and music downloads. The second cheque for one million pounds would be handed over to Police Charities from some of the proceeds of the fourth night of Martha's sell-out concerts at the 02.

Martha, Vikki and the soon to be Mr and Mrs Owen graced the King and Prime Minister with their presence. Stanislaw Nowak was told by the Palace he would not be welcome.

The King announced that thanks to Martha, the Amelia Cohen Foundation would continue to raise money for music lessons and instruments in schools. He graciously accepted the invitation to become the Foundation's Patron and said he looked forward to future fund-raising concerts and events.

Margaret Wallace embarked on a forty-six-day Mediterranean cruise without her husband. Explaining why former DAC Keith Wallace had taken early retirement was easy to her friends – however, finding face-saving reasons as to why her husband had not been selected to stand as their MP was more difficult. The cruise had been paid for from Wallace's redundancy pay-off. The irony of using the cruise to consider her future without her controlling husband was not lost of Mrs Wallace.

Danny and Daisy will return in *End Turn*,
the third of the trilogy...

There may be more?

ACKNOWLEDGEMENTS

THANK YOU

As usual a novel cannot be written without the knowledge and help of many people – all of whom must be thanked for their kind and generous support.

Many very well-known TV, radio, music, former colleagues, and personal friends have helped me with deep background to ensure the tittle-tattle of real life, show business, PR and the law are as accurately portrayed as a novel allows and showbusiness is in real-life – including: PR consultant, Lydia Owen; broadcaster and voice-artist, Alan Dedicoat; cinematographer and visual effects artist, Trevor Burgess; Spice Girl, Melanie Chisholm; author and novelist, Mark McCrum; Parliamentary Under Secretary of State David TC Davies, MP for Monmouth (at the time of writing!); John Malpass. Kirsty Malpass and Ginny Kay for their detailed typo spotting; Sarah and Guy Bowden for their creativity, fabulous suggestions and for reading early manuscripts; author and screenwriter Matthew Hall for his advice getting me started in this absurd novel-writing past-time; Alison King, for the lyrics to 'Captivity'; my daughter, Vikki Byrne (who is nothing like the Vikki in this trilogy) for the cover design; Sara Starbuck for her sage editorial counsel; Robert Orchard, for his journalism and political wisdom; Julian Phillips and Kevin Doolan for their specialist legal knowledge and for not taking the piss too much; Joshua Howey de Rijk and Jonathan White at Troubador Publishing for their great support; Ben Cameron, Debbie and the team at Cameron Publicity & Marketing for attempting to bring my novels to the attention of a wider audience; and last but not least my wife, Sue, who has supported me all the way through the process of creating these novels – and who sent me down to my sh'office in all weathers to get them finished.

There are others I'd like to publicly thank but who wish to or must remain anonymous – several will probably be well known to most readers.

Thank you one and all.

This is a work of fiction. The mistakes are mine and mine alone.

BY THE SAME AUTHOR

FICTION
Bandwagon (the first Danny and Daisy showbiz thriller)

NON-FICTION
The History of Castration
The History of Diabetes
The History of Contraception
The Cardio-Protective Effect of Wine

PRAISE FOR 'BANDWAGON'

THE FIRST IN THE DANNY AND DAISY SHOWBIZ THRILLER TRILOGY

A gripping show business thriller – This accomplished novel is compelling, and I recommend it highly. An investigative journalist explores the murky side of showbiz in a fast-paced novel that is well-informed, explores topical global crime issues, is gripping and tense, whilst managing to throw in much wit and good humour as well as romance.

I dare you to put this down – Can't remember when I last devoured a book at such pace. If I had to go anywhere in the house or garden, Bandwagon came with me. I couldn't let it out of my sight, feeling such a responsibility for the safety and welfare of the good guys and girls, and such fear and contempt for the bad guys.

A look at the murkier side of show business – A great read, romping along through London, Wales, and Europe, giving so much detail that I imagined I was right there with Danny, Daisy, and the other characters. A world of the music business, radio, TV, and the high life, all expertly portrayed in a good story.

Like good food, you want to come back for seconds! More Please! – A very enjoyable fast paced read, you will not want to put it down! The technical detail, on The Entertainment Industry is spot on. Having worked in 'the game' for some time I understand the pressures. Very well portrayed, and current in its storytelling.

A real page turner. Enjoyed every minute of it – The main characters of Danny and Daisy felt like real people, I loved the interaction between them – and the story couldn't be more current. It also felt like a good inside look at how these big events by touring artists are staged and their relationship with the all-important press. Enjoyable crime thriller with a human touch.

From the off I knew I was going to enjoy this book – A great debut novel about the music industry and the 'circus' surrounding it. From the off, I knew I was going to enjoy this book. It does flip backwards and forwards to explain the back story… All these stories are essential for the novel to coalesce, and they segue seamlessly without detracting from the pace of the novel. It's a fast-paced book, without feeling rushed and the ending left me wanting more.

Mystery/Back Stage of a Rock Concert: Yes, please – What a fun read, full of interesting characters and some details on the work that takes place behind the scenes of a rock concert tour. The book moves at a quick pace which is accomplished in part by the short chapters and the short sentence structure that help the reader increase their reading speed. The intrigue pulls the reader along without relying on unnecessary cliff-hangers and tension to maintain interest in the book. It is easy to read, and the writing encourages the reader to read 'just one more chapter' before putting the book down.

International Intrigue with a Rock'n'Roll Backdrop – Bandwagon takes you behind the scenes of the music industry as the Martha Movin' Out tour heads into its final week of rehearsals with lots of logistics, lingo and a little name dropping. The book moves into thriller territory when Martha herself disappears and several shady characters enter stage left. Danny returns to his investigative reporter roots, and with the help of Daisy, the show's PR manager, begins digging into real story behind Martha's disappearance and the Movin' Out tour.

Read it in a day! Gripping! – Great book, very well written with plenty of knowledge of the subject matter. Lots of interesting places, scenes, and detail. Very hard to put down!

Gripping page turner. A great (and authoritative) read – and bang up to date.

Absolutely loved it – Started and finished Band Wagon in the week and absolutely loved it. You've done such a fantastic job – I can't believe this is your debut novel. I really connected with your style – especially the intricate attention to detail that so many people gloss over, forgetting that it's often the small details which help to very powerfully build the world the characters are inhabiting in the reader's mind. Your extensive research and connections with the industry paid dividends – lending the work an authenticity and helping to ground the fiction in a real-world sense.

Fun thriller set convincingly in the world of showbiz – This is a great fun read, full of lots of well-informed detail about the world of showbiz, clearly written by an insider. The star goes missing, can the show go on? Investigative journalist turned celebrity radio reporter Danny Owen is a likeable and believable lead character, who soon finds himself drawing on his old skills as he struggles to find the star and save the tour, along with the star's PR Daisy deVilliers. The villains the pair encounter are nastily realistic and keep the suspense ticking over nicely until the last page. Danny likes his smart London clubs and his food – and is even more appealing for that.

Hard to put down! – A great read fast paced and very current. Good twists and turns but with no detail left out. Very easy to read style. Hard to believe it's a first book, more like one from a seasoned best-selling author.

'Bandwagon,' *the first in the Danny and Daisy showbiz thriller trilogy,* is available from all bookshops and online.

ISBN: 978 183859 298 1

Search on: Bandwagon Richard Cobourne

Signed copies, and for Book Club and speaking engagement enquiries please contact via:
Bandwagon@RichardCobourne.com

Reviews and ordering information at: www.Cobourne.com